TOWERS FALL

ALSO BY
KARINA SUMNER-SMITH

The Towers Trilogy

Radiant
Defiant

TOWERS FALL

TOWERS TRILOGY
BOOK THREE

KARINA
SUMNER-SMITH

Talos Press

Talos Press books may be purchased in bulk at special discounts for sales promotion, corporate gifts, fund-raising, or educational purposes. Special editions can also be created to specifications. For details, contact the Special Sales Department, Talos Press, 307 West 36th Street, 11th Floor, New York, NY 10018 or info@skyhorsepublishing.com.

Talos Press is an imprint of Skyhorse Publishing, Inc.®, a Delaware corporation.

Visit our website at www.talospress.com.

10 9 8 7 6 5 4 3 2 1

Library of Congress Control Number: 2015947592

Cover design by Rain Saukas
Cover images: Thinkstock

Print ISBN: 978-1-940456-41-6
Ebook ISBN: 978-1-940456-44-7

Printed in the United States of America

Dedicated with love to my Opa,
Siegfried Schnepf
1932–2015

Part One

PRAISE FOR *RADIA*

"Inequality, economics, and postapocalyptic necromancy combine persuasively in Sumner-Smith's ingenious, insightful debut. . . . With a clean, evocative style, a clever transposition of corporate warfare into a feudal future, and a strong, complementary pair of protagonists, Sumner-Smith's Towers Trilogy is off to a captivating start."
—*Publishers Weekly*, starred review

"This beautifully written page-turner is top-notch. A world that comes alive, rich and magical; character you want to spend time with; a heroine to root for; trust, friendship, and belonging—*Radiant* has it all!"
—Ed Greenwood, creator of The Forgotten Realms®
and *New York Times* bestselling author of *Spellfire* and *The Herald*

"I can't remember the last time I was as excited about the start of a new fantasy series as I am about *Radiant*, the first in a promised trilogy."
—*San Francisco Book Review*

"In penning her novel *Radiant*, Karina Sumner-Smith steps into the top ranks of a burgeoning generation of authors who are changing the face of science fiction and fantasy. With characterizations that won't let you go, deeply textured world building, and prose that sings, she offers a book that deserves to become a classic."
—Catherine Asaro, Nebula Award–winning author of *Undercity*

"If C. J. Cherry wrote fantasy with a futuristic feel, it would have a lot in common with this book, especially the protagonist. Excellent work, and recommended."
—Michelle Sagara, *New York Times*
bestselling author of *Cast in Flame*

"Sumner-Smith's writing is assured; her Xhea, prickly and inward-looking, feels right, and her world—a world where magic is currency, and the Towers that have most of it cast long shadows across those who can't even ascend to them—feels lived-in and real. I loved it."
—*The Magazine of Fantasy and Science Fiction*

"Karina Sumner-Smith's smashing debut is a page-turner of the highest pedigree."
—J. M. Frey, award-winning author of *Triptych*

"Long story short, you need to read *Radiant*. It's got the right blend between fantasy and sci-fi to appeal to fans of either genre, very realistic characters that you want to read more about, and enough mysteries and curiosity to leave me, at least, salivating over the sequel."

—*Bibliotropic*

PRAISE FOR *DEFIANT*

"*Defiant* is a compelling novel of character. Once I picked it up, I couldn't put it down again, to such a degree that I walked to the train station *still reading*. Now *that's* something I haven't done for a decade. Tight, tense, and effortlessly readable, its climax is a thing of nail-biting intensity, and it ends with revelations, and more change to come. I can recommend it wholeheartedly."

—*Tor.com*

"Like its predecessor, *Defiant* is a brilliant cross-genre piece that blends elements from many sources so that the result is something new and never-before-seen. Looks like Karina Sumner-Smith has scored another hit with her second novel, offering a spellbinding story and characters who are sure to captivate a wide audience."

—*The BiblioSanctum*

"Impossible to put down! Sumner-Smith has outdone herself in this thrilling sequel with higher stakes, darker magic, and a bond of friendship that proves unbreakable—even in the face of war. Readers will be desperate for the conclusion!"

—Jessica Leake, author of *Arcana* and the forthcoming *The Order of the Eternal Sun*

"This novel is just as well written as the first one, and . . . it careens to an explosive conclusion that will leave readers hungry for more. It's an excellent novel that is hard to put down."

—*San Francisco Book Review*

"It's one of the best post-apocalyptic urban fantasies I've ever found . . . I can't wait to read the trilogy's conclusion."

—*Bibliotropic*

"The first two novels are riveting . . . after the brilliant start with *Radiant*, Sumner-Smith may have accomplished that rarest of feats, actually surpassing her first novel with the sequel."

—*Nerds of a Feather*

Chapter One

Sitting in a concrete alcove that had once been a doorway, her cane tucked beside her to keep it from the ash, Xhea stared at the ruin of the Lower City market. If she closed her eyes, she could almost imagine the market as it had been, a riot of sound and movement.

Gone now. There were no tents there anymore, that familiar chaos of stained awnings and makeshift shelters; no ancient mall structure at their center, like an egg in its nest. There was no pushing crowd, no smoke from cooking fires or the stinking generators, no shouts of vendors hawking their wares.

No buildings. No homes.

Only a span of ash and absence.

Xhea wanted to turn away. For all that she knew the market was gone, burned to the ground in Rown's senseless attack, the sight of that empty, black stretch still had the power to rob her of breath.

Even her alcove was but an illusion of the familiar. This corner of the building still stood, in spite of everything, but the rest had fallen, leaving only a pile of cracked and broken bricks to be picked over by scavengers.

Illusion or not, the corner was a comfort. Xhea did not know how many days she had spent tucked away here over the years, making herself available to her ghost-afflicted clients. More, truly, than she could count. She knew this alcove in all seasons, soaked by rain, parched by summer sun, turned cold and uncomfortable by a rime of old ice.

Everything comes to an end.

The last time she had sat here waiting for customers was . . . Xhea blinked in sudden realization. It was that late spring day when Shai's father had come to her with a quiet, meditative ghost bound to his chest. It was strange remembering her friend that way: a hesitant spirit, worth nothing more to Xhea than the renai—the magical currency—her care might generate. That was but a few months ago; it felt a small forever.

The ghost that she had once so disdained now stood watch, scanning the burned-out market with a wary eye, magic flickering about her fingertips.

Out in the rubble, lit by the early-morning light, some few people still searched. Not for much, anymore. The bodies had long since been taken for burial, and the few possessions that might have been reclaimed from the wreckage were long gone. Even so, some stayed, sifting through the ash and ruin for nails and bits of wire, the hardened puddles of melted plumbing pipes—she knew not what else. Their backs were bent, their hands stained black from the search.

Yet it was not the searchers that drew Xhea's attention, or the rubble through which they combed, but the other figures in the midst of that desolate black. Ghosts. People had died here— more than she wanted to think about. People had died here and some few remained, lingering, bound to this place or the memories that it contained.

"They're still here," Shai said softly. Xhea didn't need to see her face to know that she, too, watched the dead.

"Ghosts aren't all like you," Xhea murmured. "Some are only pieces of their former selves."

Thinking pieces, of course; pieces that remembered being alive, being human—pieces that even kept some fragment of their personalities. Yet trauma hurt a ghost as surely as it did a living, breathing person; and trauma to a soul, without flesh to house it, was harder to heal. For many, there was no trauma worse than that of death itself.

Xhea looked back to the market's ghosts. Most, she thought, didn't know what had happened. They didn't understand that they were dead, or didn't want to believe it.

She recognized the ghost of an older woman who had owned a shoe stall. The woman was going about her business, as if her stall stood before her, as if her wares needed to be made or a customer was requesting a repair. Closer, there were a few ghosts that just . . . stood there. Staring, perhaps, in confusion, unable to comprehend that the desolation surrounding them was the ruin of their former homes.

There were more, too—more than even she could see. Ghosts hidden inside the burned and fallen buildings that ringed this place; ghosts curled and cringing against what had once been the ground, buried now by untold layers of rubble. She could feel them, each like a distant ache, a bruise on the landscape.

"I don't like to see them like this," Shai whispered. "Can you . . . ?"

Xhea shook her head.

They would be aware of her soon, she knew, drawn to her presence as she was drawn to theirs. Once she would have avoided this place as if it were cursed—as she had avoided any place thick with ghosts for as long as she could remember. Medics' wards. Edren's arena, where the gladiators fought. The twisted streets and alleys of the contested territory at the ruins' eastern edge, fought over by gangs like a single bone amidst a pack of hungry dogs.

Once, too, she might have waded among the ghosts, cutting their tethers, freeing their hold on the living world and all its untold joys and sorrows.

Once—but not anymore.

Xhea watched the ghost of a young man wander though a fallen building, his face shining with tears. He called out; the name, a female name, could have been his wife, his sister, his daughter. A friend. Xhea did not know, only watched as he searched.

"No," she murmured to Shai. "Not yet."

She would speak to them; perhaps she would cut the tethers of some, or offer what release her dark magic could provide— when they were ready. That would be their choice, in the end. Not hers.

Everyone needs time to mourn.

Little though some were afforded that luxury. For casting a shadow across them all, living and dead alike, stood Farrow.

Farrow had been the tallest and the richest of the skyscrapers, a towering structure some sixty stories high whose pale façade, wide glass panes, and broken balconies had been visible throughout the Lower City. While Edren, Orren, and Senn were clustered near the center of the Lower City core, Farrow had stood some distance apart, the ancient condominium watching over a wide stretch of territory.

Farrow's people were the Lower City's magic workers, the strongest casters on the ground—and they had all been working in secret toward the dream of transforming their earth-bound skyscraper into a floating Tower.

They had failed.

Xhea had been there as Farrow rose into the sky, shaking, shuddering. She'd heard the wail of Farrow's living heart as it was birthed by a century of collected magic—magic that had flooded through Farrow's walls in an instant. So much planning, so much time and effort; so much magic and blood, so many lives. And for nothing.

For Farrow had risen higher than any of the other skyscrapers, higher than Xhea had believed possible—and it had not been nearly high enough. They had not bridged the gap between the ground and the City above, where the Towers rose and fell as they slowly spun around the golden pillar of the Central Spire. They had failed—and, failing, had begun to fall.

And the Lower City—or, rather, the living entity formed of dark magic that existed within her home—had reached up and caught the falling structure at Xhea's behest.

Farrow now towered above the blackened ruin of the market like a sentinel, its glittering windows and pale façade all but lost within a tangle of black that wrapped around it like huge vines. They were not vines, for all that they had been grown, but tendrils formed of asphalt and plumbing pipe, concrete and wire and earth. Dead things, inert things, given life and shape by the inhuman intelligence that existed within the streets.

Looking at the ruin of the market and the broken people that searched it—looking at the ghosts that wandered through the ash, every one of them alone—was enough to stop her breath; but it was only as she looked at Farrow that Xhea understood that everything had forever changed.

The Lower City was alive like the Towers were alive—and now it was waking.

That entity was supposed to be sleeping—supposed to be healing from the damage that Rown's weapon had wrought, and from the loss of Farrow and the sudden exertion of its recapture. Healing as she was, as they all were. No longer.

Xhea closed her eyes, concentrating, trying to tune her senses with will alone.

There.

The living Lower City's song had been faint within Edren's walls, just a whisper of sound at the edge of her hearing. For days that sound had followed her like the memory of a song sung in dreams, only its echoes recalled on waking. Now, standing so close to the Lower City's living heart, she could hear it, *feel* it, as she had but once before: shifting like a restless ocean beneath her feet, the rise and fall of its song all around her.

And try though she might, she could not shake the feeling that it was calling to her.

"Do you hear that?" Xhea asked Shai. "The Lower City. Its song . . ."

What could she say? It sounded different than it had when the Lower City had first woken, she felt that clear as breathing, little though she could name the change. She couldn't even describe the song; couldn't recreate the sound, though she had tried.

It just sounded *wrong*. That was the word that had come to her, time and again as she listened, curled in her cot in one of skyscraper Edren's back rooms. As the days passed, that feeling of strangeness, of wrongness, had deepened. The living Lower City had not responded to the ribbons of magic Xhea had sent into the ground, imbued with question and concern. Or if it had responded, she'd neither heard nor understood its reply.

She'd come here in the hope that its voice would be clearer.

"There's something," Xhea started, then shook her head, frustrated. "It's saying . . ."

But Shai already understood. "Talk to it," she said. "Take as long as you need; I'll watch over you."

Xhea placed her hands on the ashy concrete beneath her. Her magic came easily now, needing no anger or pain to spur its rise. She sent small threads of power questing into the earth—then more magic, stronger magic, until it poured from her like a dark river. She felt that power as if it were a part of her, the tendrils of magic as real as her outstretched arms.

Anxiety was swept away by that tide, and a feeling of calm settled in its wake. Xhea understood the damage that dark magic did to her body—she knew that it was killing her slowly, blinding her, inhibiting her ability to heal—but in such moments she could not bring herself to care. With magic running unchecked through her body, she felt strong. She felt *whole*, all her mistakes unmade, all her broken pieces joined.

She was stronger now than she had been but weeks before. When she'd been in Farrow's care, the dark magic boy Ieren had called her weak—and had, later, been impressed by her growing magic. As if that diluted shadow had been anything close to what she'd been capable of wielding.

Now, with Shai's presence to hold her steady, it felt like there was nothing she could not do, nothing at all beyond her grasp.

Steady, she told herself, willing away that false confidence. *Concentrate.*

Xhea let her magic sink deeper into the streets and the tunnels and the earth that held them, reaching for the entity's heart. As their magics mingled, she felt the living Lower City's slow attention turn toward her.

"Hello," she whispered. "I'm here." She pushed her words into the flow of darkness, making her power vibrate with meaning.

A pause, and then the Lower City's song surged in answer. It sounded like nothing human, that song; no human voice, no instrument, had such range or layered complexity. It was beautiful in a way that made her shiver and want to pull away.

Xhea did neither. Instead she asked, "What is it? What's wrong?"

Again, there came that pause, as if the Lower City was considering her words. Its reply, when it came, was another surge of magic and meaning—flashes of images; impressions of sound, movement, emotion—that, for all their strength, Xhea struggled to understand.

It was easy, it seemed, for a vast magical entity to understand one small girl; another thing entirely for her to comprehend the complexity of its thoughts. The idea was humbling, even frightening.

A stream of magic was not enough, she realized. The last time they had spoken, when she'd first noticed the living Lower City's existence, magic had been all around her, thick in the air; magic had suffused her body, her breath, and her thoughts. What was a little river of dark compared to that?

For the first time since she'd left Farrow, since so much of her home had burned, Xhea let her magic flow freely. It roared up within her, a storm unbound, and she directed it to the ground. A moment, then she pulled, not just letting the power flow from her but also drawing back as much magic as she gave. From her to the living Lower City and back again, dark magic traveled in an unbroken loop.

She felt as the Lower City recognized the invitation inherent in her gesture, her desire to listen, to speak. There came a surge of magic—

A deafening chorus of joy and worry and welcome—

And, beneath that, something else. Something darker.

Pain. Betrayal.

Xhea gasped and she was falling—

She could not feel her body. She could not feel her hands, but she could feel the streets and the broken rubble of the market. She could not feel whether she was hot or cold, could not feel the ashy earth beneath her; instead, she *was* the earth—she was the ground and the buildings and the magic that filled them all.

She was the Lower City—and she hurt.

A second passed, an hour, a year—she did not know; there was only the magic. Anyone else might have been killed by that communion. As it was, she fought not to lose herself entirely.

"Slower," she told it—or tried to.

A moment, then the rush eased. Instead, she saw images, felt sensations: *Dark water, falling. Rain cascading over her, through her. The warmth of a thick blanket. The comfort of a full stomach.*

It meant magic, Xhea realized. Dark magic: the Lower City's food, its body and blood.

She'd seen it herself: the Central Spire, the great floating pillar around which the Towers spun, gathered the wisps of dark magic created by the City and poured it on the ground in a thick, roiling column. Dumped like waste, that magic poisoned the people that lived below—and had, over time, sparked life in the barren ground.

That rain turned hard, stinging. A storm at midnight, winds raging. A blanket too thin to keep her warm, no matter how tight she wrapped it. The aching hollow of hunger.

The hurt of loss. Betrayal.

Something had changed in the magic poured down from the City above, Xhea understood at last. For though that magic fell, night after night, something was different. Something was wrong.

The sensations continued, cascading through her one after the other as the living Lower City sang and sang.

Pain, sharp and burning—

A twist of smoke turned dark, and darker still—

Acrid smoke, a child's cry—

"No," she said again, "slower, not so much—"

But there was more—layer upon layer of images, sensations, meaning—and Xhea could not catch them all, could not hold them.

She was lost, overwhelmed; every way she turned was wrong, and then she was falling, falling.

Darkness.

Magic was a cold, dark lake, and Xhea surfaced gasping. Her body felt weighted, heavy against the concrete; her chest heaved as she struggled to remember the rhythms of breath.

But Shai was there, the ghost shining like a beacon; Xhea reached for her with shaking hands. She touched the tether that joined them and felt—stronger, somehow. Steadier. Felt some of Shai's magic flow into her through that link, balancing the tide of dark.

"The Lower City," Xhea said, and then had to break off, coughing. Sweetness, why hadn't she thought to bring water? Still she tried: "The Central Spire is—"

"Breathe," Shai told her. The ghost knelt by Xhea's feet, her blond hair falling forward like a shining curtain. "It's okay, just breathe."

It took time to steady her breathing; longer to calm her heart's frantic beat. Xhea held to Shai with hands and tether both, as if the ghost were her anchor to the world.

It was so easy to be overwhelmed by magic—and the living Lower City was nothing but magic. So easy to lose all sense of time and place and herself.

"How long?" Xhea whispered. More than a minute, for all that her communication with the Lower City had seemed to run at the speed of thought. Her eyes were crusted with the salt of dried tears; her tongue was thick, her throat parched. The light's angle had changed, too; Farrow's shadow, once long and thin as it stretched across the barren ground, had grown short.

"Nearly four hours."

Shai's voice held no reproach, and yet Xhea started nonetheless, making the charms and coins bound into her hair clink and chime as they fell across her shoulders.

There came a sound, then, echoing around them. Not magic, but a sound in truth: a clarion call that rang out across the Lower City and echoed through the twisted streets and alleyways. A sound that came from above.

Shai turned, her hands rising in reflex, some half-formed spell twining about her fingers like a slender ribbon.

"No," the ghost said. "They can't—"

Again the sound came, louder—and it was familiar, for all that Xhea had never heard it before. It was a sound described in stories, a sound not heard for decades—at least not here on the ground.

Would that it had stayed that way.

Out in the burned ruin of the market, people had stilled. They stood now with blackened hands slack at their sides, their mouths agape, whatever small objects they had reclaimed from the rubble dropped to lie forgotten at their feet. The ghosts, too, stopped and turned, the sound enough to break into even their grief and loss and denial.

As one, they looked up.

The sound came a third time, loudest of all. The dust shivered with it, puffs of ash rising; windows rattled in their panes. The voices that had cried out in fear or surprise from the first two calls now fell silent, leaving that high, shimmering note to echo through the Lower City uncontested.

Xhea closed her eyes.

Days, she thought in slow despair. For days she had heard whispers of the Lower City's song, awake and in dream. It had been calling for her.

Calling for help.

She'd ignored it, or failed to respond, and each was its own kind of failure. Now she understood—but it was too late.

Chapter Two

The Messenger fell from the Central Spire like a shooting star, haloed in brilliant light. It wasn't necessary, Xhea thought; surely the sound had been announcement enough. Yet the Messenger glowed so brightly she had to raise her hand against the glare, helpless to do anything but stare.

Xhea watched as the figure came to within a stone's throw of the ground. A male Messenger, unless she missed her guess. He wore a uniform that she knew only from stories, pale and edged with light, the aggressive cut suggesting both speed and strength. She knew the uniform was white and gold; in her black-and-white vision, Xhea saw not just white, but faint, detailed patterns, as if poems were written into the fabric.

Even without the uniform, they would have known the man was from the Spire from the blur of glowing magic where his face should have been. It cascaded like a waterfall, endlessly flowing, and only suggestions of features showed beneath: dark shadows of eyes, the horizontal slash of a mouth.

As shocked as Xhea felt—as much as the shock showed on the faces of the gathered onlookers, a crowd that grew larger by the moment—Shai's expression was worse.

"A Messenger?" the ghost whispered. "*Here?*"

Messengers only went to the City's elite—Tower council members, the best casters, those who ruled in thought and deed—bringing word of things too important to be borne by spell alone. A spell could be intercepted, if with difficulty; a spell could be twisted or changed by a talented caster. But a Messenger? Never. Their identities were hidden, their loyalty unshakable. And the penalty for interfering with one—or with a message they bore—was death.

Only twice before had a Messenger come to the Lower City, and one of those times was so long ago that Xhea suspected the story was more legend than truth, a tale grown large in the telling. The other time . . .

Xhea shook her head. That time, nearly a century before, there had been a plague in the Lower City. Shipping routes to the ground were shut down as even the poorer Towers refused to do business with the infected. Lacking resources, the skyscrapers struggled to help their own citizens. The unaffiliated—the poorest of the Lower City dwellers—were left to fend for themselves.

Bodies, it was said, were piled along the curbs and dumped in back alleys like refuse.

Anyone with the contacts in the City—or the strength left with which to send a message—pleaded for help from those above. But weeks passed before the Central Spire sent an acknowledgment. Their response, delivered by shining Messenger, had been four words.

No assistance is forthcoming.

"He's not here for you," Xhea told Shai. She meant the words for comfort, but they sounded harsh, accusing. She tried again: "He's here because . . ."

Because the Spire is trying to kill the living Lower City.

Or so the entity believed. It was a preposterous thought; the words caught behind her teeth. But Shai didn't notice, only stared up in horror.

Slowly, Xhea pushed herself to her feet with aid of her cane, then took a few careful steps from the wall that shielded her. She wanted to run, to hide, and knew there was no point in either.

Judging that the crowd beneath his feet had grown large enough, the Messenger held his arms wide. Spheres of light flew out from the motion, scattering in every direction. Xhea flinched as one flew over her head, expecting a spell, a bomb, a shock of light—

"Magical relays," Shai murmured, seemingly stunned; her attention never left the Messenger. "They project the sound of his voice."

It was true. "People of the Lower City," the Messenger proclaimed, and Xhea heard not just his words but their echoes. It sounded like dozens of people spoke in unison: a ringing choir made of a single voice.

The Messenger waited until those echoes faded. "People of the Lower City," he repeated. "Draw near."

The gathered Lower City dwellers, suspicious, moved no closer. The Messenger continued, his upper-City accent clear despite the distortion.

"By order of the Central Spire, all inhabitants of the Lower City are required to evacuate immediately. The Spire has claimed this territory as its own. You have three days to leave the area."

There were gasps, shouts—Xhea knew not what else. She couldn't hear over the sudden sound of her heart pounding in her ears.

Three days. Xhea blinked, stared, swallowed. *Three days.* The words didn't make sense, no matter that she repeated them like some terrible mantra.

Again the Messenger gestured. A coiled spell flew from his outstretched palm and expanded into a great pane of light. No, not a pane, but a map. An aerial view of the Lower City spread across that surface, depicted in perfect clarity. Even from this distance, Xhea could make out roads, rooftops, and the few stunted, scraggly trees that managed to grow in the Lower City core.

Though her feet were firmly on the ground, that sudden twist in perspective was dizzying. Xhea gripped her cane to keep herself steady, wishing she could look away.

Like a dark tide, gray washed across the map, flooding out from the center. Xhea tried to judge the shade; it was probably red, she thought, or maybe green. Wider that stain spread, and wider, until almost all of the Lower City was darkened by its shadow.

"The Central Spire claims this territory," the Messenger repeated. He gestured to the map as if any might have missed it; as if every face in the crowd wasn't uplifted, features writ with stunned dismay. In contrast, the Messenger only seemed bored.

The living Lower City was right. If Xhea had harbored any lingering thoughts that she'd misunderstood the entity's meaning, they were banished. Why else would the Spire want to claim this territory? The ruins of the city that had come before and the homes made within those painstakingly preserved structures had no true value to the Spire, nothing worth the effort it would take to claim it.

Until now.

She had wondered, distantly, what the Central Spire thought of recent events in the Lower City. It was clear that the Spire cared little for the people on the ground, nor for how those people might suffer as a result of the dark magic poured down upon them, night after night. The Spire did not care that Lower City dwellers' own magic was thin and weak; that they died young, or sickened frequently, or were poisoned by the very walls around them, the ground beneath their feet. That they could not go underground without being overwhelmed by the pain of the dark magic that had soaked into the earth through those untold years.

And the living Lower City itself? For, she'd thought, surely the Spire knew what they had made—what their dumped waste magic had created. The Towers were no different, born of the power poured into them; they were living entities that existed within the grown metal of their structures, for all that those structures knew no ground.

It had never occurred to her that the Spire had not known of the living Lower City's existence at all—not until it had reached up at Xhea's command and caught a newborn Tower as it fell from the sky.

"It's my fault," she whispered, too quietly even for Shai to hear.

Maybe it was true. But it was Farrow's fault, too—Ahrent Altaigh and the casters he led, for forcing their skyscraper's transformation too early, too quickly. It was Rown's fault for creating the desolation and the chaos that had sparked Farrow's desperate rise, and now made Farrow's new location and the tangle of black that held it so very apparent, even from above.

Xhea barely knew anyone in Farrow, then or now, for all that it was the place where she'd been born. She didn't *care* for anyone there. And yet, she had not been able to just let them die, smashed on the ground for others' mistakes.

Would you change it? Xhea asked herself. *Knowing this would be the consequence, would you let Farrow fall?*

She did not know, only felt her stomach drop away at the thought.

Sound grew as the gathered crowd understood. They shouted about their homes, their businesses, about the food supply and the dangers in the ruins beyond. Their panicked voices raised in overlapping clamor.

One onlooker shouted louder than the rest: "This is my home!"

The Messenger lifted a hand as if to wave away the words. "Not anymore."

Mutters, beneath that—shocked, disbelieving, angry.

"You want us to evacuate?" another asked. "And go where?"

A man's voice added, "Is the Spire paying to evacuate us?"

"You may go wherever you can afford," the Messenger replied, his cultured tones weighted by scorn. For a moment, Xhea saw what he saw: a gathered crowd of tired, sweaty people, digging through the rubble for garbage. The nearest buildings were burned and fallen, all tumbled bricks and shattered concrete; the farther buildings were aged and leaning, with sooty laundry hung over balcony railings.

What use in saving these people, these huddled, needy masses? Who would bother to lift them from the ground, to feed and clothe and house them, when all they would offer in return was yet more burden? No magic to provide, no skills, no renai. No use.

"Xhea," Shai said—and pointed.

Xhea blinked as a ghost stepped from the light of the Messenger's halo where she'd hidden, tight against his body and those protective spells. She, too, wore the Spire's uniform, even in death—but it was not pale, like the Messenger's, but darker. The ghost's features swam in Xhea's vision as if blurred by the memory of a shimmering mask. Her hair, though, was distinctive: a cascade of dark, shining curls utterly at odds with the stark look of her uniform.

Her red uniform, Xhea realized. She was an Enforcer—or the ghost of one.

If sight of a Messenger in the Lower City was a shock, a uniformed Enforcer would have made everyone flee, screaming, as fast as their feet might carry them. As it was, Xhea stood as if rooted, cold sweat slicking her skin.

If a Messenger was the embodiment of the Spire's voice, an Enforcer was their strong arm, the will of the elite made flesh. Xhea saw no weapons on the ghost—though they would have had no power in death. Then again, few Enforcers needed anything so crude as a weapon.

The ghost stepped away from the Messenger and descended, the thick, near-invisible tether that joined them stretching as she went. Unseen by all but Xhea and the gathered dead, the ghost of the Enforcer began to methodically search the crowd. Xhea watched as she stepped close to one person after another, looking at their faces, gauging their reactions. Some stood like stone, attention fully on the Messenger, while others shivered as if with sudden chill.

Xhea turned back to the Messenger and stared for all she was worth, letting her unfeigned shock and dismay control her expression. Even so, she couldn't help but track the ghost's progress from her peripheral vision. Couldn't help but notice that the ghost focused on women—young women, even children, especially those with dark complexions and hair.

She's looking for me.

"Shai," Xhea murmured, trying not to move her lips. "Stand away from me, and keep your magic—"

"I know," Shai replied. Already she'd moved as if to the end of her tether's limits, and now damped her Radiant glow until that light was only a glimmer, as if it was nothing more than the memory of sunlight on her skin.

But ghosts had always been able to sense Xhea's presence. No matter that she looked like just another Lower City dweller, slack-jawed and afraid, she could not hide her power from a ghost.

She could run—or try. She was rebuilding strength in the knee she'd injured months before, healed and scarred though it was; but even with her brace she couldn't move quickly—or, given the coins and charms in her hair, quietly. And for all the noise and restlessness of the crowd, people moved *toward* the Messenger, not away. Running would make her an instant target.

Target for what? She did not know—and really didn't want to find out.

Ghosts could not hurt her—but the Central Spire? The Spire controlled all dark magic and its use within the City. If they had heard of her existence . . .

If? Xhea asked herself mockingly. Just a few months before, she'd traveled to the City, snuck into Tower Eridian, and shown her dark magic in front of the Tower's gathered citizens. She'd *poured* that power into Eridian's living heart, wounding it. If anything, she should be grateful that it had taken so long for the Spire to track her down.

The Messenger kept talking, his stilted words plain and obviously scripted.

"What do you want with my store?" a man cried. "What do you want with my home?"

"The Central Spire has claimed this territory," the Messenger replied. "You cannot remain. Nothing else must be explained."

"There's *nothing* in the ruins," a woman yelled over the Messenger's bland statement. "No shelter from the elements, nothing to protect us from the walkers!"

Others joined in.

"I don't want my children to die!"

"You can't do this!"

On and on—growing loud enough to drown out some of the Messenger's reply. In the streets beyond, where the Messenger's bodiless voice echoed, Xhea could hear more shouts, the clamor of other angry voices—but no words.

Xhea realized she'd lost sight of the ghost of the Enforcer, and dared not search for her. Instead she took a cautious step back, and another, trying to look as if she feared only the Messenger or the crowd at his feet. Trying to slip into the protection of the corner of the wall, out of easy line of sight—and from there, away.

Besides, she reasoned, ghosts couldn't hurt her. If the ghost spotted her leaving, what could she do but flail at the end of her tether and watch Xhea run away?

Another careful step. Another.

A question made the crowd grow quiet, and it came from an older woman who stood some span from the Messenger's floating feet. There was nothing aggressive about her stance, though every line of her thin, aged body spoke of someone who would not be moved. She looked up, strands of white hair blowing about her face.

"What if we don't go?" Her voice carried across the crowd, almost as if she, too, used a spell to be heard. The streets echoed with the defiant sound of her voice.

The Messenger had no scripted answer. Instead, his shoulders rose in the suggestion of a shrug. He said, softer, almost amused, "Then so be it."

Silence fell—an ominous silence. Xhea saw more than one person bend to the ground, gathering rocks. Before anyone cast a stone, the Messenger lifted his head, spread his arms wide and proclaimed, "Three days! This is your only warning."

At his gesture, the map of the so-called "evacuation zone" popped like a soap bubble, only a glimmer of dispersing magic to mark where it had once been. There was more magic in that spell—more magic, even, in its fading exhaust—than most people here would generate in a week.

"There you are," a voice said.

"Xhea, no—" Shai started, but it was too late.

Xhea turned on instinct and met the eyes of the ghost before her—eyes that wavered and shifted, as did her face, as if seen through running water. But she saw the ghost woman's smile, a slow lift of dark-painted lips, as Xhea realized her mistake.

Xhea flinched away, pretending she'd just been looking at the angry crowd, but it was too late. The Enforcer ghost moved toward Xhea, her tether stretching beyond anything Xhea had seen occur naturally. Except, she saw, it wasn't a tether at all, but a spell. There was no child on the other end of that line, siphoning her spirit like milk through a straw—but it was the same. A dark magic binding.

Closer the ghost came, and closer still, white teeth visible through the dark slashes of her lips as her smile grew wider.

"And here I thought finding you would be difficult. I suppose you're not clever enough for that." The ghost tsked. "Ah, well. Makes my life easier."

It was Shai who replied, moving to intercept the Enforcer. "Stay back," she said. Perhaps she meant to sound hard, or menacing. She sounded afraid.

Xhea stopped abruptly as her shoulder blades hit concrete— the wall that she'd thought might shelter her. It was no shelter now, only a trap, closing off her limited avenues of escape.

She's just a ghost, Xhea told herself. *There's nothing she can do.*

The words felt like lies—for as she stared at the Enforcer's blurred face and the fierce halo of her hair, she realized she could feel the ghost before her. She felt stronger, more real, than any of the dead but Shai; something about her drew Xhea's eye and attention both, luring her in.

No, she realized. She didn't feel the ghost, but the hidden spell she bore.

"Run," Shai cried, diving between Xhea and the Enforcer. Shai's hands were already raised, shining with magic, as she made herself into a barrier through which the other ghost might not pass.

Too late.

The ghostly Enforcer had no magic of her own, neither bright nor dark; it did not matter. As Shai made to strike her down, the woman simply *pushed*, her hands hitting Shai in the chest as her leg swept Shai's feet from under her.

The move shouldn't have worked—neither ghost was subject to gravity's dictates—and yet the beliefs of the living died hard. Shai tumbled, fell—and the other ghost caught her arm and cast her away, as if she were nothing more than a ball to be thrown. Shai screamed as she flew.

In the scuffle, Xhea tried to escape. But, despite the plastic brace, her knee buckled beneath the strain of sudden movement. Xhea cried out and nearly fell, catching herself at the last minute and swearing all the while.

When she looked up, the Enforcer stood before her. The ghost raised her hand to the center of her chest where her tether was bound—and where, hidden inside her heart, a spell waited. A dark magic spell, shining like a dark pearl—and something else. At the gesture, the spell emerged into the ghost's hand; a flick, and it was airborne.

The spell expanded into a great, shimmering net that enfolded Xhea as it fell. She felt as each of that net's strands touched her skin, sinking through the fabric of her jacket and pants as if they were nothing. The spell *burned*.

Xhea opened her mouth in a soundless scream. Her knees gave way, suddenly boneless, and her bad knee twisted as she crumpled.

Sprawled on the ground, Xhea wanted to writhe, to scratch at her skin—anything to escape the burning spell that crawled over her and sank into her flesh. But she could not move; she only lay there, paralyzed, gasping for breath.

Above, the Towers glittered as they danced, spinning almost imperceptibly around the Central Spire. As she watched, the Messenger rose, the spells around him flaring like shining wings and sending him soaring skyward. He had never once touched the ground.

"Bye now," said the ghost of the Enforcer. Her blurred lips formed a thin and terrible smile, and then she was yanked into the air in the wake of the departing Messenger.

As the spell sank into her, Xhea did not surrender to unconsciousness; she fought it all the way down. And lost.

Chapter Three

Shai flew, tumbling, disoriented. She had no sense of ground or sky; only of motion, sudden and swift, and something that was almost like pain, echoing through her.

No, she thought. *Xhea!*

It was only as she fell to the pavement—fell *through* it—that she remembered gravity did not affect her; nor should the other ghost's blow. It was instinct and a lifetime of experience that made her flail and fall. Shai halted her wild descent, then rose, reorienting herself. Angry voices swelled as the Messenger's last words echoed through the Lower City, creating a confusing cacophony of sound.

Shai had been prepared for an attack—had woven defensive spells in newborn reflex—and then the ghost had just . . . *hit* her. She'd never been hit before. It *hurt*.

Except, she couldn't quite say what hurt, or how. Strange as the feeling of the ghost striking her chest and kicking out her legs had been, the pain didn't seem to come from those points of impact. Rather it washed over her, through her; pain without focus or source.

Xhea's pain, she realized. And it grew worse by the minute.

Since they had been rejoined, both she and Xhea had noticed a change in the nature of their link—one that went further than the transfer of magic, bright and dark, that happened naturally. Other things occasionally traveled that length: emotions, sometimes, or thoughts, faint and strangely blurred by transmission.

What she felt now? There was no softening of that pain's edges; only sensation, raw and ragged, that raged down the tether and into Shai's chest. She flinched from it, breath gone short. Or, if this was Xhea's pain blunted, she dared not think what Xhea felt.

Shai caught her bearings. There was the corner of the fallen building with its alcove—and there, on the ground before it, was a dark, huddled lump. Xhea. Of the Enforcer ghost there was no sign; only the spell she'd cast remained, a glittering net that settled over Xhea's fallen body.

Settled over her, and sank into her.

With a cry Shai flew to her friend's side, her own magic flaring in response to her sudden fear. Xhea lay as if boneless, mostly on her back, her cane some distance from her outstretched hand. Her head was turned to the side, her hair a wild tangle around her face, coins and charms glinting.

"Xhea?" Again Shai called, and again. No response, not so much as a twitch. *Unconscious*, Shai thought—though she could feel some echo of Xhea's pain washing through her.

But it was the spell that held Shai's attention—or what was left of it. For what moments before had been a gleaming net of bright magic had become but glints and glimmers of light spread across Xhea's exposed skin. The rest had already been absorbed. *No wonder she's in pain.* As Shai made to grab for the spell, thinking to pull it from Xhea's face—to unravel it, unmake it, *get it off her*—even those thin strands flickered and faded.

Xhea's dark magic had burned the spell away to nothing.

Shai exhaled in relief. "She'll be all right," she murmured. With the spell gone, Xhea's pain would ease and she would wake.

Whatever the ghostly Enforcer—or whoever had sent her—had intended with that spell didn't matter now. They'd failed. Xhea was going to be fine.

And yet . . .

Shai's hand went to the spelled tether that joined them, her brow creasing. For, though Xhea's pain had momentarily eased, it was now returning—a sharper, edged pain. Shai cringed as its echo stabbed into the pit of her stomach.

She looked deeper.

Shai had thought the spell was a net of bright magic. But as that net burned away, a second spell was released: one of dark, coiled magic, sinuous and slow. As Shai stared, that power sank into Xhea's blood and flowed through her body, darkening her hands and arms and face like a spreading stain.

Delivery system, Shai thought in shock, *and payload.*

She knew how to read bright magic spells clear as any book; she was even learning how to weave them. Yet though she could see that it was a spell and not pure dark magic that flowed through Xhea, Shai could no more understand it than she could one of the ancient, forgotten tongues.

Having infiltrated Xhea's body, the spell contracted, its power concentrating in Xhea's chest like a storm cloud.

Shai did not know what it was doing, or why, and she did not care. For as the spell worked, Xhea's skin went waxen pale and her lips darkened with a tint of blue. Sweat broke out across her forehead and dribbled down her cheeks like tears, and her eyes flickered beneath their closed lids as if she were caught in some terrible dream.

"Stop it." Shai wished she sounded strong rather than frightened. Wished she could force that strange dark magic to respond to her command. "*Stop it!*"

She reached, her own magic flaring. No spell there, no clever weavings of thought and image and memory; only need and the raw force of her power.

I'm sorry, Shai thought, and stabbed a ray of bright magic into Xhea's chest as if it were a blade.

There was pain then—hers, Xhea's, it was all the same. Shai struggled to think, struggled to keep her power flowing. Still she reached, grabbing the dark magic clotting beneath Xhea's breastbone and slicing through it with ease of breath. Dark magic could destroy bright, yes—but enough bright magic could also burn away the dark, sure as night yielded to sunlight. One only needed enough power, and the will to wield it.

Strength of power Shai had never lacked—and will? Anything, it seemed, might be learned.

Shai shredded the dark spell, wincing at the pain of every cut—gritting her teeth and shouting, as if the sound might make that power flee in terror. She cut it away from Xhea's hands and heart and face, ribbons of magic dispersing like smoke from windblown candles. She cut and cut and cut.

And watched as the spell regrew.

No, Shai realized, drawing back in horror. It had tapped into the wellspring of Xhea's power and now turned her own magic against her, using it as fuel to rebuild the spell-strands that Shai had torn away.

Shai could do nothing to stop it—only watched as that magic wrapped around Xhea and coiled tighter like a noose.

The pain was less, now; Shai could draw breath without wincing. It was no relief. On the ground, Xhea shook and trembled as if she were freezing. Her lips were blue, and her fingernails; her eyelids seemed almost bruised.

A noise made Shai look up—a concussive bang that echoed around the ruined market like rattled stones, followed by screams. The crowd had only grown in the Messenger's absence.

Perhaps some people had run to find shelter or loved ones— or even to follow the Spire's command. But more had gathered here or come to stand in the streets nearby, and now raged up at the Spire's lowermost point. Shai could not understand what the crowd shouted, only listened as their voices grew louder until it seemed the very ground should tremble with the force of that anger, that fear and hate and rage.

What she'd heard had only been a firework, she realized; smoke trailed above the crowd. But it might have as easily been a weapon or a spell; it might have been a rock hurled toward the Spire only to come tumbling down on the heads of those gathered.

Shai felt a wash of fear that wasn't for herself, wasn't even for Xhea. This crowd was angry and only getting angrier. Soon there would be bruises and blood—if not worse.

The crowd, too, was pushing closer. Xhea lay near the wall's shelter; the fallen building's rubble formed a low barrier that would slow any approach. Even so, with people flooding into the burned-out market—and the number who already shouted, red-faced, with their ash-blackened fists raised to the sky—Xhea might be trampled in minutes.

Again Shai turned to her, wishing she could gather Xhea in her arms and carry her away. Away from the crowd, the burned market, the Lower City—all of it. The desire was so strong it nearly clogged her throat. *Or perhaps*, she realized, swallowing, *that's the tears.*

"Oh, don't cry," she said, disgusted. What would Xhea say if she saw her like this, crouched and curled and *weeping*?

Xhea's eyelids flickered, opened.

"Xhea?" Shai cried. But Xhea was not waking. Her eyes rolled back in her head until only thin slivers of white showed, and she began to convulse. Shai swore and did the only thing she could think of: she wove a spell to cushion Xhea's head, keeping her from harm until the seizure had passed.

Even as Shai lowered Xhea's head gently back to the pavement, she tried to think of a way to make that spell bigger, more powerful—something strong enough to lift and carry Xhea's whole body.

As if no one would notice an unconscious girl floating by.

And if they did—what would they do? Shai did not know, only feared it as the crowd grew and surged around her, all those voices becoming one great roar.

Not knowing what else to do, Shai wove a shield spell like the one she'd used to protect the market from the brunt of Rown's magical attack. This shield was much smaller, only arcing over Xhea and the cane at her side, with the edge closest to the broken wall open to let in air.

As the spell came into being, the noise level dropped. It was no blessing. For now Shai could hear Xhea's breath: thin and faltering gasps that became thinner and weaker by the moment.

Are they killing her? Was that what the spell had been for—Xhea's slow but certain death? Because if so, it was a horrible way to die; even Rown's hunters might grant a more merciful death with the serrated edge of one of their blades.

Shai reached again for the spelled tether, suddenly thinking: if she could not slice away the dark spell from the outside, perhaps she could destroy it from the inside out. She made her power flow inward, no longer shining but funneled through the tether that joined them. Into that power, too, she channeled all the feelings that churned within her, that fear and desperate hope, as if emotion were a lifeline that she might cast for Xhea to grab.

There was no pain now, no hurt—but nothing else came in its wake. Where Shai usually felt some measure of Xhea's magic flow back into her, as if repaying the power she provided, now there was nothing, not even an echo of dark.

Still she poured all of her magic down their link—enough magic to shield a skyscraper or save a man's life; enough magic to fuel a Tower, enough magic to set the sky alight with gold and green and blue. Enough magic, she hoped, to keep her friend *here*—living, breathing. With her.

She felt, too, as the tether that unspooled from her heart grew stronger, wider, that length of near-invisible energy shimmering between them like heat from flat metal.

Stay with me. Shai watched as Xhea's breathing faltered. *Please, stay with me.*

At last, the dark spell writhing in Xhea grew still.

Shai stared at it, buried deep within Xhea's chest, but could not tell where the spell ended and Xhea's magic began. Yet that magic? She shuddered to see it. For once where power had filled Xhea, dark and steady, now there was only a small point of perfect, darkest black. A hard stone of magic caught in the chambers of her heart.

A long moment passed, then Xhea drew a shuddering breath, and another. Some of the painful tension left her limbs, and her shivering, spasming muscles relaxed to let her lie bonelessly, sprawled across the ashen pavement.

It should have been a relief—and it was, knowing that Xhea lived. Watching as her breathing steadied and slowed; watching as the blue left her lips. But she did not look well and she did not wake.

Around them, the crowd grew and grew. So many voices were raised in anger, in fear—and there was no easy outlet for those emotions. *Haven't we been through enough?* Shai thought to them, seeing their twisted faces, their hands raised with fists or weapons high. But it was to the Central Spire to which those words were best directed; the golden Spire that floated, serene, oblivious, at the heart of the City above.

She did not understand what they had done to Xhea, or why. She did not understand the Spire's command, sudden and immovable. She did not know what they wanted with this broken ground, or these burned and fallen buildings, or the ruins beyond.

No one did. And as they screamed and raged, wept and ran, Shai huddled over Xhea's body and held her—or tried to.

For when she reached out to touch Xhea's cheek, that golden skin gone waxen and pale, her fingers passed through as if she were barely real. Shai gasped and drew back, more shocked than when she'd been struck.

"No." Shai reached for Xhea's hand—wanting to touch those fingers that curled toward Xhea's palm like a flower's wilting petals. Wanting to hold Xhea's hand in her own, as she had so many times before. Yet though she felt resistance, it was only like passing her fingers through sand.

"Absent gods, Xhea," Shai whispered. "What have they done to you?"

There came a knock on the shield spell.

Shai jumped and turned.

Behind her stood Torrence, the sandy-haired bounty hunter who had worked to abduct Shai and Xhea both—and had succeeded in stealing Xhea but weeks before. They were allies now, Xhea had told her; Shai failed to believe it.

Torrence stood casually, his hand upraised to knock, every line of his posture saying that he cared not a whit for the people who ran and pushed and shouted but feet away. His eyes, and whatever truths they might tell, were hidden behind a pair of dark, battered glasses—artifacts, Shai thought, or something modeled on an ancient design. No City citizen would create, never mind wear, anything half so garish.

Behind him like a hulking shadow stood his partner, Daye.

Since Farrow's fall, the pair had tried to tail Xhea day and night—attempting, they said, to protect her, and only seeming to achieve a mutual feeling of frustration. "Listen," Xhea had told them at one point. "*You* were the ones trying to abduct me. Now you've stopped. There, problem solved."

Torrence had only laughed, while Daye, predictably, had said nothing at all.

Shai had never liked the pair, no matter what Xhea said. That morning she'd been glad that they managed to slip from Edren's walls without the bounty hunters. Now, she felt she'd never been so glad to see anyone.

Torrence knocked again, the spell shivering beneath his knuckles, then seemed to look directly at Shai. *Just the glasses,* she reassured herself, and felt unnerved nonetheless.

"Little ghost, little ghost," Torrence said in a sing-song voice, "Let me come in. Or I'll huff—"

Daye pushed him aside, none too gently. "Is she hurt?" Daye asked.

The woman's voice was quiet, but clipped and hard. She didn't bother to search for Shai, nor try to direct her words toward her. Daye only stared at Xhea, her eyes intense despite her impassive impression. In spite of everything, Shai liked her better for it.

She dropped the spell, and the crowd's roar rushed over her like a wave. Torrence stood straighter and gave a quick nod.

"Spell's down," he said, suddenly all business. Daye moved to kneel at Xhea's side.

She did a visual inspection first, scanning Xhea's outstretched arms and curled legs, the length of her torso hidden beneath her oversized jackets with its many pockets. Eyes narrowed, she watched the rise and fall of Xhea's breathing, then leaned close to peer at her face. At last she reached to feel Xhea's pulse—and when Daye's fingers touched Xhea's neck, the woman did not stiffen or jump, only hesitated then drew back slowly, as if surprised.

"What is it?" Torrence asked.

"I can touch her."

Shai stared, aghast, but Torrence only shrugged. "Well, that makes things easier."

He stooped to grab Xhea's cane as Daye knelt and gathered Xhea in her arms. Shai could only watch, feeling anxious, useless, as Torrence scanned the area—and drew his knife.

It was not like Daye's knives, the wicked blades that she wore on each hip. Knives, Shai knew, that Daye had used to stab Mercks, supervisor of Edren's night watch, before she left him to die alone in the cold and dark of the underground. Torrence's blade was short and tapered, no longer than a man's finger; though the way it glinted in the sunlight made Shai stiffen nonetheless.

What is he . . . ?

He can't . . .

The thoughts did not form, only anger, fueled by her growing anxiety. The last thing this day needed was blood.

"If you don't want anyone to get hurt, ghost girl," Torrence said in her direction, his eyes hidden beneath the dark glasses, "you might want to help clear the way."

He can see me, she realized, shocked.

Then Shai pushed such thoughts aside—for as Daye lifted Xhea into her arms and stood, her friend gave a low, frightened noise like an animal in pain. Xhea's brow creased, yet her eyes remained closed; and her hands, curled now together and tucked close to Daye's chest, trembled.

Again Shai touched the tether that joined them and sent a wave of magic and reassurance down that length.

"You're going to be okay," she whispered—and then wondered whether she meant the words to comfort Xhea or herself.

"Quickly now," Torrence said. Cane in one hand, knife in the other, he stepped into the crowd. He did not lead with his weapon but with his shoulders, moving almost like a dancer as he pushed people aside and cleared a path for Daye to follow. Shai's fingers danced in sudden inspiration: if she twisted her shield spell just *so*, and made it smaller, more maneuverable, she could nudge this man aside and stop this woman from walking forward . . .

Step by careful step, they made their way to safety.

Chapter Four

Xhea opened her eyes. Blinked, cringed, and thought better of the idea.

She lay for a long moment in the blessed darkness behind her eyelids, feeling the ground hard and uneven beneath her, hearing an angry crowd some distance away. Closer, there were the sounds of many footsteps—a road?—and a hushed conversation.

Don't want to move, she thought. As long as she stayed motionless, nothing hurt. Even her scarred knee felt strangely numb.

She'd lie here forever if she could, swaddled and safe in this strange drifting state, this place where pain was only a memory. But she rarely got what she wanted.

Xhea cracked open a cautious eye. She lay in an alley between two crumbling brick buildings, the scents of moss and mold and stagnant water thick in the late summer air. Above her were crisscrossed laundry lines heavy with sheets and clothes. Prayer flags—long scraps of cloth patterned with charms—hung limply from a nearby window, bleached pale by sun and rain and snow.

Nearby, Shai paced. The ghost seemed anxious; her feet were six inches off the ground, and when she turned at the end of each line of steps, her shoulder passed through the brick wall of the flanking building.

Closer, sitting behind her, Xhea could just make out two shapes, their shadows stretched across her. Low voices murmured.

She felt like she used to when she'd used bright magic as a drug, unknowingly keeping her own power at bay. This was like the moment when the bright magic had dwindled to nothing, the color leached from her vision, her euphoria burned to ash and weary lethargy; the moment just before the headache came, and the shakes.

Sweetness, she thought. *What happened?*

Memory later; sitting first. Xhea forced herself upright—and groaned as a wave of dizziness all but knocked her unconscious again. Clutching her head, she sagged back to the ground, swearing.

"Xhea!" Shai rushed to her side. "Are you okay?"

"Ow," Xhea muttered. She held her head until the dizziness passed, then rubbed her eyes as if to scrub away any desire to close them again. Then slowly, slowly, she pushed her way back to sitting.

"Ah," said a voice from behind her. "Not dead after all."

"Don't sound so disappointed, Torrence."

She made to turn, but Shai was closer, the ghost pressing into Xhea's space with a near-panicked expression.

"Are you all right? How do you—I mean, are you—?"

"It's okay, Shai," Xhea said quietly. *What happened?* she thought again. She hadn't seen Shai this upset since . . . well, since she'd thought that Xhea was about to die. And, no matter how strange she felt, death didn't seem terribly close. "I'm okay, just a bit dizzy."

She reached for Shai's hand. Shai all but grabbed her—then yanked her hand back as if burned.

What—?

But her fingers, Xhea saw, were trembling. *Right on time.*

Trying to hide that weakness, Xhea placed her hands on the damp ground and pushed herself around until her back rested against the nearest building. The alley was wider than her legs outstretched, but not by much.

Blocking the alley's mouth sat Torrence and Daye—though of the latter, Xhea could see only her back. Daye watched the street beyond, a knife unsheathed on her lap, her hands resting on her knees, still as stone. Xhea caught glimpses of people in the street, some of them with arms laden with clothing and other belongings, most of them running.

Torrence watched her quietly, his eyes hidden behind night-black glasses.

"No escaping you, is there?" Xhea said. She meant it as a joke, but the words fell heavily into the silence between them.

Torrence said softly, "No, darlin', there isn't—and you should be glad for that."

"What happened?"

"We thought you could tell us. Something knocked you flat, and your friend there," he nodded toward Shai, "hasn't been able to tell us what. But she's pretty upset."

Xhea said the first thing that came into her head: "You can *see* her?"

"I think he can see my magic," Shai said at the same time that Torrence replied, "Stop changing the subject."

Xhea raised an eyebrow. *Sore point, Torrence?*

The bounty hunter's vision had been damaged in Ieren's attack in Farrow, when the dark magic boy had attempted to pull Torrence's spirit out of his living body through his eyes. Had Ieren succeeded, Xhea's sometime-ally would have become food: his ghost devoured in an attempt to balance the power of Ieren's dark magic, while his body would have been empty, living. A night walker.

The attack had sensitized him to light and magic, but she'd thought that he wore the sunglasses only to hide some unsightly damage to his eyes themselves. Poor as he was, Torrence had been nearly magic-blind, only able to see magic spelled to be visible—but now he could see Shai unaided. Bright as the ghost was to Xhea, only powerful magic users could catch a glimpse of Shai—or, rather, of her Radiant magic.

Interesting, Xhea thought, glancing from Shai to Torrence and back again. And, she realized, not the point.

Because something in Daye's watchful pose and the chaos of the street beyond—something in Shai's frantic worry, and the strange feeling in Xhea's head and heart and hands—made her remember. *The Messenger.*

"Three days," she whispered.

The Enforcer ghost—and the spell. She remembered that net of light arcing over her, remembered the searing pain as it wrapped around her. Remembered, too, the ghost's blurred smile and her mocking wave as she departed.

There was no sign of that spell now, though she pushed up her sleeves to check; no sign, either, of its purpose. Just a spell to knock her out, she supposed—make her easier to transport. Yet if that had been the first stage of an abduction, it had been foiled—little though she wanted to admit that to the bounty hunters.

"Xhea." Shai made an effort to hide her fear. "Can you use your magic?"

"For what?"

"Anything. Anything at all."

Xhea frowned but lifted her hand, palm up, and called her magic to her—and then stared. Where there should have been a ribbon of black power, there was nothing. Not so much as a wisp.

Harder she tried, and harder, attempting to force her magic to flow. *Anger*, she thought—for that had always bid her power to rise; but no matter the emotion, her hand remained empty.

At last she understood why she kept remembering the first moments when a payment had burned from her. Those were the times when she'd been most empty: no bright magic left, and her dark magic forced down as far as it would go. The times, she'd once thought, that she was almost normal.

"I think they bound your magic," Shai said.

Bound, she realized, as her mother had done all those years ago: wrapped a spell around Xhea's power so tight that it seemed she had no magic at all. Yet that had been a weaker spell; Xhea, too, had been weaker, smaller. Given how her power had grown in the brief time since she'd snapped that binding, she would have thought it impossible to force it back down. Otherwise, wouldn't the Spire bind all of their dark magic users for a time, to prolong the children's lives?

Yet clearly it *was* possible. Xhea stared at her empty palm and no matter how she reached for her magic, she felt only its weight, hard and cold within her.

"What happened?" Torrence asked again. "The Lower City is up in arms over the Spire's announcement, and to find you in the middle of it . . ." He shook his head. "That's no coincidence, darlin'."

Xhea explained in curt, clipped sentences what had happened: the ghost's appearance from the Messenger's shadow and the spell she'd cast; her own pain and paralysis before passing out. She relayed, too, what Shai said had happened after. Bare though the ghost's tale was, Xhea heard in her voice an echo of her panic.

Xhea realized, too, that she was probably the only living person in the Lower City who understood why the Spire wanted to attack. That was more important than what had been done to her, or why.

"We're—what? About four blocks from Edren?" She recognized the alley now, though it wasn't part of her usual territory. Wasn't, either, anywhere on the normal route between the market and Edren.

Torrence nodded. "The streets are messy. Getting even this far was, shall we say, not the easiest. At least not with you unconscious."

"You carried me?"

"Daye."

Daye had a pain tolerance roughly equal to that of a stone wall. Xhea had seen the woman take more than her share of blows—had even seen her stabbed in the muscled flesh of her arm with little more reaction than a grimace of distaste. She'd carried Xhea once before, when they'd been inside Farrow, and though Xhea's magic had been exhausted and there had been layers of cloth between them, it had clearly not been a comfortable experience.

But this? There were blocks and blocks between them and the market, and that trip would have been slowed further by the crowd and the burden of Xhea's body.

Are you okay? Xhea caught the words before she spoke them, choked them back. Instead she said, "Well, that must have felt great."

Daye did not shift or turn, only lifted her shoulders in a fractional shrug.

Torrence explained: "Your touch doesn't hurt. Not like it once did, anyway. A little discomfort, some numbness. It's easier to touch you now than when we first met, years ago." He sounded almost apologetic.

Of course, she thought. *Because of the blighted binding.*

Xhea shook her head, frustrated. At least she still had the ability to see ghosts. At least she could still *see*. However much they bound her magic, no one could make her anything other than what she was.

At least the spell had not damaged her connection to Shai. Even bound, magic flowed between them, though Xhea doubted that Shai received anything more than a trickle of power from her. Their connection, it seemed, was more powerful than anything cast against them.

Yet Xhea's only real power had been stolen from her. She was suddenly as she'd always thought herself: a small girl with no magic, only the strange and sickly talent of seeing ghosts.

No, less. She couldn't even walk unaided.

Xhea took a deep breath and pushed her despair away, like a dark secret she could close in a box and ignore. *Bigger problems*, she reminded herself, *than your own feelings of inadequacy.*

"I can walk now," she said. "We need to get to Edren. I need to talk to Lorn."

Torrence gave a mocking grin. "I think he's going to have a few more things on his plate than what happened to you, darling girl."

Xhea glared. "Everyone knows that the Spire's going to destroy the Lower City," she said, "but I know *why*." Or, at least, she knew what the living Lower City had told her in that overwhelming rush of thoughts and impressions, tangled images and memories.

Torrence blinked, and Daye turned around slowly—not to look at Xhea, but at her partner. Daye's face was impassive as ever, and yet Xhea got the impression that she was laughing at him.

He seemed to come to the same conclusion, and waved his hand at Daye as if shooing away a fly.

"Well," he said, rising, "why didn't you say so?" He handed Xhea her cane with a flourish, then bowed and gestured toward the alley's mouth. "After you."

The way to Edren was blocked by angry crowds. Xhea followed in the bounty hunters' wake, letting them slice through the edges of that crowd like a knife through soft flesh.

Some people were heading toward the burned-out market— or, perhaps, toward the Spire itself, though its bottommost tip was a few hundred feet from the ground. Others carried weapons on their belts or slung over their shoulders, some already drawn as if to threaten absent aggressors. One man even carried a heavy length of pipe with its end sharpened into a crude point, though it was obviously unbalanced and useless as a spear.

And what are you going to do with that? she thought to him scornfully as she limped past. *Throw it in the Spire's general direction until they relent?* More rage than sense, in her estimation; but that was cause enough to give the whole lot a wide berth.

Yet just as many people appeared to be running away, toward homes or families. Some few, their arms full with belongings, appeared to be heading to the ruins already.

Few enough buildings were left standing out in the ruins; fewer still with any hope of being made habitable—many of which had already been claimed as replacements for those that had burned. Building materials were at a premium; so many people needed nails or boards or sheets of metal to replace sagging roofs, all in the hope of creating something that could keep them safe when night fell—and from freezing when winter arrived.

Xhea shook her head. Whatever their motive, the Spire's pronouncement was a death sentence for the Lower City. Their lives and livelihoods were precarious as it was; many of the displaced wouldn't make it through the winter unless they fell on the mercy of friends, family, or one of the skyscrapers. Indenture contracts were signed that way; normal folks became Rown hunters, and hunters became gladiators in Edren's arena. There were countless ways to lose one's self and soul, and in times of desperation one Lower City dweller or another had found them all.

None of which even touched what the loss of the market had done to the Lower City's food supply and the delivery of the various goods supplied by the poorest Towers—the few, above, who deigned to do business with the Lower City. *The few desperate enough to need the renai.*

It was one thing to have lost so much already. But to lose everything? Every building, every home, every street. The skyscrapers themselves. Everything that lay beneath. It was too much, almost, to comprehend.

Soon, one's affiliation wouldn't matter, Edren or Orren or Senn, Rown or fallen Farrow. One and all, the Lower City dwellers would starve, or freeze, or be torn apart by the night walkers when the rotting walls gave way to those insistent hands. People would kill each other for shelter, or a morsel of food, or a blanket.

Herself included. That is, if this sweetness blighted binding spell didn't kill her first. Xhea tightened her grip on her cane. Already her magic, bound into that cold, hard knot, pressed against the inside of her breastbone like an insistent finger. Her stomach ached.

Just get to Edren, she told herself, as if the skyscraper and her allies within had any hope of keeping such fates at bay. She stared at Torrence and Daye's backs, clung to her cane, and tried to hurry her steps.

She felt Shai's presence, too, just behind her left shoulder; felt the light of her Radiant magic fall upon her like sunlight. Xhea glanced over her shoulder. To her eyes, Shai looked worried, but no different; yet her expression did nothing to hide the emotion that Xhea felt from her.

Anger. Sorrow. Loss.

And not just about the Spire's pronouncement. There was something terribly personal in the feelings—a hurt that Xhea sensed but could not explain.

Was it right to acknowledge such things? Emotions sent to her seemingly without Shai's knowledge or intent. Xhea felt as if she was prying into the ghost's heart and mind without permission, and she shied away from such intrusion.

Yet it seemed wrong, too, to know that her friend was upset and to ignore it.

As they turned down a side street that was calmer than the main thoroughfare—if barely—Xhea caught Shai's eye.

"What is it?" she murmured, quiet enough that Torrence and Daye might pretend not to hear.

Shai shook her head, and let the distance between them increase by half a step. "It's nothing." She forced her lips into a smile.

Maybe she should have let it go, let the ghost speak to her in her own time—if at all—and yet Xhea couldn't stand the sight of that flat, fake smile. Couldn't stand the thought that Shai was lying to her.

In the street some ten feet ahead of them, a fight broke out. Two men grappled, with a third encouraging them with shouts and curses. No weapons drawn, only flying fists and faces flushed dark with anger.

Torrence and Daye stopped as one, then ushered Xhea toward the shelter of the buildings at the road's edge.

"Let me handle this," Torrence said. At Daye's look, he raised his hands, his unsheathed blade held like an afterthought. "Diplomacy first, right? *Then* you can bash their heads together."

Daye nodded.

"Gentlemen." Torrence's loud voice carried. He pushed his way toward the fighting men, while Daye gave Xhea a look that said she was not to move.

Xhea ignored her. Instead she turned to Shai, who stood now at her side with her head bowed and her restless hands clasped together. The facade was cracking; even were it not for the link that joined them, Xhea would have known her misery.

"What is it?" Xhea asked. "What is it really?"

"I . . ."

"Shai," she said. Just that.

"Really," Shai said. "I'm just being silly." She looked away, tears standing in her eyes.

"Don't." It wasn't a request, wasn't a plea, for all that some part of her wanted to beg. Whatever had happened, whatever she'd missed when unconsciousness had claimed her, it mattered. If it mattered to Shai, it mattered to her.

Please don't turn away from me, Xhea thought, little though she could say the words.

Yet perhaps Shai heard nonetheless. She took a shuddering breath and moved closer, her steps almost hesitant. "Take my hand." The ghost's own hand, when she reached out, was shaking.

Xhea frowned, not understanding, but did as the ghost asked. She reached, taking Shai's hand in her own as she had done so many times before, in fear and in comfort, in hope and in reassurance—and felt her fingers slide through.

It was not like touching any other ghost. Though she could interact with the dead, most ghosts felt like little more than a heavy, chill fog. But Shai? Shai felt real to her—real in every possible sense of the word.

And now this.

She knew it was only a consequence of the binding; there wasn't enough magic left in her hand to push against Shai's power. But even when she'd exhausted her magic rescuing Shai, months before—even when people had been able, briefly, to touch her skin without pain—Shai had been able to hold her hand.

It's not just a simple binding, is it? Xhea realized. *They've done something more to me. Something else.* The thought made her feel cold.

"We're still together," Xhea said then. She touched the spelled tether that linked them; it was strong and wide and unbroken. "We're still bound."

"I know," Shai whispered. She glanced away, embarrassed. "I told you, I'm just being foolish."

Except Xhea felt it too: an ache deep within her, a feeling that she could not name, to have Shai here—and yet so far away. Untouchable.

While the living could touch her with only mild discomfort. Despite all the times she'd wished she could banish the pain of her touch, the change now felt like a loss.

"There we go," Torrence said, returning. He dusted his hands on his legs. "No problem." His knife, Xhea noted, had been put away, and he wore an expression of boyish glee that usually accompanied violence. Again they pressed forward, and Xhea spared but a glance for the men sprawled and groaning on the ground—all three of them. A little boy stooped beside them, hastily searching their pockets.

Shai spoke, clearly searching for a way to change the topic. "What did the Lower City tell you," she asked, "before the Messenger came?"

Xhea shook her head. That conversation had ended not an hour or two before; already it felt like a lifetime.

So as she walked she spoke to Shai under her breath, relaying her conversation with the living Lower City—if conversation was even the right word. The experience had more in common with throwing oneself into a flooding cistern than it did with talking.

"The Central Spire was trying to poison it," she explained. "Or so it believed."

"For how long?" Shai asked, and her voice was approaching normal.

Xhea shrugged. "A few days after Farrow fell, maybe?" It was hard to tell; sentient earth had a strange concept of time's passage.

"How do you poison a creature made of magic?"

Xhea frowned. It had been so clear; but some of her understanding—her comprehension of the entity's message—had been lost upon waking.

At Daye's direction, she turned down an alley to dodge a group of upset people gathered outside their homes. Torrence took one look at the woman at the crowd's center—a woman who pointed at the building's rooftop as she wailed something unintelligible—and shook his head. *Avoid, avoid.* Xhea wasn't inclined to disagree; she'd take the alleyway's thick muck over that nonsense any day.

"I think," she said to Shai, "that they did something to the dark magic that they dump on the ground. Twisted it somehow, maybe turned it into a spell."

"But it didn't work?"

"Obviously."

"And what did it do to the people down here?" Shai asked. "All that magic." It was a question, Xhea realized, embarrassed, that she'd not considered.

"I don't know."

Had it done anything? How could it not? Yet she could only wonder how it had affected the bright magic users around her. Sweetness and blight, she hadn't even noticed it herself.

Except, looking back, she wanted to say that she *had* felt that change, the twist in the cascade of black. As if she could dump all her restless nights and hard, bleary mornings not just on the Lower City calling out to her, but on the Central Spire. The myriad pains of her life bundled up into a neat package and laid at their collective feet.

Perhaps it was even true.

"If they want to kill the Lower City, why don't they just stop dumping magic down here? Cut off the food supply. Let it starve." The words sounded harsh, coming from Shai; but, hearing the anger in the ghost's voice, Xhea knew what she meant. Why kill thousands of living, breathing people instead of just one creature? Why kill so many when you're just cleaning up your own mess?

Because we're nothing to them. No worth that's not measured in magic. Xhea kept the words behind her teeth. Perhaps she should be thankful that the Spire had shown enough concern to give warning—that the Lower City dwellers had been given three days and a chance to leave.

She snorted. As if she should feel grateful that they had been gifted with a slow death, rather than a quick one.

Xhea stumbled and clutched her cane to keep from pitching forward into the muck. *A stone*, she thought, *a crack*—and it was only as she gasped that she realized her sudden unsteadiness came not from the ground underfoot but the spell that bound her magic.

It pressed against that hard knot of black power, surging, stuttering. Xhea staggered to a stop, clutching her stomach as if she might reach inside herself and calm the sudden riot of power. Her magic was moving—not rising, as it once had, but twisting with precise control and intent. But not her control—not her intent.

Torrence called her name; she heard running footsteps. Something cold and strange passed through her shoulder, and it was only as she gasped that she realized it was Shai, trying and failing to hold her. Again the spell surged and she stumbled, disoriented, as the world seemed to flip and turn. She swallowed heavily.

But there was a sound. Xhea pried open her eyes, not remembering having closed them, and looked around. The sound cut through the background noise, drowning out the shouts and calls and the distant woman's unintelligible wails. It was high and sweet and almost musical, rising and falling in a rhythm that reminded her of breath. It wrapped around her and bid her stand, bid her stay; it made her want to let her mind just drift away.

"Do you hear—?" Xhea started, and then realized that the sound was coming from her.

"Xhea," Shai said. And again, louder. "Xhea, you have to stop."

Xhea forced her eyes open once more and blinked. "Stop . . . ?"

The sound was like a lullaby, soft and sweet. It calmed her fears. Or maybe it was the magic itself that created this gentle place in her own head—that took away all the fear and panic, and told her she was safe.

That thought alone was enough to make her catch her breath as a rush of adrenaline surged through her. Safe? On the Lower City streets? Oh, that was never true—but especially not now, not *here*.

"You're making that sound," Shai said. "It's your magic."

It was her magic, but not her will. Xhea felt the spell within her stealing her power—using it, twisting it. She fought back, but still that song rose, echoing.

Then, as suddenly as it had started, the sound faded and vanished. Gasping, Xhea leaned on her cane and struggled to calm her breathing. At last she looked up, meeting the intense looks of the ghost and two bounty hunters before her.

"It hijacked me," she managed. "It used my magic."

"For what?" Torrence asked.

Xhea shook her head. But Shai replied, "It's a tracking spell."

"No," she said, but had no words, no logic, only that flat denial. *They couldn't have—they can't—*

To lock her magic away was one thing—but to use it against her? She shivered, too shocked and appalled even for anger.

"A tracking spell," she managed. "But who . . . why . . . ?"

Daye spoke quietly, her words like small, hard stones. "We'd better hurry."

Better run, Xhea thought, *before whoever's tracking me arrives.*

Torrence nodded. "Come on. We're nearly there."

They walked in silence the rest of the way to skyscraper Edren.

Chapter Five

Inside skyscraper Edren's main meeting room, Shai stared resolutely out the window. The pane was cracked in one corner, and hazed with untold years of dirt, but was clear enough for her to see outside.

She couldn't see the market from here, only the dark shape of Farrow held aloft; she couldn't see the crowd that roared and surged at its base. Instead, she peered down onto the streets below and the rooftops of nearby buildings. On one roof, she could see a woman frantically dismantling some sort of antenna array, coiling up wires and pulling down the corroded metal tines that reached skyward like branches. On another, a pale-skinned man sat with a sleeping infant in his lap; the man's head was bowed and his shoulders shook as if with sobs.

Behind her, Edren's ruling council was meeting. Arguing, really. If she let those familiar voices pour over her like autumn rain, they sounded little different than the crowd outside. She'd thought . . .

Shai shook her head, frustrated. She'd thought that coming here would make everything better. They seemed foolish, now, those beliefs that had grown in the dark of her subconscious; she pulled them out into the light where they curled and crisped to nothing.

Somehow, she'd believed that, here, Xhea would be safe—that they might deal with the binding or the call it sent out, and protect Xhea from whomever wanted to muzzle and claim her. She'd thought that Edren would have explanations, if not solutions. As if Lorn Edren, or Emara, or any of the people gathered now around the battered table behind her could say anything, *do* anything to change the fate that now bore down upon them like a Tower in full flight.

It was not that she'd been lying to herself. It was only that instinct had shouted louder than sense, telling her, *Go home and everything will be okay.*

She didn't know when some part of her had begun to think of Edren as home—and doubted now whether anything could be made okay. Again she shook her head, as if denial might push back reality or the despair it birthed.

There, she thought. Outside the window she watched a spell rise. Up close, she knew it would have been a shining sphere of magic, with rainbow hues shimmering across its surface. From a distance it was no more than a bright glint, like a star lifting skyward.

A message spell. And not the first she had seen.

Shai waited a long moment, not listening to the debate behind her, not watching the small moments play out on the ground below. Just waiting.

And—*there.* Another spell rose, brighter than the first, faster, lifting from the Lower City's far side where Farrow had once stood. A long moment, and then another lifted from a neighborhood nearby; and another, flying upward from somewhere near Senn.

In the time she had stood here, Shai had seen so many message spells fly to the City above that she had lost count. Edren, too, had sent messages upward. They were probably sending more even now, as the council debated.

Those messages were requests for help sent to the Towers. Some were going to the skyscrapers' allies and trading partners, the poorer Towers on the City's fringes; others to the richer Towers that they'd courted or from which they'd sometimes bought goods. She imagined some were going to extended family members or one-time friends—anyone and everyone who now had full citizenship, no matter how distant the tie. She'd even seen a few rise to the Central Spire itself, begging, she imagined, for mercy. For an explanation. For a stay of execution.

But in all the time she'd watched, Shai had not seen any message spells fall to the Lower City in reply. Nor had she seen any fly from one skyscraper to another, no matter that the clogged streets made hand delivery impossible.

All the hands outstretched, pleading for help, were raised to the sky.

"They should be working together," Shai said at last. "The skyscrapers, all of them." She turned to Xhea, who sat at the meeting table's far end.

Xhea looked at her incredulously. "You think that's going to happen? After what Rown did?" She spoke softly in an attempt not to interrupt the discussion, but heads turned toward her nonetheless.

Shai knew what Rown had done. She had seen the dead and the dying—dead children, even. She had stood in the burning market, the air thick with smoke and embers, and exhausted her magic defending against their attack. She knew the weight of blame that rested squarely on Rown's shoulders. But the actions of the leadership—the actions of some hundred of their citizens, truth be told—should not condemn them all.

She knew, too, the edges of Edren's feud with Orren—the murder of Orren's ruling family in the war ten years before, and the assassination of Lorn's father, Verrus Edren, which Shai had witnessed. There would be other stories, other feuds and wars and betrayals.

Whatever the weight of the skyscrapers' history and politics—whatever retribution they deserved—it was not this.

"If there was ever a time to forgive and forget," Shai started, but the words weren't right. They dried in her mouth like dead leaves; they crackled between her teeth. She didn't know who, in the end, she was trying to convince. Those that needed her words couldn't even hear her.

So Shai schooled herself to calm as Xhea explained to Edren's gathered council what she had learned from the living Lower City. She, like Xhea, tried to ignore the councilors' expressions of skepticism and scorn, their reactions tempered only by Lorn and Emara's complete belief.

The cold reality of the situation was setting in, now that the first rush of confusion had passed. Shai stared at her hands, the window, the wall, and tried to keep herself still.

Except as she watched, her hands curled into fists, seemingly of their own accord. She was angry, she realized. She was so, so angry. She wanted suddenly to scream or cry, to throw something, to rage at—what? The Central Spire, the City above? The desperate poor themselves? She did not know, only felt the emotion as if it were a burning rock lodged low in her throat.

She knew that once she would not have cried out at the Messenger's announcement, or thought the crowd's anger to be just. Once she wouldn't have spared a second thought to the Spire's actions, or to the fates of the people on the ground. It wasn't that she had been callous or cruel; only that such matters would have been, in every possible way, beneath her.

Shai had come to terms with the person she'd been, or was trying to. Even so, the shame was a weight, heavy to bear.

At last Xhea finished her explanation and sat back while the councilors discussed the possible import of her words.

"What is it?" Xhea asked her, little louder than a whisper.

Shai gave an awkward half-shrug. "I don't know what you mean."

Xhea pointed to the spelled tether and all that link now implied. Even if no words had traveled down that length, she had felt some echo of Shai's distress.

"Do you have an idea? Something you could recommend? Because if you do I'll tell them, you know I will."

Shai took a deep, shuddering breath, suddenly unable to hold Xhea's gaze.

Did she have something to recommend? She should. Here she was, the supposed dead-girl savior of the Lower City, the one who had shielded them as Rown fired on the unarmed, the one who called down rain from the blue sky to put out the fires.

And she had nothing. Nothing at all.

For the first time, living or dead, her power was inconsequential. Before she had felt helpless, ignorant of the workings of her own magic and limited by the stark realities of her death. She had thought herself useless, had been frustrated by her inability to enact change or control her fate—but never before had she been powerless.

She looked down at her hands, their Radiant glow, and knew that she could give every spark of power she'd generated in life and death and still have no chance of fighting back. No chance of protecting those around her, or defending them.

Not against the Central Spire.

"I don't know what to do." The words made her want to weep. She was supposed to help them—she was supposed to *fix this*—and could do nothing. She couldn't even help her friend.

If being a Radiant had no value, what good was she? Just some ghostly dead girl, hanging on past her expiry date.

"Me either," Xhea said. "But maybe Edren or one of the other skyscrapers . . ."

But in the history of the City, no one, no matter how rich or influential, had crossed the Central Spire. Not ever. Before today, it had never occurred to Shai that anyone would want to. The Spire was no government, no commanding body; they only maintained the structure in which the City operated. They kept peace between the Towers; they approved mergers and acquisitions; they even dealt with the Towers' worst criminals. But for the most part, they let life in the City run its course, each Tower operating under its own rules, its own patterns of living, without any interference.

As it should be. Or so she had always believed.

Yet the Spire had power, one that—if what Xhea had shared was true—was based on their rigid control of the rare talents of dark magic users. Children, all, who were needed to create the bindings that had held Shai to life, despite her body's pain and failure; bindings that had tied her spirit and her magic alike to Allenai, sending her vast power into the Tower's coffers and its heart. They alone could create the bindings that tied Radiants to their Tower, in life or death.

Without the Spire, the whole City would slowly crumble and fall. She was nothing compared to the Spire—none of them were.

"How do we even know the girl is telling the truth?"

The belligerent voice from midway down the table made them both turn. The man that Xhea referred to as Councilor Horse-Face leaned forward and waved a dismissive hand in Xhea's direction. In taking over Edren's council, Lorn had cleared out many of his father's handpicked councilors—but not, it seemed, all.

Emara Pol-Edren responded—the tall, dusky-skinned woman who commanded just as much of this skyscraper these days as did her husband. "Don't," she said, and if her voice was soft it was not yielding. "We don't have time for pointless arguments, Councilor Lorris."

Councilor Lorris waved again. "Fine, fine. But what does that even mean, that the Spire wants to destroy some magic creature? I don't see how it helps us."

"It gives us insight into the Spire's motivation. It helps us predict and plan."

He laughed then, loud and mocking. "Predict *what*? The method of our execution should we choose to stay?" He looked around the table. "That is what you're trying to find, is it not? A way that we can stay."

"We're trying to find a way that we can stay *alive*," another councilor replied, but Shai didn't see who, didn't turn to seek his face.

Lorn Edren saw to the heart of the matter. He spoke, his voice a bass rumble, directing his words someplace above and behind Xhea's head: "The Lower City is a creature of magic just like the Towers. Shai, how would you kill a Tower?"

For all that she was visible only to Xhea, Edren's officials were aware of Shai. Of those, Lorn and Emara alone attempted to speak to the empty air where they sensed her presence. Usually, she appreciated the effort. Today, seeing Lorn speak to the wallpaper near her left shoulder was just one more frustration.

Even as she considered his words, Shai shook her head. Towers struggled for position, they fought for altitude, they merged—and sometimes, very rarely, split—but they were not killed. But Towers could—and did—die. Everything living had its end.

"You don't kill Towers," she said. "They grow old and weak. They slip to the City's fringes. They fall from the sky."

Xhea relayed those quiet words—then held up her hand to forestall interruption. She seemed to know, even before Shai herself did, that there was more.

Struggling to fill that sudden silence, Shai thought: *They could be starved of magic—but what else?*

"Dark magic." Shai looked to Xhea. "Your power balances out bright magic, unravels spells. Theoretically, couldn't enough dark magic kill a Tower?"

"Theoretically," Xhea said with a shrug. "But do you really think they'd dump enough raw bright magic on the Lower City to kill it?"

Thinking of the currency that magic represented, Shai shook her head. "No," she started—only to have one of the councilors speak over her, responding to Xhea's words.

"Pure bright magic doesn't kill," he protested.

"Shut that man up," Xhea snapped.

Shai felt a surge of gratitude. As if he could tell a dead girl what had or had not killed her.

"I don't know what good a physical attack would be," Shai said, warming to her topic. "Nothing living could move against the dark magic of the Lower City and survive. And you said that the living entity's not just part of the buildings, it's the ground itself."

Xhea nodded and conveyed the words. "Throwing rocks doesn't seem particularly effective," she added. "But what if they destroyed all the buildings, ripped them up, scattered the rubble wide . . . ?" Even as she spoke her eyes grew distant, considering the implications of her own idea.

"You could hurt it," Shai said. Towers sometimes lost great chunks of themselves to offensive spells, or in failed hostile takeovers. Such wounds caused the Towers pain, hindered their movements and damaged their systems; bad wounds could take years to heal. She thought, too, of what Xhea had said when she first discovered the living Lower City's presence: that it felt the loss of Farrow, ripped from the ground.

"You could hurt it," Shai said again, "the way a person would be hurt by the loss of a limb. But it might survive such a loss."

"So if it's a physical attack, they'd have to—what? Scoop out the whole of the Lower City, earth and tunnels and all?"

"Is that even possible?" Lorn asked quietly, his words measured, considering.

"Theoretically," Shai said. Because, if she tried, she could imagine the spell one might weave to achieve such an end—or, at least, that spell's beginnings. Despite her instinctive ability with magic, she knew too little of true spellcasting to construct such a complex working.

Besides, even if she could design the spell, Shai would never have enough raw magic to power it. But the Central Spire? It was possible.

"But," she added, "even if you ripped it whole from the ground, it would still be alive—at least until it starved, lacking new magic."

Xhea conveyed this, then suggested, "They could drop it from a great height. The whole of the Lower City lifted into the sky, taken somewhere distant, and let fall."

"Sounds inefficient," a councilor said—a small, pale woman that Shai didn't recognize. "Not just the cost to scoop it out, but to move it."

"You don't catch and release something you want to kill," Emara said shortly. She was right.

"I think we have to assume a magical attack," Shai said. "But think—pure magic would be likewise inefficient. It'd just be a battle of force, magic against magic, until one ran out of power."

Never mind that such a battle would require the City to lose some significant portion of their net worth—which she doubted anyone would accept willingly, or without great need.

"A spell, then."

Shai nodded. Of course, saying "a spell" was about as useful as saying "a weapon"—the range between a pointed rock on a stick and the Towers' layered defenses was so wide as to be ridiculous. Even so, it was a place to start.

"Xhea, remember what you said about Rown's attack? That the shot from their defensive spell generator scored a line on the Lower City's living heart. It damaged it, right? Even if only a little."

It was Xhea's turn to nod as she relayed Shai's thought to Edren's council.

"That was just one defensive spell generator," Shai continued. "One, used inexpertly. Every single Tower has dozens, if not more."

"And how many does the Spire have?"

Shai considered; the question had never occurred to her. The Spire's shape was smooth, a long, slender needle, tapered at each end, with the wider undulations of platforms spaced along its length. Nowhere did defensive spires bristle along that form, as they did on the Towers; she turned the image of the Spire over in her mind, but could not remember seeing spell generators, no matter how small.

But the Spire was protected. Though she could not say from whence they emanated, protective spells surrounded the Central Spire like great, shimmering veils. Even in daylight, when the Towers' spells grew dim, the Spire's golden light shone.

Maybe the whole Spire is a spell generator. The thought made her uncomfortable and she could not say why.

"I don't know," she said instead.

"But—if that's all this is about, killing this thing—then we could come back, couldn't we?" Councilor Lorris said. "They don't want our possessions. We can just take everything of value into the ruins by the Spire's deadline, guard and protect it while they cleanse the Lower City of this creature, and then we can return home. Once the thing is dead, the Spire won't care what we do. We can go back to our lives. And if we're fast enough, we could even gain some advantage over Orren and Rown in the process."

He sat back in his seat, smug.

"Absent gods," Shai murmured. "That man is such a fool."

Xhea rolled her eyes in disgust. "Tell me about it."

More than a few of the councilors looked at the man as if he had lost his mind, but it was Xhea who turned to him in a clatter of charms, her jaw set.

"Look," she said. "Rown had one half-broken, underpowered spell generator trained on the market. Do you remember what happened when they did that? Hmm?" She spoke as if he were a child; his face reddened with every word. "If the Spire or the whole City above was to fire upon the Lower City with even a fraction of the power at their easy disposal, do you actually think anything would survive? *Anything*?"

"They do that, and we'll burn. All of us."

Shai blinked. For a moment she had become lost in the enjoyment of turning the ideas over in her mind, exposing their myriad facets. She'd almost forgotten that this was not theory; that they were discussing the destruction of the very walls around them, the ground beneath their feet, every home and structure that she could see out that dirt-clouded window and beyond.

Lorn spoke into the silence. "We have to proceed, then, as if we can never return. We have teams investigating and holding potential territory in the area directly beyond the arena; we can start there. I asked for a list to be drawn up of the critical systems that cannot be moved beyond Edren's walls ..."

At Lorn's words, the small, pale councilor got slowly to her feet. She was silent—and her silence seemed to have a physical force, spreading across the table like the ripples from a thrown stone. When all eyes were on her, she spoke.

"Why are we discussing fleeing as our first option? Running, hiding, salvaging what we can." She looked from one person to another, and though her eyes never lifted toward Shai, even she felt that gaze like an accusation. "We're going to give up our homes, just like that? Why aren't we trying to fight back?"

"Better our homes," another councilor said quietly, "than our lives."

"And what good are our lives out there? What you're discussing is the end of Edren, the end of everything we've built, everything we've preserved—everything we *are*."

"Edren is more than these walls," Emara said. "More than territory."

The councilor gave a thin, tight-lipped smile. "And you know as well as I do how little those other things will be worth out in the ruins. If we're our people, then leaving means our people are going to die. Or did you mean less tangible things? Loyalty, trust, togetherness—how long do you think those values will survive? Or do you forget, gladiator, what desperation can do to a person?"

"I hung up my blades, *Councilor* Tranten." Emara's voice had gone cold. "It has been years since I fought for spectators, you know that. Nor is this a show to be put on for the Spire or anyone else's amusement."

Again that smile, a thin gleam of teeth. "Better polish those blades then, *Councilor* Pol-Edren. Looks like you're going to need them."

Into the sudden quiet there came the sound of a distant crash, then shouting. Emara and Councilor Tranten turned as one, their eyes going to the door. Others started speaking, rising from their chairs. Xhea glanced at Shai and that look was all she needed.

"On it."

Shai sped through the wall into the hall beyond. Only one of the black-clad security guards stationed outside the door remained; the other had run to the end of the hall, jammed the elevator doors open, and was now attempting to hold the stairwell door shut.

"We need backup!" he shouted into the microphone clipped to his shoulder.

A device on his belt crackled, and then came a torrent of words, all chopped and garbled by static. Multiple people spoke over each other, voices tense, shouting.

"—on the fifth—"

"—seven through nine, repeat we have—"

"—can't hold!"

As Shai listened, wide-eyed, one word stood out: *intruders*. She froze, remembering the last time intruders had walked Edren's halls. Remembering the metallic smell of blood, the red sprays on the wallpaper—

The clashing blades, a man falling to the floor—

And Lorn screaming her name as he attempted to defend his father's body. Shai shook herself, struggling to push the memories aside.

Quickly now, she told herself. No matter what her fear said, she'd faced worse than a few armed thugs. Taking a deep breath, Shai let herself fall through the floor.

On the floor below, she arrived just in time to watch a pair of heavily armed intruders take out an Edren security guard—and not with the blades or projectile weapons they carried, but a spell. The speed was shocking. One moment, the guard had the intruders in his sights, demanding that they lay down their weapons. A whip-like flash of light, and the guard's eyes rolled back in his head. He crumpled to the floor, boneless.

An intruder kicked the guard's battered gun across the floor and kept walking.

"Seventh floor," the intruder said, her voice clipped. "All clear." No radio; a spark of a message spell leapt from her lips.

On the sixth floor, and the fifth, Shai found more of the same: Edren guards no more than huddled lumps on the floor, sprawled in doorways or pushed against the baseboards, their radios crackling unanswered. Most were not wounded—at least nothing worse than a bloody nose or a messy cut. They were still breathing.

Despite the sudden outcry, the intruders had done much of their work in silence. Where Shai expected to find fights or tense standoffs, there were only intruders, fallen guards, and Edren citizens huddled behind closed doors.

The intruders themselves wore mismatched clothing, protective vests and jackets or sometimes dark T-shirts that displayed muscled arms and the hard expanses of their chests. No insignia that she could see—not Rown's or Orren's or anyone else's. Their weapons were an odd collection of knives, projectile weapons, and short, hard clubs—chosen, it seemed, entirely by preference.

They should have looked like common thugs, and yet . . . didn't. Shai looked from one to the other, trying think through her haze of panic. *Their clothing is new*, she realized. Mismatched though the pieces were, she saw no fraying edges, no patches, no rips or stains. Their weapons, too, seemed pristine—and worn almost for show.

They have magic. Real magic, not the bare glints and glimmers of the ground-bound poor. Despite their attempt at disguise, they used magic unthinkingly, like a reflex—something no Lower City dweller ever did.

They're City citizens, Shai thought in shock. Their accents, when they spoke, only confirmed it. *City citizens here, acting like common thugs. But why?*

She hesitated, caught between mounting a defense and rushing back to the meeting room, when a sound from the stairwell drew her attention. Footsteps, slow and steady. Climbing. She moved closer. A man appeared, and unlike the armed thugs that surrounded him, he reminded her of a real City citizen: neat and clean and civilized. A business man.

He showed no surprise to see the guard slumped on the concrete landing with one side of his face red in a way that promised a bruise's dark bloom.

"Hit this one a bit hard," one of the intruders said, apologetic.

The City man didn't bother to shrug. "Leave him." He resumed his ascent.

"Not much farther," said one of the others, consulting a device. "Four floors up and down a hall."

The meeting room.

Suddenly Shai remembered the tracking spell within Xhea calling out, singing that strange, high song. Was this who it had called—this man and his makeshift army? The thought made her go cold, any plans for a defense unmade like a spool unwinding. She fled, following the line of her tether.

Outside the meeting room, the two guards she'd first seen had already been felled, and two City thugs stood outside the door, leaning against the wall as they waited. Inside, the councilors had barricaded the door with a stack of chairs.

"Are you okay?" Xhea asked, seeing Shai return.

Shai nodded. "They'll be here soon." She relayed what she'd seen as quickly as possible, impatient as Xhea repeated her words to the councilors. Every moment, the intruders grew closer; the businessman, whoever he was, was coming here. She heard, at last, footsteps in the hall outside.

"The tracking spell," Shai said. "Xhea, could this . . . ?"

Xhea shook her head, her eyes never leaving the barricaded door. There was no time to run, or any way to break free. Nowhere, in this bare room, to hide.

"City citizens?" asked Councilor Lorris. "But who? Why?"

No one spared him so much as a glance.

The door moved, hitting the stacked chairs with a clatter. The chairs shifted—but the councilors knew their business; they did not fall.

Shai felt a surge of fear and anger, the emotions confused and tangled. She could not tell which were hers and which were Xhea's—because magic flowed between them, hard and fast, though neither of them had called it. Though, now, only one of them *could*.

In that moment, Shai felt as she had in the hours just after their renewed joining: more solid. More real.

Almost alive.

And angry. So very angry. *Is this how Xhea feels?* If so, Shai couldn't imagine how the girl stayed so seemingly calm, her face impassive.

"A barred door?" called a muffled voice—the businessman. "Is this any way to treat a guest?"

Lorn's head came up and he stared at the door, taken aback.

"Is that . . . ?" Emara whispered. Lorn nodded.

"A guest?" shouted Councilor Tranten, her voice sharp. "Don't mistake a blade for an invitation."

Lorn raised his hand, asking for silence, and though the councilor chafed at the request, her brow drawn low and lips thinning, she complied.

"Remove the barricade." Lorn moved forward, grasping a chair and hauling it aside. Others reluctantly joined him—all but Xhea, who clutched her cane, and Councilor Tranten, who looked like she would burn the chairs to ash with her glare before she deigned to touch one, never mind move it aside.

When the last chair was gone, Lorn swung the door wide. Two armed intruders entered, hard and fast, their weapons drawn—but Shai was ready. Before the councilors could do more than flinch, Shai's magic flowed from her outstretched hands.

A wall, she thought. *Clear as glass, hard as iron.*

Power shimmered into shape at the thought, sheer force of magic accomplishing what skill could not. She could not have made the stun-spells that the intruders deployed against Edren's security; she could not have created the spells on their weapons. Yet *this* she could do without hesitation.

She wanted to laugh as the first thug hit the barrier and stumbled back, dazed; the second man halted just in time, his surprised expression almost comical. Shai wanted to laugh but could not; the sound stuck in her throat, tasting like tears.

Lorn was on his feet, chairs ignored, his calm expression and steady breathing belying the sudden tension in the room. It was Emara, standing at his side, who opened and shut her empty hands in frustration, as if wishing she could reach for the blades she no longer wore.

"Shai," Lorn said. "Let them come."

But he hadn't seen what she had—didn't understand how quickly their spells might lash out. Though blood had not been shed in this room, threat of its fall was heavy all around.

She had failed the guards outside, she knew that now. She'd been too slow to arrive, slower to react. She would not fail again—not when Xhea's life was at risk.

"Shai." There was steel in Lorn's tone, the word sliding toward command.

"Don't make me," she said to him. "Don't do this."

But her voice, unheard, echoed into silence. Shai closed her eyes and let the spell fall.

Chapter Six

Xhea did not recognize the man who came through the door, flanked by armed guards. She was, apparently, in the minority. More than one of the gathered councilors muttered darkly as he arrived.

"Lozan," Councilor Tranten said as if the word were a curse.

Lozan? But that's—

"A Tower." Shai's expression was dark with distaste. "I knew it."

More than that, Tower Lozan was Edren's primary trading partner in the City. Yet Xhea could not whisper to Shai without drawing attention in what was an already tense room.

"Mr. Deryan," Lorn said carefully. "This is a surprise."

"Mr. Edren. Lor . . ." The man rubbed his neck as if in embarrassment—clearly feigned. "Lorren, was it?"

"Lorn."

"Ah, yes, Lorn. My apologies. I remember that now, from my aide's notes from our first meeting."

"Our meeting three days ago, yes," Lorn replied dryly. "A meeting that was scheduled a week in advance, I recall. Something about your busy schedule . . . ?"

"As always." He laughed as if at a shared joke, while the room around him stayed silent. From the looks on the councilors' faces, Xhea wasn't the only one who wanted to hit the guy in the mouth with a rock. With four armed and seemingly ill-tempered men standing with weapons drawn, even Xhea didn't consider it for long.

"Please," Deryan said. "I didn't mean to interrupt. Councilors, feel free to take your seats." It didn't sound like an invitation. Slowly, the councilors moved to comply, taking chairs from the pile and returning to their places around the table under the watchful eyes of the Tower guards. Xhea followed suit, dragging a chair across the floor as loudly as she could, and delighting in the metal squeal that resulted.

Deryan watched. Xhea felt him notice her, picking her out as the one who did not belong. It wasn't difficult: in amongst the skyscraper's leadership, here she was, a scruffy teen with ash-stained hands, a twisted wood cane, and chiming, braid-tangled hair.

You wonder why I'm here? Xhea met his gaze without flinching. Held it. *Keep wondering.*

At last Lorn was seated, Emara at his side, and only then did Deryan gesture for a chair to be brought to him.

"Now," he said, "you must be curious why I'm here."

"It looks," Lorn said slowly, "like you are here to take advantage of our current situation." He cast a meaningful look at the four armed men that covered the room with their weapons.

Xhea was startled by Lorn's tone—or, rather, Addis's. For though it was Lorn's voice, deep and resonant, she heard only Addis in those careful, modulated words. She'd barely met the true Lorn, though knew he would have tried to kill Lozan's representative by now—or made a show of the attempt. But Addis only stared, his face revealing nothing, and Xhea imagined that she could see the true spirit that lived inside his brother's body.

"Come now," Deryan said. "A Tower assault force stealing from its allies, ground-bound though they might be? Oh, I don't know. Doesn't seem like it would be good for business, now does it?"

"Nor for one's sterling reputation," Lorn replied dryly.

"Sterling reputation. I like that." The man smiled. "No, we're just here to discuss a few routine matters."

"Routine matters require armed guards?"

"You had armed guards outside this very door, my dear man. Trying times and all that."

Armed guards that Shai had said were unconscious and incapacitated. At least Xhea couldn't feel any newly made ghosts. That was something.

"In light of the Spire's recent pronouncement, I was reviewing Edren's file. The history between our organizations goes back many years, does it not? Some forty-five years, all told."

"From when my grandmother ruled, yes."

"Indeed, indeed." Deryan looked pensive. "And during that time, we have each kept to the letter of our bargain—isn't that so? Lozan providing tools and materials to make repairs, plans for spells beyond your knowledge, and Edren paying in . . . well, any number of valuable things. Renai. Raw materials. Warm bodies."

Xhea's heart sank. Edren had sold them *people*?

She wasn't naive; she knew that the Towers brought Lower City dwellers above, indentured them or paid them pittances, sometimes even dangling hope of citizenship as the lure to encourage more work, longer hours, less renai. She knew that some people who went above were never heard from again, and though she hoped that some had found happy endings, she wasn't so foolish as to believe it.

It was only knowing that Orren did not have the lock on that particular market, for all that she'd scorned them for it. *Edren sends gladiators,* she guessed, *or the people who train them.* She had heard a rumor that out on the City's fringes one could find rougher entertainments than thought proper in the central Towers, games of wit and spell and blood that mirrored those fought in Edren's arena. What better place to find trained participants?

At least, she hoped he meant gladiators.

"I don't really see—" began Councilor Lorris, his flushed-red face puffing up in indignation.

"Councilor," Lorn said sharply, and the man fell silent. Lorn looked again to his guest. "Yes," he said.

"And—remind me—what was the term of our most recent agreement?"

"Five years from date of signing. An agreement my father made eight months ago."

"Ah, yes, that's right." Deryan nodded. "It seems that we have a bit of a problem here, you and I." He gestured around the room, as if to include Edren's angry ruling council in the conversation. "Edren is going to be in violation of that contract."

"Explain."

"The contract stipulates delivery deadlines, minimum production thresholds, that sort of thing. Yet you and yours are being evicted from the premises. It seems unlikely you will be able to meet even a fraction of those requirements if you are cast into the wasteland." Deryan pointed toward the window, seemingly to indicate the ruins beyond the Lower City. "Similarly—and I hope you'll forgive my directness—but if you're dead, you will be likewise unable to provide either services or recompense." He smiled as if at some witticism.

Xhea ground her teeth in an effort not to speak.

Though her magic was bound tight, anger had always bid it flow. It pushed now against the bindings—pushed hard—and she gasped at that sudden pressure. The binding spell did not bend, did not yield; it stole the magic and twisted it.

Xhea knew what was coming. She grabbed the chair's armrests to keep herself still.

Her bones vibrated as the spell called out. Its high, sweet voice sang in time to her thudding heartbeat. Goosebumps lifted across her skin.

Here, the spell seemed to say. *I'm here, right here.*

It was all that Xhea could do not to sag in her chair, eyes half-lidded, and lose herself in that song. Calm was not the right word; it was like being high, lost in a wave of perfect sensation. If one of the Tower guards turned a weapon on her, she might not move, might not rise—and that realization, which should have terrified her, brought no fear.

Shai knelt before Xhea and reached for her hand—then flinched. Instead, she leaned forward and looked into Xhea's eyes as if she knew how hard it was for her to cling to this place, this moment, and not be swept away by the spell's song.

"Look at me," she said. Xhea blinked and stared. She suddenly noticed the way Shai's pale eyelashes curled, and that there were small, dark flecks in the gleaming silver of Shai's irises. Brighter Shai glowed, and brighter; bright enough that Xhea could not look away, did not want to.

"Can you control it?" Shai asked.

Xhea shook her head. But she was not angry anymore—and, calmed, her magic no longer fought the binding, depriving the spell of its fuel. Bit by bit the sound faded, the shivering sensation dwindling to nothing until she only sat, disoriented and uncomfortable, clinging to the arms of a battered chair.

She could breathe again. She could think.

Carefully, Xhea looked around; in the whole room, only one living face was turned toward her. Not Lorn or Emara, not even Deryan, but one of the Tower guards. He blinked, looking at Xhea in no little confusion—and then to the space where Shai knelt, haloed in magical light. He rubbed his eyes with the back of one hand.

"Obviously, you are concerned by our situation," Lorn was saying, his words calm and measured. "We thank you for that. I assume you're here to offer assistance?"

Despite her lingering discomfort, Xhea wanted to laugh. As if such an offer would be accompanied by armed personnel, unconscious guards, and hostages.

Deryan inclined his head. "Of course we're concerned. Loss of this agreement could have unfortunate impacts on Lozan's operating revenues for years. I'm here to see that any such losses are minimized."

Emara spoke, her expression bland. "How charitable."

He continued as if there had been no interruption. "We are seeking whatever payment may be made now. There might be some individuals who would be of value to us. Of course, compensation would be at a lower rate than usual, given the extra effort and renai required to feed and house individuals at short notice, and for such an extended period." Again, that smile. "After all, our Tower is not a hotel."

"How many of our people might be of value?"

Xhea had the sudden feeling that Lorn would sell every last Edren citizen if it would save their lives. She did not know whether the sudden pressure in her chest came from hope or dismay. Maybe both.

"Perhaps thirty? Thirty-five? We would have to see the individuals in question first, of course."

Edren had hundreds of citizens inside the skyscraper—thousands in their expanded territory. And Xhea doubted that Lozan would be interested in those most in need of saving: the babies and children, the pregnant women, the elderly.

"Even so," Deryan continued, "that leaves a lot of debt unaccounted for."

Lorn laced his fingers together, and Xhea had the feeling it was to keep from curling his hands into fists. For all that his face seemed impassive, his dark brown skin gleamed with sweat.

"Debt," he said, "for services that you have not provided?"

"I see you need to review your contracts more carefully. I'll have a copy sent with the relevant sections highlighted. But yes, while Lozan is responsible for providing variable levels of supplies in response to stated need, including advances against future needs, Edren must provide regular payment—or pay penalties. Penalty or contractual service for which, I'm afraid, you're on the hook."

"What is it you want?" Lorn ground out, his façade cracking. Emara stiffened, and no few of the councilors; it seemed only Lorn's raised hand, asking for silence and stillness, kept them from doing more.

Deryan's smile was cool, calm, professional—and did absolutely nothing to hide his delight. "To begin, we'll take your magical storage coils," he said, "and all they contain."

Lorn did not speak; he did not have to. Nearly every councilor around the table was on their feet, Lorn's earlier request for silence entirely ignored. He did not seem to mind. The councilors shouted, their words overlapping in anger and outrage.

"You can't possibly—"

"—Edren's *entire* net worth—"

"I'll see your blighted head on a pole before—"

Xhea couldn't help herself: she laughed. And once she started laughing, she could not stop. Exhausted, her fear and anger gave way to something that was probably hysteria.

"Of course," Xhea said at last, wiping away her tears of mirth. "Of course."

"What?" Shai asked. "What is it?"

But it wasn't only Shai who was staring at her—wasn't only Shai who was asking her what was so funny. No one else in the room seemed amused.

The storage coils, she thought, smothering laughter. *The magical savings of every Edren citizen—of the skyscraper itself— taken all at once.*

It was, perhaps, a stroke of genius.

"The poorer Towers," she said, directing her words to the councilors. "They're as much scavengers as we are. What do you bet that there are blighted corpse-crawlers like this guy visiting every skyscraper? All those trading contracts suddenly come due—or maybe some are actually honest about it. Taking everything because we have no future use anymore."

"Xhea . . ." Shai started.

Councilor Lorris looked like he wanted to throw Xhea from the room. "How is that funny?" he demanded.

"Don't you see?" Xhea shook her head in a clatter of charms. "We leave, the poorer Towers take everything, and we die. We stay to defend what's ours? The Spire kills us all."

Again she laughed, because it was suddenly that or burst into tears.

"No way up," she said. "No way out."

Deryan looked Xhea up and down slowly. There had never been much of her, and what he saw was worth only his disdain.

"And who are you?" he asked.

Xhea grinned and leaned back in her chair. "I'm Edren's spiritual advisor. Expert on ghostly matters."

"Xhea." This in a warning tone from Emara. Xhea shrugged; she owed this man nothing.

Lorn moved, reclaiming his opponent's attention—and acted as if Xhea had not spoken. "The storage coils are integrated into Edren's walls and all of our systems. What you're asking is no small task. I could no more hand over the storage coils without work and preparation than I could hand over my own leg."

Deryan turned away from Xhea, forgetting her. "No such care is needed, my dear man."

"But we need *time*," Councilor Lorris said, his horse face screwed up with dismay. "I mean, you can't possibly think—"

"Hmm, yes. Three days, and all that." Deryan smiled. "Sounds like you'd better get cutting."

The shock was beginning to wear off. Xhea studied him—this so-called Mr. Deryan—the way she used to study a potential client, looking for the tells that said whether he was a safe bet or more risk than the hassle was worth. If he'd come to her, asking for help, she'd have run the other way, as far and as fast as she could.

Too many pieces didn't add up. There he was, wearing his expensive suit with their bright-spelled cufflinks, his hair newly cut, his City accent plain in every word. Yet she'd met business owners and gang leaders, seen the rulers of no few skyscrapers—and none would have stooped to this kind of inefficient hand-waving. He was enjoying himself too much.

He's not the one in charge, she realized. *He's just Lorn's contact—maybe some low level intermediary.* She snorted softly. She'd been taken in as easily as the council; score one for the showy entrance.

When she looked, she could just see the glimmer of fine-woven spells hidden in the whorl of his ear and the dark strands of his hair. She couldn't read their lines of intent, but was willing to bet that he was taking orders—and that someone higher up the chain of command was listening.

Councilor Tranten spoke next, her unblinking eyes fixed on Deryan. "To begin," she said flatly.

He turned, eyebrows rising in question.

"You said, '*To begin*, we'll take your magical storage coils.' What comes next?"

"Ah, yes, very good." He sounded as if he were an instructor and Tranten some particularly clever student. "The storage coils are a good start. Easy money, shall we say. But that's hardly much magic, is it? Not nearly enough to cover your debts."

"If they just want raw magic," Shai said, "maybe I could . . ."

Xhea shook her head, wishing she could speak unheard. "No," she whispered, the sound of her voice little louder than breath. "Think what they'd do."

If Tower Lozan was desperate enough to steal the storage coils of a ground-bound trading partner, their reaction to an unbound Radiant would be obvious—and drastic. Except for her brief flare to get Xhea's attention, Shai had kept her magic damped; and of the five Lozan citizens in the room, only one guard seemed to suspect her presence. For that, Xhea was grateful.

She couldn't help but think that in all the Lower City, Edren was hardly the greatest prize—or the only one to have alerted their trading partners of their plight. Even with once-rich Farrow out of the picture, one would have thought that Senn would have been a more appealing target, or Orren, trade agreements be blighted.

As if she had the same thought, Shai drifted back to the window, frowning as she looked outside.

"What, then?" Lorn asked. "You want the life savings of the entire skyscraper, some thirty-odd of our citizens, and what else?"

Deryan just smiled. "Why, everything, of course."

"Define *everything*." Lorn's voice made each word a threat. The guards heard the change in his tone for what it was; in unison, the two closest to him lifted not their weapons but their hands, magic glimmering around their fingertips. Lorn only had eyes for Deryan.

"Even Towers need new materials. Some of these old buildings have useful metal in the walls—wiring, plumbing pipes, elevators, and the like. There are artifacts that may be of value. Organic materials can enrich our soil or be sold to the growing platforms. None of it is top quality, to be sure, but it can add up."

From the window, Shai said, "They're everywhere."

Xhea glanced to the ghost. Deryan's words echoed around her, through her, as if from a dream.

"It's not just Lozan. There are aircars on Senn's roof—new models. I can see armed guards in some of the streets. Orren has been surrounded by people wearing Tower Elemere's sigil, holding off troops who are from—" Shai frowned, shaking her head. "Zie? Tolair? I'm not sure."

"What if we sold them to you?" Emara asked. She touched Lorn's arm, not holding him back but reminding him to stand steady. "We could come to an agreement."

"We already *have* an agreement. Lozan is acting within its rights as stipulated by its terms."

"To take what you're attempting to claim is yours by right, you'd have to destroy everything—our homes, our livelihoods, these very walls."

"Indeed."

"Our people need safety, Mr. Deryan," Emara said, fighting to sound reasonable. "Assistance to help face what is to come. If Lozan could—"

Deryan shook his head. "Oh, my dear woman, you're under the misapprehension that this is a negotiation. It is not. I am telling Edren's council what is going to happen so that you can make efforts to direct an appropriate response and reduce loss of life. If you do not choose to do so, well . . ." He raised his hands and shrugged broadly. "You shall be responsible for the consequences."

"This skyscraper is ours," Lorn said. "This territory is ours."

"Not anymore."

Xhea listened in angry silence as Deryan outlined the evacuation plans for Edren and its former territory—plans, he explained, that were already underway.

They did not have three days to find safety and shelter; they had hours. Xhea wished for her magic if only so she could fell Deryan with the ease with which his men had knocked out Edren's guards. She wanted to lay him out cold and flat, wanted to kick him while he was down—and knew that it would make no difference.

She glanced across the table and saw the calculating look on Councilor Tranten's face. Watched as the small, pale woman ran through the same scenarios as Xhea, and came to the same bleak conclusions.

Say they hurt Deryan and his guards; say they killed him. Then what? Lozan's forces held most of the skyscraper; they'd acted swiftly while Deryan spoke, and had found Edren's defenses little challenge. Edren's citizens were now hostages to ensure the council's cooperation.

All the while, Shai stood at the window and gave whispered reports of the other skyscrapers' fates. Edren was lucky; Lozan was their primary trading partner, and the only Tower with which they had a detailed agreement. Orren's so-called wealth was being split between two Towers, while a tense standoff was occurring outside—and, it could only be assumed, inside—Senn, as no fewer than four Towers fought for salvage rights.

Xhea was planning a quiet escape from the meeting room when Deryan's words made her go still.

"Oh, one more thing," he said. "We've noticed, in the last while, an increase in Edren's raw magical wealth. Would you care to explain the source?"

Lorn's expression did not change. "Gambling," he said. "We introduced new options at the arena."

"Gambling, is it? Because I heard an interesting rumor—a rumor that Edren has a new ally, of sorts. A newfound resource."

Lorn watched him, volunteering nothing—and the rest of the council, miracle of miracles, followed suit.

"I heard a rumor," Deryan said, "that you had a Radiant."

Silence.

Deryan looked from one quiet, unmoving council member to the next. His face changed, losing some of its cheerful aggression.

"It's true?" he breathed. "How could you—I mean, when . . ."

"It's easier to show you," Lorn said slowly. He turned to Xhea.

He wouldn't, she thought. *He can't. Sweetness and blight, Addis, you can't possibly . . .*

Except to save the people of his skyscraper? To save what he could of their lives and their future, crumbling around them? What *wouldn't* he do?

"Xhea," he said. "Go and get Addis. Tell him that we need to tell our friend, here, about the Radiant."

Xhea stared. Blinked—and comprehension dawned.

"Okay." She grabbed her cane and rose.

"Slowly," Lorn added. "We don't want any misunderstandings."

Xhea nodded and started for the door, Shai at her side. *She should run*, Xhea thought, wishing she could truly speak to the ghost without words. Wishing she could raise her hand to the tether and push understanding down that line: *Get out, get away, before they realize that you're here.*

As if words could force Shai to leave her. Xhea knew that protective look on Shai's face. Xhea had no real way to defend herself right now, and Shai wouldn't leave her undefended.

Cursing in silence, Xhea walked toward the door, feeling every eye in the room on her. *Nothing to see here*, she thought at them, and suppressed a smile as a Lozan guard opened the door to let her go.

"Wait," another guard said. Xhea hesitated and glanced back.

It was the smallest of the guards, a shorter man who lacked the muscle-bound look of his colleagues. The one, she realized, who had seen Shai.

The smallest, weakest guard; she suddenly bet that meant he had the strongest magic. Sure enough, when she shifted her vision, the light of his magic was the brightest in the room. Well, brightest of the living.

The guard did something similar, squinting—and then shifting to look at the air at Xhea's side. The empty space where Shai stood.

His eyes widened. "Stop her!"

Xhea ran.

Her gait was not pretty—she stumbled more than she ran, heavily favoring her damaged knee and wincing at the pain—but it got her out the door. Behind her, Shai flared brightly. It was the worst thing she could do against four City citizens watching for her presence—but there wasn't time to stop her.

"Run!" Shai cried. Xhea felt more than saw the spell that Shai cast; there was a flash, then a wave of heat washed across Xhea's back as if someone had opened an oven behind her.

Two more Lozan personnel waited in the hall. She caught a glimpse of their expressions: bored and amused, seeing her as neither threat nor challenge.

It didn't matter that she had no real defense, or that her magic was bound; she could *see* their power. She ducked beneath the spell flung at her, then spun toward the nearer man, aiming her cane at his knees. He shifted as his colleague cast another spell.

Then Shai was there, knocking the spell from the air like a troublesome fly, and driving both men back against the wall, her shield spell used like a battering ram. Again Xhea felt that wash of heat as she staggered toward the stairwell.

A Lozan man shouted, but Xhea focused on Shai's words: "Not the stairs—the elevator!"

The elevator gaped wide, a knife sheath jammed into its door mechanism. Without her magic, Xhea realized, it would be safe for her to use. She hurtled toward it and stumbled inside, yanking the sheath from the mechanism as she passed. She leaned hard against the elevator's far door, gasping and shaking and gritting her teeth against the pain in her knee—and, even so, she couldn't help but laugh at the Lozan guards' expressions as the doors rolled closed.

She hit the button for the lobby, and laughed in relief as it lit. *Not a magical sensor, thank absent gods.*

Shai joined her a moment later.

"Score one for the dead girl," Xhea said.

"Alert's gone out," the ghost told her, ignoring the comment. "They'll be ready for you."

So much for the element of surprise. Xhea looked to the numbers atop the door, slowly ticking down.

There was only one place that she could run to evade pursuit—her and Shai both. Because if they grabbed the ghost and took her away, there'd be no point in cowering and hiding; there'd be no point in anything, really.

"When we stop, I'm going to distract them," Shai said. "You run."

"Shai, you can't—" Xhea started—then stared.

Because Shai held her hands before her, light pouring from her palms like water—and in midair it transformed into shadow. *Dark magic,* was Xhea's shocked thought—but no, that was impossible. *Illusion spell,* she realized a second later, as the shadow took the form of a girl.

Third floor.

Second floor.

Lobby.

Xhea pressed herself into the elevator's front corner, hidden from sight as the doors rolled open.

As far as illusions went, Shai's wasn't particularly good. It was little more than a moving shadow in the form of a person, shapes flying about its head that seemed like a flurry of braid tangled hair. It rushed from the elevator in a strange, desperate silence, running for Edren's main doors. Shai's fingers danced like a puppeteer's.

Bad illusion or not, it grabbed the attention of the Lozan personnel stationed in the front lobby—and held it. Shouts, commands to stop, the sizzle of a shock stick flaring to life—such sounds were music to Xhea's ears.

"One," Xhea whispered. She gripped her cane harder. "Two . . . Three."

She did not run—couldn't—but moved as quickly and as quietly as she could from the elevator toward the stairs. All around the lobby, Lozan men were stationed. All around, too, she could see the black-clad lumps of Edren's guard—some twitching and cursing, held by shining restraint spells, others still as the dead. *Mercks*, she thought. But she kept her head down and *moved*.

She was halfway across the lobby before the ruse was detected, and nearly to the stairs before anyone thought to turn. Shouting, they moved to intercept. A shimmering barrier appeared between Xhea and the front door; another sprang to life before her, blocking her from the stairs to the ballrooms above.

But she wasn't running up. By the time her pursuers realized she was going down, it was too late.

Despite her heart hammering in her ears, she couldn't help but hear the shouts and swearing in her wake. Again the Lozan men tried to raise a barrier before her, or throw a binding around her, or snatch her up with an invisible hand. Shai was there and she was faster, stronger than any of their spells; she unraveled each as they flew toward Xhea and tossed them aside like so much waste.

At last Xhea reached the lower level's dusty floor, and stumbled into the darkness. Behind her, she heard some of Lozan's men attempting the stairs. But they were City citizens; they would not get far.

Oh, how her knee hurt—Xhea wanted to fall to the floor and clutch it, press her hands against that too-hot flesh as if touch might reduce the pain—but made herself keep walking. Slower now, steadier, leaning heavily on her cane.

Xhea glanced to Shai. "You were amazing," she said.

Shai's expression was almost comical, and she stammered and fumbled for words. "I didn't . . . I mean, I . . . thank you." The ghost blushed.

Gratitude, Xhea knew, was something she rarely voiced. *Old habits die hard and all that.* Shai deserved better.

"No," Xhea said, feeling suddenly awkward and forcing herself to speak anyway. "Thank you. I couldn't have done anything to stop them." Even now, it hurt to admit that—but if she had to rely on anyone, at least it was Shai. It didn't feel like being rescued; time and again, they saved each other.

To distract herself from her own feelings, Xhea asked, "I kept feeling heat from your attacks. What were you doing?"

If anything, Shai only blushed harder. "I just thought they'd be afraid of the shield if it radiated heat—that they wouldn't get close enough to counter it. That it would be, I don't know, *surprising*. So I twisted the reheat charm they use in the Edren kitchens into the spelllines."

Xhea stopped, staring.

"I don't know any offensive spells!" Shai cried. "What was I supposed to do?"

But Xhea was laughing—not at Shai, but the idea that they'd just evaded members of a Tower assault team with an overpowered version of a spell used to keep tea warm.

Better to laugh than cry, she thought. *Better to run than give up in despair.*

It was too much to think about, and so she only walked, holding fast to her cane. Side by side, Xhea and Shai made their slow way from Edren's basement into the cool, dark tunnels of the underground.

Chapter Seven

Xhea pushed aside the last of the temporary repairs to Edren's bored-through barricade and slipped into the corridor beyond. Guilt felt like a tether, drawing her back. Again and again she thought of what must be happening in Edren above them. Lozan's forces moving from floor to floor, taking over. That tense, crowded meeting room. The fallen guards.

There's nothing you can do. She could only run and hide, and she tried not to feel ashamed at the necessity. Shai was a treasure no Tower might ignore, and her only weakness was Xhea, the mortal girl to which she was bound.

With Shai at her side, Xhea left Edren behind. She walked to the abandoned food court where she'd seen Ieren for the first time—where she'd fallen, where Mercks had been stabbed. His blood remained on the tiles, dried now into a patch of black.

Then they went farther, out into the branching shopping corridors beyond. The floors were thick with dust, the ceilings stained and sagging where they had not collapsed entirely.

The halls were lined with the dirty glass panes of former storefronts, shadowy lumps and toppled displays all that was left inside.

Everything was dark, and breaking or long broken; everything smelled of age and decay. The underground was silent but for the scuff of her boots, the soft chime of her hair, the tap of her cane against the dusty tile.

Home, Xhea thought. She smiled sadly.

For all that she knew the Lower City's streets and the ruins beyond, this was her true home. There were other markings here—marks left by Torrence and Daye, and the few others poor enough to withstand the pain of traveling below, however briefly—but most of the paths in the dust were made by years of her footprints. There, to the left, she'd hidden a cache of food and a spare blanket last winter, just in case; a little farther on, beneath a broken elevator and the fractured skylight somewhere above, was one of her many rain barrels.

But this place felt different now. Almost strange, as if the dust of her absence had settled on every surface, though little more than two months had passed since she walked these halls with regularity.

Or maybe it was only knowing that, no matter what happened, she could never return. Perhaps some part of the underground would survive the Spire's attack; perhaps the deepest subway lines might not fall, or the ones farthest out in the ruins. Perhaps there would be some place left where, for all the dust and dirt, the chill and silence, her heart would sing *home*.

But she did not think so.

Xhea's years here had not been good or easy. For all that some hidden corner, some forgotten artifact, some glimpse of a scuff made by her own, smaller hand made her smile, she was not so sentimental that she forgot what her life had been like. The hunger, ever-present; the pain. Cold days and colder nights; the times when everything froze solid and she faced the very real risk of dying, alone and huddled in too-thin blankets. Beneath it all, the hurt of loneliness, so raw that she should have bled from it.

The pending loss of these halls seemed like a dream. How could a place that had existed for so long be destroyed so suddenly? The city that had come before had existed for untold hundreds of years; the Lower City for untold hundreds more. It seemed impossible to imagine it gone.

But then, this whole day seemed impossible, more dream than terrible reality. She felt that at any moment she might wake and find everything normal, balance regained. She'd be in her small room on Edren's ground floor, listening to the clatter from the skyscraper's kitchen. Or she'd be in one of her rooms down here in the tunnels, ready to head out to find the day's customers. And the market would not have burned, and Farrow would stand where it always had, and . . .

Shai would not be with her. Xhea winced at the thought. For all the pain the past few months had birthed—for all the strange consequences of their meeting, and their decision to remain together—she could not imagine returning to a life without Shai. It would be easier to cut out her own heart and cast it aside.

Xhea looked up, thinking to say something, thinking to tell Shai—oh, she didn't even know. The words were slippery, hard to catch and harder to speak. Even so, she'd opened her mouth to try when something caught her attention.

She hesitated, looking at the corridor to their left.

"What is it?" Shai asked.

"I never went down here," Xhea murmured, staring at that hall. "I always knew it was dangerous, but I never thought why." There were many places like that underground—places where the tunnel risked collapse, or that flooded with rainwater, or where the sewer pipes had ruptured.

"It looks normal," Shai said. And it did. It was a straight corridor with shops to either side. Midway down, there had been a leak; the ceiling tiles were stained dark and sagging, the ground patterned with debris from flooding.

The only real difference between that hall and the one in which they stood was that, there, no footsteps marred the dust. Not a single one.

"It does," Xhea agreed.

But at the end of the corridor there was . . . nothing. No light, nor its absence; only a vast span of darkness that had both shape and presence. Darkness that radiated, as if shadow had the same properties as light.

The Lower City's living heart.

"I never questioned why I didn't walk here. I never heard it. Never *felt* it. Not once."

Except, with its power filling everything around her, how could she not? Despite her ignorance, she had to have felt something from this hall and the entity at its end, if only enough to keep her away.

The underground was silent, but there was sound too, now that she knew how to hear it—sound that had nothing to do with the air or her ears. If she let herself listen, it was all but deafening, an echoing choir of inhuman song.

It called to her.

Xhea stepped forward, raising her free hand as if to feel the heat from a fire. Another step, another. She should not go closer; she knew the danger. Yet that darkness drew her, step by step.

She wanted reach out with more than her hand—wanted to understand the thoughts and words and images of the living Lower City's song—but didn't have even the faintest wisp of power. She knew what would happen if she tried to overpower the binding on her magic: the tracking spell would call out, and all but incapacitate her.

Perhaps it had no power over her here, so close to the Lower City's living heart. Perhaps the tracking spell's call would be muffled by the layers of earth and air between her and her unknown pursuers.

Perhaps. But she did not think so.

"Xhea."

She glanced back. She hadn't realized how far she'd walked until she saw the ghost standing ten feet behind her.

"Please come back," Shai said. "I can't follow."

Because the dark magic that wrapped around Xhea, whispering to her of comfort and home, was as a storm wind to Shai. It pressed against her, flattening her clothes to her body and whipping her pale hair behind her like a tattered flag.

"I can't speak to it," Xhea said, bereft. "I can't tell it what's happened. I can't . . ."

"No." Shai's voice was soft. "Xhea, come back."

Xhea looked back at the Lower City's heart. She did not have her own magic, but felt the calm of the Lower City's power wash through her nonetheless. She wanted to keep walking and fall into that darkness as if it were a pool of cool, clear water.

"It can still hurt you," Shai said. "Perhaps not your spirit, but your body. You know what that much dark magic will do."

"It will kill me." Xhea's voice was dreamlike and slow.

"Yes. Come back to me."

"Does it hurt?" Xhea asked. "Death?"

Because she was not afraid, staring into that ache of black. It sang of welcome, now and always; and its magic, as it surrounded her, felt like the crisp, clear air of a new spring day.

It took a long, slow moment for Shai to respond. "Death? No. But dying . . ." She shook her head. "I don't want you to die."

"I don't want anyone to die," Xhea said, and it was true. "Yet we do, don't we? All of us, in the end."

"Xhea," Shai said. "Look at me."

Xhea turned, hard though it was to tear her gaze from the Lower City's heart—all that dark magic, the glorious chorus of its song. She made herself look at Shai—and found that she could not look away.

Shai glowed, but not her usual soft, comforting light. Magic shone from her, fierce and brilliant; light radiated from her like wings, holding back the darkness.

Yet it was not Shai's magic that drew Xhea, but her expression. She was afraid, but so beautiful in her fear. Her silver eyes were wide but determined, and she had one hand outstretched, reaching for Xhea if she might span the space between them by will alone.

Oh, Shai could not rival the Lower City's darkness. If she walked into its heart, it would surely extinguish that fire as easily as Xhea might blow out a candle's flame. But she would do it, Xhea saw. If she kept walking, Shai would follow.

"Come back to me," Shai said again. "Please."

And Xhea felt everything that Shai did not say, hope and fear and longing flowing through the link between them.

Xhea did not realize she was walking until suddenly she could breathe again. Another step, another, and she reached with her free hand for Shai's outstretched fingers—and in that moment it didn't matter that they could not touch, that death now stood as a barrier between them. She only reached and reached, and her eyes never left Shai's, not for a moment.

At last Xhea collapsed on the dusty floor, Shai at her side. For a moment she just lay there, staring at the ceiling. Everything was so very much brighter, away from the Lower City's shadow.

I could have died. Xhea poked at the thought as if it might birth some fear or horror that she had not felt.

She had not wanted to die, only to . . . what? Touch the living Lower City's heart? Let the magic surround her, flow through her until there was nothing left?

That's just death with another name, she told herself, and knew it to be true.

"Don't do that to me," Shai said. "Please. Not ever again."

"I'm sorry," Xhea whispered, wanting to take the ghost's hand.

But she did not make that promise. Couldn't. Neither of them could be other than what they were.

For a time they walked in silence, fleeing the sound of the Lower City's heart. Up one corridor and down another, taking a long flight of stairs one slow and careful tread at a time. Resting, sometimes, as she was able.

Xhea's knee wanted her to stop, but she could not, would not. She had always thought best when she was moving, as if her body's motion might shake free some forgotten fact or twist the world around her until she might see it from another angle. But what possible solution could she find by taking another step, another flight of stairs? What might she earn from the pain of her motion beyond fresh bruises and stiffness to greet her with the morning sun?

Her mind raced. *We need to gather defenses, or help others to fight the poorer Towers, or create some sort of weapon, or . . .*

Her imagination failed her. That, or her will to lie to herself.

"Can you think of a way to stop them?" The words slipped from her mouth unbidden. "The Spire. Lozan and the other Towers. Any of it."

A long moment passed, then Shai shook her head. "No." The desolation in her voice said what the word did not.

Xhea stopped, resting her free hand on an age-grimed railing. Her stomach twisted at the thought of the empty air beyond that railing, the long fall to the shopping corridor below; and so she looked at Shai's face, at the water-stained ceiling above them—anywhere but down.

"I keep trying," Shai said. "I keep thinking that if I try hard enough—if I were clever enough, powerful enough—then I could fix this. Make them stop, or turn the Spire's attack aside, or . . . I don't even know."

"Let me guess. You've thought of a shield, a weapon of our own, some way to reflect the Spire's power back at them—"

"A way to disperse the magic of their attack harmlessly, or create a storm to knock them out of the sky—"

"—finding a way for everyone to escape to the ruins and not starve, not freeze to death this winter—"

"—using your dark magic to undo some key point that holds the whole City together—"

"—falling on our knees and begging them not to do it—"

"—working together, just the two of us, to *stop them*."

"Oh, right," Xhea said, pretending to slap her forehead. "Our secret plan to save everyone. What was it again?"

"Magic, of course."

Xhea laughed, she couldn't help herself—nor, after a moment, could Shai. They laughed until tears ran down their cheeks and the empty halls echoed with the sound. *Hysteria*, Xhea thought, and laughed some more. It felt good, in spite of everything.

At last Shai said, "Maybe if it was one Tower."

"Or two."

"Perhaps. Maybe then we could do something. But this . . . ?" There was no fear in Shai's expression now, none of the anger and panic that had defined their afternoon. Only blank shock—confusion as to how it could have all gone so terribly, awfully wrong. "Nothing I could do would have any effect on the Central Spire."

Tell her she's wrong, Xhea told herself. Hadn't she always fought back, no matter the odds? Fought to stay alive, fought to be something, anything, but another abandoned child ground to nothing in the dirt of the Lower City streets. Together, they'd fought Allenai and Eridian, just the two of them. Xhea had fought the death sentence of her injury, and the weight of her depression; she'd even fought Farrow, in her way.

And Shai? She was a Radiant, one of the most powerful magic wielders in the City, living or dead. The power she could bring to bear made the magic of even the City's elite seem dim by comparison.

There should have been nothing that could stand against them. Xhea smiled. Oh, if only.

Tell her she's wrong, her heart said. But she couldn't.

Instead, Xhea raised her hand to the spelled tether that joined them as if the gesture was a question.

"It's growing stronger," she said. "The link. Or changing, maybe, as we use it."

A nod.

Xhea remembered her earlier wish that she could speak to Shai through that line. "Do you think that there's some way we could use it? Speak to each other, or send messages?"

"It didn't work before," Shai reminded her.

Xhea shrugged. It was true—they'd tried. But that had been only days after their joining, when they had started to realize that more flowed between them than magic.

Besides, she knew that a tether could carry sound; even now she remembered Shai's scream echoing to her all the way from Eridian when the Tower had attempted to bind Shai to those walls. And who knew what else the dark magic binding she'd wrought could do? For all that she'd woven that dark length, its workings remained a mystery.

"We can at least try."

Shai touched the tether almost hesitantly, and light swirled around her fingers like a flower's petals unfolding. That power flowed into the tether, vanishing.

Xhea closed her eyes, trying to concentrate only on the tether and the message that Shai had sent through it. Before, the sensations and images had struck quickly and without warning. Now, she frowned, struggling to detect anything at all.

Was there such a thing as emotional static? If so, that's what she was getting: the magical equivalent of white noise.

There. Xhea blinked and drew back as something hit her with an almost physical force against her sternum. A rush of heat, and then a wave that felt almost like sorrow, almost like longing, washed over her. She caught a glimpse of . . .

"A chair?" Xhea opened her eyes and blinked in confusion.

"It worked?" Shai sounded surprised.

"If your goal was to convey an important message about the existence of sad furniture, then yes, I guess so."

"What do you mean, sad?"

"Melancholy, maybe?"

"Oh." Shai looked embarrassed. "I was trying to share with you an image of my room at home. I mean, in Allenai. Where I grew up."

Xhea snorted. "You send a meaningful image of your childhood, I get a sad chair. This method of communication is not without its problems, I see." She laughed like none of it mattered, and tried to shake off the lingering sadness. Tried to avoid thinking about the meaning of that sorrow.

Instead she reached for the tether. It wasn't until her fingers touched that line of slippery, energized air that she realized she had no idea what to send. She was suddenly afraid, in a way that defied logic, of what she might project down that link without meaning to.

No secrets, she thought. *No lies. Not anymore.* True as those words were, Xhea couldn't help but wonder what Shai would think of her if she heard the restless thoughts that even now flickered through her brain, edged, cutting. She didn't want to see her friend recoil; didn't want to see the disappointment on her face when she learned who Xhea truly was, in her heart of hearts.

Stop it.

Xhea sent the first thought that came into her mind, twin to Shai's own sending: an image of the apartment where she'd lived when she was younger. The wide, dirty windows lit with the sunset's fading gray, dust motes swirling in the bands of light. The smell of dinner cooking, a jumble of food scraps boiled and called soup. And a figure sitting, head bowed, in the corner of the room. A slim needle glinted in her hand as the girl made stitch after careful stitch in a blanket made from clothing too torn to be mended.

Abelane.

Shai's eyes flew open. She stared at Xhea in silence.

Why did I have to send that? It had to have been the sorrow and nostalgia in Shai's sending that conjured the image from the depths of Xhea's mind.

"I saw Abelane," Shai said. "Sunlight and windows."

"Yes. It worked."

But Shai's look was so intent that Xhea wanted to turn away, or shrug, or say something, anything, to deflect that attention. She didn't expect Shai's next words.

"You were happy."

Xhea blinked. Of all the words to describe her childhood, "happy" had never made the list. But that day? That moment?

"Yes," she said softly.

It hadn't been anything special—no celebration, no holiday, nothing. Even so, it had been a moment that she remembered, even clung to; an image that surfaced when she felt the most alone.

The memory of being loved.

She did not need that memory now, did not turn it over in her mind the way she once had, as if it were a stone to be worried smooth by her attention. Did not need to rage over it the way she had at other times, the truth of her abandonment made clear.

"It worked." Shai's smile was like the sun coming out.

"I don't know how it helps us," Xhea said, for all that the idea had been hers in the first place. "But now we know. Next up, our amazing magical plan to save everyone."

Shai's smile dimmed. "Right."

They worked for hours, discussing every possible idea, no matter how strange or outlandish, as if it might save them. As if it might hold a faint glimmer of hope that they might tease out into the open with their careful, patient questioning.

To no avail.

At last Xhea went to rummage through some of her old food stashes in the hope something might have survived, whole and edible, in her absence. She paused only to stare up a broken escalator to where, stories above, dwindling daylight filtered in through the shadows.

Three days, Xhea thought. Three days and the first was gone.

In the Lower City, night was falling.

Part Two

Chapter Eight

That night, Shai lingered at Xhea's side long after the girl had fallen asleep.

Xhea had gone to one of her rooms, a small space hidden in the back of a store where she'd slept many times before. It wasn't home, not even a temporary one; only a dusty corner with a makeshift bed, some stale water, and a bucket in the corner. "What else could I possibly need?" Xhea had said, lowering herself carefully into the nest of blankets. Her knee, it seemed, hurt more than she wanted to let on. She'd lain back, and within moments was lost to the world.

Shai knew she should stay. This was not just any night when she might walk through the empty Lower City streets, alone but for her thoughts and the other dead. The poorer Towers held the Lower City now, or would shortly; and Lozan, at least, was looking for her. How many other Towers would have heard rumors of the Lower City's Radiant by now?

It wasn't safe, and yet she was drawn outside, as surely and as strongly as she'd once been pulled by her tether.

She believed she could help people.

Shai had not thought of any way out of the impending disaster. Even so, there were a thousand small tasks that needed doing, all of which might be sped along by a bit more power or a small spell. She thought of the things she'd done when her magic had been waning, before she'd discovered that Xhea was still alive. She'd healed wounds and bolstered ailing people fleeing the fire, supported a falling wall just long enough for rescuers to drag a man to safety.

Surely there was something she could contribute now.

It wasn't fear for herself that made her hesitate. Shai looked down at Xhea's sleeping face, the tangle of her charm-bound hair spread across the blankets.

She couldn't help but think of the image that Xhea had sent to her of Abelane sitting in the apartment they had shared when Xhea was young. The details had been hazy, like the memory of a dream; but the rush of emotions that had come with it had momentarily robbed Shai of words. That feeling of pure, simple happiness—washed away, hard and sudden, by . . . what? She struggled to name what she had felt. If emotions had a color, these had been as black as Xhea's magic.

Shai thought she'd understood what Xhea had felt at being abandoned as a child; thought she'd known what had driven her, shaped her, in the years that followed. After all their quiet conversations—all the things they'd discussed and confessed, just the two of them—she thought she'd understood Xhea better than anyone.

Perhaps she did. But what she felt in wake of that memory hadn't been anger at being left behind, or a sense of injustice or even pain. It had been a weight of inevitability; a cold grief and an acceptance of her loneliness as the only thing she truly deserved.

Shai never wanted to be the one to cause such feelings. But here, with Xhea asleep, there was nothing Shai might do but watch and wait.

"Sleep well," she whispered at last. "I'll come back soon. I promise."

Above, the world was dark and cool. The shadows in the streets shifted as the Towers lit the darkened sky, and the wind eased through the empty spaces, sending scraps of garbage scraping across the ground like dried leaves. That much, at least, was normal. But the rest?

Shai looked around, eyes wide.

She had traveled alone through the Lower City's streets night after night, until she knew these streets better in Towerlight, moonlight, than she did by day. Where usually there was silence, here there was noise, motion, light.

Doors were closed, and each building's lower windows were boarded over. But higher, where heavy curtains usually blocked the candlelight, lights shone like beacons. Sounds, too, echoed through the empty streets: voices shouting, arguing; things being moved; the scrape of heavy items being pushed across the floor. Nearby, someone was weeping.

They're packing, she realized. *Getting ready to flee.*

But it was more than that. Because as she watched, a door to a nearby building opened and two people stumbled out, a man and a woman, laughing. Between them stretched a glimmering spell upon which rested a heavy spool of wire, which they took down the street to an aircar parked in the middle of the road.

Rising, Shai saw more aircars on the building's roof—new aircars, polished to a mirror shine—being loaded with what Shai would have once called scraps: buckets of nails and lengths of heavy metal pipe, pieces of wood and boxes filled with personal belongings. Materials that the Lower City dwellers would surely need if they were to have any chance of creating safe shelter out in the ruins.

Fuel for the Towers. For all that the Towers were beings of magic, their physical forms were made from other things. The eldest, largest Towers rarely needed to augment their structures, even during significant renovations; younger Towers—and poorer Towers—knew no such luxury. The things they were pulling from the buildings were not the highest quality, but the price, as they said, was right.

Shai watched as the pair maneuvered the heavy spool into the aircar's storage compartment, laughing and joking as they settled it with their other spoils. Perhaps they thought their voices quiet, their lights dim; perhaps they thought themselves cautious.

Not cautious enough.

Shai turned away. Yet farther, she saw more of the same: desperate Lower City dwellers packing, shouting, sometimes fighting with City citizens who used spells to hold back fists and knives alike with ease. In some places, people of the poorer Towers had taken over the buildings entirely, forcing out their inhabitants.

Small spells, small ways to help, she'd thought; but what was she supposed to do in the face of *this*?

A cry in the street made her freeze, then turn back the way she'd come.

The pair stood near their aircar, its storage compartment gaping wide—but a third figure had joined them in the street. A night walker.

The walker was a woman, or had been in life—a life that was long behind it now. The walker had obviously spent some untold months out in the ruins; its clothes were but dirty tatters, so stained that Shai could only guess at their original colors. The walker's skin sagged from its face and hung loose from its arms as it raised them, making Shai think that the living woman had been larger in life. Almost, she could imagine it: the rounded flesh of the woman's belly and breasts, her wide, glowing cheeks as she laughed, the softness of her arms as they wrapped around a loved one. Gone now, that body and the person who had once owned it.

She'd seen this walker once or twice before over the past months, though never so close. It was slower than some of the others; looking at the scabbed, infected ruin of its feet, Shai understood why.

The City citizens had cringed at the walker's appearance, but now, watching its slow approach, they straightened, some of their fear leaving.

"It's just an old woman," one said, wrinkling her nose—as if that seeming old woman wouldn't tear her apart if it reached her. The other raised his weapon. It was a shock gun like those carried by Tower security, used to shut down dangerous situations before they got out of hand.

The spell flashed from the gun's barrel, lightning quick, and hit the walker square in the chest. The walker jerked back, then stumbled and fell to the asphalt, its body twitching.

The man laughed dismissively. "How easy they fall—with a little help."

"Keep watch," the woman replied, unimpressed with his bravado. "There might be others. "

Shai watched the walker. Shock guns did not kill; they incapacitated their targets with pain. One shot was often enough to immobilize, if not knock a person unconscious for minutes at a time.

But night walkers no longer registered pain.

In silence, the walker rose to its broken feet with a swiftness that Xhea would have envied. It glanced toward Shai, its pupils contracting at her dim light—then back to the City citizens. The latter were far closer. The walker started toward them.

Step. Step. Step.

The pair pushed the spool of wire deeper into the aircar's storage compartment, trying to create room for another load. Beneath the noise of their efforts, the sound of those slow, steady footsteps was lost. Shai wanted to cry out and warn them—even as that angry, hurt part of her said to do nothing.

If they wanted to take everything good from the Lower City, shouldn't they have a taste of the bad? They had come here to steal—and not from the dead, but the living. They'd written off the Lower City dwellers, down to the smallest child.

Poor though their Towers were, their wants were nothing compared to the needs of the Lower City. Still they took, and took, and took.

Step. Step. Step.

The man looked up and exclaimed in surprise, stumbling back as he fumbled for his shock gun. Again he shot the walker, the spell hitting the creature on its shoulder and reverberating through its body. The walker stumbled but did not fall. It stared unblinkingly at the man before it.

Step. Step.

He shot it again and again. The walker's muscles twitched and spasmed. Its skin reddened from spell-burns, and it blinked, half-blinded with every shot.

Still it came for him.

At last the gun's storage coils whined, bordering on empty. The man hit it against his hand as if a jolt might fix it, and stumbled back until his back hit the wall of the building behind him.

Instead of panicking, the woman had prepared a spell—a quick twist of power meant to bind and incapacitate. Shai recognized the simple spelllines from the self-defense training she'd received as a girl. Simple though the spell was, it was clearly not one the woman had oft practiced, and fear did terrible things to one's accuracy.

The woman's first shot went wide—but her second, hastily woven, hit the walker square in the face. It stumbled, slowed but in no way bound by the magic that wound around its face and neck. It righted itself, and reached for her.

Enough, Shai thought, breaking herself from her immobility. Anger had goaded her to many things these past months, but these people's blood and screams would solve nothing.

She did not need a spell. Instead, Shai descended to the ground, raised her arms, and let her power flow.

She had held her magic damped on instinct, hoping to avoid detection. Now she relaxed that control. It felt like letting her hair down from a too-tight braid at day's end; it felt like falling back onto fresh sheets and exhaling.

Magic radiated from her as if she were the dawning sun, sending long shadows racing across the darkened pavement. The City citizens cringed, raising their hands to shield their eyes from the sudden glare.

The walker had frozen mid-step; now it turned toward Shai.

Her light transcended the magical spectrum, shining into the visual one. As that light fell full upon the walker's face, it flinched; its mouth opened as if to cry out, but no sound emerged.

Shai thought of Torrence's new sensitivity to light and magic—and Xhea had saved him before the dark magic boy had done more than begin to draw his spirit out through his eyes. She could only imagine how much stronger that sensitivity would be to one who had known no such salvation.

The walker moved toward Shai as if there was no one else in the world. The City citizens, behind it, were forgotten; the walker paid them no more attention than it did the broken ground beneath its feet.

"Get back inside," the City woman was saying. "Come on, get up—*get up!*"

The man just stared, his spent shock gun hanging from limp fingers. But not at the walker, Shai saw, but at her—or, rather, the featureless glowing figure that he surely saw in her stead.

"It's true." The words were soft and reverent.

Xhea was right: rumors of Shai's presence had spread far beyond Edren's walls. Yet she did not fear these two—not here, not now. The walker filled the whole of her attention.

I have to do something. But what?

Because seeing it here—seeing even City citizens, unprepared, made all but helpless by its approach—she could only think of the Lower City dwellers cast into the ruins, left to the walkers' absent mercy. There were more people than there were safe walls to hold them.

Somewhere nearby she heard a panicked scream and the crack of a spell discharging. The sounds' echoes danced around her. Hers was not the only walker in the streets, or the only one to have spotted prey.

Shai looked at the walker. She could try to bind it or incapacitate it. She could try to kill it; perhaps she *should* kill it. She tried to think of how many innocent people she might save, as if such thoughts could help her conjure the sharp, vicious spell she would need to accomplish the task.

The walker stared at Shai, enraptured by her light, and did not move. It barely seemed to breathe. For all that the walkers were alive—though their hearts beat and blood flowed through their veins; though they ate, when they could—she could not call the thing before her one of the living. There was no person behind those staring eyes; only a body, empty and echoing, and the needs that drove the flesh.

As Shai watched, something seemed to leave the creature— some coiled tension or yearning; some pain that had nothing to do with the wounds of its failing body. As the light of her magic poured over its gaunt face, for just a moment it seemed not to be an empty shell of flesh, but the memory of a person. Shai imagined that she could see something more, as if kindness or humor might be written in the lines of one's face, the curl of aging fingers, the grown-out cut of tangled, dirty hair.

She knew, then, that she could not kill it—could not kill *her*; yet neither could she allow the walker to remain.

There came a flash and a spell struck Shai's chest—or tried to. Like all else, the twist of magic flew through her; there was less substance in her glowing, ghostly body than in a gust of wind. Even so, Shai jumped in surprise, reading the spell's intent even as it discharged harmlessly in the street.

A defensive spell, she realized. *A spell meant to catch and bind.*

The City woman stood with her hands raised, looking confused. The woman hadn't hit Shai by accident, aiming for the walker, but on purpose. Even as she watched, the woman started another spell—a stronger, more complex weaving—her eyes never leaving Shai's glow.

Trying to catch the Radiant ghost, Shai thought, her dismay transformed to irritation. *Just another treasure to haul home from the ruins.*

With a flick of her ghostly fingers, Shai unraveled the woman's half-woven spell, then turned away. She moved slowly, putting space between her and the walker—and step by uneven step, the walker followed.

Down the street and around the corner, Shai led the night walker out toward the ruins, moving just slowly enough that the creature might follow. Farther she went, out to where only a few of the buildings had inhabitants; farther, where the roaming gangs held more sway than the skyscrapers; and farther still.

Shai wasn't sure when the second walker joined her, or the third; only heard their footsteps in echo of the first. She glanced back. She recognized one of them, an old woman who wore only the tattered remains of a dress that hung down to mid-thigh, her legs like thin branches, her knees swollen. The other was newer—a young man that she had never seen before.

Soon they reached the edge where the Lower City surrendered to the ruins beyond—the place that had been marked in red on the Messenger's map.

In the days since the market had burned, she'd come here each night to watch as people claimed these structures, finding the empty hulks and gutted buildings that were strong enough to house themselves or their families in some semblance of safety. In some, roofs were being built, walls reinforced, holes patched and mended. In others, the glassless windows were being boarded over—or, better, bricked with stone, chunks of concrete, and rough mortar.

Homes for the people displaced by Rown's attack, homes to replace the buildings that had burned. Homes, too, for those who had fled Rown itself, abandoning their allegiance to the skyscraper in wake of the attacks—though those were far fewer in number.

Homes that were now being abandoned. Already, Shai could see places where that new construction was being torn down, bundled up, and dragged into the ruins. While the skyscrapers' leaders planned and pleaded, and crowds gathered in the burned market, shouting and brandishing stones, there were other Lower City dwellers who were quickly and quietly leaving.

Shai could see hints of their presences around her: faint, candlelight flickers inside gutted hulks, hastily extinguished as the walkers' footsteps neared; dimmer lights, less than the glow from banked embers, of people's magic, their rare spelled possessions, and the power of their makeshift defenses. She tried her best to avoid them as she led the walkers onward.

She didn't know how many walkers were following her now; she'd stopped looking back, not wanting to see their blank faces, their empty, staring eyes. Instead she watched as the buildings gave way to rubble and the rubble to rounded stone; she listened as the walkers' footsteps no longer crunched along broken asphalt but kicked loose rocks, swished through grass, rustled through leaves.

So far from the Lower City's dark magic, things grew. Grass and flowers. Trees, in places; some stunted and twisted, but others growing strong and tall, destroying crumbling foundations with their insistent roots. It smelled different here, too; less of garbage and sewage and things left to rot, and more of earth and pollen and wild flowers' faint perfume.

At last, Shai stopped. This was far enough. She could return to the Lower City without difficulty—but the walkers? Too far to go and return before daylight, she judged. Their burrows were out here somewhere, little places where a once-human thing might curl and hide from the sun that burned their eyes.

Shai turned—and there he was.

She had gathered a crowd of some twenty night walkers; they stared blankly up at her, their faces so different, their expressions identical. Her eyes went only to one. Shai lost the ability to breathe, to think; all her words were suddenly gone, as if her mind were a street that the wind had scoured clean.

The walker stood in the shadow of what had once been a wall, shielded from both the multi-hued Towerlight and Shai's own soft luminance. His head was lifted, unkempt brown hair hanging limply into his eyes. His clothes were muddy and torn, nothing familiar in their shape or color. Shai did not move or speak, yet he responded nonetheless, his mouth opening as if to reply.

Her father.

No, Shai thought. Her father was dead, she knew that; he was dead as surely as she was, though his body still walked. Even so, her heart clenched at the sight of him.

It had been little more than four months since she'd seen him alive, shortly after her own death; less since her first glimpse of his empty body in the subway tunnels beneath the Lower City.

He had changed much since then. His face was heavily lined and hollow-cheeked, his eyes lost in sunken shadow. His body, beneath the frayed and stinking ruins of what had once been fine clothes, was bent and broken as if he bore the weight of untold years.

He was her father, and . . . not. For when he moved toward her—and he did, stepping closer until he was hemmed in by the other walkers—there was nothing in his posture or gait that spoke of the man she'd known; nothing in his expression that told of the father she'd loved. Only the slow and steady footsteps of a night walker.

Shai shivered, wanting to scream or weep, she knew not which. She wanted to reach for him, as if anything of her father might remain in that ruined shell of flesh; she wanted to run away as far and as fast as she could, as if speed or distance might separate her from even the memory of this moment and the blankness of his eyes.

She floated, standing in midair a good five feet from the ground—but as she looked into the empty face of the man who had been her father, Shai found herself sinking. Her feet touched the earth light as a falling leaf, and she sank no further.

The closest walker reached for her, and another; gathering her magic, she pushed them aside, clearing a path to her father. She reached for his face as if she might cup his cheek in her hand—and hesitated. She could not touch his face or flesh; her hand would pass through unfeeling. But it was not that which stopped her hand and made her fingers curl toward her palm like a wilting flower's petals, but a painful realization.

Here he is, after all this time.

She could not count the nights she had spent looking for him, searching the ruins as if she knew no other purpose. Her searches had become routine, a pattern of thought and action long stripped of expectation. Time had numbed her to hope; it was easier that way. Or maybe it was only that she never quite knew how to stop.

Yet here he was. She had found him.

Now what? The thought echoed in the recesses of her mind.

She'd seen so many walkers—more, she thought, than any living person. Young and old, male and female; she'd come to recognize many on sight. She recognized, too, when a new walker joined the crowd: healthier, stronger; their hair not yet matted; their clothes not yet stiffened by weeks of sweat and rain and grime. The walkers that died? Those she did not mark, only wondered at the absence of their familiar features as weeks passed.

Again and again Shai had wondered what she'd feel upon seeing her father again. Now, looking at the starving ruin of his face, she could only think, *Not this*.

Not this ache, as if her insides had been hollowed out. No hope, now; no joy. Even her grief and anger withered—that, or grew so all-encompassing that she could no longer see their edges.

Father. The word was on her tongue and it felt like a lie, bitter and hard-edged. He just looked at her. His expression did not change; the rhythms of his breath remained slow and steady. Only his eyes revealed that he saw her, his dilated pupils contracting from the light of her magic.

No recognition there. No reaction.

Shai took a long shuddering breath as she finally understood the words she had repeated in the silence of her mind. There was nothing left of the man she had loved, nothing of the man he had been. *Nothing*.

Only this.

The next thought came more slowly and, she knew not from where; it was just there, a sharp presence in the center of her mind.

I could kill him.

She could not touch him—but she had her magic. For all that bright magic was the light of living and growth, it could kill; of course it could. *She* could kill—couldn't she? She had the power; she had, perhaps, the motivation.

But the will?

She wanted to laugh at the absurdity, or cry. Tears won, as they always had. She ignored them, letting them fall glittering to the uneven ground.

She couldn't kill him; she didn't have to attempt the spell to know its inevitable failure. She hadn't been able to hurt a night walker she'd never known; how could this be easier? Which left her—what? Only the tears, and the span of seconds that rolled by, slow and inexorable, within the walkers' sight.

Instead, Shai closed her eyes and rose, higher and higher, as if with enough distance she might leave even memory behind. Higher and higher, until the walkers might see her as nothing but another Tower, another light glowing in the sky.

Shai tilted her head back toward the City, the Towers, the stars, and she thought of nothing at all. She felt the whisper of Towerlight as it brushed across her face, magic on magic. She tried only to breathe.

She did not open her eyes until she knew the walkers would have gone, moving on to other ruins, other worn paths, other places.

Gone, all of them.

Gone.

Shai had never been brave.

There had been times when her mother had told her otherwise, sitting at Shai's bedside wearing her office clothes. "You're so brave," she'd say sometimes. "Try to be brave," she'd say at others, when the pain was bad and getting worse, as if bravery might bring Shai hope or strength or oxygen.

When things truly got bad? Shai's mother hadn't been there at all; only her father, quiet and calm. He'd held her hand, and steadied the shaking glass as she tried to take a sip of water. He'd slept in the chair by her bedside, curled uncomfortably into a too-tight ball just so he'd be there. He'd told her stories.

Even then, that word had made her angry. *Brave.* Where was the bravery in illness? She'd had no choice. And if sometimes she had wept or screamed, if she been afraid or wanted to close her eyes and just *stop*—and she had, more times than she could remember—did that somehow make her a coward? No, to be truly sick wasn't about bravery or cowardice. Merely endurance.

At last, she'd found something she could not endure.

It wasn't weak to run from the creature that had once been her father; it wasn't cowardice that made her squeeze her eyes shut so she wouldn't see him walk away. She told herself that truth over and over, and every time the words tasted like lies.

Shai finally looked down. There were no walkers beneath her anymore, only a span of empty ground.

Pretend that everything's fine, she told herself. *Pretend that nothing's changed.*

And do what?

She thought of the need that had driven her from the underground—the belief that she could do some good. Heal a wound or ease some anonymous hurt; fix a crumbling wall or lighten some heavy burden.

Her small spells felt as nothing now; grief burned her magic to ashes.

Instead, she looked farther into the ruins. There was no light that wasn't reflected from the City above: all was calm and silent.

No one out here but her and the walkers, and she didn't think that either counted. Only an untold expanse of time-smoothed ruins stretching from here to . . . she didn't even know where.

Why are you here, Shai? she asked herself in silence. In this place, in these ruins—in the living world at all. *Oh, absent gods save me. What am I doing?*

Never had she felt so alone.

Yet, as she floated over the dark entrance to a half-collapsed basement, she saw a glimmer of light from inside. She hesitated, thinking, *Just Towerlight reflecting from glass shards*, then turned back. Again she saw it, that faint glimmer—not true light, but magic.

It was a man, she saw, lying curled around a knife with a spelled blade. The knife was unsheathed, the metal glowing faintly with magic. The concrete wall was at his back, and he used a heavily stuffed bag as a pillow. Even in the darkness, his eyes were open, watching.

What's he doing?

But Shai already knew the answer. For that bag wasn't the sign of a hunter caught out in the ruins after daylight; and the knife, held in his white-knuckled hand, trembled with every breath. He could hear the night walkers, as surely as she could; he was only here because he had to be.

He was walking away from the Lower City. Away from the skyscrapers, the buildings, the food supply—away from the Towers, the Spire, the magic, the threat. Away from all of it.

He wasn't the only one. For as Shai rose, shocked, she caught a glimpse of a figure perched atop a crumbling wall, much as Xhea had done that long night shortly after they'd met. No magic, there, to betray the figure's location; it was only the movement of hair in the wind that caught Shai's eye. Again she saw a bundle at the figure's side, a dark patch that surely represented the whole of their belongings—or everything they could carry.

Farther out, and farther still? She found more. Ones and twos, mostly; few families this far out, fewer that one might count as elderly.

These people weren't just abandoning their homes and seeking the shelter they might carve from the fallen buildings. They were heading out to the badlands, taking only what they might carry. Or maybe they were walking farther, out into the world beyond.

Shai stared at the far horizon, untouched by Towerlight, lit only by pinprick stars. She did not know what was out there, if anything. The thought was enough to pierce her haze of grief— and it filled her with something that could have as easily been named excitement as fear. Because there was a whole world out there, little though she'd considered it in life or death; there was more to this life than the City and the Spire and those crushed beneath the floating Towers.

For a moment, it was all Shai could do not to flee toward that great unknown—to run and run and never look back.

She raised a hand to the center of her chest—to the tether, spelled with dark magic, that joined her to one small, hurt girl curled alone in the darkness beneath the Lower City. Shai wanted to run, but would not—could not. Not alone.

Instead, she took a deep breath and started her journey back to the Lower City.

Chapter Nine

In memory, Xhea watched Farrow as it fell. All the weight of that pale, ungainly structure as it struggled through the air, broken concrete dropping from its shattered base like hail. The fountain of magic from its peak, cascading into a shimmering bubble that flared and flickered and failed, while the magic coursing through its walls tried to spark life from the inanimate.

In the early morning light, there was no glow, no magic, only the wan sunlight on its black-wrapped surface. Farrow's height drew the eye, as did the twisting chaos of the grown tendrils that held it aloft; its shadow stretched long and dark across the burned market. Yet for all the changes that had occurred in the weeks since Farrow's hard landing—the makeshift doors bored through the encircling vines, the stairs hewn into those black sides—nothing seemed to have changed at the skyscraper's peak.

Squinting, Xhea could just see them: two defensive spell generators—long spires of bound metal and spellwork—that stabbed skyward from opposite corners of the skyscraper's rooftop. They had been meant to protect Farrow as it rose and fought for position in the City above. They were makeshift things, broken and rusted, purchased from a Tower; and they would have served only until Farrow could have changed its shape and grown its own spires. Even so, Xhea remembered the defensive spells that had fountained from them like water, and the protective bubble of magic that they had created. The beginnings of Towerlight.

Gone now, those spells and the magic that had powered them. But as Rown had so adeptly proved, defensive spires also made effective weapons.

Shai returned to Xhea's side, falling from the sky at a speed that made Xhea's stomach lurch. The ghost slowed and steadied herself effortlessly, landing feather-light beside her.

"They're intact," she reported. "No obvious signs of damage. And there's no one up on the rooftop."

Xhea nodded and looked at the spires, slim lines silhouetted by a patch of pale sky. Rown's defensive spell generator was conspicuously absent—either hidden or stolen, if Xhea had to guess. Given the death and destruction it had caused, she hardly mourned its absence. But that left only Farrow's two spires, hopelessly far above.

"You sure you can get the generators down here?" Shai asked skeptically. "I can reduce the weight and help try to balance the load, but . . ."

"I'm not sure of anything," Xhea said with a small, harsh laugh.

"Okay, we get the generators, and then what?"

Xhea shrugged. "Then we have options."

"Two spell generators won't be enough to defend against the Central Spire," Shai protested—and not for the first time.

"No," Xhea admitted. "But if not the Spire, then the Towers. If not the Towers, the walkers." She looked back to the ghost. "It's something, Shai."

Something that felt terribly, awfully like hope. Xhea tried to crush the feeling.

Yet she couldn't help but imagine a great dome of power arcing over the whole of the Lower City, shining as it repelled the Spire's attack. *Foolishness*, she told herself; she might as well push the Spire with hands alone for all the difference it would make. Even Shai's power was but a glimmer compared to the Central Spire's.

But if not that, then perhaps they could bring the spell generators out to the ruins—cast that dome over the broken ground where the Lower City dwellers sheltered, so that they were protected not by walls but by spellwork. Even if Shai could not maintain the protection forever, perhaps it would be enough for them to start building something new—homes and defenses, weapons and plans.

Three days. For the first time since she'd heard those words echo through the streets, Xhea began to believe that the Lower City might have a future—the people, if not the buildings or the entity itself.

It was enough to push her forward, no matter how her stomach churned at the thought of climbing the makeshift stairs that snaked up the dark tendrils to Farrow's doors. No railings, no smooth surface upon which to walk. It mattered little that no one had yet slipped and fallen from those pathways; the thought alone made her feel faint.

"It's okay," Shai said softly. "You'll be fine. I won't let you fall."

Xhea tightened her sweaty grip on her cane and nodded. She wished suddenly, desperately, for Torrence or Daye on that long, dangerous climb; for the comfort of a solid body and a drawn weapon between herself and those who might seek to claim her. She did not know who had bound her magic, but there was no end to the list of those who might seek to claim Shai for her power.

Not helping.

Xhea forced herself forward, trying to ignore the crawling feeling between her shoulder blades of being watched. Trying not to think of how easy it would be to claim her from Farrow's exterior like one would pluck a grape from its stem.

But as she walked into the chill of the skyscraper's shadow, it was not fear that made her slow, but the Lower City's song. A shiver ran across her skin, raising goosebumps; and her heart sped up, trying to beat in time.

With every step that song grew louder, stronger, until she felt that she was not walking toward Farrow but some echo of the Lower City's heart. Again her magic tried to rise and flow from her in echo or answer, and again she pushed it down, fighting that surge of power. So exposed, the last thing she needed was the tracking spell calling out her location.

The first step of the winding pathway stood before her, an uneven gouge in the grown vine; yet it was her hand that reached for the surface of that black structure.

Xhea gasped as she touched it. It felt smooth as a time-worn stone and slightly cool, not yet warmed by the late summer sun—but it was the power it held that made her catch her breath.

Home, that touch said. *Home*, as if there was anything in the grown structure that might have been comforting or familiar.

Only magic, she realized. For all that the living Lower City's awareness spread to every building and street within the core territories, it was only this structure of reshaped rubble that it possessed entirely. It was only here that the entity lived as the Towers lived, its magic and consciousness an inextricable part of the vines that held Farrow, its magic flowing through the materials like water.

That structure vibrated in response to her touch. Xhea no longer had to strain to hear the song; it rose around her, swelling in welcome.

Oh, how she wanted to reply—to have even the thinnest thread of power to send into all that dark. She had nothing, only the cold, hard stone that her magic formed inside her, and the fear of what would happen if she tried to fight the bonds that held it.

"Hello," she whispered instead, as if the Lower City might hear and understand. Wishing she could push her thoughts through that single point of contact, or shape understanding from fingers alone.

Does it know? she wondered. Did it hear the Messenger's announcement, or feel the chaos within these streets? Did it understand that the end of its life approached with the inexorable speed of the rising sun?

She did not know, only leaned against that surface as if it were her only hold on the world.

"Xhea," Shai said behind her. "The ghosts . . ."

She didn't need to continue. Xhea could feel the market's gathered dead turning to her; turning, in truth, toward the living Lower City's rising power. Shai's presence was the strongest, yet she felt the others, too, like distant points of pressure arrayed behind her. They drew closer, struggling against their tethers.

She understood that pull; she could not look away from Farrow's grown base. Its dark surface rippled, shapes and shadows racing from her touch like patterns in gray oil. Beneath her hand, something moved.

Startled, Xhea recoiled—and saw a crack where her palm had rested. That crack widened like curtains being drawn back, vines shifting and moving until a space had opened before her. It was a hand's span above her head, little larger than the shape of her standing body. She stared, mouth agape.

Alive like the Towers are alive, she thought again. *And this ground its claimed body.*

What else might it do, given the chance? A chance, it seemed, it would never have.

"I think it's an invitation."

"An invitation for what?" Shai's voice held a hint of fear—and Xhea understood.

She trusted her desire to walk into the Lower City's dark magic as much as she trusted the sudden impulse to leap from a building's crumbling edge.

She thought, too, of the only time she'd seen a Tower's transformation up close, in Allenai's forced takeover of Eridian. Their walls had transformed into something that moved like living water, flowing and shifting until there was nothing she could name a wall, a floor, a ceiling. Neither Tower had hurt its citizens, but had instead drawn them into their living flesh, holding them close and safe.

Xhea stared at the space before her, smaller than any rough-hewn coffin, and wondered if it was the same. *But to keep me safe from what?*

Only then did she turn, that thought more powerful than even the dark magic's call.

There, on the market's far side, stood two men. City citizens both—and not, unless she missed her guess, anyone from a poor Tower. It was easy, now, to look beneath the surface of things—and a body was no more barrier to her sight than a wall or ceiling or the ground itself.

Magic glowed deep within their hearts, bright and steady and strong. Spells, too, were woven through their clothing and glittered about their ears and lips; magic imbued the plain, heavy rings that each wore on their right hands.

They had not seen her, not yet—but they were seeking. She watched as they walked into the market and scanned the gathering people. No angry crowd this morning, no scavengers out in the ashes; only people who carried all that they owned on their backs. Even so, the pair made only a cursory attempt to blend in, the threat inherent in their stances enough to make Lower City dwellers step aside without question.

They could be looking for anyone, she told herself, and did not believe it. She'd seen bounty hunters work before; these were only richer, better-equipped versions of the ones she knew. She could only be grateful that they weren't Enforcers.

The smaller of the pair tilted his head as if listening, and for once Xhea was glad of the binding around her magic; the pain was reminder to not fight its control.

Instead, she stepped farther into Farrow's shadow—and then, pushing past hesitation, into the dark chamber it had created.

Xhea expected Shai to protest. Instead, the ghost rushed after her, her brilliance lighting that small space far better than the dawning sunlight. Sunlight that vanished as the dark tendrils moved and shifted around them, making room for Shai and then closing them into a space shaped like palms cupped together. The sound of Xhea's breath echoed off the close walls.

Xhea shifted, turning to look at Shai. The ghost's face was but a hand's span from her own. It was only here, so close, that she noticed that Shai was taller than she was; though they stood all but toe to toe, Xhea had to tilt her head to meet the ghost's pale eyes.

Silence settled over them, between them. Xhea's breath caught.

"Well," she said softly, and had to swallow past the sudden tightness in her throat. "This might have been hasty."

"But they can't see us here." Shai, too, whispered.

"No."

Again, silence stretched between them. Shai's face was but a breath away from her own. Xhea was suddenly aware of her shallow breathing, her clammy palms, the way her hand trembled against her cane's metal top. Magic flowed between them, with other things caught up in that tide. Thoughts, flickering lightning-fast; emotions too tangled to name. Xhea's heart raced, pounding against her ribs, and she did not want to think why.

So she touched the cool surface of the wall beside her, and shivered as a trickle of dark magic flowed into her through that contact. It calmed her, steadied her, even as she struggled to slow her breathing. She blinked, forcing herself to look away from Shai—to look up at the uneven peak of the small space around them, and imagined the caught skyscraper that loomed somewhere far above.

"How long do you think it will hide us?"

Shai's shrug was almost graceful; she, too, looked upward. "How long do you want to stay hidden?"

Again Xhea swallowed, choking back her answer. *Focus*, she told herself.

"I don't think that 'forever' is workable in this situation."

Shai gave a soft laugh, glancing back to Xhea's face. "In this situation? So little is."

No kidding.

Xhea tried to think only of the defensive spell generators up on the rooftop, dragging her thoughts back to where they belonged.

"Maybe," she started, only to stop in surprise as the walls around her shifted once more. It wasn't anything like she'd imagined, that motion: no shuddering, no grinding sound of stone-on-stone; only a smooth flow, as if these surfaces became liquid and re-formed at the Lower City's command.

A path opened before them, spiraling upward.

Xhea looked at that path; it was not nearly as steep as the stairs carved into Farrow's sides, not nearly as rough or rocky. *Still a very long walk.* Even so, she was grateful. She stepped forward and felt the moment that Shai's light no longer fell full upon her face. That magic had been like sunlight, warm and ever-present; outside the sphere of Shai's radiance, the shadows felt cold.

"Stop," Shai said. Xhea hesitated, then turned, coins and charms chiming as her hair fell across her shoulders. Shai's thoughts, it seemed, had run a similar path to hers. "It will take a long time to walk that far. And then all the stairs in Farrow to get to the roof."

Xhea nodded, but Shai hesitated a long moment before continuing, her voice so soft it was little more than a whisper.

"I said I wouldn't let you fall. Perhaps I can help you fly."

Xhea wanted to stare; wanted, in truth, to smile. Yet for all of Shai's impact on the living world, the things she knew how to do were hardly physical. She could heal and transform and protect, create great workings of shimmering light—but lift someone? They couldn't even touch.

"But how . . . ?" she tried. "But you . . ."

"That's not a no," Shai said, and moved closer until there was barely any space between them. "May I try?"

Xhea nodded shakily.

"Hold to me."

Hold? Xhea couldn't bear the thought of reaching for Shai and having her hand pass through unfeeling, only mist and magic where her heart said there should be a person, warm and real. Instead she drew her cane toward her body, clinging to it.

Magic flared, bright and warm, and wrapped around her, pushing back the darkness. Shai's expression was intense, her face lit with a joy so sharp it seemed almost to cut.

A dream fueled this spell, Xhea thought—a dream or a memory or some powerful thought, she knew not which; she only saw its echoes as brilliant spell lines arced around them. Or perhaps she could imagine, for as she stared at Shai all she could think of was their fall together from the City above, Shai's arms holding her, her magic flaring about them like wings.

Xhea gasped as her feet lifted from the ground.

Did the path before them change? Xhea did not look, could not see; Shai, before her, seemed to fill the whole of her vision. It did not feel as if they took that slow, winding path. Instead they rose like a bubble through that twining, coiling black— and the Lower City's grown tendrils reshaped around them.

No time seemed to pass, or perhaps it was an hour, a day— Xhea did not know, only stood blinking as Shai set her down on solid ground once more.

"I . . ." she started.

Shai smiled and slowly, slowly drew back.

Xhea took a long, shuddering breath, feeling as if she hadn't inhaled in forever, and made herself look away. The ground beneath her was black and smooth—yet the walls, the ceiling? Xhea blinked and blinked again, then walked in a slow circle, staring at the space in which she found herself.

It had been an apartment once. Crumbling plaster clung to the ceiling, while paint flaked from the walls in long, gray curls. There was a doorframe, a blackened window. At waist height, all of that ended: the walls broken off unevenly, cracked and scorched. Below, there was only black.

"Farrow," Xhea whispered.

Shai slipped through the wall, then peeked back. "The hall is clear."

Xhea struggled through the half-open wreck of the door. Only Shai waited beyond. Carefully they made their way down the ruins of the hall and into the stairwell.

It was dim there, closed-in and quiet. The only source of true light filtered down from high above. Xhea grabbed the railing and started to climb, her brow drawn low. There were no candles, no light spells, not in the stairs or in the halls they slowly passed. No sounds of life or movement that were not her own. Around her, Farrow rose tall and silent.

Has everyone already left? Because long before the Messenger's arrival, she'd seen them—Farrow citizens abandoning these dead walls, their backs laden with whatever they might safely carry. She had not envied them the long, precarious climb down to the ground. Others had made a makeshift pulley system by which goods might be lifted or dropped from the skyscraper's higher levels—though Xhea had only ever seen things being taken away.

Not that she blamed them. For all that Farrow proper still existed, she'd yet to see a wall without cracks or other structural damage, where the living Lower City's black tendrils didn't invade the structure entirely. Perhaps things were better, stronger, more habitable in the levels above; but she did not think so.

Xhea had only climbed a half-dozen flights of stairs when something made her slow—something other than the pain in her knee and the growing shortness of her breath. She stopped on the next landing and turned, frowning.

Beside her, Shai too had paused. The ghost moved without speaking, one shining hand raised. She pressed her hand to the wall and let it sink into the concrete.

Xhea pushed the stairwell door open and peered into the hall beyond. Only silence here; only stillness. Nothing that might cause the disturbance that even now brushed against the edges of her senses.

Not a ghost. Not the living Lower City. But something.

A moment passed. "Xhea," Shai said slowly.

But Xhea was already nodding. She had followed that instinct and looked up, changing her eyes' focus to see past the stained ceiling above her, and the one above that.

There, near the building's peak, was a glow. It was faint, and flickered like an erratic heartbeat—far brighter than she would expect from any Lower City citizen. Brighter than any person who was not Radiant.

Magic, Xhea thought. *Bright magic—here, in the midst of so much dark.* Bright magic not in human form, not forced into a storage coil or running through the wires in the walls, but formed into a glowing sphere of light.

A Tower's heart.

Xhea met Shai's eyes, the ghost's shocked expression a mirror of Xhea's own, and whispered what they were both thinking.

"Farrow is still alive."

Chapter Ten

Xhea did not ask where she needed to go, little though she knew Farrow; she did not wonder what she would find at her destination. She needed only time, and the strength to climb, and felt as if both were failing her.

If the floors below had felt quiet, Farrow's thirty-fourth floor felt like the underground: so long deserted that absence had become a physical force. The sound of her footsteps, her cane, her hair, her breath: all seemed loud in that long corridor, each sound only emphasizing the silence.

The doors to the rooms were closed; no spellcasters or medics walked between them. Of the magic she'd once seen shining within these walls, spells and charms alike flaring to life in Farrow's concrete bones, there were only flickers like embers burning to ash.

"Hello?" Xhea called, neither expecting nor receiving a reply.

She pushed open a door; it was not locked. Inside, there were four empty medical beds, rumpled sheets and the trailing wires standing testament to the one-time occupants. A fifth bed held a person—or, Xhea realized, a person's body.

The man's pale, freckled skin had turned waxen, and the stained sheet that covered him up to his chest lay unmoved by the rhythms of breath. His IV had run dry, and the wires attached to his shaved head, wrists, and above his heart were only wires; no magic flowed along their lengths.

Xhea did not recognize him—did not think that it had been her hands that had held those wires, her magic that had bound them, metal to flesh and the spirit beneath. She did not think so, but did not know, and uncertainty made her stare long after she should have turned away.

"They're just leaving him here?" Shai whispered, shocked.

"It can't have been long." As if that were any excuse. But Xhea did not want to touch that death-pale cheek to see whether it had gone cold and stiff. Instead, she closed the door.

She did not open any of the other doors. Empty beds, beds occupied by the dead or the dying: she could not stand to see any of them. Instead she walked, head bowed and cane clutched in her unsteady hand, toward the skyscraper's center. Toward its living heart—even if the transformation was nothing like any of them had imagined.

"This way," Shai said, urging Xhea in her wake. There was a glow before them, a dim and sputtering light that Shai dwarfed unthinkingly.

Xhea needed no encouragement. She could hear Farrow's heart now, more than she could see it: a faint song that quivered through the walls, not breaking the silence but deepening it. She tried to put words to the sound and could not; not its tone or pitch, not its melody. Only its rhythm seemed clear, and it was a thrum like blood through thickened, aging veins: a slowing beat of weariness and hurt.

Here. They stopped. This section of hall looked like any other, closed doors with peeling paint, the carpet worn to tatters and showing the glue-stained concrete beneath. But from around one of those doors came a light, and the air tingled against Xhea's exposed skin. She touched her cheek, as her fingers and face grew slightly numb. *Bright magic*, she realized. It was a haze in the air, and Xhea had no magic of her own to push it back.

Shai slipped through the door, leaving Xhea to fumble at the handle with fingers gone clumsy from pins and needles. No lock here, either; the door swung wide.

There were no beds inside, occupied or otherwise; no trailing wires, no IVs. Only a ruin that had once been the far wall, rubble scattered across the floor—and Farrow's heart. Seeing it, Xhea could not look away.

In her brief time in the City, Xhea had seen the hearts of some dozen or more Towers. Each had been different, vibrating at its own frequency, glowing its own shade—its own colors, she supposed, little though she could see them. Each, had she known then how to hear them, would have had its own song. Yet, for all their differences, every Tower's heart was a massive sphere of pure bright magic that shone like a miniature sun. Each had been as big across as the Lower City market, some even larger, and had been haloed with flaring arcs of pure power.

Farrow's heart was no larger than one of the bundles of tied rags that Lower City children kicked through the streets, and as uneven. It hovered inside a hollow smashed in the far wall, the drywall around it ripped aside in great chunks. It shone, but dully—its light was gray like old silver, dented and tarnished, and it sputtered and flickered as she watched.

In the heart's shadow, a man sat on a chair that was more rust now than metal. His hands were curled in his lap, his pale skin turned bone white with plaster dust, his salt-and-pepper hair speckled with flecks of concrete. It smelled as if he had not bathed for some days.

He did not look up as Xhea entered, nor as Shai glowed brighter, dispelling the gloom. He only stared at Farrow's heart as if it were the only thing left to him of value—and perhaps it was. If he had reached out, he could have held it in his hands. He did not try.

A moment passed, and then the man spoke.

"It's dying," said Ahrent Altaigh, his words low and uninflected. He spoke as if Xhea had always been here, beside him; as if she had not left, had not ruined everything with that leaving.

Xhea looked at him, the man who had stolen her away—the architect of Farrow's rise and fall—and felt no anger. She should have, perhaps; yet it seemed that he was as ruined as his home. All the resentment she'd harbored, all the fury, fizzled away to nothing.

"It was stronger than this?" Xhea asked.

But of course it had been stronger, brighter. She'd heard the wail of this heart being born, felt the pain and numbness of its raw energy. Once, the whole Lower City had seen its glow.

"It's dying," Ahrent Altaigh said again, "because they are dying, one after another, as we knew they would." He meant the people they'd bound to Farrow's walls, magic and spirit both. She'd seen the truth of that. "It's dying because the people of Farrow are fleeing. No reason to stay and every reason to leave."

He turned.

There was little in that face of the man she'd known. Oh, his features were the same—that sharp nose, the strong chin—but his expression belonged to another person entirely. Gone was that passion that had burned within him like fire; gone was that unthinking confidence in posture and word and movement. His dark eyes were like sunken hollows, and his hands lay limply in his lap.

"You're still here," Xhea said quietly.

He smiled, a pained twist of his lips. "There is nowhere else for me to be."

It was only then that she saw what he had attempted. There were cuts in his arms to which he'd bound wires with medical tape and strips of knotted fabric. The dust that coated his hands had stuck not merely to sweat, but to blood—old now and dried. Blood, too, coated some length of the wire that stretched from his arms to the flickering heart, and had dripped to pattern the floor.

He had no dark magic binding, like those that she and Ieren had woven for Farrow's so-called volunteers; no link of magic and spirit, as was needed for any true connection to a living Tower. He had only his own attempts. Bright magic spells flickered around his scabbed-over wounds, and Xhea saw in their lines of intent some hint of the spells' purpose: to tie, to bind, to make his magic flow.

She wanted to ask why he'd bothered with the wire—why he'd bound himself here, when he might have simply lifted his hands and let his power flow. Yet, watching that wire, she could see: flawed though the transfer was, his spells worked regardless of his attention. In sleep or awake, that trickle of power would flow from him, sure as blood.

But one man could not fuel a Tower, no matter how strong the man, no matter how small the Tower's heart.

"I tried to cut it free," Ahrent Altaigh said. "It wasn't supposed to form inside the wall. In the plans . . ." He shook his head, his eyes focusing on something far away—the reality that had never come to pass. "So much did not go according to plan, not least of all this. I could not move the wall and so I tried to cut it free. Thinking that there was some way, some hope . . ."

It was Shai who spoke: "A heart cannot live outside its body, neither human nor Tower."

There was no need to pass along the ghost's soft words. Ahrent already knew.

Xhea looked again at the flickering, fading remains of the skyscraper's once great dreams. No magic flowed in from Farrow's bound citizens, or so little that it made no difference. Were they dead, then, all those people she had bound? All those anonymous faces—and one that she had known. Marna, her grandmother's wife—Xhea's only tie to the family she'd once had.

No wonder it was dying.

Xhea stepped forward, her hands upraised as if Farrow's heart was a small fire at which she might warm herself. Ahrent moved to stop her, his dusty, bloodied hands plucking ineffectually at her sleeve. His weakness, too, showed in every movement, and Xhea wondered when he'd last eaten.

"Don't," he said. "You can't—"

"I won't hurt it," Xhea said, but still he tried to stop her.

"Let me." Shai slipped past Xhea and Ahrent both, making Ahrent shiver as she neared. He looked up, his eyes widening. They grew wider as Shai cupped the flickering heart in her hands and let her magic flow.

Farrow reached for that power and drew it in greedily, sucking it back the way a starving child drank soup: near choking on sustenance. Even its hunger was nothing compared to Shai's power. As fast as it absorbed her magic, she sent it more and more, letting it eat its fill.

A moment, and then Shai drew in a sharp breath. "Xhea, it's—" The ghost broke off, turning the whole of her attention to that tiny, flickering life.

"Hello," Shai whispered, her tone turned soft. She smiled.

At last Ahrent seemed to understand, and he sagged into his rusty chair with something that was almost relief.

"Your Radiant." The words were bare; Ahrent Altaigh seemed too worn, too exhausted for wonder.

"She is not mine," Xhea said, "any more than I am hers."

"Yours, then," Shai murmured absently. For a moment, Xhea could not breathe.

She made herself look only at Farrow. Already, the flickering heart had become steadier, its light brighter. Its song, too, was changing; Xhea imagined that she could hear in that faint, whispered chorus of notes some hint of the entity it could become—yet it would need more than a few minutes of a Radiant's power to become anything greater. It would need a lifetime, and they had only a day.

"Shai," Xhea said. "If we can't move it . . ." She could not bring herself to finish the sentence. There had been so much death, so much pain and loss to create this small, inhuman entity. She did not blame it, no more than she could blame an infant whose mother died giving birth. But what was the use in saving it now if it was only going to be destroyed tomorrow?

Or perhaps that was all they could do. Perhaps they could not save it; perhaps they could not save anyone. But Shai could make the moments before its death hurt a little less.

It doesn't deserve to suffer. None of us do.

Xhea stood at Ahrent's side as Shai held the newborn Tower and gave it light and life and hope in these last few days before its end.

Xhea watched Farrow's light grow brighter; felt magic thicken the air like fog. Too late did she think of the consequences.

As the heart's magic strengthened, her own power tried to protect her—and slammed hard against the barrier of its binding.

Xhea gasped as the tracking spell called out. The sound vibrated through her bones.

Control the magic, she thought. *Push it down.*

It was easy as holding her hand in a fire.

Again the tracking spell called out—louder this time, stronger—and the sound and its vibration almost drove her to her knees. *Here*, it cried. *Here, here, here!*

"Xhea?" Shai's voice sounded distant, lost beneath the spell's call.

Farrow's growing power no longer just tingled across Xhea's skin but burned, too hot and too cold, as it sank into her. She drew in that fog of power with every breath, and it numbed her from the inside out. Yet bright magic counteracted her power—suddenly her dark magic did not fight against the binding but struggled, twisting and writhing as Farrow's light burned it away to nothing. Deprived of its fuel, the tracking spell's song sputtered and died, and Xhea sagged forward, her mind echoing with that sudden silence.

Her relief was short-lived, for still Farrow's magic washed over her, sank into her, burning. Xhea blinked, struggling to focus. She looked at Shai and saw a glimpse of cream-pale skin and shining blonde hair, a spark of blue eyes as the ghost turned to her—and then very little at all.

She was blind without her magic.

Xhea stumbled back, thinking only: *Get away.*

Her shoulder blades hit the far wall and she fumbled for the door, her numbed fingers dropping her cane.

"Shai." She could barely hear her own voice. "Shai, I . . ."

Shai must have turned to her, for the heart wailed as Shai's magic was drawn away. Xhea felt Farrow reach for that sustenance, magic flaring and grasping—and Ahrent gasped as the newborn Tower pulled hard on the only available source of power.

Xhea tried to crawl, but could not support her weight. Instead she reached out with clawed hands and dragged herself across the floor. She could only think, *Away, away, away.* Something cold fluttered against her arms, her shoulders—Shai's ghostly hands. She felt Shai's rush of fear as if it was her own.

Thinking felt like drawing stones up through thick mud. *I can't stop it,* she realized. She couldn't get far enough, fast enough, and the bright magic burned.

In desperation, Xhea reached for her magic—that cold, dark lake; that hard, painful stone—and *pulled.* Her magic was bound, but Shai's was not; and as Xhea struggled to call her power, fighting binding's constriction, she felt some of Shai's strength flow into her. She could not see Shai, but the ghost was suddenly with her, real and present, her emotions pouring into Xhea with her magic.

Fear and love and anxiety wrapped around Xhea like strong, steadying hands. She was weak, blinded, unable to stand; but Shai believed in her.

Xhea pulled harder on her magic harder, willing it to break the bindings that held it and roar free once more. Again her power rose, and again the tracking spell stole that magic, calling out louder.

Here, here, here!

No, Xhea thought. It was *her* magic, *her* power—she would not have it turned against her. Xhea screamed as she fought, but could not hear her own voice; she drew on her power with all her strength, all her will, and forced it past the binding.

Crack!

Xhea gasped at the sharp shock in the depth of her chest. The tracking spell warbled and sputtered, then fell silent, and Xhea sagged to the ground, suddenly boneless. For a moment, the only sound was the high-pitched ringing in her ears.

The binding had cracked, she realized slowly, and the tracking spell had been destroyed, unraveled by the force of magic she'd pushed through it. She felt the last shards of the spell fade away.

A thin stream of dark magic trickled free of the damaged binding and washed through her, thin and weak but *there.*

She drew a deep breath, for she could suddenly inhale again without pain. She blinked, and she could see in blessed black and white.

Shai hovered anxiously, while Ahrent had fallen from his chair and lay sprawled on the ground. Farrow's heart shone behind them like a broken moon, glowing tarnished silver.

Tarnished . . .

The thought, half-formed, was swept away by the physical relief. Xhea blinked, and let herself sag against the floor, staring up at the ceiling. Shai stood over her, her light like a second sun. Bright magic was thick in the air, but the dark power in her blood now held back the worst of it, and the silence as her magic flowed felt like a blessing.

It was not.

"The tracking spell is gone," Shai was saying. "And there's damage to the rest."

"I know," Xhea murmured, rubbing her aching eyes; she felt none of Shai's obvious joy. She sat slowly, aching, then felt the ground around her for her cane. Her knee throbbed, but not so much that she could not stand. And she would have to stand, she knew; she would have run if she could. But where?

Fear that was too cold, too hard, to be panic lodged in her stomach. Because in the tracking spell's final moments, Xhea had heard something respond to its call. Not Farrow, or Shai, or anything around them. Something far distant.

Something above them.

Sweetness.

Ahrent lifted his head and groaned. That bare length of copper wiring had been pulled from his arm in the fall, and blood dribbled a slow track down his arm. *It wasn't necessary,* Xhea wanted to tell him. Not the wire or the blood—but what did it matter now?

"We have to go," she said, ignoring Ahrent. She struggled to her feet and stumbled back, heading out into the hall and away—

away from Farrow's heart and the glow of its magic, away from Ahrent and his wounds and accusations. Away, away, away.

Shai followed—and so, staggering and unsteady, did Ahrent.

"Wait!" His voice cracked. For all his new weakness, he was angry now, coming toward her with blood dripping black from his outstretched hand. "You can't just leave. Not again. Not like this."

Unheard beneath his words, Shai asked her, "What is it?"

"I have to get out of here." Xhea leaned heavily on her cane. "Go as far and as fast as I can. I think—"

She froze. The words evaporated from her mouth and mind—for there, on the edge of her senses, Xhea felt something else. A presence—

No, two presences. More. They were above her and somewhere to her right, and drawing closer by the moment. *Ghosts*, she thought, and her blood ran cold.

"Too late," Xhea whispered. "They're coming."

"Who is?" Ahrent asked. "What did you do? What—"

Xhea wasn't listening. "It wasn't just a tracking spell, was it?" She looked to Shai for confirmation. "Wasn't just tracking where I was, but whether I tried to use my magic. Whether I *had* any magic."

If she was powerful enough to unravel the tracking spell—if her magic had the strength to crack its binding—did that count as "off the charts"?

She laughed; it was a tired, bitter sound. She should run, she knew—but where could she flee that a ghost could not follow?

"Who's coming?" Ahrent asked again. He blinked, stunned. "What's happening? What have you done?"

"We have to get away from the heart," Shai said suddenly.

Xhea had barely taken a step when there came a muffled thump from somewhere above, and the walls around them vibrated. Ahrent stiffened, his hands rising into a defensive pose, heedless of his fingers' exhausted trembling.

Ghosts, Xhea thought, *don't try to knock in a hole in the wall.* But who would the Spire send after a rogue dark magic user?

Someone with a lot of magic or a very big gun. She didn't like either option.

Shai was right—they had to get away from Farrow's heart. Perhaps the Spire would not care about Farrow any more than the thousands of other living beings in the Lower City, but she could not be sure. Xhea stumbled into the far stairwell, not running away from the intruders but toward them.

Behind her, Ahrent was saying, "You can't leave. Xhea, you have to—"

She ignored him, leaving him struggling in her wake.

Again there came that deep thumping, and the walls shuddered. The hair-fine cracks that patterned the concrete widened, and dust trickled down. Trying not to think of the weight of the building above her, Xhea grabbed the railing and hauled herself up the stairs.

"Do you have a plan?" Shai asked.

Xhea glanced back. If her expression did not tell Shai everything she needed to know, then perhaps the emotion echoing between them did. Regret and sorrow and determination.

It was that last to which she clung as if it were fuel enough to keep her moving.

"You can't just give up," Shai said. "Not here. Not now."

"It's not giving up."

Oh really? some part of her replied. *Then why aren't you running?*

But there was nowhere to go, no way that she could physically run. And for all that she'd cracked the binding, she had access to no more than a trickle of dark magic.

The Spire cared little for the Lower City or anyone in it; they'd tear Farrow apart floor by floor if that's what it took to find her, no matter the human cost. There was no standing against the Spire.

She thought again of the defensive spell generators on Farrow's roof. If Shai could reach them, power them—if she could, perhaps, find someone to transport them to the ruins . . . Oh, Xhea did not know what good it might do; it was such a thin, tenuous hope, and yet she clung to it as if it alone might spell salvation.

But not for her.

"If I surrender," Xhea said, "they'll only have me." *Such a noble sacrifice*, she mocked herself in silence. "You'll be safe. You just can't come with me."

"Don't," Shai said, and there was nothing left in her voice of the hesitant, fearful ghost Xhea had met all those months ago. "That isn't your choice to make."

Xhea reached the top of the stairs and took a shuddering breath before pulling the door open. Her hands were numb; her fingers shook. Weaknesses that she could do nothing to hide. Xhea stepped into the hall and tried to walk as tall and as strong as her damaged knee would let her, pretending that her cane was not a support but a weapon upon which she deigned to lean.

Anything to keep from looking at Shai or facing her sudden anger. Xhea wanted to take Shai's hand to bridge the sudden gap she felt yawning between them. Instead she walked.

"No," Xhea admitted. "No, it's not. But I'm *asking*. They're going to take me, and—"

Kill me. That was the thought that rose, no matter how she tried to push it away. She was a dark magic user—a powerful one, if she understood correctly—and the only one outside of the Spire's control. Ahrent had told her once that her dark magic made her more valuable even than a Radiant, and far more rare; that dark magic users—and the spirit bindings they created— were the key to the Spire's power over the Towers. Xhea knew that whatever the Spire wanted of her, she would not, could not comply.

Not unless there was some way they could force her. Not unless they had leverage.

Shai.

Dead though she might be, Xhea knew that the Spire could still hurt Shai—or use her against Xhea. Destroy her ghost. Sell her to a Tower for her power—did it really matter which? None were possibilities that Xhea could bear to contemplate.

Perhaps something of her thoughts showed on her face, for the ghost's expression turned bleak.

"Don't ask it of me," Shai said. "Don't make me stay here while they take you."

"I can't stop you," Xhea said instead. "I won't. But I don't know where they're going to take me, Shai. I don't know what they're going to do. And you . . ."

"I know what they'd do to me." The words were like an admission of defeat.

This hall was a mirror of the one below; it, too, had once housed the bodies of the volunteers bound to Farrow's walls. It, too, felt empty, silent but for the pounding and scraping against the building's exterior.

Xhea pushed open a door and walked inside, following the sounds. No beds here anymore, no inhabitants, living or otherwise; only a span of dusty carpet and a chair in the far corner. A few cracks of daylight shone through the far window. The rest was covered with black strands that wholly blocked their sight of whoever or whatever was outside.

But Xhea could feel them. She could hear them pounding.

"Then what's the point?" Shai whispered. "If you're not here, what's the point of any of it?"

"Maybe you can save people. Use the defensive spell generators. Help them save themselves."

"And you?"

You can't help me. No one can. The words floated between them, unspoken.

Xhea laughed and tried to grin; it was either that or weep. "Maybe I won't die."

There came another hard, echoing impact against Farrow's exterior walls, and the room around them shuddered.

Again, and spider web cracks appeared in the window's ancient glass.

Again, and daylight shone into the room, brighter and brighter, as the living Lower City's grown tendrils were torn away. Outside, Xhea caught glimpses of an aircar's side, the shimmer of spell exhaust, the bright flash of something that might have been metal or spell.

Xhea looked back at Shai. There was nothing to do but wait.

Don't let them take me. The words were on her tongue and yet she choked them back, tasting tears.

Don't leave me alone.

Instead, she raised her right hand and held it hesitantly before her.

Shai looked at her, looked at that hand, and then raised her own in a perfect mirror. Slowly she pressed their hands together, palm to palm.

Oh, Xhea's magic was so weak. She had less power now than she had even that first night she'd spent in Shai's company, the first night her magic had risen. Just a thin trickle of dark slipped through the cracks in the binding.

But it was something. *Please, let it be enough.*

And there, whisper soft, came the feel of Shai's hand against her own. She felt the warmth of Shai's magic, the chill that said ghost, and she didn't see either because she could not look away from Shai's eyes.

Xhea was suddenly aware that, joined though they might be, this might be the last time she saw Shai. The thought was sharp enough to cut.

There was so much she wanted to say and she did not have words for any of it.

The exterior wall tumbled down. Dust and shards of glass flew into the room on a gust of hot air. Shai did not move and yet power surged from her. Light arced around them, bright, gleaming, as it effortlessly held back the debris. Intruders forced their way into the room, shouting, and Shai did not look away from Xhea's face. Did not so much as blink.

"Let me fight them," Shai said. "I could push them back—we could escape into the ruins. The badlands. Farther. I can do it, I know I can."

How she wished she could. Once, she would have taken that offer without a second thought; she would have run from this place laughing and never looked back.

"And then what?" Xhea whispered. "Everyone will die, Shai. The Lower City will be destroyed. You're their only hope—and me?" She smiled, or tried to. "I'm your only weakness."

Tears welled in Shai's eyes.

"Save them," Xhea said. "I'm not worth it."

"You're wrong," Shai told her, but she let her hand fall.

Slowly, Xhea turned to face the masked people who now stood inside, silhouetted by the gaping hole and the daylight streaming in. If she had any doubt of who had come to claim her, it fled.

There were two men and a woman, each tall and muscular, and they wore the Spire's uniform, masks and all. Their uniforms were not white like the Messenger's, but a dark gray that Xhea knew to be red.

Bound to each was a ghost.

Like their living counterparts, the ghosts wore that dark gray uniform, their features blurred where a mask of light had once shone. They stood at attention, vigilant even in death, and Xhea wondered foolishly how the Spire had earned such everlasting loyalty.

Enforcers, all.

She could feel them—had felt them, even from so far away. Something about these ghosts was so cold, so abhorrent, that her flesh shuddered to have them near. The living Enforcers made her want to step back, but the dead ones made her want to turn and run.

Instead, Xhea squared her shoulders and forced her lips into a grim parody of a grin. Perhaps the expression could hide the tears that threatened to fall.

A male Enforcer stepped forward, dragging his ghost at the end of a wide, dark-spelled tether.

"By order of the Central Spire," he began.

"I know, I know," Xhea said impatiently, waving her free hand. "Let's just get this over with."

Xhea did not scream or fight as she was pushed into the back of the armored aircar that hovered outside the hole in Farrow's wall, much as she wanted to. Instead she ducked her head and sat quietly, gripping her cane as if it were a lifeline, tasting bile. The living guards took seats across from her. The ghosts were somewhere behind her. She did not know why she felt their presences so strongly, why having them there *hurt*.

She did not turn; she could not stand to see Shai alone behind her.

The ghost Enforcers, though they had clearly seen Shai, had done no more than glare at her before walking away. Narrow orders, Xhea could only suppose, and gave thanks for that small mercy.

The aircar rose, its engine whisper-quiet. Only the changing light and the shifting view of Farrow's damaged side revealed that they were moving.

Xhea called upon her magic. With effort, she forced a thin trickle of dark past the binding, down through her hands and into the seat below her. Her last aircar trip to the City had nearly ended in disaster when her magic had unraveled the car's spells as they flew. Surely this car, with spelled magic shining from its windows and doors, from the blighted seat cushions, would be no less vulnerable.

No more than a whisper of power had left her hands before the Enforcers around her stiffened.

"Stop it," said one, his tone hard, commanding.

"The car's reinforced against your power," the woman said, almost cheerfully. "But keep it up, and I'd be happy to knock you into tomorrow."

Xhea rolled her eyes. Yet she lifted her hands in surrender, and released her hold on her magic.

As they circled and rose, she peered out the window, ignoring her stomach's lurch as she looked down and down and down. They had barely risen above the tops of the skyscrapers, but already the Lower City was spread out beneath them. It seemed so very small. On the ground, the skyscrapers seemed huge, dominating the landscape—but from on high? They were nothing, just crumbling sticks in a sea of ruins.

Xhea mentally traced the ring from the Messenger's map on the landscape before her, marking the Spire's target and all that lay within. Marking the limits of the living Lower City.

Xhea grew very still, her eyes going wide.

"We're fools," she whispered at last. "All of us, such fools."

"You can say that again," muttered one of the Enforcers disdainfully.

But Xhea only had eyes for the Lower City. Small as it seemed—all those tiny buildings, all those scattered homes dwarfed by the Towers above them—the whole of the Lower City was huge.

All of this time, Xhea thought in a daze. *So long trying to figure out what the Spire will do, how it will attack the Lower City.*

How could none of us think to ask why?

Chapter Eleven

Shai stood in the emptiness where Farrow's destroyed side surrendered to open sky and watched as Xhea was taken from her. Watched the armored aircar rise, surrounded by a shimmering halo of spell exhaust; watched it circle, higher and higher, heading toward the Spire.

Was it better, letting that departure be a choice? Knowing that they allowed the distance that grew between them, a widening gap that soon even Shai's gaze could not traverse. Her choice to stay, Xhea's choice to leave her behind—did it really matter which? In the end it felt the same.

It felt wrong.

Don't be foolish, she chided; the words took on her mother's oft-critical tones. Shai knew that she could at that moment—at any moment—choose to follow Xhea, just rise like a bubble through the air and walls that separated them until she stood once more at Xhea's side. Somehow that made everything worse.

"Don't go," she whispered—words said far too late. Or perhaps she should have said, "Take me with you."

Shai looked away from the Spire, from its golden glow and the Towers slowly circling it, back to the market's burned-out rubble. Only ghosts stood there now, staring about them in desolation.

She rose and looked farther. There were more people—more, truly, than she'd seen ever gathered in the market, more than she'd imagined lived in the Lower City. In every direction they streamed out from their homes and skyscrapers, taking every road, every alley, every path leading out. No destination, Shai thought, but away.

"These people need you now," she told herself, as if she might conjure resolve from her sudden desolation. She heard Xhea's words, echoing in memory: *Maybe you can help them. Help them save themselves.*

She tried to push away the thought that echoed through her mind like thunder. *If you're not here, Xhea, what's the point? Without you, what does any of it matter?*

These people needed her—or they needed her magic, the spells she might weave. They did not, truly, need *her*. But now was not the time to debate the distinction.

She remembered what her mother had said to her once after Shai had complained to her about the frustrating, awful unfairness of being Radiant. No comfort there, as her father might have offered; no hug or kind look. It was not, she'd thought later, even truly her mother who had responded; only Councilwoman Aliane Nalani, speaking on behalf of Allenai's ruling board.

"Making a difference is exhausting and thankless," she'd said, "but you do it anyway, because you have to. Because you can."

Shai touched the tether that joined her to Xhea and tried to send calm through that link, little though she felt it herself. She wished she could feel something, anything in reply. But there was only the wind, sweeping through her as if she was not there at all.

Shai returned to Farrow's rooftop where the two defensive spell generators were mounted, seemingly untouched since the skyscraper's disastrous rise and fall. She examined each, peering closely at the main spires and their various cross-spars, rusted and twisted by age; then looked deeper at the spells embedded in the metal. Battered and damaged as the generators were, the spells within were perfectly sound—and far more efficient than anything she might create.

Xhea's plan was sound, little though Shai knew how to bring it to fruition.

She struggled with the bolts and rusted screws for what felt like an hour, her spells ineffective, her hands sliding through unfeeling, before—in a fit of anger—she gestured at the generator's mooring with hand and magic both. The gesture was little more than instinct. Yet her hand sliced through it like a knife through warm butter, leaving the edges of the cut smooth and shining.

For a moment Shai just gaped—only to spring into action as a gust of air almost knocked the generator from the rooftop toward the ground. She wove a spell in haste and threw it at the tilting spire; it accomplished its end more with sheer force of power than its spelllines. Watching the twisted length fall to the gravel of Farrow's roof with a clang, Shai couldn't bring herself to care.

The other generator she managed to slice free more slowly, and pushed it to the rooftop. At last she stood, looking from one to the other, and wondered how she could get them out to the ruins.

Lorn, she thought. Surely she'd find some help in that quarter—and Emara had always been more sensitive to Shai's presence than most. She could find one of them, write out what she needed—

A glance at Edren told her she'd find no help there. Lozan transport trucks crowded the ancient hotel's rooftop and were being loaded, it seemed, with whatever wasn't tied down.

As she watched, a spell detonated deep inside the skyscraper. A flash lit the windows of Edren's seventeenth floor, and the whole building shuddered, bits of brick raining to the ground.

Even if there were a way to stop the Central Spire's attack on the morrow, Shai suddenly wondered whether there would be anything left of the Lower City to save.

But surely Edren's citizens would be gathering out in the ruins somewhere—Edren's citizens, and the other Lower City dwellers. Such distinctions mattered little now; she'd try to help them all.

"Where are Torrence and Daye when you need them?" Shai looked around as if her words might conjure the bounty hunters from the roof's shadows, only to sigh in irritation.

She tried, again and again, to push the spell generators together, thinking to lift them with a spell the same way she'd lifted Xhea; she could carry them herself. The generators rolled and scraped and banged together, rising but a bare few inches off the roof's surface before falling back with a clatter.

Lifting Xhea had been so easy. She hadn't even thought, hadn't really tried; the magic had just been there, flowing like an extension of her will, wrapping around Xhea's slight body so gently—and then they'd just been rising.

Lifting Xhea had been so easy, and now Shai struggled to raise two small lengths of metal from a rooftop. The absurdity of the situation made her want to give up and just let the hours pass, one after another, until the end.

She wasn't supposed to be anyone's savior, yet she felt the weight of their lives nonetheless—the weight of all her unmade choices, settling over her hands and eyes, pressing on her chest. She couldn't even save the one person who mattered to her. Not when it counted.

Shai leaned back and stared at the sky as if that might stop the tears from welling. Stupid to cry instead of fighting to do more, and yet Shai did not know what to do, how to gather the will to keep going.

Is this how Xhea felt? The thought came as if from nowhere. All those years she'd been alone. Was this what her life had been like, day after day of this emptiness, this helplessness, this rage and hurt and sorrow?

Shai shook her head and tried to just let the sunlight wash over her, through her, as if it could burn away her weakness. Above, the Towers rose and fell on currents of bright power, oblivious to all that happened below.

Why don't they help? Because they had the power—if not enough to stop the Spire and its plan of destruction, then at least to aid the Lower City dwellers. People were going to die; it was inevitable.

She'd heard talk of sending armed bands to kill every walker they could find; of plans for security perimeters and armed lookouts, scouts, and absent gods only knew what else. And, as much as she wanted to believe otherwise, it wouldn't be enough.

No shelter, no resources—only what they could claim from the rubble. No trade meant no food, or only the little they could safely grow and raise themselves; and even beyond the destructive range of the Lower City's power, that was little indeed. People were going to starve and be killed by the walkers; people were going to kill each other fighting for resources. No sanitation, no sewers, no infrastructure—illness would follow shortly thereafter.

And winter was but months away.

One Radiant was nothing against such things. But the Towers?

Shai watched their graceful movement. They could assist with food, water, shelter, protection. If only one Tower contributed, just one of those glittering, brilliant hundreds, everything would change.

But the skyscrapers had called out to their every contact in the City above, every trading partner, every distant family member, every childhood friend who had made it in spite of the odds—and it had come to nothing. Worse than nothing.

The Lower City echoed from another explosion—not inside Edren this time, but Orren. Shai glanced toward the precariously leaning skyscraper with its ragged top. A hole had been blasted in its side and aircars hovered around it like wasps.

She could not stand to see that slow destruction, and so she looked up—and her eyes fell on a familiar Tower.

Allenai.

Slowly, Shai sat up. The Lower City dwellers might not know anyone in a position of power in the City, anyone in one of the greater Towers—but she did.

More than spell generators, more than healing spells and reinforced walls, perhaps this was what she could do. Perhaps this was how she could save them: not with her own hands, weak and fumbling; not with her magic; but by finding help among the powerful.

Shai did not remember making a decision; she just found herself rising.

At long last, and all alone, Shai went home.

Home.

Allenai did not look much like her home anymore—at least not from the outside. Once the Tower had been in the classical shape: a single wide platform in the center with great spires jutting up and down. Like a spinning top, Xhea had once described it—no matter that countless smaller platforms and defensive spires had marred some of that silhouette.

Now only the peak looked the same; Allenai's bottommost half, which had absorbed Tower Eridian, was entirely unfamiliar. Multiple living platforms now bloomed from its central axis, making the Tower look like a waveform pattern turned on its side. Only its color was unchanged: that deep purple-toned maroon that shifted and shimmered in the sunlight, red and blue sparking from its depths.

It should have been beautiful; it should have reminded her of orchid blossoms and fresh-picked plums. Yet, staring at the Tower that had once been her life and safety, Shai could only think of bruises.

Inside, too, everything had changed. She knew that no Tower could undergo a merger and retain all of its halls and familiar sights, but seeing those changes was a shock.

The public halls were full of shoppers, visitors and citizens alike, many with tea or sugar-dusted pastries in hand. A spelled breeze flowed through the winding walkways, smelling of new leaves and fresh air and ripe peaches. Nearby, a musician played a light-harp, his dancing fingers conjuring birdsong-like trills from its beams. Around his head swirled some dozen pinprick sparks of renai spelled to transfer at the song's end; they were marks of favor—and the onlookers' generosity.

Signs of a healthy, prosperous Tower.

Shai should have been glad to see them. And she was: the guilt she'd harbored over her abandonment of Allenai was washed away by that sight. Yet she recognized little in the scene, not the walkways or the domed ceiling above them, not the arches or fountains or even the musician's song. How could this be her home when she knew none of it?

Worse, the sight made her angry.

Shai glanced at her hands. They were as they had always been: soft, uncallused, and haloed with light, her ghostly skin untouched by blood or dirt. After the past weeks, her hands should have been black with both; her nails should have been cracked and torn; her fair skin should have been dry and patterned with small cuts.

Lower City hands.

Looking back to the crowd before her, Shai thought of Xhea's failed attempt to get herself kicked out of Tower Celleran, months ago. Xhea had screamed at the crowd that they weren't better than her, that they hadn't earned their lives of luxury and ease, but were born to them. They'd been handed gifts that were forever outside Xhea's reach—outside the reach of any Lower City citizen, no matter how hard they worked. All because of their magic.

For the first time, Shai didn't just understand Xhea's anger but felt it herself, deep in the pit of her belly.

These people had their own problems; their lives had their own hardships, their own stresses and disasters and threats. She knew it, and yet she only saw the smiles, only heard the laughter. She saw manicured hands holding cream-filled pastries up to pink, painted lips and the perfect white of their teeth as they bit down.

You're not here for this. She repeated the words until they felt like truth. Even so, it was hard to turn away.

Shai didn't think to wonder whether her home—the one she'd shared with her parents for all seventeen years of her life—would be where she expected, not until she was rushing toward it through familiar halls. Due to her mother's position, the Nalani family had lived in Allenai's higher levels, and those seemed largely untouched by the merger. Even so, the layout might have changed during those first tumultuous weeks, whole homes shifted like marbles inside a shaken container and settled into new positions.

Or worse: what if her mother had sold it? Councilwoman Aliane Nalani's husband and daughter were dead; would she have even wanted to remain by herself?

You don't need to go home, Shai told herself. She wanted to find her mother to beg for help, and her mother had never worked from home if her constituency office was open. Her work schedule had always been relentless, and Shai had suspected that she'd liked it that way, despite protestations to the contrary. Councilwoman Nalani had risen before dawn each day, and often worked long into the night. Those days that they'd been supposed to do something together as a family, Shai's mom had manipulated their schedule to assure that she could get in a few hours of work anyway—and Shai had never seen her delay the receipt of a message spell.

She was not eager; the thought of returning home made her feel ill. Yet she moved as if drawn, toward that familiar door and then through it, unable to stop her momentum.

Shai had never thought of her house as big—yet it was. The open space before the front door felt as large as the lobby in skyscraper Edren, if cleaner and in much better repair. Rooms spread about her: the formal living room to her left where her mother had received important guests, and the dining room beyond; the library to her right, its shelves heavy with books, its wall adorned with a huge oil painting of a tree. Before her, a wide staircase swept up to the bedrooms, her mother's home office, and her father's small studio; while off to one side was the hall to the kitchen and the solarium and the family room with its squishy couches where Shai had liked to lounge. Above, the small daylight spells bound to the antique chandelier that her mom had found so charming glinted in the hanging crystals and patterned the ceiling with shards of rainbows.

It wasn't the sight that caught her breathless, tears pricking her eyes, but the smell.

If asked, Shai would have said that she couldn't remember what her home had smelled like, though she'd lived there all her life. She would have guessed that it smelled of clean air, perhaps, or growing things, or even the sharply floral scent of her mother's favorite perfume.

But it was *this*, the scent that suddenly overwhelmed her—a scent of fresh bread, of cinnamon and sugar. Beneath that, there was the ever-present smell of the living, mossy carpeting that most Towers preferred—a smell that had always reminded Shai of sweet clover.

Her home smelled of cinnamon buns and earth. How could she have forgotten?

Shai struggled for breath, pushing back the need to sob. *Silly ghost. You have no lungs, no need for oxygen, no need to breathe at all.* But the desire to cry, it seemed, went deeper than the demands of mere flesh and blood.

She moved from room to room—not walking now, only sliding like a tear across glass. Her fingers passed through the bronze statue on the table in the front hall; her touch did not disturb the fine layer of dust that had gathered on the kitchen's wide marble countertops. She glanced at the framed photographs on the walls, seeing her younger, smiling face and no hint of her current reflection.

Shai flowed through her home, feeling every bit the ghost that she was. Feeling, somehow, that if she could just touch something—a doorframe, a light switch, the cover of a book she'd read to tatters—that it all could be undone: her illness and her death, her absence from this place, and everything that had filled those strange, difficult months.

There was a photo of Shai on the mantle in the family room, above the fireplace where only spelled flames burned. In it, she was young—twelve, maybe thirteen; she was golden and happy, sunlight shining in her blond hair, her face alight with joy. Wasn't that who she truly was?

Not anymore.

Shai went upstairs. Her mother's home office was empty, as she'd known it would be; but, as in the kitchen, dust had settled across the desk's surface. She shouldn't be surprised—her mother had likely lost herself in her responsibilities, staying at the office at all hours, pretending that if she just worked long enough she could escape the weight of memory.

Her parents' bedroom was similarly empty, the bed neatly made, her father's glasses resting atop a book at the bedside. It looked as if no one had slept there in months. Yet Shai paused, sinking as if she might sit on the bed, and stared at those glasses. Stared at the absence around her, empty and echoing, and could not help but see her father's face. Not the face she had known and loved, but as she had seen it last: gaunt and blank and starving.

She remembered, too, the thought that had come like a lightning strike from the night sky: that she could kill him. Not that she could heal him, or ease the pain of his countless hurts; not that she could care for him as he had so long cared for her. She'd thought only of death.

Horrible as that thought was, she could not say it was wrong. Because she looked at those glasses and their dust-patterned lenses, and couldn't pretend that he would have wanted otherwise.

Wasn't that what he had done for her at the end? In stealing her away to that broken, impoverished Tower; in finding Xhea to help with her ghost. He'd not offered Shai healing or hurt's ease, for such things had become impossible. He'd not given her new life or freedom—for such things, if they existed, were denied to her because of what she was and the permanence of her binding to Allenai.

He'd only found a way to stop it, the hurt and the need and the power that underlay it. He'd found a way to let her die.

Shai remembered dying, and the moments that had come before. She remembered how she had felt, what she had thought, hard though it was to do so. Though she had feared death, in that moment the choice he and Xhea had offered—the choice to die—had felt like a gift.

To her. She didn't know whether her father had felt the same in the end. And Xhea? Shai almost smiled. Never before had she known anyone with as many complicated and oft-conflicting feelings as Xhea. In this, she thought, Xhea's joy would have been equal to her guilt and sorrow.

But if death had been a gift to Shai, did that make it right to kill her father? Or rather, kill his body. Her father was, now, unable to make that choice. Some dark magic child had ripped his spirit from his living body and consumed him.

His spirit was not lingering in this world, had not left for whatever might wait beyond. He was just . . . gone.

Truly gone.

Maybe it wasn't Shai that was the ghost here, but the house around her; for she had changed after death—she had, in her way, tried to live—while this place had lingered, caught in a reality that no longer existed. Waiting for her father to come home, to lie down in this bed, place the glasses on his nose and flip his book to the place marked with a green ribbon. Waiting for Shai to return to her routine of school and homework and outings, the many things she did to forget her illness; or, even, waiting for Shai to curl once more in her bed, sweating and in pain, staring at the ceiling as the hours passed. All of them waiting for her mom to come home.

Shai took a long, slow breath and wiped away tears that she didn't remember crying.

Time to go to Mom's office, she thought, rising. There were far more important things at stake than her own grief.

Even so, she hesitated at the top of the stairs. Turned.

She would not return here, she knew, not ever again. Before she left, there was just one last place she had to go.

The door to Shai's bedroom was closed. The nametag that had been there since Shai was little—the one bearing her name in her own clumsy, child's hand—hadn't been re-hung; hadn't, in all likelihood, made it back from that broken Tower where her father had taken her to die. She could see where it had been, a faint, bleached shape against the door's natural wood.

Closing her eyes, Shai slipped through the door. When she opened them, she might have stepped back in time.

There was no hospital bed there anymore, no medical equipment, no IV or monitors or the countless bottles of pills that had clustered on her nightstand. Instead, her childhood bed had been replaced, pulled from storage absent gods only knew where, and topped with a blanket patterned with blue flowers. Next to the bed was the chair in which her father had sat and slept during the years of her illness—the chair that she had sent an image of to Xhea.

The curtains were drawn, hiding the spelled window panel and the sunlight beyond. For all that their home was near Allenai's core, every room had a window with a view; this window, with its blue curtains, had been Shai's only glimpse of the world outside for a very long time. Even with that view hidden, its light shuttered, she could see the pieces of her old life everywhere: her certificates on the wall, her books and trinkets on the shelf, her best attempt at watercolor painting framed and hung.

And there on the bed lay her mother.

At first Shai did not see her, not even as her Radiant light spread though the room like a candle's golden glow; she only wondered why the bed had been left rumpled and the frilled-edged decorative pillows cast aside. Then she watched as the blanket rose and fell in the rhythms of breath. She stepped closer, hesitant, and saw unwashed blond hair spread in a messy tangle across the pillow.

Shai's breath caught and she stared, trying to believe that the huddled, unkempt woman lying here, asleep in the middle of the afternoon, could truly be her mother. Lying here, Shai realized, as if she had not risen for days.

"Mom," Shai whispered. But Aliane Nalani could not hear her daughter—would not, even if she shouted—and Shai's heart ached to know it.

Ached, too, to see her lying as if she were broken. Because whatever Shai had expected of her mother, it was not this.

Shai crept closer. It was wrong to say that she'd never seen her mother in her room, here at this bedside, for all that the lie felt like truth. Yet it'd seemed that her mother had only ever been passing through, had stopped by for a quick word, had peeked in when Shai was sleeping.

"Your mother's gone to the office," her father would tell her so many mornings, "but she checked on you while you were asleep." Shai had thought he was lying, not out of malice, but in an attempt to make her feel better. To make her feel loved by the one person who had never had time for her, no matter what Shai tried.

But a memory returned to her now, one she had always believed a comforting dream: her mother standing over her, seen through eyes all but closed. The feel of a cool hand pushing back sweaty hair from her face; the feel of lips, soft and dry, feather-light against her forehead.

Dream or memory, she was not sure—and it didn't matter. For Shai moved slowly, softly, as if her tread might wake the woman lost in this unhappy, graceless sleep, and leaned over the bed. Brushed her hand over the sweaty tangles of her mother's once-perfect hair; kissed her forehead with trembling lips.

Tears fell, glittering. Her own, and her mother's.

Aliane woke then, or perhaps just opened her eyes, and stared unseeing as tears rolled down her face to darken the pillow beneath her cheek.

Shai knelt before her, willing her mother to sense her. She reached for her mother's hand, lost beneath that too-heavy blanket. Her hands slipped through blanket and flesh and the mattress beneath, and only once before had Shai felt so bereft of touch or its illusion.

A sense of a presence, a flicker at the edge one's vision, a half-heard whisper—these were the ways Xhea said most people sensed ghosts. But then, Shai was no ordinary ghost.

All her half-made plans, all the ways she'd thought to communicate, the spells and clever tricks that she had learned in the weeks past—they were gone as if she'd never known them. Gone or pushed away, for she did not know what she might write with her pinpoint light; knew no gesture she could make that would speak when she could not.

"Mom," she said again, louder, her voice breaking. Shai willed her mother to see her, to know that she was here.

Perhaps she did, for Aliane's eyes went wide. A moment, then she slowly tried to raise her head from the pillow.

"Shai?" she whispered. Then: "I'm dreaming." Such broken hope and sorrow in the words.

"You're not," Shai said, unheard.

But if her mother could not hear her voice, she could see her— or see, at least, the light that she cast. Though Shai's had been the most powerful magical gift within her family, it was not because her parents had ever wanted for magic—her mother especially.

Instead of speaking, Shai reached again for her mother's hand, glowing brighter as she did so. Brighter, until her glow lit the room, throwing shadows across the wall; brighter, as if someone had thrown open the curtains and let the sunlight pour inside; and brighter still.

Aliane gasped softly, as if finally realizing that she was awake. Realizing that her dead daughter sat before her, full of Radiant light.

"Shai," she said again. "You've come back. You—"

Shai shook her head.

"Can you speak?"

Again Shai shook her head, and then raised her shoulders in a broad shrug. Her mother seemed to understand. Even so, Shai sparked a light and wrote in midair.

Only like this.

Her mother struggled to sit.

Sitting, Councilwoman Aliane Nalani looked down at herself in dazed disbelief, as if this was her first moment truly conscious for a very long time. She touched her hair and grimaced, then held her hand before her, seemingly surprised to see it tremble.

"What must you think, to see me like this?" She laughed thinly, the sound doing nothing to hide her shame. "Falling apart."

At that moment, Shai was glad her mother could not hear her. There was no need to disguise her sudden loss for words.

"If I go take a shower," Aliane said, as if it were a foreign concept, "will you be here when I come back? Can you stay?"

Shai nodded. At that moment, there was nowhere else she could imagine being.

Chapter Twelve

All her life, Xhea had dreamed of Towers.

She'd only had pictures and stories on which to build her fantasy, snippets of overheard conversation that she wove into her imagined life like glimmering threads. Stories of rich food and bright, open halls; stories where no one hurt or cried, grew sick or felt pain. A place where hunger and cold and want could not reach her.

But she'd never thought to dream of the Central Spire—not before she'd met Shai. For all that its presence dominated the landscape above, it had never seemed like a place she might visit. It had been more like the moon: beautiful and wholly untouchable.

When Shai spoke of visiting the Spire, she spoke mostly of the sky gardens. Rose gardens with winding pathways surrounded by heavy blossoms, the air heady with perfume; wild gardens with trees that grew tall and thin as they struggled toward the sun; topiary gardens with trees shaped into dancing ladies and rearing horses, mythical creatures and birds taking flight.

There was more to the Spire, too: homes and offices, shops and galleries and theaters. There was a prison, where the worst of the City's criminals were sent; there were courts and offices for the magistrates.

Yet as the armored aircar settled to the ground in an open landing bay low in the Spire's downward point—as the Enforcers led her from the car and into the Spire proper, pushing her as fast as her limping gait would allow—she could not help but look around in surprise. Whatever she'd expected of the Spire, it was not this.

Bare walls, stark and unadorned. Wide doorways with heavy doors that rose and fell at their approach, clanking and grinding like shielded metal. No mossy covering on the floor. Air filtered and tasteless and utterly without scent; air blank like white paper.

When they'd taken her, she'd expected—what? An official to greet her, perhaps; someone to try and convince her of her value to the Spire. Maybe a bribe, like Ahrent Altaigh had tried in Farrow—plentiful food and clean water, a comfortable home, knowledge and respect and clean clothes—as if her allegiance might be purchased. Maybe even a cell, some dark room with no windows, where her eventual release would be a reward for good behavior.

Instead she was processed as if she was not a person but a thing, some strange artifact pulled from the ruins of the city that had come before. She was examined, measured, and cataloged. No greetings, not even as she was passed from one white-coated person to the next; only bare, necessary words.

"Lift your arms."

"Turn."

"Stand up."

"Look here."

"Hold your breath. Now breathe out. Again."

She had only one living Enforcer to guard her now, and the dead one bound to his chest. But even he did not speak—at least not to her; only led her from one place to the next with rough efficiency.

It was only as she stood, arms outstretched as the man before her prepared some sort of spell, that she realized: there was almost no magic here, neither bright nor dark. Not in the walls or the floor beneath her feet, not on the doors through which they passed or in the lights along the ceiling.

"Hold still." Xhea turned to look at the man. She moved one arm, then the other; shifted her weight and winced as her bad leg protested.

"What are you doing?" she asked as she had no half-dozen times before. She slid one foot forward, tilted her head—small, inconvenient motions.

The man huffed out his breath in displeasure, and met her eyes.

"I'm measuring your magic. Now *hold still.*"

Xhea froze, inside and out. Her power was restrained by the binding spell, its pressure like a weight on her chest; yet she'd been pushing against it in an effort to force that small crack wider. Now she pulled her magic to her like a snail vanishing into its shell and held it tight, hoping that no trickle of black emerged.

Sweat beaded her forehead. She closed her eyes.

"Binding's secure," the man said at last. "But who unraveled the tracking spell?"

Xhea huffed out the breath she hadn't realized she was holding. "I'm very talented."

"Rather the opposite." Xhea could not tell whether he sounded pleased or disappointed at that revelation. He looked to her guard. "She's safe enough to handle, if it comes to that. We'll have time for a more detailed examination in a few days."

"She done here?" the Enforcer asked.

"For now."

It should have been a relief. Yet as Xhea gathered her jacket and cane, it was all she could do to keep from pressing her hand against her stomach, as if that might ease the cold, unhappy ache that had nothing to do with her magic.

Another aircar ride, this one to another location in the Spire no more than a few stories away.

"What," she asked her guards, living and dead, "you never heard of elevators?"

They did not deign to reply.

But it was clear, as they moved beyond the landing bay, that they'd brought her someplace far different. There was carpet beneath her feet—not the mossy covering she knew from her time in the Towers, but real carpet, soft beneath her boot soles. The walls were pale but faintly patterned. There were numbered doors at regular intervals along the hall and paintings hung between them. Xhea glanced at the images as she passed. A sunset. A branching tree. A flower.

The hall, too, curved gently, seeming to form a ring; Xhea wondered if she kept walking whether she might eventually walk the whole circumference of the Spire. Huge as it was, it had few living platforms, and none were as wide as a Tower's. For the first time, Xhea considered just how many levels the Spire might have within its slender length, floor upon floor layered atop each other like a teetering stack of dishes.

At last the Enforcer stopped at a door and pushed it wide. Mechanical door handle, Xhea noted—not a touchpad or magical sensor in sight.

"In here," he said, gesturing to the room beyond.

A sudden pressure between her shoulder blades sent her stumbling through the door and nearly sprawling onto the carpet beyond. Xhea fought to regain her balance, breath gone short, then turned back to glare.

No faces there: only a shining mask of magic, and a blurred set of features. Still, she could imagine his unkind smile as the ghost Enforcer gave her a brief wave.

"Enjoy your stay, princess."

The door closed and a heavy lock clicked home.

Xhea looked around. Despite the lock on the door, this was not the cell she'd imagined; nor was it the luxurious accommodations she'd assumed would be omnipresent throughout the City. It was just a room—one of a small suite—though it was clean and neat and comfortably furnished.

She took a slow circuit through the rooms. A living room with a soft gray couch and chair, a bathroom with a shower, a bedroom, and a kitchen with laden cupboards. No one else there; no signs that this was anyone's home. Everything seemed new, plain, untouched.

"Hello?" she called. No echo: her voice vanished in the space like a stone thrown into dark water.

She wanted to lie down; she wanted to close her eyes, wanted to scream or rage or weep. Instead she limped slowly to the kitchen and methodically filled her arms with the contents of the fridge and cupboards. When she could hold no more, she brought the food to the table.

Sitting was a relief beyond words, her knee's ache having grown to a hot, throbbing pain; only that hurt had been enough to distract from her stomach's insistent demands. She'd barely eaten today. Barely eaten, truth be told, the day before that. One by one, she ripped open packets and pried lids off of containers, then began eating their contents.

Cookies with swirls of cinnamon. A sandwich layered with tender meat, juicy tomatoes, and lettuce so fresh that it crunched. A bowl of self-warming soup with rich, spicy broth. In spite of herself, she enjoyed every bite.

Xhea peered around as she chewed, refocusing her eyes. Here, as before, there was no sign of spells—no sign of any magic at all.

It wasn't just the lights and door handles that were fully mechanical; for the span of at least three or four stories up and down and in every direction, she could see no spells on the structure, no ribbons of magic snaking through the walls. Here, in the City where the use of magic was omnipresent, there was nothing.

She pushed the thought aside.

There would be time, she judged, before a representative would come to offer what threats or promises they deemed appropriate. First they would make her wait, simmering in her own anxiety. She rolled her eyes at the thought.

Time passed.

When the chair grew uncomfortable, Xhea rose and paced, limping heavily but attempting to keep her muscles from stiffening. When she tired of dragging herself across the same patch of carpet, she flopped down on the couch in the main room and stretched her legs.

Silence all around her, broken only by the sound of her movement, her breath.

Was this the prison of which Shai had spoken? If so, it was a strange one. Xhea thought again of the curving hall outside her door—all those numbered doors, and the locks on each. Locks controlled on the outside; locks, she realized, that were set oddly, as if out of a small child's easy reach.

Not a normal prison, then, but one designed to hold her. Or, rather, people like her.

Reaching with her other senses, she felt them. The distant pressure that spoke of ghosts—and, farther, a faint sense of something cold and dark that drew her, like Ieren had.

Dark magic children and their bondlings.

The thought was frightening. They were only children— but children with power. Children who'd grown up knowing how to use this magic that had suddenly risen within her, and who had use of that power even now. Despite the crack she'd created and the trickle of power she could conjure, the man had been right: the binding on Xhea's magic was strong and holding.

She could break it, she thought, as she had broken the binding that her mother had created for her as a child—but not quickly. A week, perhaps; a few days if she really tried.

Not fast enough.

There was no clock. There were no windows through which she could watch the sun pass overhead, the Towers rise and fall, the shadows shift across the distant ground. There was only the sound of her breath and the beat of her heart, each poor at marking seconds.

What do they want? she wondered. Because if she understood what the Spire wanted of her, she could avoid being caught by surprise. Did they want her magic, her willing assistance—or only to remove her from the situation? Ensure that they controlled every dark magic user, no matter how weak.

Time passed.

Xhea yelled at the ceiling, cursed and shouted and demanded that someone come see her. She screamed until her voice cracked and her throat ached. She tried to smash every dish upon the floor, threw a vase at a wall and awkwardly kicked it when it refused to break. Something, anything, to gain a reaction.

Nothing worked.

Time passed, and time passed, and time passed.

They can just leave me here, Xhea realized at last. An hour, a day, a year—what did it matter? *They can just lock me in here and do nothing until it's too late.*

Perhaps the Spire officials were watching her, waiting until she'd been broken down by boredom and isolation. Or perhaps they already had what they wanted: an uncooperative dark magic girl, and access to the escaped Radiant ghost to whom she was bound.

And if you had evaded them? asked a quiet voice, hard and bitter. *What then?*

Oh, the mockery there. For she knew the thought that underlay it, the belief that lingered unspoken: that she might have saved them, she and Shai together. Saved everyone, the whole of the Lower City, from the Central Spire's wrath.

Two girls and their magic winning against the power of the entire City above. Somehow.

As if.

Once she wouldn't have cared what happened to the rest of the Lower City. She'd cared little for anyone else—why should she, when they had obviously cared so little for her?

But something had changed, because she would save them now, if she could. All those people she didn't know and probably wouldn't even like—the angry ones and the awful ones, the families and the City folks fallen on hard times, the orphans and the people that everyone else had forgotten about. The dregs of humanity. The people no one wanted.

The people just like her.

She'd abandoned them. No matter her intention, she'd stopped trying.

Xhea took a long, shuddering breath and forced herself to her feet. *Bruised and battered*, she thought, *but not defeated.* She wasn't going to sit or sleep, pace or fret, when she could be doing something. Anything, no matter how small.

Xhea turned again to the locked door. *Mechanical locks*, she thought—and smiled. They were treating her like she was just any other dark magic child, small and helpless and raised in captivity. She was not.

They'd left her no tools; they'd searched her pockets and taken away anything that could possibly be dangerous or useful—but they had not searched well enough. Carefully, Xhea fished a thick, tarnished needle from the seam of her pant leg. Her good needles were hidden—but this? It was big and strong and near impossible to break.

Big enough, strong enough, to pick a lock.

Chapter Thirteen

When her mother returned some fifteen minutes later, dressed in a soft robe with her hair twisted up in a towel, Shai was ready.

Over the past weeks, she had tried to create a spell that would allow her to speak to someone other than Xhea. Her attempts had not all ended in failure, but the sounds she was able to create—screeches, whispers, echoing booms—refused to make spoken words. She'd thought speech was nothing but sound shaped by mouth and lips and tongue; yet the intricacies of those movements were frighteningly hard to replicate.

The day before, seeing the message spells rising from across the Lower City, she'd wondered if there was some way that she could shape, if not sound, then at least her intent—images, perhaps, or captured thoughts. Such things were theoretically possible, though she'd had no time to experiment.

Instead she'd done what she could: as her mother had showered, she'd written her arguments in light across the air—and then recorded those patterns into a single large spell sequence.

"Shai," her mother said—and stopped. Though Shai waited, haloed in light, the blinking sphere of the spell hovered in the middle of the room, demanding attention.

"From you?"

Shai nodded.

Aliane touched the spell. It read her magical signature, and then unfurled like a golden ribbon unwinding.

Its first two words were simple, written in Shai's own hand: *Hi, Mom.*

Aliane's breath caught. She looked from Shai to the words, the tips of her fingers pressed against her lips.

The ribbon reworked itself, new words writing themselves across the air, and her mother had no further chance to look away.

Shai had never had her mother's ability to construct strong, rational arguments, nor had she ever particularly excelled at debate; being put on the spot had made her want to shrink into herself, as if a hunched posture and a face flushed red could deflect attention. Here, now, she had tried nonetheless, attempting to explain her situation and that of the Lower City in the clear, precise terms her mother preferred.

Her words were rushed, inelegant; she winced to see them, even knowing she'd had time for nothing more. She explained that the Lower City was alive. She told of the Messenger and the Central Spire's declaration, and the invasion of edge-cast Towers that had quickly followed—but mostly she shared what these things meant to the people on the ground.

Shai asked for Allenai's help. An intercession, a message sent to the right person in the Spire, even protection against the poorer Towers. At the very least, Allenai could provide help for the refugees themselves—food or clean water or the construction of new shelter out in the ruins.

Something. Anything.

Shai's message ended in a shower of fading sparks, but her mother did not move, only stood as if frozen.

"This?" Aliane asked.

Shai blinked, not understanding.

Her mother turned to her, incredulous. "*This* is where you've been? *This* is what you've been doing?"

Shai almost stepped back. It wouldn't have been the first time that her mother's words had made her physically recoil; each felt like a slap, weighted by judgment.

"There you are," Shai whispered, knowing her mother would not hear. There was the mother she'd known—and whom she'd resented and wanted desperately to please in equal measure.

Aliane Nalani stood taller, that defeated stoop straightening as if Shai had injected steel into her spine. Her chin rose as if she wished to look down her nose at her daughter—never mind that she and Shai were the same height.

"So many nights I wondered what had happened to you, how long you'd lingered bound to that *girl*—and you were down there the whole time. That's who you want to ally yourself with? Deadbeats and criminals and people too stupid to make anything of their lives?"

Once, such words—or even the tone in which they were spoken—would have been enough to make Shai crumple. She would have muttered apologies and fled.

Now such reactions made no sense. She felt no shame or recrimination, only anger. It was a slow, hot burn.

Shai called forth a light and stretched it, creating glowing letters in the air between them. Not gold, this time, but a harsh, pure white.

One word, scrawled large: *NO.*

"I didn't come here to fight," Shai said to her mother, because she couldn't stay silent. "I don't need this."

Her mother kept speaking as if that message did not hang before her, casting stark shadows—as if Shai's words were of no consequence. "You returned for those people on the ground. Not for *your* people, not for Allenai."

Don't, Shai wrote. *It's not like that.*

"Not for me," Aliane said, her voice gone quiet. "Months since you died, and you never once came back for me." All at once that steel was gone from her; she folded in on herself, body hunching as if grief struck a blow to her chest.

What could Shai say? It was true.

She had searched the ruins for her father, night after night; she had sat at Xhea's bedside during the girl's long, fraught recovery. It had never once occurred to her that her mother might need her. No, that she might *want* her.

Shai had known that her mother would mourn; of all the things one could say about her—hard and driven and political—she was not a monster. Her worst cruelty had been her absence.

And mine? Shai thought suddenly. For if she'd ached for her mother all those years, was it so hard to believe that her own absence could create a similar pain? But not a temporary one; death was a barrier rarely crossed.

Shai opened her hand, relaxing the fist she didn't remember making. She made to reach out—but her mother was speaking again.

"Go," Aliane said, her voice low and hard. "If that's all you're here for, then go."

Shai stared, not believing the words.

"The world does not revolve around you, Shai, even though you think it does."

As if wanting to help the people of the Lower City was the selfish act. Angry tears stung her eyes. Hers, it seems, was just another pointless message bubble sent skyward, for all that she had delivered it herself. Just another plea rejected out of hand.

What did you think was going to happen? she asked in savage silence. *That she'd care just because you asked it?*

What Tower would spend so much renai without any prospect of future profit? They had systems to run, people to feed, investors to satisfy; all more important than helping the dirty, anonymous masses. And there was no good publicity in crossing the Spire, even if they tried to spin their actions as a misguided attempt at charity.

Shai bowed her head in defeat, choked back her anger, and walked away. She pulled her magic to her as she went, and the room darkened in her wake.

"Wait," her mother said.

Shai hesitated. Some part of her wanted to storm away, as if the sight of her disappearing back was the only answer she need give. But she didn't want that to be the last interaction she had with her mother. Not for either of them.

She took a steadying breath and turned.

"I didn't think . . ." Aliane started, and then stared as if she had no idea how to go on. Shai glowed brighter, that soft radiance an encouragement.

Again she tried: "Since you and your father . . ." But those words, too, caught in her throat. Then the look that Shai had always thought of as her mother's professional mask dropped over her features, blank and unyielding. Breath after breath, Aliane regained control.

How Shai had once envied that control, that expression that hid everything and gave away nothing and never, ever yielded. How she had hated it, even as she'd tried to school her own features in its hard reflection.

"I've had a lot of time these past weeks to think. Too much, perhaps. When you can't change the choices you made, sometimes that's all you can think about. What you should have said or done differently. It can eat you whole."

Shai nodded, making the gesture broad enough that her mother could see it from across the room. Reconsidered and stepped closer, reducing the gap that her angry steps had opened.

Aliane tried to smile. Failed. "I couldn't save you from your magic. I couldn't give you the life I so desperately wanted you to have, and couldn't change the world to make your path easier. I think I stopped trying, stopped hoping that things could be different. That was my mistake, and I regret it."

There was, Shai thought, a stiffness to the confession that made her think it was not entirely spontaneous. They were words, perhaps, that her mother had repeated in her mind these past months—words she never thought she'd be able to tell Shai.

It was not an apology; Shai didn't know whether she deserved one. Need a parent apologize for their choices? Need their child? Because she, too, wanted to apologize; wanted, foolishly, to collapse into her mother's arms and beg forgiveness for the hurt and sorrow she had created just by living. By her magic, and the destiny it entailed.

By fighting, in the end, her fate and magic both.

She wanted to beg forgiveness, but would not—because, out of everything, that was not the part of her life she would do differently. Though she'd made mistakes since her death, learning to stand up for herself was not among them.

"What you're asking, Shai," her mother said softly, "for Allenai to intercede with the Spire, to create protest—dissent— among the Towers . . ."

"I understand what it would mean," Shai said. "Of course I do."

Her mother couldn't hear her; even so, she seemed to understand.

"I'll try, Shai, but I can't promise anything." She shook her head, and Shai tried hard not to see defeat in that gesture. The known futility of the effort. "This time, I'll try. For you."

It was, in the end, all she could ask.

Anger didn't just disappear; nor did the complex tangle of emotions that knotted beneath that anger, complicating and fueling it. For the first time, Shai understood Xhea's desire to pace. Anything to burn out the frustration.

Yet she could not stay in her home, could not stare at her mother's grieving face any longer. Instead she walked through Allenai's halls, past the library and her school, past the swimming complex and the upper shopping promenade and the paths that led to the offices at the Tower's peak. At last she found her way to the garden at the Tower's center, where trees had grown vast beneath Allenai's living heart.

She paused, looking up. Allenai's vast heart shone so brightly that she'd always thought it pale. Now, with no true eyes to blind, she could see the truth: color churned deep within it, a thousand fractal shades of red and violet, silver and blue. Staring at that complex, swirling magic, she couldn't help but think of Farrow's dark and sputtering heart, held in her incorporeal hands.

Gasping. Flaring. Dying. Its soft light tarnished gray.

Just one more thing she couldn't bear to think about.

Shai closed her eyes and floated. Lost, aimless, she drifted, allowing the Tower's light to fall upon her upraised face, her outstretched hands, her tired and aching heart.

Magic could not wash away hurt or anger, though sometimes it seemed that way. She felt Allenai's power pour over her, shine through her, and imagined its warmth was akin to silence.

No words echoed through her head, again and again—not her mother's or Xhea's or even her own; no recriminations or regrets. Even the sound of the wind through the trees below her, the distant sound of voices, the burble of a nearby fountain, faded to nothing.

Quiet was peace—or so she had believed. She had always loved Allenai's central garden and the silence that could be found on its pathways. Allenai's garden was not as large as some Towers boasted, not as showy as others; it was not as wild or glorious as those in the Central Spire. But it was hers—or it had been.

Now, as all else fell away, the quiet she'd so prized felt like stagnation.

If she stripped away the words and the anger, the frustration and the futility of everything she'd tried, what was left? She felt like an insect caught in a spider's web. To do nothing was to allow death to creep close as if accepting its inevitability. But to fight would only wrap her tighter and tighter in those invisible bonds, earning nothing but fear.

Shai's hands curled into fists and slowly relaxed. She sighed, struggling to calm herself.

There are always the spell generators, she thought, thinking of the metal spires left on Farrow's rooftop. She'd lost but a span of hours on her futile mission; that was not the same as defeat.

Yet it felt that way, because for a moment she had believed that she was going to turn the tide. She snorted softly in derision. As if a single plea might save the Lower City when nothing else had.

Her mother would try to help—but for all her previous optimism, Shai knew those efforts would come to nothing. *A*

dead girl and a grieving Councilwoman on compassionate leave.
Some champions.

She understood what Allenai's council would say and the reasons they'd give to remain impartial. What possible benefit could Allenai gain from intercession? Much to risk and little to gain. Shai had come asking, but what value could she offer in return?

Only herself.

That was the true reason she was angry. Not her mother, not even Allenai; only herself. For she held a solution in her hands as surely as she'd held Farrow's heart—and she did not know if she was strong enough to use it.

She could surrender—willingly return to the fate she'd feared all her life, and had so narrowly escaped. Allenai's council would not turn her away. In return she could demand that they help the Lower City and its people.

But here she was.

Above her, the intense magic of Allenai's heart roiled. All the magic of Allenai's citizens concentrated there, flowing in before surging back out to the Tower's systems. Some part of her magic was surely there, too, little though she could see it.

Her magic, and that of Allenai's other Radiants, bound to these walls. Because there were others, few though they were. As a child, she'd only known one. Again and again she'd asked to meet the others, only to be put off, her questions turned aside, until after her Last Binding. Then, still wearing her long, plum-colored dress from the ceremony, she'd been brought to the chamber above Allenai's heart where the other Radiants lived.

Though "lived" wasn't strictly the right word.

She'd stared, stricken, at those crystalline boxes, unable to hide her horror. "They're just beds," one man had told her. "Just like hospital beds." Another had explained that the Radiants were alive and comfortable within, that the Tower cared for their every need—that they felt no pain or hunger, but slept, dreaming beautiful dreams.

Shai hadn't been able to see those shapes as anything other than glittering coffins.

In the time leading up to her death, she had tried not to think of those boxes or the people they held, the Radiants' features obscured by the faceted crystal. Now they were right there, just on the other side of Allenai's heart. Like her, neither truly living nor wholly dead.

I could go back, she thought. *To save the Lower City, I could just surrender; dream those beautiful dreams. Perhaps it won't be so bad.*

She shook her head. It wasn't that she was scared—or, rather, it wasn't only fear that stopped her. But giving herself to Allenai would mean surrendering Xhea as well, or severing the link between them. Shai's power would belong to the Tower, every last spark—and Xhea would die, consumed by her dark magic's hunger.

She could surrender herself—but Xhea? Never.

Shai wanted to fly up to that room—not to join the other Radiants, but to free them. She could imagine unraveling the dark magic bindings that held them to broken life unending or tied their spirit to a body not their own.

But her actions would not be seen as mercy, but sabotage. Without the Radiants' power, Allenai would starve, as Farrow had. The Tower's systems would become erratic, its businesses would struggle, its council would lose political power. Bit by bit, the Tower would slip through the sky, losing hard-won position and altitude.

Allenai would fall.

She could imagine it: the great living structure hitting the ground and shattering, the force of impact too much for even a Tower to handle. All of Allenai's people cast to the earth like confetti.

No, she could not free the Radiants. She knew it, even though the desire shuddered through her like a second heartbeat.

"I'm sorry," Shai whispered.

As if in reply, Allenai's heart flared. A great arc of power rose from its surface like a rope of silver flame, and passed through her incorporeal body. Shai gasped in shock.

Then again, in sudden realization.

For she thought of holding Farrow's heart cupped in her palms. Neither Farrow nor Allenai was human; she'd been told, time and again, that creatures of living magic did not understand human motives or feel human emotions. She did not believe it.

A Tower's heart was not a spell; it had no lines of intent, no spell anchors, no magical signature. But in the shifting gray patterns of Farrow's magic, she had seen meaning—as if thought and emotion had swirled before her, written in light and shadow.

Farrow had been afraid. It had been lost and hurting and desperately lonely.

She hadn't heard a song like Xhea described. Even so, Shai had wondered, *Is this what she feels when she speaks to the Lower City?* Maybe it was different; but—as she'd looked into Farrow's very being, felt its life press against her hands—she had not thought so.

What was Allenai but that same creature, that same heart, writ large? It was older and more complex, its body so vast that it had once seemed the whole of her world—but it was the same, too, in the end.

If she could speak with one, why not the other?

Allenai's council might not be swayed by her plea, and dismiss the arguments Councilwoman Nalani mustered in the Lower City's favor—but what if Shai ignored the council entirely? Why couldn't she beg help from the Tower itself?

Shai rose, rushing higher as if buoyed by hope. Allenai's flaring light filled the whole of her vision.

Unprotected, there was danger in drawing too near to the raw magic of a Tower's heart—but, dead, she had nothing to fear. So close, Allenai's magic swept over her like a strong wind, making her hair fly about her face. It was warm, even hot, but Shai did not fear burning; instead, her own power flared in echo as if she might rival that light.

It won't know me, she realized. Because this wasn't just Allenai anymore, wasn't quite the same heart in whose light she'd bathed as a child. It was Eridian, too, or a new entity created from the merging of each—she knew not which.

Even so, Shai reached out with not fear but hope. She touched Allenai's heart with a single shining hand.

Light. White, sharp, blinding.

Magic so intense that it erased thought, sensation, memory.

A moment passed, an hour—Shai did not know. White surrounded her; it was a color, a shape, a texture. White like the taste of spring rain.

And then: color. Faintly at first, she saw light touched with gold—sunlight. There came a whisper of some darker shade, like a cloud hinting at rain. Then more: a blush of pink, a flicker of orange, a slow twining tendril of green.

It's speaking, Shai realized. Speaking or thinking, or perhaps there was no difference between the two. Speaking—but not to her. Despite her magic, Allenai hadn't even noticed her presence. Against its immensity—the power of so many citizens, so many Radiants, so many lifetimes—she was so very small.

For a moment, Shai wanted nothing more than to lose herself, flow into that light the way water flowed into a pool. Because for all its raw power, there was peace in the Tower's heart.

Beautiful dreams, Shai thought, unbidden. She pushed away the thought and the desire from which it was born. Instead, she spoke.

"Hello," Shai whispered. Only words—because, despite her skill with weaving pure magic, she did not know how to shape a pattern of greeting. What shape spoke of awe or peace, hope or supplication?

The Tower responded.

Shai had never heard magic, like Xhea could; but for a moment there seemed to be a sound like a vast chorus on the edge of her hearing. She could almost taste Allenai's magic, sweet and sharp and lemony.

She pushed the sensations away, trying to focus only on those that she might understand.

Color, shape, pattern. Light swirled in response to her greeting, purple and blue spirals lit with wire-sharp sparks. Allenai was surprised, she realized; it was curious, but hesitant, unsure. Shai reached for it with fingers outstretched, afraid that the being of light and magic for which she'd once lived would reject her.

Instead, magic flared in answer.

It was only color and light; but in those patterns Shai saw arms opening wide to embrace her and soft lips smiling. She felt warmth close around her like a soft blanket. She smelled cinnamon buns and earth.

In a language that had no words, Allenai spoke: *Welcome home.*

Shai wanted to weep, or perhaps to laugh. She did both, tears and sound alike flowing into Allenai's living heart.

Is this what I've been afraid of? There was no pain here, no strife; no need, even, to struggle. She felt the Tower around her and the lifeblood of its magic flowing through its walls; she felt the bright sparks of its citizens and saw hints of their lives, all those myriad loves and hopes and sorrows. She felt the swirl of Allenai's defensive spells, and the rise and fall of the other Towers, and the ground so far below.

Lost in wonder, Shai forgot herself and simply drifted, warm and welcomed and home.

She did not realize that she was dissolving until her tether to Xhea pulled her back with a shock. Power flowed into her through that link—not bright magic but dark, reminding her of other things. Solidity. Life and breath and the pains of living. Sunlight to sunset, dusk to night. Stars' bright sparks against the sky's perfect black.

Two hands, touching.

Shai took a deep, shuddering breath, or tried to, and pulled herself back from the edge. As she drew away, she felt Allenai's questioning—saw its brief confusion as a swirl of orange and blue.

But she had a purpose. With her mother, she'd had to craft a careful argument. Here, there was no need for such struggle.

Instead she thought of the Lower City as she'd first known it—those broken buildings, those broken people—and what she'd come to learn. The Lower City as a living, changing entity.

"The Lower City is alive," she whispered, and sending the words the way she'd pushed a thought to Xhea through their link: the knowledge carried by magic.

She'd thought to start simply, and yet felt Allenai's sharp curiosity; it pulled at her, thoughts swirling. Thoughts, words, magic: they flowed from her without her conscious bidding, a trickle of information that became a stream, a river, a flood. The Messenger and the chaos in his wake; the Central Spire's orders, and the belief that the Spire's true goal was to kill the living Lower City.

Allenai pulled, and Shai found herself thinking of the Lower City—of the streets and buildings and the twisted underground passages; of Farrow held aloft in its black vines; of the people, running, struggling. In memory she saw the Lower City's heart, that span of impenetrable black, and Farrow's, small and stuttering within her ghostly hands. She saw the City citizens and their spool of wire, the denotations within Edren—the people of the poorer Towers taking and taking and giving nothing in return.

When Allenai started drawing on her memories of her life and death, her fear of her Radiant magic and a lifetime bound to Allenai's walls—when it pulled forth thoughts of Xhea and what she meant to Shai—she drew back.

"Enough." Shai retreated until only her outstretched hand touched Allenai's heart. The Tower's patterns swirled in confusion, but it complied.

"Will you help us?" she asked.

Its reply was cascading blue and gold, magic that smelled like citrus and cherry blossoms, burning leaves and tar. Shai stared into the chaotic patterns, no longer able to tell one shape from another—unable to tell one color from another, so fast did they flicker before her.

Yet she could put words to that chaos. *Let us think, small light. You have given us much to consider.*

"My thanks," Shai whispered.

She did not know how to convey her joy at this communion or her sorrow at leaving. Such things didn't need words; they shone from her like light. Deep within Allenai's heart, something swirled in reply.

Shai frowned and looked closer, thinking she had misunderstood—for it had seemed to speak of loneliness. How many thousands lived within Allenai, in Eridian-that-was? How many Radiants were bound to this heart? She did not know—yet none, she realized, truly spoke to the Tower. Not awake and aware; not as she had just done.

Small light, it had called her; or, perhaps, *spark*. It was almost a term of endearment. In spite of everything, it made her smile.

"I'll come back," Shai murmured. "If you'd like that. If you want me to."

Magic arced around her as if it were dancing. Shai laughed, because that was answer enough.

Chapter Fourteen

Xhea looked out cautiously, but the curving hall was empty. No guards outside, no one waiting for her. Smiling, she slipped the needle back into its seam, then stepped from her room, pulling the door shut behind her.

There was no use going back toward the landing bay and so she crept in the opposite direction, her hair pulled over her shoulder to quiet its chime. Some few of the doors she passed were locked, but others had their bolts drawn back.

Xhea paused at one of the unlocked doors.

If they locked the children in, then an unlocked door would mean that there was no one inside—or that the room was used for something different. There could be something useful there, or a way out. She cautiously turned the handle.

The door cracked open to reveal a room identical to the one she had left—and entirely different. It was the same structure and layout, yet there was no way she might mistake the two. While her room had been stark and impersonal, this looked like a home—a messy one. The couch in the corner was piled with blankets, the table with books, the counters with plates and meals half-finished. A child's paintings were roughly tacked on the far wall, none hung higher than Xhea's shoulder.

Standing there, her hand on the door handle, she felt something else: a slight pull, an ache at the edge of her senses. A person and a ghost.

They're not all locked in after all.

Footsteps approached from one of the adjoining rooms. Xhea recoiled and hurriedly pulled the door shut. Yet she'd hardly walked much farther down the hall when the sound of voices reached her, speaking quietly, laughing; a little farther, and they seemed like all she could hear.

There was no running; no point, even, in trying. While to her right doors continued at wide, even intervals, on the left there was only a wide open space from which she heard the voices. She could not pass by unnoticed—and behind her there was nothing but her own room, yet more locked doors, and the landing bay.

She hesitated, weighing her options, before tightening her grip on her cane and squaring her shoulders. Xhea turned the corner and walked into a wide, open room filled with children.

Dark magic children, each with a ghost tethered to hands or heart or chest.

Four kids gathered around the wide table that dominated the room's far end, books and papers spread before them. The oldest among them seemed perhaps ten years of age—and a very small ten at that. Others, obviously younger, sprawled across the floor, playing with wooden blocks and fighting over puzzle pieces. In one corner, a cluster of kids gathered around a man in a pale gray Spire's uniform, that familiar cascade of magic obscuring his features as he read to them from an open storybook.

Some of the ghosts stood in a circle nearby, their tethers drawn taut, looking like parents keeping half an eye on their kids while they discussed the neighborhood gossip. A few others floated, eyes closed, oblivious.

Children and ghosts alike looked up as Xhea entered, her hair chiming. The Spire's servant cautiously lowered the book to his lap.

"Hello," said a little girl on the floor. Her long, dark hair was in braids. "Feeling better?" She smiled, the expression sweet and welcoming.

Another boy—one of the eldest, sitting at the table—grinned. "Hey. Didn't think they'd bother to let you out. Thanks for the swear words." They'd heard her shouting, then; heard her throwing things and demanding to be freed.

Xhea moved closer, acknowledging neither greeting. There, in the room's far corner, she found what she was looking for: two ghosts huddled together not to chat, but seemingly for warmth. One was a man, large and muscular, whose pale-skinned face was bruised dark, his shaved head crisscrossed with scars. His right eye was swollen shut and seeped shadowed tears—bloody tears, though she only saw gray. His other eye met Xhea's gaze, hard and angry, as he tightened his arms protectively around the ghost he held.

That ghost was a girl who might have been Xhea's age when she'd died. Dusky skin that Xhea guessed to be light brown, her close-shorn hair standing in uneven spikes. She did not move, only stared blankly as if lost in a haze of grief.

The man's fingers were gone, and his hands—holding the girl to his chest—had turned hazy. But the girl had no feet anymore, no calves, no hands or forearms. Though she was visible, she no longer looked quite real; Xhea could see through her as if she was made only of mist.

Xhea wanted to go to the ghosts, kneel before them and . . . what? There her imagination failed, for she could think of nothing that might undo what had been done to them. Instead she followed their tethers to their anchors: two of the older dark magic children, both at the table. She gauged the look of each, and wondered what might happen if she lunged and cut both tethers.

She imagined two children like Ieren, powerful and far better trained than she was, raging out of control. Imagined what the others might do if she suddenly attacked one of their own.

She felt the cold, bound knot of her power, all but useless.

Even so, Xhea curled her free hand into a fist to keep from severing those bonds regardless.

"Where's your bondling?" asked the boy tethered to girl's half-eaten ghost.

He, at least, had understood the direction of her stare. His expression was less friendly now, and he watched warily as if unsure whether, lacking a bondling of her own, Xhea was going to make a play for his.

"Not here," Xhea replied flatly. She touched the tether that joined her to Shai, as much for reassurance as to demonstrate that she already had a ghost.

He frowned, perplexed. "Why do you allow your bondling such freedom?"

"Allow? She is not property."

The boy shrugged. "You can command her to do whatever you want. Why let her run around? Something could happen to her."

"Is that a threat?" Knives were less sharp than her tone.

"Hey, kiddo," said an older voice, interrupting.

She turned, expecting to see the man in the Spire's garb—yet though he had risen, it was only to flee, the storybook abandoned on his chair. It was a ghost who spoke, an older man who stepped away from the gossip ring, moving toward her.

"You've had a rough day, but let's not get off on the wrong foot, okay?" He smiled, white teeth gleaming, and gestured to the table. "Why don't you have a seat and tell us your name? I'm Darsen, and this is my little boy Amel."

Amel was perhaps four years old. The child blinked at her with wide, dark eyes.

The wrong foot? Xhea thought incredulously. Except it was clear that these gathered people, children and ghosts alike, saw her not as a visitor but a new addition to their number.

"You're old." This from Amel; his ghost—his father?— reached forward to shush him.

"Amel," chided the girl with the long braids. "You know we don't talk about age here."

Because age was correlated with power—the more powerful the dark magic, the quicker it killed its user. Xhea's age was like wearing a sign around her neck that declared her to be weak. It was not scorn she saw in the children's eyes as they processed this fact. It was pity.

"Yes," Xhea said. "I'm old. I have a ghost—a bondling—but I'm not like you." The loathing in her voice, the way she looked from the dissolving ghosts to the children—children doing their schoolwork, reading, *playing*, as if those spirits and their pain were beneath even casual notice—made that point clear.

"Child," Darsen said. "You don't understand."

Xhea turned to him in a clatter of charms. Darsen was an older man, or had been when he died; he was a City man from his accent and tailored clothes and the coiffed sweep of his graying hair. The tether connecting him to Amel was a heart tether, thick and strong.

"No," she said, harsh, condemning. "I don't."

But she'd felt that hunger—the need to consume a ghost to counterbalance the effects of dark magic on her body and soul. As that hunger had grown, it had overridden her thought, fear, compassion. Now, as in days past, Xhea tried not to think of what the hunger might have driven her to do had Shai not returned.

And that same hunger in a child? she asked herself. *Do you think a little kid could have so much restraint—or understand the consequences of their actions?*

And, unlike her, they didn't have a Radiant ghost to save them.

"Not all are taken," Darsen told her softly, gesturing to the other ghosts. "Not all are hurt. Not for a very long time."

Xhea had the feeling that there was more he wanted to say, and only the children's presence stopped him.

They were, Xhea realized, only children. They had not had her life. Despite the challenges of their magic and the hunger its use engendered—despite all that the Spire made them do—they had never known a life where everyone living shied from their touch. They had always had each other.

She envied them that, if only a little.

But she did not want this life. There was no place for her among them, not now or in any of the years past.

"Not for a very long time," Xhea said to Darsen, "isn't the same as not at all."

"No. It isn't." Yet he smiled at Amel, and reached for the boy's head as if he might ruffle his hair.

Xhea looked to the ghosts she'd named gossiping parents, and wondered if there was some truth to that thought. Each had a tether near as wide as the one that connected Darsen to Amel, unspooled from their hearts.

Did they kill their parents? If so, they'd been forgiven, or the parents had gone willingly; Xhea wasn't sure which she found more upsetting.

"Don't tell me they chose this." Xhea pointed to the two ghosts in the corner. Because she'd heard that lie once already, and wasn't so foolish as to believe it a second time. "Don't pretend this is what they wanted."

"They're just prisoners," said one of the children.

Another shrugged, confused by her objection. "Their lives are forfeit." She sounded like she was quoting something oft-heard. "There's a cost to being a criminal."

A cost? For even the worst crimes in the Lower City, punishment was swift, if no less final. No one deserved a slow torture of unmaking. Xhea realized that if she searched the Lower City's nighttime streets, she might find them: the ghosts' bodies, empty eyes staring as they walked.

She swallowed her angry retort, though it pained her, and instead asked: "Is that where you get the bondlings you take from the living?" Because that's what Ieren had attempted when he'd grabbed Torrence—to replace his bound ghost with the spirit of a living, breathing man.

"Sure," said the older boy. "Them, or sometimes people like *her*. Nobodies." He gestured behind Xhea.

She turned. Right behind her stood a woman wearing the Spire's uniform, a stack of folded towels held in her arms. The Messenger's uniform had been white, and the Enforcers' were that dark gray Xhea knew to be red, but this woman wore a nondescript pale gray. *Green*, Xhea thought, *or perhaps blue*. Of her face, Xhea could see nothing; only that shimmering mask of magic.

"I'm sorry," the woman started—then froze, staring at Xhea.

Maybe the new girl bites.

"She counts as expendable?" Xhea gestured to the woman. "Why, because it's her job to bring you towels?"

As if the answer could be anything other than yes.

The older boy shrugged again, still confused; the expression was mirrored on the other children's faces. "Sure," he said. "She's a criminal, too. A nobody."

"No face," said one of the girls on the floor, her angelic face framed with cute, blond pigtails. "No name. Nobody."

"Laney's not nobody!" one of the smaller kids protested, only to be shushed by his friends.

Xhea watched as the "nobody" woman backed away, then hurried down the corridor without a backward glance.

She, too, wanted to leave. *These kids can't help you. They can't help the Lower City.*

But she could use one as a hostage.

The idea made her go still; she knew the children's value. She was larger and stronger than any of them—and immune to the pain of their touch.

But who could she threaten? And what would she demand?

Before Xhea could move, the girl with the long braids abruptly stood. "I don't like you," the girl declared, turning up her nose. "You're too angry. It makes you ugly and mean."

Xhea would have said that the girl was no more than six years old; given her experience with Ieren, she added a few years to that tally. Standing, the girl came only to Xhea's mid-chest. Despite both the girl's apparent age and stature, the others deferred to her—even the ghosts.

Her own bondling—a man—huddled at the far end of his tether, refusing to even look in their direction. It was another of the ghosts who tried to object, saying, "Lissel, listen, if you'd just—"

The girl, Lissel, knocked the objection aside. "No," she said, force of command behind the word, and the woman fell silent. "I don't think we should let her be like this. I don't think we should talk to her at all until she learns to behave."

Xhea looked down at Lissel with unfeigned scorn. "And who put you in charge, little girl?"

"I'm first, here!" she said, stung—and apparently not realizing she had already broken her imperious decree.

"First what?"

"*This.*"

Lissel held her hand before her and smoke wreathed her fingers, spiraling into the air in a sinuous column. Magic—and not mere wisps of gray, but magic deep and black. Yet it was not its shade that made Xhea hesitate, but its shape; as she watched, that single column split and split again, bursting outward until the girl held a tree of dark magic on her palm.

Xhea had marveled at Ieren's control—but this was beyond anything she'd imagined. It reminded her not so much of her own power, but Shai's, that bright magic creating fractal patterns between her hands. Perhaps Xhea's own magic, unbound, was more powerful; but she had nothing approaching that kind of control.

This was not the first time someone had tried to intimidate Xhea into compliance. Growing up on the Lower City streets, there had always been someone bigger and stronger than she was, and the discomfort of her touch had been slim protection. If someone had shown off the way this girl was now? There were two choices: hit them harder or run away. Sometimes both.

Her hand tightened on her cane, preparing to swing, but Xhea made herself draw back. *Just a child*, she reminded herself. Hurting the girl would earn her nothing.

Instead she said quietly, "I see."

Lissel looked triumphant. Her hands dropped and the magic faded into the air.

"Is everything okay in here?"

Xhea turned. In the doorway were two more "nobodies" in the Spire's uniform—clearly nervous, yet walking forward nonetheless. One reached up and touched her neck; the shimmering mask of magic fell, revealing a woman's face.

"Everything's fine," Lissel chirped. She smirked at Xhea before flouncing away, the other children making room for her as she went.

The Spire's servant watched Xhea warily. "I didn't realize you would be joining us already." Polite-speak, Xhea figured, for *How did you get out of your blighted room?*

She smiled. "I was just leaving."

When Xhea returned to her rooms, there was no one waiting inside. Not the official she expected at every turn; not a jailer or guard. Not even a ghost.

Yet someone had been there while she was gone: her food wrappings had been taken away, the dishes she'd thrown had been cleaned and placed in the cupboard, the vase she'd attempted to smash righted and filled with leafless sticks.

The servant, she realized.

Again she heard the child's words: *No face, no name. Nobody.* She'd seen four of those so-called nobodies, the people tasked to serve and watch over the dark magic children—and who risked their hunger and fickle wrath each day.

Prisoners, indeed.

On her walk back, Xhea had tried every door, locked and unlocked; those that opened had been clearly the children's rooms. She'd found nothing useful—no stairwells, no utility closet full of tools, not even a blighted window.

Now she moved through her rooms, restless, irritable. Useless. She wanted to hit something, wanted to spit—and the pain in her knee didn't help. At last she flopped back onto the bed, upon which fresh sheets had been laid—and then couldn't resist lying back, just for a moment. She'd never felt anything so comfortable.

Xhea stared at the ceiling—a perfect span of unstained white—and tried to think. She could run—but where? She could damage her rooms, or the halls and communal spaces beyond—but to what end? She could fight or scare or hurt the dark magic children. And none of it would help her escape or prevent the Lower City's fate. Time felt like sand, running through her fingers.

Perhaps she should stay safe and quiet, giving Shai a chance to act before the Spire's attack tomorrow. As long as they were bound, Shai's magic would flow, strong and steady. Surely, Xhea thought, that was something.

It didn't make her feel any better.

Tomorrow. If she looked, would she see the weapon spell the Spire meant to cast upon the ground being woven somewhere above her? Refocusing her vision to see pure magic, Xhea looked at the ceiling—and beyond.

For a span of a few stories, there was nothing: no light, no spells, only a blankness that she understood to be no magic at all. Nothing that dark magic might reach or destroy. Beyond that? Oh, there was magic there—but unlike anything she'd seen.

Raw power shone in intense spots, their light all but blinding. *No*, she realized. *Not spots—channels of power.* They were rivers of power that flowed along the Spire's length to its peak, lost in the sky; it was only her perspective beneath them that made them look like round points of light.

Farther, there was a ring of light that had to be a living platform, spells thick in its walls and floors, bright pinpricks of people moving within. Higher, there was another living platform, wider than the first; higher, another. No matter how far it seemed she looked, she could see no end to the Spire's levels.

Yet she could see no sign of the weapon they meant to turn against the Lower City—no sign of any disruption at all.

Unless the weapon is the Spire itself. The thought was disturbing—yet it made a strange kind of sense. For it was the Spire that poured dark magic on the ground; if it could channel that power, and channel bright magic as she saw above, surely it could be a conduit for a spell. It was, after all, the greatest of the Towers—if one could call it a Tower at all.

Despite its slender shape, the Spire was huge almost beyond imagining. But then, so was the living Lower City. In memory, she saw it: the Lower City stretched beneath her, all those broken structures—and the expanse of shadow beneath. She had felt how deep into the earth that power spread; far deeper than the Lower City was wide.

Again Xhea thought, *Why would the Spire want to destroy the living Lower City?* She smiled, the expression thin and tense, and did not open her eyes.

For seeing it there, that huge creature of living dark magic, she had realized: it was a threat. The Lower City was the only magical entity, bright or dark, large enough to rival the Spire's power.

And if the Lower City might rival that power, might it not best it?

Alive, the Lower City was a threat to not only the Spire, but the whole of the City above, all of the Towers. No wonder they wanted it dead.

And the Spire itself? It would have to kill another living magical entity, one that had offered no threat but that of its existence. *What does it think?*

Xhea stared into the brilliant light above her as if written in those patterns she might see evidence of the Spire's empathy, or meaning, or regret; but there was only magic, only light. No matter how far she looked, or how hard, she could not see the Spire's heart.

Xhea was still frowning over that absence when sleep came to claim her, dragging her down into darkness.

Chapter Fifteen

Night was falling.

Slipping through Allenai's exterior wall, Shai was startled to find that the sun was but a brilliant sliver on the horizon, the hazy sky lit orange and red. Closer, everything was falling into shade and shadow, and heavy clouds in the east threatened rain.

Hours had passed since she'd spoken with her mother; hours upon hours lost to her seemingly brief communion with Allenai's living heart. Longer than she would have thought possible.

The spell generators. She had thought she'd have hours to create the spell that would enable her to transport them to the refugees in the ruins; hours, too, to help set them up and prepare for nightfall. No hope of that now.

Even so, with a spark of magic sent to Allenai in farewell, Shai fell toward Farrow. The wind did not touch her; and the Towers' nighttime defenses, as they came to life around her, let her pass unhindered.

As she descended, she looked at the Lower City cast in the sun's ember glow. The shadows of the skyscrapers were stretched long and dark across the broken ground. Any other day, this was when the Lower City dwellers would be returning to their homes and barring their doors. Yet even from so high, she could tell that there were people in the streets—and not just those from the poorer Towers.

Shai slowed her descent as she tried to understand what was happening. Watching as people stumbled from their homes—watching them fight and shout and hurl rocks at the buildings in which they'd lived. No, she realized; not at the buildings, but the people who had stolen them.

They're being evicted, Shai realized in horror. For all that she saw fights and struggles, the flash of blade and spell alike, it was clear: the people of the poorer Towers now controlled the Lower City.

Not everyone had surrendered to the Towers, or gone willingly. There were bodies lying in the streets, seemingly whole and uninjured; the spelled weapons from the City above made death so much cleaner.

Shai landed feather-light on Farrow's gravel rooftop, and looked at the spell generators in dismay. *One thing at a time.* She tried to block out all else, focusing on one of the generators. But she had no clever thoughts now, no rush of image and emotion to help her shape her power; her fear was a cold, sick weight in the base of her stomach.

Every time she blinked, she saw those bodies lying unmoving.

See the spell, she told herself instead, trying to draw upon her magic lessons as a child. What had her teacher told her? *Understand the shape of the spell you're creating before you call forth the first spark.* That was, after all, how everyone else wove magic.

As her breath fell into a calming rhythm, she closed her eyes and imagined them: the spell anchors, solid and true; the lines of intent, which captured the spell's meaning whole; and the many spell lines, which would weave together to execute that intent.

Lift. Stabilize. Transport. It was, she realized, like an elevator's propulsion spell wrought in miniature.

Yet Shai had only begun to weave the spell anchors when there came a loud, low thud from nearby. Shai jumped, her head jerking up and her spell scattering as she spun toward the source of the noise.

There. One of the shorter buildings visible in Orren's territory was now surrounded by a billowing cloud of dust, and even from so far distant she heard debris hitting the ground. She heard screaming.

She moved to the edge of Farrow's rooftop, watching as another detonation blew out part of the building's wall. A moment, then the building crumbled in on itself and collapsed— only to have the falling pieces caught by a spell. Sparking bright, the spell sorted the rubble, pulling metal rebar, pipes, and wiring to a shipping container and casting the rest aside.

Shai stared, aghast—then forced her gaze back to the generators. Xhea's plan was good, but not one that Shai could execute on her own. At least not in time to save those who were even now hiding in what scant protection the ruins could offer.

Out in the ruins beyond, fires glowed. Some were small, hidden lights—the kind of fire that might be quickly extinguished. Others blazed high and bright, as if to defy the darkness and the dangers it held. But night was falling; the walkers would arrive soon.

She needed another plan, quickly.

Perhaps she could create a simple version of the spell the generators emitted, which she could use to create a shelter. But her spells woven on instinct were inefficient; she would use too much magic, exhaust herself—and Xhea, too, as she drew on the girl's power—long before dawn.

What they needed now was not magic, but real, strong walls.

Shai's eyes went wide. *The warehouse.*

When she had first come to the Lower City, that first day in Xhea's company they had visited the warehouse of one of Xhea's contacts: a City man, Wen, who bought and sold artifacts from the city that had come before—or had in life. His son, Brend, had attempted to manage the business since Wen's death, though his father's ghost had lingered in the warehouse.

Yet it was the warehouse itself that caught her attention, not its contents. The building itself was something found nowhere else in the ruins: a new structure, large enough that it might house hundreds. But the refugees would never find it; spells hid the building and subtly warned the curious away.

Abandoning the generators, Shai fled toward the ruins and tried not to listen as another detonation echoed through the streets. Another Lower City structure crumbled in her wake.

In the once-deserted streets surrounding the warehouse, much was as Shai had imagined: people huddled behind makeshift barricades or inside fallen structures, weapons raised in readiness. No walkers yet, not while the sun's light cast the streets in bloody red and shadow—but they would already be waking. Soon they would rise.

Shai wanted to help the family she saw in a nearby hulk of a building. Small children cowered in the far corner, their parents and two eldest siblings standing over them with bleak, scared faces and knives in their hands.

She wanted to help the people she saw but a block beyond—a larger group that stood not behind walls but in the middle of the street in a great ring, a roaring bonfire at their backs and a stacked-high pile of rubble before them.

She wanted—

But no. Instead she slipped through the wall of the warehouse into the captured daylight beyond. She gasped at the mess within.

At first Shai thought that refugees must have found their way inside and trashed the artifacts, searching for anything valuable. Instead of the rows of shelves that she remembered, their contents stacked and neatly labeled, there was chaos. Shelves emptied, artifacts cast to the ground; shelves pushed askew or even tipped. Against the far wall, a shelf leaned drunkenly, spilling dozens of small objects across the ground: spools and wires and small wooden boxes, batteries and shining discs and things she could not name.

Nor was the warehouse silent. Near its center she heard sounds: rustling and thumping, a scrape as something was pushed across the floor.

"Wen?" Shai called softly as she moved toward the noise. "Where are you?"

A pause, then, "Here," came the reply, his voice as quiet as hers.

The old man's ghost was sitting at the wide wooden table in the building's center, half-moon glasses perched on his nose like an afterthought. A few small artifacts were spread across the table before him, but they did not hold his attention; he looked only at the man who moved through the shelves nearby.

"What is he . . . ?" Shai's voice trailed away as she watched the man sort through the shelves' contents with frantic haste. She recognized him, though she'd only seen him once before: Brend, Wen's son.

Like those outside, Brend looked as though he had not slept in days. His hair was a tousled mess, his eyes heavily shadowed; and the rumpled and dust-smudged appearance of his clothes was in sharp contrast to their cut and style. Still he worked, digging through the artifacts, placing some objects into the box at his feet and casting others aside.

Shai watched in perplexed silence.

"Xhea's friend. The Radiant." Wen nodded at Shai, recognizing her glow if not her face. He turned back to his son. "Night is falling," he said, as if in explanation.

"Yes," Shai said in slow agreement.

"He was moving slower before, taking more care, even wrapping the artifacts for transport. Now he just says that over and over. 'Night is falling.'"

Wen had not been beyond the warehouse walls, Shai realized; his tether would not let him pass so far. He did not know what was happening in the world beyond.

So she told him, in spare, stark words, what awaited the Lower City when tomorrow dawned. Told him too of the people outside these walls, and the walkers that would come when darkness fell.

For a long moment, Wen was silent. "I think," he said at last, "that he wants to let them in."

Watching Brend, Shai couldn't help but agree—and felt no little relief at the realization. She would not have to find a way to tell him what had to be done, or struggle to pull away the shielding spells and open the doors to those outside. Brend was here, flesh and blood, and could do such tasks without difficulty.

Except, she couldn't help but wonder: "How did he know?"

For she'd seen the City above—or at least she'd seen Allenai, where people strolled about their business as if this were any other day. There had been no announcement of the Spire's intent; no need for such an announcement to be made. Yet here he was, packing.

And she remembered: Brend, like his father, was a citizen of Eridian—or had been. Eridian was no more; since the takeover, he would have become an Allenai citizen. Had her mother spread the word, requested help? Had Allenai itself?

Shai pushed such thoughts aside.

"He can't save everything," Wen said. "I don't know why he's trying." But his voice betrayed something else beneath the words.

"Why do you think he's trying?" Shai asked softly.

There was a pause, punctuated only by the sound of Brend grabbing another artifact and trying to make room for it in the already full box.

There were so many possible answers, Shai knew. This warehouse had been a key part of Wen's business, and was now Brend's; it was, if not the whole of his livelihood, then at least part. Pride was another answer; or perhaps this was just an attempt to make what he could from these resources before they were destroyed or used or taken. The actions of the poorer Towers on a smaller scale.

Because Shai remembered what Xhea had said about Brend—what Wen hadn't said in words. What she saw written in Wen's face now, as he watched his son attempt to pack that box.

Brend had never loved the warehouse. He had never loved this work—not the artifacts or the people he had to deal with to acquire them, Xhea not least among them. He had only a fraction of his father's eye for value, and little of Wen's head for business. Yet he had kept this place and its contacts—had continued doing the work, though he struggled and swore and only slowly improved—and for what?

"For me." Wen took off his glasses. The old man was not crying, Shai saw, but it seemed that was only a matter of will. "He's trying for me."

Trying to save what was left of his father's legacy.

No, Shai realized, her imagined breath catching in her throat. *Trying to save what's left of his father.*

It was a goal she understood all too well, despite the difference in their circumstances. There was no way to bring life back to the dead. Brend could no more see or speak to his father than Shai could to hers; they were gone, each in their own way, their haunting of flesh and spirit a reminder of what had been lost.

Yet Brend knew, too, that his father lingered here. Xhea had conveyed messages between them; she had, time and again, reminded Brend that Wen was here, watching—bound not to a person, but a place.

Brend lifted another item and looked around, trying to find a box not already filled to overflowing. Trying to find a place to put the item he held now in his shaking hands—whatever it was. But for all the distress evident in his fingers' rough trembling, it was his face that made Shai go still.

He was weeping. Not in the way that Shai had seen her own father weep, and then only rarely. Not the way that men were told to weep: tears choked back, forced down, suppressed with anger and will and a facade of indifference. Instead, tears flowed down his cheeks freely and dripped from his stubbled chin; his breath caught in his throat. He brushed those tears away almost absently, only trying to see past them that he might finish his work.

His father's work.

Yet it was work that would know no end—not if he were to open the doors and let the refugees inside.

It seemed Brend's thoughts followed a similar path, for at last he drew a long, shuddering breath and stopped moving. He looked down at the metal thing in his hands, its surface pitted with rust and water stains, the plastic of its electrical cord cracked with age; then slowly lowered it to the ground.

"There's too much," Brend whispered—speaking, it seemed, to the warehouse around him, empty but for the artifacts and the two ghosts who hung now on his quiet, defeated words. "Too much for days, never mind hours."

"I didn't tell him . . ." Wen said. "I never asked . . ."

He looked away—looked to Shai. "The dead don't get choices anymore, do we? All our choices have been made, all our days are in the past. We only get to linger, and watch as everything we built begins to crumble."

Xhea should be here. Clumsy as Xhea was with matters of life and death—matters, truly, of emotion—she knew Wen far better than Shai did. *Perhaps she would know what to say.*

Shai's hand reached out as if of its own accord. Her fingers touched Wen's shoulder, and—when he did not draw away—rested there in comfort.

"We still get choices," Shai said. "There is always a choice. Even here. Even now."

Hadn't she struggled with similar thoughts? The weight of hopelessness, sorrow, and regret; thinking that there was nothing she could do, no matter what she tried. Yet she, unlike Wen, had power.

Wen did not shrug off her hand, yet neither did he acknowledge her words; he only turned away, bowing his head. A long moment passed, then he stood from his chair and walked toward his son and the mess that surrounded him.

"Is this why I stayed, then?" Wen asked softly. "For the knowledge that nothing truly lasts forever? Because I knew that. I knew that nothing I built would last much beyond the span of my days. And yet I had the hope . . ." He shook his head. "Foolish hope."

Before him, Brend closed the box and carried it to a pile of other boxes seemingly packed with similar haste. Carefully, he wove a spell, and in its twisted strands Shai could see simple commands: *lift, carry, hide.* One by one, the boxes rose and moved in a neat line up to the warehouse's second level.

Shai asked, "Why did you stay? If not for this, then why?"

Wen looked around, his tired gaze scanning the shelves and the artifacts, the table and the mess and the daylight spell that lit them all.

"In the hope that something would last. Memory, perhaps, or hope of recollection." Again he shook his head in slow denial. "Do you know how long the city that came before stood? Or the civilizations that came before it? Because the things I found in the ruins—the things brought to me, the things I saved and protected—told far more than our scant histories ever did. So many people. So many lives we can barely even imagine. I could not bring them back, but I'd hoped . . .

"Time takes away so much. No," he said then, his voice turning angry. "Time takes away *everything.*"

"Yes," Shai said, because it was true. She suddenly felt like she could breathe again. "It does. All of this will be gone one day. Your warehouse and the artifacts. The Lower City and the Towers and the Central Spire. Gone like the city that came before is gone. Only dust and ash and ruin, and then not even that. Gone, even, from memory.

"And yet we're here."

Wen looked at her, startled. Her words, it seemed, were not the comfort he had expected—nor the confirmation, perhaps, that he'd sought. Because for all that she agreed, Shai's voice held none of his despair.

"Wen." Shai moved to stand before him, not as a young girl to an aged companion—not even, truth be told, as a friend. Only as a ghost: a creature of memory and magic, will and hope and regret. She lifted her incorporeal hands to his shoulders and stared into the watery expanse of his old, tired eyes. "Tell me. Why did you stay?"

Wen made to move, to turn away, but Shai held him. She watched as emotions played over his features with the speed of lightning: hurt and anger flashing to sorrow and grief and things that she could not name.

"For him," Wen said at last, and his voice was broken. He looked to his son and Shai loosened her hold, letting him turn, leaving only a single hand resting on his shoulder. "For Brend. He never loved this work, but what else did I have? This is all I knew how to give to him. And I thought that maybe if he was here, and I was here, then maybe, maybe . . ."

Wen blinked and looked away. Swallowed hard and closed his eyes. "Then maybe," he whispered, "Brend could forgive me."

Shai did not know what had happened between them; whether Wen spoke of some great hurt, or only the many small things that might build a wall between a parent and their grown child. It did not, in the end, truly matter. For she thought again of her own mother, curled in upon herself; she thought of the things that she herself had done or failed to do. She knew the hurt that could exist between people who loved each other, and how anger and disappointment could weave through that love until it seemed impossible to tell one from the other.

"And him?" she asked instead. "Why do you think Brend is here?"

Wen opened his eyes and looked at his son. They seemed so alike in that moment: not just their dark hair, the shape of their eyes, the line of nose and jaw that spoke of their shared blood, but their expressions. The way their heads bowed toward the floor and their shoulders sagged with something that Shai could only name defeat.

Then slowly Brend straightened.

"Dad?" he said. Not in reply to anything Shai or Wen had said; for him, there was only the sound of his own unanswered words. Still he spoke. "Dad, if you're here—"

Shai released Wen, and the old man turned to his son. Reached for him with one unsteady hand.

"I'm here," he said. "I cannot be anywhere else."

Wen was bound by his tether, unable to leave this place, this piece of his history and all the fragments of the past that it contained. Yet Shai did not think that he meant those physical limits.

"Dad," Brend said again, raising his voice. The word echoed, catching in corners and returning in flicks and flutters like the sound of a bird's wings.

"Yes. I'm here."

A pause, then: "I can't save it," Brend said. "Everything you've built. I've tried but there's not enough time."

Brend looked to the ceiling and captured sunlight fell upon his upturned face, shining across the tracks of his tears.

"I'm sorry," he whispered. "I'm so sorry. But I tried, Dad. For you, I tried."

The things that one will say when no one's there to hear.

Because she'd seen how Brend stood when Xhea was present: the stiffness of his posture, his forced and overly formal manner. There was none of that now; only an open vulnerability that Shai thought Brend shared with no one.

Yet his father could hear those words—words that one might whisper at a funeral, bowed over the casket. Words said only when it was far too late to change anything.

The past could not be changed, or their words truly shared. Shai was not Xhea, able to give voice to the dead; and this was not the time to pass messages with her airborne light.

No need, in the end, to stand between these two.

"I'm going to dismantle the spells," Brend said, and his words had the sound of a decision made. "I'm going to open the doors and let them inside. There are kids outside, Dad. Little kids and their families. Other people, too—people who will steal the things you've built. People who will destroy them and feel no regret. People who . . ." He shook his head, wiped away his tears.

"I'm sorry," Brend said again. "I know I'm not the son you wanted. But I tried."

He went to the warehouse doors, hidden these long years behind layered spells. The building was disguised as a ruin—a place in no way fit for shelter or protection. Spells, too, were used to provoke feelings of nervousness and caution; spells that pricked the deepest part of the human brain, saying: *Danger. Threat. Don't go here.*

One by one, Brend unraveled his father's complex workings, and one by one the spells fell. Shai had not been aware of the pressure of the bright magic flowing through the warehouse's walls, only felt as that power faded away.

In silence, the two ghosts followed Brend as he threw open the warehouse doors and stepped into the gathering darkness, the light from the daylight spell shining out into the ruins like a beacon.

Beside her, Wen watched as his son called out to the family that Shai had seen in the nearby ruins, knives clutched in their hands. Already, they had been staring—shocked, Shai thought, at the building that had suddenly appeared before them, no destroyed hulk but a structure strong and straight and true. They stared, too, at Brend as if he was but a mirage, a dream of salvation that would vanish if they reached for it.

"Hurry!" Brend called, beckoning. "Inside, quickly, before the walkers come."

That word—walkers—got them to their feet. The parents and elder siblings created a ring around the younger children, guarding them as they hurried across the street, their few belongings bundled on their backs.

They stepped inside the warehouse and their eyes went wide, blinking at the light and the laden shelves. But Brend had already ventured forth again. Through the open door, Shai could hear him calling to other Lower City dwellers, inviting them into the warehouse's shelter and protection, asking them to spread the word.

Slowly, refugees filed inside and claimed corners of the vast space, fitting themselves in between the shelves. Shai watched as once again Wen looked around at what he had built, his expression so different than the one he'd worn but moments before.

"If I'm to have a legacy," Wen said slowly, "it won't be this place, will it? Not these walls, not these things. Not anything I found or sold."

He knelt unseen by a little boy's side. The boy's pale skin was smudged with dirt and ash, the tracks of tears creating bright lines down his cheeks. But he was not crying now. Instead, he sorted through a stack of artifacts under his older brother's watchful eye, and exclaimed over the things he found there. He held up some sort of kitchen instrument, two whisks connected by gears turned by a small hand crank, and puzzled over it. Spun the crank, and laughed as the whisks twirled, heedless of the rust that cascaded down or the grinding sound of the old metal.

"But maybe I can be remembered for this." Wen lifted his eyes and looked at his son, ushering more refugees through the doors. "I can be remembered through him, and what he did this night.

"It won't last," Wen said, and the words sounded like a revelation. "Time destroys everything. But it matters *now*."

Shai smiled as she said, "Yes."

Perhaps there would come a day when someone would weep over the history they would lose here; the history, too, that would be destroyed in the Spire's attack tomorrow. All the pieces, big and small, that spoke of the city that had come before and the world in which those ancient people had lived; all the pieces of lives so different from their own that they were nearly impossible to imagine.

But here, now? Looking at that child laughing—looking at the refugees as they stumbled inside, their fear turning to wonder—there were no regrets.

Wen watched as Brend worked, an urgency and passion in his movements that made the City man all but unrecognizable—at least to Shai. In Wen's face? There was only love. Only pride.

"He's a good man," Wen said. "Isn't he? A good person."

Shai had barely spent more than an hour in Brend's presence, and yet she nodded. For whoever else he was, whatever else he did, she could not watch him save families, save children, and say anything else.

"He is."

"I'm so proud of him." Wen smiled and looked to her. "Will you tell him that? Can Xhea? Please tell him." Tears stood in his eyes, bright, shining, and he did not brush them away.

"He already knows." Shai took Wen's hand, warm within her own. Already it felt fainter, less substantial. "But we'll tell him anyway."

"Thank you." His voice was almost too quiet to be heard.

Wen did not say anything else, only stood smiling as he watched his son. Shai held his hand and stood with him, feeling his fingers become as mist within her grasp, watching as the light of his surviving spell shone through him. Watching as one legacy fell, slowly, slowly, and another grew around them.

At last Wen slipped from the world and was gone.

It was a long moment before Shai moved. She did not laugh or weep—only felt the world echo around her, soft and slow, as some part of her yearned to go in Wen's wake.

But she was needed. Shai reached for the tether bound to the center of her chest and held to it, drawing strength from that bond—strength that had nothing to do with magic and everything to do with the person at the other end of that line.

Why did you stay? She had asked Wen that question; yet it had been so long since she'd asked it of herself.

Once she'd felt torn, drawn toward so much unfinished business that it seemed she was but a rag toy that threatened to tear in two. So many failed responsibilities, so much guilt and regret; and through it all the weight of her own failure.

If such things were not gone now—and they weren't—they no longer had the power to hold her. No more did they drag at her, commanding her attention in their silent, recriminating voices.

No, for all that she struggled to make a difference—make things better, if only in some handful of small ways—there was only one reason that she stayed. One thing, beyond all else, that was worth transcending death.

Xhea.

Perhaps they could not save everyone; perhaps there was no way to stop what was happening, no matter what they tried. But they had already rescued each other more times that she could count—in more *ways* than she could count. Shai would do everything that she could to help these people, because she didn't know how to do anything else; but in the end it was for Xhea that she stayed.

In spite of everything, something in that thought made her smile.

Shai looked around. Some of the refugees had already sent armed runners into the ruins to find and guide others back to the warehouse. Inside, shelves were being pushed aside as people found places to sit and breathe and believe, if only for a moment, that they might live until dawn.

Through it all, Brend was there, seemingly in his element—directing, instructing, distributing goods and soliciting recommendations. *Wen was right to be proud.*

They did not need her. But there were only so many people who were within reach of the warehouse, and the span of newly inhabited ruins was vast indeed. So many remained unprotected, hoping that the dark and quiet might hide them.

Too many targets for the night walkers to find. Too many dark hours remaining until dawn.

With one last look at the warehouse and the people now safe within its strong walls, Shai sped out into the night.

Chapter Sixteen

A noise woke Xhea from a deep, dreamless sleep. She froze, every muscle tense as she listened.

She heard the click of the apartment's door closing. Footsteps—soft, muffled—in the room beyond.

Xhea assessed her options. She had her cane and the blankets in which she curled; though, lost in those blankets' embrace, Xhea did not think she could rise quickly or quietly. She had no knife, no spell, no way to cause a distraction. If she screamed, would anyone respond? She doubted it.

The footsteps that crept toward her were not a child's, not another dark magic user. Eyes closed, feigning sleep, Xhea looked into the magical spectrum and saw the glow of bright magic in the hall beyond—a dull glow in the shape of a person. As she watched, the intruder came to stand in the open bedroom door and rested a hand on the doorframe.

Xhea drew hard on her power, stifling a gasp at the effort; the binding was little looser than before, and she paid for the thin thread of magic with pain. Yet the intruder did not pull a weapon or gather a spell, only stood in the doorway, watching.

Xhea hesitated then looked closer, seeing not the Enforcer she'd expected, but only a stoop-shouldered person, their breath quick with fear.

Slowly, Xhea sat and opened her eyes.

"You're awake," the intruder said. Her voice was soft, her words subtly distorted by the masking spell over her face.

It was one of the servants Xhea had seen earlier, the one who'd carried the towels. Yet there was something else, too. Something in the woman's stance, the way her long-fingered hand clutched at the doorframe—something, perhaps, in that voice—was familiar.

"No thanks to you," Xhea muttered. The words came without thought; the fear that had bound her tongue was leaving her, as was the tide of adrenaline on which it had been borne.

Still, she didn't want this woman—the Spire's servant, the so-called nobody—to see her hands shake, and so she shrugged and carefully pushed her nest of blankets aside.

Xhea expected an apology; strange, that desire, yet she only noticed it when an apology was not forthcoming. That more than anything made her turn back to the servant, narrowing her eyes.

She had a slender build, her curves hidden by the uniform's severe cut. Her callused hands were marked with half-healed cuts and bruises, and her skin was pale in a way that made Xhea think it had been a long time since she'd seen sunlight. She was a woman, no scrawny teen like Xhea herself, and yet she didn't look old.

She held nothing: no towels or sheets, no cleaning supplies, no message, spelled or otherwise. She only stood, poised, as if waiting. As if unsure what to do next.

"What do you want, anyway?" Xhea asked, sounding every bit the angry adolescent she surely looked.

"Manners," the woman snapped, and Xhea blinked. The woman, too, seemed to take a mental step back, as if surprised that word had come from her mouth.

And something in that word, or the speaking of it—

Something in her tone, or the subtle shift in her stance—

Something, something—

No, Xhea thought suddenly, almost violently, and recoiled from her thoughts as if they were knives.

Yet they lingered, growing stronger as the woman moved toward the bed and Xhea at its end. *I'm trapped*, Xhea realized; the woman stood between her and the door. Even so, she was not afraid.

Because she knew this woman. There was something about her that, in spite of everything, said safety.

Comfort.

Home.

The woman touched the neckline of her uniform, unbuttoning the collar to reveal a shining ring of metal around her neck. Xhea would have said it was a necklace; yet despite its shine, it looked neither decorative nor beautiful. Magic flowed through it in an unending loop; magic flowed from it, up and over the woman's face in a waterfall of blurred, shimmering light.

The woman hit some unseen switch and the masking spell fell away. She pushed her dark hair back from her face with one hand, fingers trembling. Tried to smile.

"Hello, Xhea," she said softly.

Xhea could not smile. She could not shout, though she wanted to; she could not weep. She could not, for a long moment, do anything but stare.

A word rose like a lump in her throat, a word that refused to be swallowed back unspoken. A name, once more dear to her than her own.

"Abelane."

"I thought it was you," Abelane said. She sounded sad, somehow, even as she tried again to smile.

Xhea just stared and stared and stared.

Because it was her, it was Lane; Xhea would know her anywhere.

She was older, yes, as Xhea was. Her face was different: longer, her chin more defined, her cheeks no longer gaunt from untold months with too little food. That face was so familiar and so strange at the same time. Abelane had to be—what? Twenty by now.

Yet, looking at her, Xhea saw neither the woman who stood before her nor the room that surrounded them. She saw only their apartment on the edge of where the Lower City surrendered to the ruins. That near-empty, dusty space with its wide windows and half-finished loft, the fire drum that had been their stove and heating both, the nest of blankets in the corner that had served as a bed.

Abelane had rescued Xhea from the streets, and for years she had been Xhea's whole world—her sister and mother, teacher and best friend. Together they had built a life for themselves out of scrap and ruin and nothing.

Xhea thought of those days, the two of them scrounging and stealing, running the countless small cons that had enabled them to keep going, keep eating, to be safe and sheltered for one more night. She thought of the nights when she had curled in the nest of dusty blankets near Lane's shoulder, close enough that she could feel the older girl's warmth, but not so close that Xhea might accidentally touch her. It had only been when she was asleep that Lane had looked her age: just a handful of years older than Xhea herself, for all that the girl had cared for her and taught her everything she knew.

For years they'd been family to each other. There were few memories from her childhood worth keeping, and Lane featured in all of them.

And then Lane had just vanished. Abandoned her or died, and Xhea had never known which was worse: the death of the only person that she'd ever loved, or knowing that Lane might have just gone without a word or a backward glance, leaving her alone.

Xhea had woken one morning to see Lane's bed empty, her quilt folded neatly, her shoes and jacket gone from by the door. She had thought Lane had just stepped out to get breakfast; but hours passed, and then days, and she never returned. Xhea had only been nine years old.

"You're *alive*," Xhea whispered, in spite of herself.

Echoing unvoiced: *I thought you were dead.*

It was the obvious thing to say; it was true. Or, almost so.

I wanted you to be dead—that was the full truth, the shameful truth, and the one that almost kept Xhea from speaking at all. Because it had seemed better at the time, young and hurt and in mourning, that Lane be dead rather than to have left her voluntarily.

Better to be alone than abandoned.

Even so, for years Xhea would wake from half-remembered dreams of a shadowy person walking away while she was helpless to follow—a figure that did not turn or acknowledge Xhea's cries, no matter how loud she shouted, how desperately she pleaded.

Her subconscious had never been subtle.

And yet here she was, Abelane, whole and healthy if not unchanged. *Not dead after all*, Xhea thought, and she didn't know whether the emotion surging through her was joy or rage. Perhaps both.

"So are you." Abelane smiled again, the faint expression lighting her face. "All these years, I worried—"

Once Xhea would have run to Abelane, thrown her arms around her—or tried. Even when she'd been young, her magic bound, her touch had been uncomfortable to endure.

Once she would have cursed at her, shouted, kicked the wall, demanded that she turn around *right now* and stay out of her life forever. Because if Lane had chosen to abandon Xhea, that choice could not be unmade or its effects undone; and, walking back through that door, even metaphorically, did not make anything right.

Once she would have wept.

Xhea wanted to do all of those things. Tears pricked her eyes and her throat became tight. She wanted to do all those things and instead did none, despite the desire, because none of them felt right.

Instead she said, "No." Her voice was low and intense. "*Don't.* Don't pretend that you cared. Don't you dare."

"You don't understand. I didn't know that you—" Abelane raised a hand as Xhea made to interrupt again, but there was no command in that gesture; and her eyes, meeting Xhea's, seemed almost to beg. "I know you're angry, and you have a right to be. But I had to come."

Whatever she wanted, whatever she was going to say, Xhea didn't want to hear it. More than six years had gone by since they'd seen each other—six years in which Xhea had existed perfectly well on her own, thank you very much, and she wasn't going to go back.

"Well, now you're here." Xhea shrugged, wishing she were standing just so that she could turn away. Wishing she wasn't swaddled in blankets like a child. "You've seen me in all my glory. And now you can go."

A moment, then: "Xhea?" Abelane's quiet voice had become quieter. She hesitated. "Is that really what you want?"

Xhea looked at that strange, familiar face.

Where was the Abelane she had known? That girl had been young and scared and entirely out of her depth, as much as Xhea herself had been—but she'd also had nerve to spare. She'd been resourceful and clever, quick to anger and quicker to forgive. Even now, Xhea knew that sometimes when she set her jaw and rolled her shoulders back she was mimicking Lane's stance when the girl had readied herself to face down someone far larger.

Given her age at the time? That had been nearly everyone.

Where was that Abelane? Because the young woman before her now stood as if expecting a blow; and though she held her head high, her dark eyes were shadowed. Afraid.

Gone, Xhea thought. Gone as surely as that small, prickly child that Xhea herself had once been. For good or ill, they were different people now.

Instead of responding, Xhea slowly pushed the covers aside. Swung her legs over the edge of the mattress, supporting her bad knee with her hands, then worked to tighten the brace through her pants. Not looking at Abelane, she reached for her cane and stood. Swayed a moment—still tired, still weary—then caught her balance.

When she turned to once more meet Abelane's eye, the older girl—woman, now—was staring in open-mouthed shock. "Your leg," she said. "Xhea, what happened?"

Xhea laughed at that, though the sound came out little louder than a puff of air. It seemed, hours before, Abelane hadn't noticed her cane.

What happened? Her life had happened; years upon years that she'd fought through alone. Almost all of the big moments had occurred following her polarizing loss of Abelane.

The collapse of the Red Line subway tunnel. Learning to live alone, finding a place for herself, discovering the ways a girl with no magic might earn what she needed to survive. Her year in Orren, and the botched resurrection. The discovery that she could travel in the tunnels below. Her clients and her business associations; the long string of ghosts she'd helped and ignored, spoken to and cast aside.

Meeting Shai and saving her.

The rise of her dark magic.

And yes, the injury that led to the cane she now needed, the knee brace, and the permanent limp to her gait. Compared to the rest, it seemed like such a small thing. Not inconsequential, but not enough to eclipse the other aspects of her life.

The thought felt almost like a revelation.

"I fell," Xhea said, and laughed. It was even true.

"Xhea, I—"

This time Xhea interrupted. "No," she said. The word was almost gentle—at least, for Xhea. No extra edge to that short, sharp syllable. "Tell me the truth. Why are you here?"

"I shouldn't be." Abelane took a steadying breath. "Do you mean here, right now, or here in the Spire, or . . ."

"All of it."

"That . . . that would take a bit to tell."

Xhea raised an eyebrow. "Do I look busy?" *Unless* . . . "Have you come to let me out?" she whispered. "Help me escape?"

Abelane only shook her head. "I don't have anything like that kind of power. I'm trapped here just as much as you are. Just as much as the rest of them."

Xhea nodded, trying—and failing—to hide her disappointment.

Abelane continued, "I just couldn't believe that it was really you. Then I thought—I mean, I hoped—" Words seemed to flee from her; she looked down, but not before Xhea saw her eyes fill with tears.

Abelane? Xhea thought. *Crying?* Maybe after a half-hour shouting match; maybe in the middle of the night, sobs poorly stifled as the memory of some daytime terror rose unbidden—but this?

Abelane, too, seemed ashamed, for she wiped the tears away with the back of one hand, the gesture quick and angry.

"Maybe we could talk," Abelane said at last. The tentative note to her voice made it sound almost like a question.

Xhea considered, looking toward the ceiling. It was only white. She could see no monitoring spells, no hint of any magic—not magic, that is, that wasn't connected to Abelane herself.

Yet as Xhea shifted her vision to see that power more clearly, it wasn't the glow of magic at Abelane's heart that drew Xhea's attention—not the reflection of her natural power—but the gleam of the silver ring that encircled her neck. It was so very bright—and yet there was something else, too. A darker core within.

Xhea squinted, trying to understand the spell's fine, complex lines of intent, bright and dark, and could not. Perhaps Shai could have, but this working was beyond her.

"Is it safe?" Xhea gestured to the collar.

Are they tracking her movements? Monitoring her words? Controlling her?

"Safe for me? No," Abelane said, and something in that word made her draw herself a little taller. She lifted her chin in a small gesture of defiance; and when she smiled, it was with some hint of her old fire. "But why should that stop me?"

For all her shock and anger, Xhea couldn't help it: she grinned.

"Well, then." Xhea gestured to the stark, impersonal room. "Here we are."

"I didn't want to leave," Abelane said. She had said many, many things since her unannounced arrival, but that was the one to which Xhea returned, rolling the words over in her mind like a stone polished smooth.

They had not gone to sit on the couch or on the edge of the bed. *Too personal*, Xhea had decided; and without a word of protest, Abelane had followed her to the kitchen. There they sat separated by the wooden table, an expanse that felt every bit as real and solid as the barrier of years that now existed between them.

Xhea had fetched another package of cookies from the cupboard and placed them on the table. A peace offering—or a gift to a stranger.

And she is a stranger, Xhea reminded herself. A stranger for all that a glimpse of her face, the sound of her voice, spoke of comfort and home.

"That's not true," Xhea replied. "We both wanted to leave. To escape to the City."

Oh, her myriad plans and schemes to find their way aloft. Xhea used to lie awake for hours, staring at the water-stained ceiling of their broken apartment, whispering new ideas to Lane in the darkness.

"To escape, maybe," Abelane conceded. Her smile was sad. "But I started life in the City, and some days it was the absolute last place I wanted to be."

Xhea nodded slowly. She had always wondered whether Abelane was a runaway; it was not a revelation. That first year together, though Xhea had been a child of no more than five or six, there had been so many basic things that she'd had to show Abelane: where to dump waste and how to bargain for food, the names of the skyscrapers and how to tell one from the other. Abelane had always had more magic than most Lower City dwellers, too, little though she'd known how to use it.

She'd come from a life, Xhea thought now, where the basics had been provided without asking. And yet she'd run and stayed away, not wanting to return. Fleeing something worse than dirt and hunger, want and ruin.

"If you didn't want to leave, why did you?"

Abelane looked down at her hands, folded in her lap.

"I had no choice."

Xhea took a long, shuddering breath. The words were, somehow, salve to that wound she still bore, scabbed over but far from healed. Even so, the response rose—*There's always a choice.* Except now she knew the edges of such choices; bad choices and worse, the making of each its own kind of pain.

That's what she saw in Abelane's face: the pain of a hard choice made and regretted ever since; a choice that she wished she had not been forced to make. Or was that only wishful thinking, Xhea seeing the things she wished to see?

Once, twice, Abelane made to speak; and then hesitated, closing her lips around the words. She looked at her hands, at the table, at that small package of cinnamon cookies—anywhere but at Xhea's face.

Xhea gave her that silence, pushing down her impatience. It was, in the end, all she had to give.

"They arrived the day before," Abelane said at last, her voice soft. "We'd been at the market—do you remember? We'd done a big trade for that lot of nails we found in the eastern ruins, and we were stocking up on food for the week."

"We bought bread," Xhea murmured. Or Lane had; with her ability to transform bright magic into renai, everything had been so much easier. At least, that's how she'd chosen to remember it.

Abelane nodded. "Bread and noodles and an onion, all wrapped and hidden beneath the cloth from my hair. Then I looked up, and there they were. If we hadn't worked for days for that bread, I would have dropped it and run."

She met Xhea's eyes, and Xhea knew what Abelane wasn't saying: how afraid she'd been. Because the first lesson that she'd taught a young, scared Xhea was that there were times to run and times to hide, times to scream and times to fight—and how to know the difference.

Running when you hadn't yet been spotted? Running instead of quietly slipping away, losing yourself in the crowd? *Clumsy and stupid and just going to get you caught*, as Lane used to say.

Still, she gave her the words: "Running would have drawn their attention."

"I nearly ran anyway, but you were there. We went home, and I tried to believe that they weren't going to follow us. That they weren't going to find me anyway."

"Who?" Xhea asked. "Who was after you?" Unspoken beneath: *Why?*

Her parents, Xhea guessed, *come to take her home—or bounty hunters hired on their behalf.*

But what Abelane said was, "Enforcers."

"No. I would have seen them."

Even if she hadn't seen their uniforms, Xhea would have seen the disruption they caused in the market. Lower City dwellers were used to City folks searching for the lost and escaped among their ranks; they were used to City criminals and the unexpectedly destitute alike, and the bounty hunters that inevitably followed their trails. But Spire Enforcers among those crowded tents? The effects would have rippled like waves, and Abelane wouldn't have been the only one running.

"They don't always wear the uniform or hide their faces," Abelane said, some of her old edge coming back into her voice. "They don't have to."

Xhea snorted. "And you do?" She gave a meaningful look to Abelane's metal collar.

She could understand why Messengers wore the mask: they were the Spire's will incarnate; not a person, just the channel through which orders and information flowed. Enforcers, too, were the strong and sometimes violent enactment of that will.

"Yes," Abelane said, and her tone invited no questions. She returned to her story. "They wore plain clothes, like any other hunter. But I recognized one—and when he moved, I could see a glimpse of silver around his neck."

"You *recognized* them?"

Abelane just looked at her.

Xhea sighed. "Even if they were Enforcers," she said, not convinced but conceding the point, "you don't know they were after you."

"They had an image of me, Xhea. That's what drew my attention—that picture, made from glimmering light."

"No," Xhea said. Because she had asked in the market, in the streets; she had asked everyone she could find, everyone who she could get to listen: "Have you seen Abelane?" She'd even shown a rough sketch, drawn by someone who'd lived nearby—a sketch she'd bought with her last piece of that bread.

No one had seen her—and no one had mentioned Enforcers or bounty hunters seeking someone of Abelane's description. That sort of thing stuck in the memory, even if it took more than a spark of renai to loosen a witness's tongue.

"I looked different. In the picture."

"Younger," Xhea said.

"Yes, and . . . different. Even you wouldn't have recognized me."

Xhea stared at Abelane, thoughts crashing together inside her mind almost too fast for her to follow.

"The Lower City wasn't the first place that you ran to," she said. "Was it?"

It wasn't really a question.

"No," Abelane whispered.

"You went to a skin sculptor?" Xhea asked. It wasn't the right term—the official term—for the people who used magic to shape flesh and blood and bone like clay; it was only what everyone called them. Though the City's elite regularly reshaped their faces and bodies to perfect their appearances, she'd not heard of such procedures being commonly used on a child—especially not changes so drastic as to leave the person unrecognizable.

Abelane nodded. "My family had power, then. Influence. They sent me to the best they could afford—new face, new name. New life. Paid extra to keep everyone silent. I fell asleep as Mirae, an eight-year-old citizen of Irlasel, and woke up Abelane, adoptive daughter of some mid-tier family in a mid-tier Tower. Jortanen."

It wasn't a Tower name that Xhea recognized. But Irlasel? It was not Allenai, not quite; but strong and influential enough that they could reach Allenai's altitude within a few decades, if not sooner.

And Mirae? Xhea shook her head. Whoever that girl had been, Xhea had never known her. Though Abelane had been young when Xhea had known her, she'd been older than eight. How long had she spent in the City above, running? How long had she hidden in the Lower City before she'd found and rescued Xhea?

"Is that your name now?" Xhea asked softly, then corrected herself: "Is that your name again? Mirae."

"No," she said. "Mirae is dead."

"Legally."

"In every way that possibly matters. I don't know who that is anymore."

"And Abelane?"

A thin, haunted smile. "Her, I'm trying to remember."

"But why, Lane?" Xhea asked, the old nickname slipping out before she thought. "What did you do?" Because she could think of nothing that an eight-year-old child could do that would require such a response.

"It's not anything that I did. It's what I saw."

Xhea waited. At last, Abelane took a long, shuddering breath, and spoke.

"Growing up, my friend Ella had a little brother who was born with dark magic. We didn't know much about it, just that his power was different and that he lived in the Spire. He came for visits, sometimes." Her eyes became distant. "Tolin, his name was. I'd almost forgotten that.

"During one of his visits, something happened. His tether to his bondling was severed, or he used up the ghost unexpectedly— even now I don't know what, only that the boy went from seeming healthy and cheerful to . . . sick. Curled in on himself, sweating, shaking."

The hunger. Xhea's stomach cramped at the thought.

"Their mother tried to get Ella and me to safety. But Ella . . . he was her *brother.* She didn't understand. When her mother turned away, Ella ran to him and grabbed him by the shoulders. I think she was trying to hug him, make him feel better. But the moment that she touched him, she just *froze.*

"Her mother was shouting, and the minder dove in to try to separate them, but it didn't make any difference. It was as if there was just the two of them, staring into each other's eyes— Ella silent and rigid as a statue, and Tolin just looking at her like . . . I don't even know."

Abelane stared at the table's surface as if the wood reflected that moment back at her, a mirror for her memory. If it had been a mirror in truth, Abelane might have smashed it into a thousand glittering shards. Xhea didn't need to see Abelane's hands to know that they were shaking.

"She didn't scream, Xhea. Didn't make a sound, not from the moment her hand touched him. But I swear she knew what was happening. Because her eyes . . ." She shook her head. "I saw her eyes before her brother covered them with his tiny hand, and she was terrified.

"A moment later, she collapsed, and only then could anyone break her brother's hold on her body. But it was too late. I'd seen him take something from her—something glimmering held in his tight little fist.

"I *ran*. Just turned and ran as hard and as fast as I could. My parents believed me—or believed *something*, absent gods only know why—and they took me away."

Suddenly Xhea remembered the first time she'd talked to Lane about ghosts. It had taken time; young Xhea had been convinced that if Lane knew about the ghosts, that she'd kick Xhea out, send her away. Reject her.

She'd told her about a ghost that she'd seen in the market, and Lane had been shocked, angry—or so Xhea had thought. Now she wondered if what she'd really been was afraid.

Over and over Lane had said that Xhea was lying, just making up stories to scare her. It had taken weeks for that sudden coldness between them to fade; longer before Lane suggested using her talent to make money. Only now did Xhea truly understand that fear.

"But why—?"

"The Spire," Abelane said. She snorted and gestured at the walls around them. "What I saw then, a dark magic child stealing a living person's spirit from their body, is a secret that the Central Spire holds very, very closely. People know that dark magic users exist—that they are rare and highly valued, that they're needed to make soul bindings that join Radiants to their Towers—but they don't know what else they do. Don't know what they *can* do."

"But what does it matter?" For how many Lower City dwellers now knew that very secret? Herself included. More, certainly, than she had fingers; likely many more.

"I don't think you realize how many spirits these children consume during their lives."

"Dozens?"

A short laugh, bleak and without humor. "At least. They need a source for all those spirits. They use the criminals sent to the prison."

A source for ghosts, Xhea thought in slow shock. For as plentiful as ghosts could be in some areas, their presence was neither predictable nor certain.

She thought, too, of the speed at which Ieren had emptied Farrow of whatever ghosts might have once lingered there. For there had been none that she'd seen or heard or even distantly felt, which was hardly the case anywhere else within the Lower City.

But prisoners?

Abelane explained, "It's part of the Spire's arrangement with the Towers. All criminals convicted for serious crimes—however those may be defined by the individual Tower—are not to be held by the Tower itself for a period of more than one year, but sent to the Central Spire for imprisonment. The Spire is contractually bound never to kill a Tower's citizen. Only hold them and, if appropriate, free them when they have been reformed. But few ever come out."

The night walkers.

If the Spire could not kill a person, why spend good renai to house and clothe, feed and care for what was only, in the end, a useless vessel? And so they were tossed, carelessly, to the Lower City. The prisoners were not killed but they died all the same, starved and broken; and sometimes they killed others before dying.

Which said nothing about what happened to their spirits, those final months or weeks or days in which they were slowly consumed.

No wonder a vacant body can always be found for a Radiant ghost, Xhea thought, dazed, remembering that Shai had said a Radiant spirit must be anchored to a living body to continue generating magic. *The Spire has an endless supply of empty bodies, which they discard, living, like waste.*

"But you're just a witness to a crime, not a criminal. Why are you even here?"

"I am a criminal, Xhea. Tried and convicted. It's a crime to attempt to evade an Enforcer or dodge the Spire's justice, and I did both. And after what I had seen? I was too dangerous to be let go—but too useful to be allowed to waste away in some cell. So here I am."

"Serving the dark magic children?"

Abelane nodded. "Making their food. Doing their laundry, bringing them new clothes, helping teach the younger ones their lessons. Telling them stories. Cleaning their rooms. Comforting them in the night when they have a bad dream." She shrugged; it was a strangely hopeless gesture.

"But why didn't you just stay?" Xhea asked, helpless to stop the plaintive note that crept into her voice. "We could have run, we could have hidden—we could have figured something out. Together."

Some part of her, it seemed, was always nine years old, waking to an empty room and pacing those floorboards long past nightfall. Some part of her was always dust-coated and desperate, searching the ruins of the collapsed Red Line subway tunnel, as if beneath a pile of crumbled concrete she could find the bloody, broken reason why she was suddenly alone.

"I escaped the market without being seen," Abelane said, "but they tracked me anyway. Some things not even a skin sculptor can change."

A moment, then: "Your magical signature."

It was a revelation. Xhea had always known that Abelane had more bright magic than many Lower City dwellers; yet she had rarely used that power. She'd paid for food when they had no chits, but only then; and all her other spells? Tricks, Xhea had thought of them. Just little tricks of magic that helped them steal food or heal a cut or quiet the sound of their ragged breath when a pursuer came too close to their hiding spot.

But what if it hadn't been that Abelane *couldn't* use her magic, but only that she was too scared to try? Terrified that any given spell might attract attention from the wrong people.

"They tracked me to our apartment. I didn't sleep that night—too wound up, and certain that at any moment there would be footsteps on the stairs and it would be them. Before dawn I looked outside and there they were, two Enforcers standing on the front step. I looked back and . . . there you were. Curled up. Sleeping.

"I knew you would try to stop me. When you got angry, there was nothing that could stand in your way—certainly not sense. And you'd touch one of them, and they'd know what you are, and they'd take you, too."

Abelane looked up, and in her face Xhea could see the girl that she'd been: fourteen years old, standing in front of that dusty window in the pre-dawn light, terrified and alone. No one to help her or stop what was going to happen; only a small, sleeping person who loved her.

"Why let them have us both when they only wanted me?"

A sacrifice.

Why didn't you wake me? Xhea wanted to ask. *Why didn't you at least say goodbye?*

But she knew. Abelane was right: nothing would have stopped Xhea. She would have thrown herself between Abelane and the Enforcers, Lane's sacrifice be blighted. She would have clung to Lane's hand, heedless of the pain. She would have volunteered to go.

And this, she thought, looking at the Spire's pale walls around her, *would have been my life.* Her mother's binding would have broken sooner—and how many ghosts would she have destroyed since then? And none of them Radiant, none of them enough to keep her safe and steady and sane.

In all likelihood, she would have already been dead.

At nine years old? She would have done anything to save Lane.

"I thought I could protect you—I thought I *had* protected you. Maybe it didn't matter in the end. You're here. But I tried."

"Six years," Xhea whispered. "You've been here for six years. While I . . ." How could she even explain what had filled those years? She lacked the words even to try; lacked the desire.

"How did they find you?" Abelane asked then. "Because you're not like them, not really. You could always see ghosts and your touch hurt, but you always had so little magic that you couldn't have . . ."

Xhea stretched her hand into the middle of the table, palm up, and called her magic. It hurt as she forced that thin, weak stream of power through the crack in the binding, down her arm and out into the air beyond. It was just a pale wisp of wavering gray, like the smoke from an extinguished match, vanishing as it rose.

Even so, Abelane gasped and pushed back from the table in shock.

"No," she said in disbelief. "Xhea you can't—you shouldn't—"

"I have their power," Xhea said. She released her hold on her magic, wanting to press her hand against her stomach to ease the pain. "But I'm not like them. What you saw—I've never done that. Not ever. I even stopped a dark magic child from stealing a living man's spirit. Ieren," she said, suddenly realizing that if Abelane had been here all this time, she would have known the boy.

Abelane nodded hesitantly.

"Ieren tried to steal the spirit of someone I knew, and I put the man's spirit *back*. He's alive. He's fine." *Mostly*, Xhea thought, but there was no need to say that aloud.

"But if you have their power," Abelane said softly, "then you need a ghost. You destroy people anyway."

Xhea curled her fingers in one at a time, feeling the chill of her fingertips against her palm. She was hungry, she realized, but it was only normal hunger.

Keeping her movements slow and unthreatening, she reached for a cookie. Abelane tensed, ready to run. Xhea pretended she did not see, as if that reaction wasn't another bruise to her already battered heart. She lifted the cookie and took a bite, using the movement to hide her indecision.

Because this could be the reason that Abelane was here, all unknowing. If anyone in the Spire had discovered their shared past, they would not hesitate to use it against her. Information, trust, cooperation—she did not know what the Spire wanted from her, only that Abelane was their best route to get it.

The Spire must already know about Shai, she thought at last. Their stories were inextricably intertwined: the Radiant spirit who had come to the Lower City, and the girl who could see ghosts who was the connection to that power. It wouldn't be a betrayal to explain that much—wouldn't put Shai in any new danger.

"I have a ghost," Xhea said. "But I would never hurt her. Not intentionally; not ever. She's a friend."

"Your power won't give you a choice." And oh, the sadness in Abelane's voice. "Do you think that they don't try? That they don't want to protect the ones bound to them? I *know,* Xhea—I know more about these children and their power than almost anyone."

"But we—"

Abelane continued, unhearing. "For most of these children, their first bondling is a parent, sometimes a sibling or other relative. Someone who loves them without question. They go voluntarily, and at the moment of their death, they bind themselves to the child."

For a moment, Xhea could but gape. *A tether,* she thought. A dark magic child as their unfinished business, the thing that they could not leave behind.

"Then the child is taught to create a dark magic binding, if they have not already done so instinctively. It holds them steadier than the tether alone—and helps keeps their power quiescent while they learn to control it. The dual link makes the ghost survive longer."

"Why are they not bound?" Xhea asked. For years the binding her mother had woven—combined with the bright magic with which Xhea had regularly dosed herself—had kept Xhea's magic suppressed.

"They are when they're young. But the longer they're around other dark magic users or powerful ghosts, the more their power pushes against those bindings. Better that they learn to control the power young than have it overwhelm or kill them unexpectedly." Abelane shrugged. "Or so it's said. It doesn't change what they do to the ghosts bound to them. Quickly or slowly, the ghosts are destroyed."

"How do you know? You can't see them."

"No," Abelane said, her voice turning angry. "But *they* can. You think it's easier for a kid to see their parent in pain if that parent is dead? And they know it's their fault." She gestured sharply. "No, I can't see what they do, but they tell me. 'Laney, his hands are gone.' 'Laney, I can't see his face anymore.' 'Laney, he won't stop crying.'"

"Abelane," Xhea started, but Abelane wasn't listening. Her voice was louder, harder, anger cracking through the wall time and distance had built between them.

"You know what's even worse? When you know the person that they're consuming. When the kid wakes up crying because their ghost is whimpering in pain, and that ghost's your dead friend, and you can't see them and you can't hear them and *you can't help them.* All you can do is try to dry the kid's eyes and console them and hope that they don't kill you next."

"*Lane,*" Xhea said, as if with voice alone she could cut through that rage. "My friend. My ghost. She's a Radiant."

Abelane froze, her mouth slightly open.

"And no, she hasn't been with me that long, but we need each other. I keep her strong and she keeps me ..." Xhea suddenly had to swallow past a thickness in her throat. "She keeps me alive."

No, more than that.

She gave me a life worth having.

With that thought, something changed within her. That hard stone of hurt and anger she'd held within her heart for so very long softened—if only a little. Because whatever had happened to Abelane, no matter why she'd left, Xhea had survived. She'd found her own way, her own strength, her own life. She was whole. She was *alive.*

She'd even found another person who loved her.

Xhea lifted a hand to the spelled tether that joined her to Shai. Though she received no thoughts or images, she felt the flow of Shai's bright magic holding her sane and steady and safe.

But wasn't the magic that Xhea cared about, not in the end. It was the person on the other end of that line.

Across from her, Abelane had grown still, her eyes wide. Slowly her lips shaped the words, "A Radiant?" Yet no sound emerged, not even a whisper.

A moment, then Abelane rose unsteadily to her feet. *Get up*, she mouthed.

Xhea blinked. All the things they'd spoken of—their shared past, Abelane's history and imprisonment, the true nature of dark magic—and only *this* concerned her? A passing mention of Shai?

I don't understand. Yet she had but to look at Abelane's face to see her fear and urgency.

In all her life, Xhea had only trusted two people without question—and Abelane was one of them. Time stretched between them, and a distance made of past hurts and unanswered questions—a wound that would be a long time healing. But this was still Abelane.

Not knowing whether she would later curse herself for a fool, Xhea followed Abelane's lead, moving toward the door. There Abelane paused just long enough to reactivate her bright mask, then led Xhea from the room, down the hall, and away.

Chapter Seventeen

Out in the hall, Abelane's demeanor changed, all trace of her sudden panic vanishing.

"Since they let you out already," she said cheerfully, "let me show you around. We can save the grand tour for tomorrow, but it won't do to have you wandering around lost, right?"

"What are you—"

Abelane stepped on her foot and Xhea fought not to yelp. But she knew the gesture; couldn't count the number of times she'd had her toes squished in just such a manner.

Abelane had been a great con artist, her acts so believable even Xhea had sometimes fallen for them. A subtle kick or pinch or Abelane's shoe grinding down on her toes had often been the only way that Abelane could tell Xhea to shut her mouth lest she ruin the con for the both of them.

"Can you not injure my *good* leg?" Xhea muttered instead, the words all but inaudible. Abelane showed no sign that she had heard, only ushered Xhea forward as she talked in a quiet, happy voice about the daily routine.

They passed door after door—most locked now from the outside, as Xhea's had been. Extending her senses, Xhea could feel the inhabitants in the spaces just beyond: the twin pull of dark magic and a ghost.

She glanced at Abelane out of the corner of her eye, trying to keep from frowning; Abelane chattered on, seemingly oblivious. It was as if when that mask went over her face, she became a different person; everything, from the way she walked to the relentlessly cheerful cadence of her voice, changed.

An act, Xhea thought; one that had clearly kept Abelane safe—or at least alive—these past years in the Spire.

As they walked, Abelane pointed out rooms in the center spaces, off the hall's left side: the common area, the playroom, classrooms, a dining hall. To their right there were only those numbered doors, stretching on and on unbroken.

"Are there really so many?" Xhea asked at last. Abelane's head tilted in question, and Xhea pointed to the doors. "Children." Because she'd seen—what, a dozen dark magic children? Seen, too, those doors closed and locked. Yet Xhea had counted some twenty rooms already, and they hadn't yet traveled even the half of the Spire's circumference.

"Oh, no," Abelane said. "The children are here, of course, but there are other rooms, too. Spaces for friends and family to visit, rooms for attendants like me. The laundry. The kitchens."

"Your room is here?" Xhea asked softly.

"Of course," Abelane said. "Where else would I go?" So much echoing unsaid beneath those seemingly casual words.

"Do you visit the rest of the Spire? Take the children on trips?"

But Abelane only changed the subject, chattering on about meal times and seating arrangements in the dining hall.

Six years, Xhea thought again. Six years had passed and Abelane had spent every day of them here, the whole of her existence limited to this curving hall, this array of rooms.

They reached yet another numbered door, no different than the rest, but here Abelane stopped, fumbled with the lock, and then ushered Xhea through the open door.

The air in the room beyond warm and damp, and the machines along the far wall were full of clothing. Abelane had brought her to the laundry.

Behind her, Abelane barricaded the door with a laundry trolley, then went to those machines against the wall and hit buttons, spun dials. There came the sound of water, the smell of soap, and as Xhea watched the clothes tumbled, cleaning themselves.

Xhea stared, distracted by a moment of unmitigated longing. Thinking: *No cold water, no harsh soap, no dry hands cracked and bleeding—*

Abelane turned to her, switching off her spelled mask once more. Even after the time they'd spent talking, the sight of Abelane's face was again enough to steal Xhea's breath. *Like seeing a ghost.*

"A Radiant?" she said, her voice low and urgent and all but lost beneath the sound of the laundry. "You brought a Radiant *here*? Have you *lost your mind*?"

"No, not here—though she wanted to come. She's just joined to me."

If Abelane raised her eyebrows any farther, Xhea thought, they'd disappear into her hairline entirely.

"I don't even know where to start with that. Letting your bondling stray that far—binding a Radiant at all—I just . . ." Abelane ran a weary hand across her face.

"I'm not *letting* her do anything. It's her choice."

"Don't be naive," Abelane snapped. "If she's bound to you, then she's tied to your will, your needs. The binding *takes*, Xhea; fast or slow it takes, bit by bit until there's nothing left. The ghost's tether might slow that process, but it doesn't stop it."

"Then we've done something else," Xhea protested. "Not just a binding. Because the magic flows between both of us, not just me taking but—"

"*Don't*," Abelane said. "Don't lie to me."

Xhea wanted to explain—but realized that Abelane wouldn't know what was happening on the ground, or have any idea of the fate that even now was but a day away from befalling her one-time home.

"She's trying to protect the Lower City," Xhea said instead. "Do you know what the Spire is going to do? They're going to destroy it all, Lane—everything. Tomorrow."

Abelane only shook her head as if such things did not, could not matter.

"If that's what you want," Abelane said instead, "then of course she is. The binding is a conduit for your will. She'd be helpless against it."

Xhea stiffened. *Is it true?* That Shai wasn't trying to save the Lower City because she wanted to, but because Xhea did.

No, worse: not just saving the Lower City—saving Xhea. Staying with her. Caring for her, now and in all the months past.

Xhea thought of that moment in Farrow, Shai but a breath away from her, holding her feather-light as they rose. The thoughts, the feelings, that flowed between them. Surely that was not all forced. Not all lies.

But what if it is? What if the only reason that Shai cared for her was because Xhea wanted her to? For she knew the depth of the loneliness that had once defined her life, and the intensity of the desire to have someone know her, understand her. Love her.

Xhea said nothing, only stared as the meaning of Abelane's words curled and crashed through her. Some fraction of that shock must have showed on her face, for Abelane grimaced changed the subject.

"Does the Spire know about your bondling? Do they know what she is?"

In all the tests, the poking and prodding Xhea had endured before being unceremoniously dumped on this floor, no one had so much as mentioned ghosts. But if they did not know, surely they had heard the rumors. Xhea nodded.

"Then you have to go. Now. You have to get out of here."

"Oh really?" Xhea looked at her incredulously. "Thanks for that, I never would have realized."

"No, Xhea, I'm serious. They'll kill you."

"That's not exactly news." Xhea gestured around the laundry room, as if the movement could encompass more than these walls and their piles of small clothes. The rooms in which she was kept; the hall, and the many rooms along its slow arc. "Nice as this is, I hardly feel like anyone's trying to win me over."

Keep her out of the way, more like, until someone had time to deal with her. If she'd been anyone else, a locked door and strong walls would have been enough to hold her.

See you tomorrow, one of her examiners had said; she'd thought he was speaking to the Enforcers, but now she wasn't so sure. Oh, tomorrow, tomorrow; one way or another, everything would change. They would come for her—and what? She would not willingly betray Shai, no matter what they offered; nor would she do the kind of work for which they trained these children, the bindings that were their lifeblood.

Abelane said, "Xhea, no one *needs* to win you over. You're old, untrained, and too weak to be useful. Don't make that face—it's not an insult. You haven't seen what these kids can do." No admiration, there; only dread.

And you haven't seen what I can do. But Xhea kept the words unspoken; suddenly, she did not want to discuss the bindings that kept her magic, now and in the past, at bay. Instead she shrugged.

"Don't start that with me," Abelane said, the gesture getting her back up. "You have no idea what you're dealing with. You think you're not hurting that ghost? *Fine*. But know that one of the kids here certainly would." She pointed angrily at the far wall.

"The older attendants used to tell stories, you know, about the last dark magic child to bind a Radiant. Years ago, now. They said that he lived to be almost twenty, and his power . . ." She shook her head, horror seeming to stop her words.

"It's happened before?"

Perhaps it was just a rumor, some old story turned into legend; the attendants, after all, seemed to have a shorter life expectancy than their charges. Even so, the thought was enough to give Xhea pause.

Yet what truly made her recoil was the thought of Shai bound to one of the children she'd seen in the common room. It was too easy to imagine Shai ending up like that ghost girl huddled in the corner, eaten away to nothing. She would fight, of course; she had her magic. But what if she was commanded not to rebel? Commanded to be nothing but a battery once more, a source of life and power, her own wants and needs entirely inconsequential.

Even now, Xhea could steal Shai's magic. If she pulled on that power—drew and drew and drew against that Radiant wellspring of light, and gave nothing in return—how long would Shai last?

The horror of that thought motivated her far more than the threat of her own death.

"I think so," Abelane said. "The worst stories are the ones that end up being true."

"Well, what, then? I never wanted to come here, and the last thing I want is for them to get hold of Sh—ah, my bondling. So if you know a way out, let's hear it."

Abelane paced in agitation, while Xhea stood and gripped the metal top of her cane until it became hot and slippery with sweat. Abelane kept muttering and then shaking her head, seemingly coming up with ideas and rejecting them just as quickly. In the machines around them, sudsy gray clothes pressed up against the little round windows, squished and smeared as they tumbled.

"Deliveries are through the main landing bay," Abelane said after some minutes. "All food and supplies come in that way, all waste goes out. Two locked doors: the door to the bay and the door to the world beyond. No aircars or elevators are allowed to park in the bay or be left unattended at any time. And there are no deliveries scheduled for another three days."

"What about letting the children out?" Xhea asked. "Their work takes them beyond these walls, right?"

Abelane shrugged. "Same deal. Guarded aircars through the main bay."

It's a prison. What did you expect? Little though she believed any of the kids raised here thought much about running away, surely if any had tried Abelane would have heard stories about that, too. Another chapter in the ever-larger book of dire tales that detailed what happened to attendants who allowed their charges to come to ill.

Xhea tried to imagine what she might do with the thin thread of power she could force beyond her binding. An attack on the guards who came for her in the morning—something quick and unexpected, like the magical equivalent to a blow across the back of the head. And then she could try to grab some keys and . . . ?

It'd never work. Fine, then—there was always her earlier idea of holding the kids hostage. She could overpower one of the smaller children and use the threat of the loss of that precious resource to force the Spire to free her.

As if she could bring herself to hurt a little kid.

Oh, where is Daye when you need her?

"There's a room," Abelane said slowly, and Xhea turned. "Just one room where the prisoner transfers are conducted." At Xhea's blank look, she explained, "That's what they call it, when the child takes a living person's spirit."

Xhea nodded, swallowing. A room used only for that violation? She quailed to think of the frequency of the so-called "prisoner transfers." But then, she had some idea of the numbers. She'd seen their empty bodies in the midnight streets. She'd heard them walking.

"Prisoners are brought in by aircar," Abelane continued. "There's a special landing bay, its doors double-spelled. But there's another door, a smaller one, that's used for the bodies."

"Bodies that are sent to the Lower City," Xhea whispered. The questions came tumbling out: "How are the bodies transported? Could you take me to that room? Do you know how to operate the door?"

"Now why would you want to do that?"

The voice made Xhea go still, and at the room's far end Abelane froze, caught mid-pace. It was a child's voice, young and high and sweet. A girl's voice. Slowly, Xhea turned.

Lissel stood in the open doorway. The laundry cart had been pushed to one side, the sound of its movement masked by the machines around them. She wore a long, white nightgown, while her hair—unbound from its braids—fell in soft waves to her waist.

Behind her hovered her bondling, a white man in his thirties wearing pale, plain clothing. Clothing, Xhea thought, like one of Ieren's bondlings had worn—the man who had come to her in Edren, screaming and raging as he vanished. There was no such energy in this ghost; his head was bent as if weighted, his shoulders slumped, his hands hanging limp at his sides. His eyes were open, and yet there was no intelligence there, just a glazed, gray blankness.

Lissel smiled, looking from Xhea to Abelane and back again, then tilted her head. "Why did you bring the new girl into the laundry room, Laney? I don't think you're allowed to do that." Sweet as her voice was, her tone said: *You're going to be in trouble.* And that Lissel, at least, was going to enjoy it.

Abelane reached for the metal band around her neck, then let her hand fall back without activating the mask. Too late for that; too late by far.

"I was just giving her a tour," she said instead, smiling. She sounded chipper once more—but Xhea, at least, could hear the fear beneath. "She wanted to see everything."

"No one wants to see the laundry."

"But she needs some new clothes. Just look at how messy she is. And the smell!" Abelane made a face, as if Xhea's supposed dirty, stinky self was a funny joke that she and Lissel shared.

As ploys went, it wasn't a bad one; Lissel had already proven herself eager to maintain her superiority. Yet Lissel shrugged, seemingly bored. "Then why were you talking about the transfer room?"

At Abelane's hesitation, Lissel smiled again. It was the smile, Xhea thought, of a hunter glad to see some small, furry thing turning and twisting in his trap. The fight might not have gone out of the animal, but it was going to be dinner nonetheless.

The girl turned to Xhea. "You wanted to see where the prisoner transfers take place? I can show you."

Abelane had to be nice to the girl; and she'd had years of experience dealing with powerful, ill-mannered children who could kill her at a whim. But Xhea had faced down things far worse than a little girl in her nightgown.

Xhea looked Lissel up and down with disdain. "Get out of here. I need nothing from you."

"I told you," Lissel said. "You're just ugly and mean, and I don't really like that."

"Does it look like I care?"

"Looks like she does." Lissel reached for Abelane and dark magic flashed like a whip of shadow; Abelane cried out and clutched at her hand. A hand, Xhea saw, that had gone white as bone, as if entirely bloodless.

With the spell, Lissel's ghost jerked at the end of his dark-spelled tether. He whimpered.

Xhea moved between Abelane and Lissel, her body like a shield; she lifted her cane in obvious threat. "You want to try that again?"

"Are you going to make me?" the girl asked, then smiled again. "Come on, I just want to show you the room. Wasn't that what you wanted? Everyone else is asleep anyway."

Without giving Xhea a chance to reply, Lissel gestured again and another thread of power unfurled, fast as thought. *Abelane!* Xhea thought, moving to block the spell—but it wasn't moving toward Abelane but Xhea herself. It wrapped around her neck, cold and tight.

Her breath caught, and Xhea became very, very still.

"This way!" Lissel said. She crooked her finger and the spell jerked forward, making Xhea stumble as it dragged her forward.

It's a test. Lissel was trying to goad Xhea to use her magic—and oh, how Xhea wished she might comply. The girl had called herself "first" here, a position dictated by the strength of her magic. Xhea, the newcomer, was a stranger in a place where the children had been raised since near-infancy, learning and testing their newfound powers together. Of course they would want to know what she could do, what risk she might pose, where she would fall in their little hierarchy.

Before, seeing Lissel shape a tree of dark magic above her outstretched palm, Xhea thought she'd understood what she faced. But it wasn't only the girl's sheer power or control that she needed to fear, but her skill.

She'd seen Ieren and thought that she'd understood what the Spire taught dark magic children.

Yet she realized: Ieren had been sent down to Farrow, and had died in the Lower City's mess and ruin. His death had been a waste, the last weeks of his life thrown away on a project that amounted to nothing. She'd assumed that the Spire had sent him because he'd been close to death. Now, watching the shocking ease with which Lissel wove complex spells—faster, even, than Xhea could have made her unbound power rise—she understood.

Ieren had been old and weak; his power had been nothing compared to Lissel's. No wonder he had lorded his talent over Xhea and hidden the truth of his age; it must have been a change for him to be the powerful one.

It's a test, Xhea thought again as Lissel gestured and sent her sprawling. *And I'm failing.*

Xhea called on her magic and Shai's strength beneath it, pushing against the binding—hoping, trying, to break it. Hoping, even, to force that crack wider, that she might have more than a bare thread of power.

Lissel glanced at her, considering. "I made that spell, you know."

Xhea raised an eyebrow, trying not to let her pain show in her expression. "Spell?"

"The binding on your power. My bindings are the strongest here—it's why they always ask me to do the most important work."

"Don't suppose you want to take it off then, do you?"

"No. Why would I want to do that?"

So I don't punch you in the neck and stuff you in a closet until morning, Xhea thought. What she said was, "You scared I'm going to be better than you? Stronger?"

Lissel looked surprised—and then she laughed, the sound full of genuine amusement. "You?" she said through giggles. "Stronger? No, I don't think so."

"Then what're you afraid of?"

Lissel just rolled her eyes. Rightly so, for no matter how she pushed Xhea could make little headway against the binding. Sweat broke out across her forehead and her breath grew short as pain built in the depth of her stomach. Only a trickle of power leaked past the binding's constriction, all but useless, and still Lissel's spell tightened around her throat.

"Come on, Laney," Lissel said, turning away. "We should show her the room. Show her how it works."

Abelane's eyes were wide, but she nodded. With a cautious hand, she reached toward the collar around her neck.

"No, silly. No masks! Leave it off."

Xhea didn't think that Abelane had been reaching for the mask switch. What other spells were embedded in the collar's metal? A communication spell? A panic button, a way to call for help?

Abelane's hand fell to her side. "Okay," she said. She did not try to fight back—and yet Lissel gestured and bound Abelane in rings of dark power at her wrists and chest and throat. Abelane cried out.

Why are you playing her game? Xhea asked herself suddenly. She pushed away the pain at her neck and chest as if they were nothing. Grabbed her cane and swung at the girl.

Growing up on the Lower City streets, Xhea had learned how to hurt and incapacitate attackers, even if she lacked the strength of most would-be assailants. But Lissel was just a scrap of a girl, her body that of a six-year-old child's, no matter her true age. Xhea could hurt her without thinking.

Even so, she pulled the blow at the last minute. The girl yelped and fell back, clutching her shoulder. She spun toward Xhea, tears in her eyes, her expression a study in outrage.

"You're not allowed to hit me!" she cried. Her magic grew stronger and darker, swirling around her like a storm cloud, and Xhea couldn't help but think of Ieren's sudden, out-of-control rages. Abelane tried to shy away, but was held by those dark bands. Even Lissel's bondling looked up, his eyes shadowed with something like dread.

Yet Xhea touched the spell at her neck and directed the gray wisp of her power toward it, and at last the spell gave way. She shook off its remnants with a flick of her fingers, and stood tall in the face of Lissel's building anger, as if all that dark power meant nothing to her.

"And you're not allowed to put spells on me," Xhea replied.

A pause, then Lissel gave a grudging nod, that sense of a rising storm vanishing as quickly as it had come.

"Laney and I are going to the transfer room," Lissel said, her tiny fingers still clutching her shoulder. "Try to catch up." This time when the spell came flashing out, it did not catch or bind, but struck Xhea across her damaged knee. Xhea cried out as she tumbled gracelessly to the floor.

Then Lissel left the laundry room, dragging Abelane and her bondling ghost thoughtlessly behind her.

Chapter Eighteen

Shai sped farther into the ruins. Darkness was gathering quickly, twilight surrendering to evening, and one by one clouds blotted out the stars.

She passed person after person, and it hurt to keep going, knowing she could help them and continuing regardless. Each time she glanced at a family huddled behind a broken wall, a lone woman perched on a high ledge, a band of men sitting back-to-back with weapons drawn, she could not help but wonder if they would live until morning. Which of these people might survive even if she did not pause to help? Which of them would die because she left them there alone?

Terrible choices; and though she told herself that she had to keep going, had to find a larger group, had to protect as many as she could at once, Shai could not help but feel her stomach twist with slow, sick guilt.

Nor were the walkers the only threat. For all that she saw groups of people banding together out in the ruins, there were those, too, who sought only to prey on the weaker around them.

As if the Towers haven't taken enough, Shai thought in disgust, watching as a young man stole from an older woman's bags as a girl—his sister, probably—held the woman down in the dust, a twist of sharpened metal held to her throat. *As if the Spire won't take everything.*

Such times—hard times, desperate times—revealed a person's true self, routine and nicety stripped away. The good and the bad and the lost; they were all here in the ruins.

Light led Shai onward, glowing from a far quarter of the ruins. Following that light to its source, at last Shai found what she had been seeking. A makeshift wall surrounded a few hundred people in a great, uneven ring. Parts of that wall were ancient foundations, but the rest was just rubble, heaped high. Staring at that mess of rock and concrete and rebar, Shai thought of Edren's underground barricade: protection built from whatever was at hand.

It was not the wall itself that held Shai's attention, but the power that wove through it. Spells had been laid upon that rubble; spells upon spells to bind the bits into a whole, to make them stand strong and true and withstand an impact. As Shai approached, she could see people working in the darkening twilight to weave more spells, bit by painful bit.

These were their life's savings, Shai suddenly understood, poured out into that broken stone. But what use were life's savings when one might not live to see dawn?

Here she could help—and not one but many. All the people working to build those walls higher, stronger; all the people huddled behind them.

As she drew nearer, already planning her reinforcements, Shai recognized people moving behind those walls. It was the tall man she saw first—a man hard with muscle, his face edged like a hatchet. It took her a moment to recall his name: Pol, Emara's father. Overseer of Edren's arena and the fights within, and, years ago, Edren's general during the Lower City's desperate war.

No fear showed in his face or movements; he only worked, directing the men and women around him. He gestured to points on a map scratched into the dirt, and the gathered forces nodded, some few saluting, and ran about their tasks.

Shai knew then: *Edren has fallen.* Not the building perhaps, though that might follow; not the soul of the place, not the people. But if Edren's wartime general was here, defending this encampment— if their gladiators were here, and their security members—they were no longer attempting to defend the skyscraper itself.

Tower Lozan had won.

But more than Edren's citizens were gathered inside these walls, and as she neared Shai saw a group of defenders ushering more people inside, all of them wearing Senn's distinctive sigil on their packs.

Now that she knew to look, Shai saw Emara nearby—not commanding, but working. She was down to a thin shirt, muscular arms glistening as she heaved a heavy stone into a secondary wall that ringed around a group of children and their minders. Councilor Tranten worked at her side, the smaller woman not lifting the stones but weaving spells over them—thin and tired spells, Lower City spells, but spells nonetheless.

Yet it was a voice from outside the walls that drew her.

"There's the ghost girl," Torrence said, and Shai looked down.

Torrence and Daye stood outside the protective wall of rubble, the pair slightly apart from a group of six others. They, like the hunters that stood near them, were armed—though not, she thought, with all the weapons to their name. Daye had her knives, while Torrence rolled a slim blade back and forth between his hands, restless.

They were used to the ruins and the badlands and the horrors that walked these grass-clogged streets. But for all the blades, Shai saw more empty sheaths—and the weapons that many raised could not have been their usual armaments. A long shard of glass, fabric wrapped around its end; makeshift blades of sharp plastic or twisted sheet metal; shivs and chains and lengths of rusted iron pipe.

Shai came to stand before the pair, though only Torrence's head swiveled to follow the movement. He was, for the first time she'd seen since Farrow's fall, not wearing his dark sunglasses.

"Have you come to rescue us, O Angel of Light?" Torrence asked her with a mocking grin. "Come to shield us from the monsters and soothe our despair?"

His words were edged, but his expression was not. *It's not in his nature to plead*, Shai thought. No more than this.

Daye did not look for Shai, only continued sharpening her blades, her gaze flicking once and again toward the ruins around them. The walkers would be coming soon.

"Ready?" someone from the other group asked—one of Edren's hunters, Shai realized, recognizing his face. "Best if we meet them farther from the walls."

"Just a moment," Torrence replied though Daye was already straightening, rolling her shoulders, readying a knife in her strong, callused grip.

Perhaps it was the weapons, or their stance, or the way that the hunters stared out into the darkness beyond, but only then did Shai realize: they were not going to defend the walls. They were going out to find the walkers.

Find them and kill them, before they could kill everyone else.

It made sense; she knew it. Xhea had told her that people had tried to clear the ruins of walkers time and again, but such efforts were costly. Walkers could come upon a man slow and steady and silent; they could surround him before he even knew they were there. They could not be intimidated; they did not feel fear or pain, and would grasp and tear at anyone who came within reach.

And no matter how many walkers were killed, they always returned, like a pool filled from an underground spring.

The plan made sense—destroy the threat, no matter the cost, and most of the Lower City dwellers would live to see morning. The idea filled Shai with horror nonetheless. The walkers were monsters, yes, but monsters who had once been people. She could not help but imagine her father's gaunt, once-beloved face as those knives sliced him open, as those clubs beat him down.

The spell generators, Shai reminded herself. She shuddered, pushing the images away, and looked at Torrence. *If they could bring the generators here . . .*

Quickly, she kindled her light and wrote in the air before Torrence and Daye both, explaining the situation in short, sharp words. Though the words were dim, just shining into the visible spectrum, Torrence squinted as if half-blinded. The hunters from the other group gasped and shied away, then drew weapons in response to this seeming threat.

Torrence and Daye ignored them.

"If we get the generators," Torrence said, cutting to the heart of the matter, "will you be here to power them? Because without you, that's just a fool's errand."

Yes, Shai wrote, hoping it was true.

"I think I saw an aircar hidden in the ruins a ways back," Torrence said speculatively. He gestured to his left.

Daye nodded and slid her knife into its sheath. "Yes," she said in her oddly soft voice. "Model VX-47 with modified lifters, cargo storage back, and new-welded towing hooks. Covered with a tarp. Low walls on two sides, backed into the corner protection. Guard on nearby wall, blind spot at his seven o'clock. Marks of footsteps in a ring—irregular patrol, one man, maybe two. A small distraction would draw them away."

Shai blinked, then glanced in the direction Torrence had gestured. No sign of any of that. *She knows that just from memory? Just from passing by?*

"Can you get it?"

Daye looked at Torrence flatly. Shai saw nothing in that expression, but Torrence raised his hands as if in surrender, saying, "Okay, okay. I just asked. You don't have to bite my head off."

Which, Shai thought, probably meant yes.

"They weren't letting many aircars out of the Lower City," he said. "It'd be tough to get in, but tougher to get out. Never mind actually grabbing the generators." He sounded, if anything, excited by the prospect. "What do you think?"

Daye leaned against the piled-high wall, considering. She looked at the ruins beyond, lit now only by candlelight, Towerlight; she tilted her head to stare at the Towers above. She was, for the span of a breath, so still that she might have been the statue of a woman—then she nodded once, shortly.

"We'll get them," she said.

Torrence grinned, then went to speak with the group of hunters, telling them to leave without them, that they'd catch up sometime later.

"Good hunting," one said, and Torrence replied in kind. The other man smiled, and there was nothing kind in that expression: the dim light and the stranger's blackened teeth turned his face into a grinning skull.

He'll keep them safe, Shai told herself. *He'll help keep walkers from reaching the walls.* Even so, she shivered.

And perhaps that would be enough. The walkers were no army, no matter their numbers, and strong walls were often enough to keep them at bay. Perhaps they would move on to seek other targets, easier targets—though that was poor comfort this night.

Despite their numbers, the refugees drew little attention. Voices were hushed and lights shielded; most made do with the flickering Towerlight.

Shai glanced up. Above them, a feud was in progress: Olton encroached on Celleran and Altaine, with their allies up in arms. Defensive spells flared across the sky, like living clouds lit with lightning, casting the ruins in shades of green and gold and blue.

Blood looked black in such light.

She pushed the thought away. *Defenses*, she told herself, and began planning spells—their anchors, their spelllines. Thinking, too, of a Tower's strong walls, of a window holding back a storm; remembering the great dome of power she'd conjured to hold back the worst of Rown's fire from the Lower City market.

Yet even as she wove the spells, light glimmering around her fingertips, she worried. Torrence and Daye would retrieve the spell generators from Farrow, she reassured herself; these defenses only had to hold out for a few hours.

Even so, some part of her whispered: *Something's wrong.*

She frowned, thinking. For she knew that the walkers were drawn to any sign of life caught beyond the barrier of strong walls—sound or light or movement—and while Shai had never seen them kill a person, the stories had been bad enough. They ate people, some said; yet, having watched them, Shai didn't think it was true. They were starving—and yes, they tore people apart and perhaps ate what was left behind—but it was not the need to eat that seemed to drive them.

Not food that made them hunger.

It was magic.

Magic that drew them and magic they desired; magic that they sought within the flesh of their victims, as if the light of that power might fill them once more. As if any amount of power could heal what had been done to them, or replace what had been lost.

Shai remembered the walkers' upturned faces, their blank attention as they followed her through the streets the night before. And she thought of the light that had drawn her to this encampment—not the light of the shielded candles that even now burned within the walls, but the spells on the defenses. The light of the small spells on people's belongings, their weapons and keepsakes; the light of the people themselves.

Dim lights, all; they were so very poor. But here, in such quantity? They would be a beacon.

Wait!

Torrence and Daye were walking away, but Shai cast the word before them, bright and shimmering. Torrence cringed from it, squeezing his eyes closed.

"Of all the blighted—" he muttered and then looked up, searching for her with tear-bright eyes. "What is it?"

What do you see? she wrote, dimmer this time.

He shrugged. "Right now? Blighted lot of spots."

The walls. The defenses. You see like the walkers now. What will they see?

"Like the walkers," he said. "Don't expect me to thank you for that comparison."

But he turned, rubbed his eyes, and looked at the growing encampment. Frowned, took a step back, and looked again.

"If this is how the walkers see," he said then, softly, "then they will be here soon."

Daye stepped beside him, and perhaps Torrence saw some question in her stance, her movement—something that Shai could not. He turned to her and said, "No. I think we should go." He looked back to Shai and said, "We'll get those spires fast as we can, ghost girl, but don't expect any miracles."

No, Shai thought, watching the bounty hunters walk away. But these people, if they knew she was here, would expect miracles of her.

Yet that thought was unfair. For all of Torrence's earlier mocking, these people were not looking for a savior. They worked, backs bent, sweat shining on their faces and dripping from their hair. They were not waiting to be saved but carving salvation out of the dirt and rubble around them, shaping it with blood and sweat and will.

And if she felt their lives like a yoke of responsibility, that was her choice. Not theirs. These people had lived without her almost their whole lives—generations on generations living and dying in these ruins—and no matter the brutality of this night, they would survive.

Behind the barricade, a soft voice began to sing. Shai did not know the song, neither words nor melody, yet she recognized it nonetheless: a song meant to lull children to sleep.

Shai did not know what drove her, yet she let her protection spell fall from her fingers and she rose, following that thread of sound. The children lay within an inner ring of defenses, some three dozen or more, ranging from near-infants to children just old enough to argue that they were adults.

In the center of that gathering was a dark-skinned young man with a child cradled in his arms. Shai watched as the young man stroked the child's softly curling hair, his large fingers so gentle; and he sang, his voice a clear, untrained tenor. The children huddled around him, drawing close as if he were a warm fire, their only light and protection from the darkness.

Sleep, Shai thought to them. *There is nothing here to fear.*

The spell she cast over them was not one that spoke of strong walls or valiant defenses, but only of slumber, soft and gentle: a barrier to muffle sound and let them rest in peace.

The young man's song continued, though now Shai had to strain to hear him; and one by one the children lowered their heads and closed their eyes. Only then did she work to reinforce the walls around them, all that piled rock and broken concrete, hoping that the strength of her spells balanced the risk of their magical light.

"They're coming!" someone cried from atop the main walls. "The walkers are coming!"

Shai turned.

Already the defenders gathered, drawn toward the source of that call. She saw Emara among their number, one of her crescent blades in her hand; the other was held by Councilor Tranten, the smaller woman standing at her side.

Nearby, Pol shouted orders—positions, formations, Shai knew not which—but the defenders moved to obey. Or most of them did. Some stood as if they'd turned to stone, staring horrified into the darkness beyond.

Some people had never seen a night walker, Shai realized. They'd only heard them: their slow and steady footsteps, their fingernails scraping against a shuttered window, a barred door. They'd heard, too, the screams of those caught without shelter, and seen the mess that was left of those unlucky few by morning.

Shai looked into the darkness—but she did not see what the living saw.

Perhaps the details were the same. The first walker to approach had been a woman in her forties—or so Shai would guess. Her hair was short, the dark curls streaked with gray and clumped with mud. She walked, slow and steady, despite the bloody ruin of her feet.

Yet from the drawn gasps and held breaths of those behind the barricade, Shai knew that they saw only a night walker—only a monster in human form. The stuff of nightmares conjured from the dark.

Shai saw a woman. She *recognized* her—not from life, but from many long nights just like this one.

She'd first seen the woman weeks before. Then, her hair had been clean, her skin unmarked, her clothes whole and unstained. She had seemed, truth be told, like someone that Shai's mother might have known: the kind of woman who would laugh over a glass of wine, debating the finer points of the latest political proposal before dinner was served.

As the days passed, Shai had caught other glimpses of the woman. She'd watched as her golden brown complexion grew dull and ashy, and her cheeks became hollow; watched as her clothes became stained, with holes in the knees and elbows. She didn't look much like a person anymore, only the monster that she had become.

There was a shout. The hunters beyond the walls fanned out, moving to circle the walker, while those inside the barricades prepared some sort of projectile weapon.

"Get the light!" someone cried. "We need to see where we're shooting."

"No—we can't risk drawing more of them!"

Shai ignored the voices and went to the edge of the barricade.

The hunters were right: the walkers had to be cut down. Destroyed, every last one of them. They weren't even truly human anymore—just living bodies. Just things.

Shai knew it, and yet blood was blood, and death was death, and she could not handle more of either. And so she rose, glowing, and drew the walker's eye.

"Ignore them," Shai whispered. "Look at me."

The woman—the walker—stopped. Raised her head slowly, blank eyes staring as she looked at Shai, and opened her mouth.

She did not speak—Shai could not call the sound that came from that parched-lipped mouth a word. It was barely more than a breath, a groan. There came a pause, then the walker inhaled, sniffing.

Not human, Shai thought. *Not anymore.*

The hunters too had frozen—not seeing Shai or her light, only thinking that the walker's sudden stillness presaged some new, vicious attack.

Shai stepped past the barrier and its defenders until she stood before the woman with her arms outstretched. Shai's body was magic—her face and her flesh, her arms and her clothing, her very sense of self. Magic, too, filled her hands as if light were a liquid that pooled in her cupped palms.

She glowed brighter, shining as if she might rival the Towers and the stars above them, shining to rival the golden Spire. She could tell the moment her light passed into the visible spectrum—the defenders gasped, and the hunters stumbled back, blinded. The walkers only stared.

Magic—her magic—was the power of life. Unshaped, it was like cool, clean water, washing the world clean. It bathed the walker's upraised face and the broken ruins around them. Shadows stretched from Shai in every direction.

Magic was the power of life, and yet she wished it could bring death. Not death like the one the hunters promised with their makeshift weapons; not death like the one she saw along the gleaming edges of Emara's long, curved blades.

Death like the one Xhea had granted to a single walker, what seemed a lifetime ago.

Death as a gift, if such a thing could truly be said. A death soft and gentle; a closing of eyes, a laying down of burdens. An end to all things—even this.

Here, now? There was not time. Because behind the woman stood another walker; behind him, another still. She could hear them now in the ruins all around, coming in from the badlands like a tide.

"Here," Shai whispered to them, rising. She opened her hands and magic poured from her. "I'm here. Come to me."

Somewhere to her left, someone screamed—an attack, Shai thought. Yet the sound broke off as Shai's light distracted the attacking walker. She heard footsteps—and, in their wake, a low whimpering.

"Ignore them." Shai raised her voice, letting the sound echo across the ruins—and why not? For if the walkers could see her magic, perhaps they could hear her. Perhaps they could look into her eyes, the way she looked into theirs—perhaps, somewhere in their lost and broken minds, they could understand.

"Forget them, all of them. You wanted magic? *Here*."

Shai stepped from the barricade, moving farther into the ruins. Upraised faces turned to watch her go—walker and human alike. But only the walkers followed.

There were so many. Shai had thought she'd seen them all, one night or another; had thought, foolishly, that she could count their numbers, some gathered dozens. Yet this was beyond anything she'd imagined.

Crack!

Shai did not know the source of the noise, only felt as something passed through her, fast and hot. It did not hurt—and yet the sharpness of the sensation made her pause.

She looked down, and watched as the first walker she'd drawn collapsed to the ground, a gaping bloody hole in her chest. *Gunshot,* Shai thought, *or an offensive spell*—and it was all the same in the end. The walker's blood—the woman's blood—flowed hot and dark onto the rocky ground.

It was foolish to weep. Better a dead walker than a dead child, a dead man, a dead woman. But watching as that once-human creature shuddered and struggled to draw her last few breaths, Shai could not help the tears that cascaded down her cheeks.

Again that sound came—*crack!*—and another walker fell. And another. And another.

She had made them into targets for some unseen marksman.

No, Shai thought, and watched as the walkers fell. Creatures that had once been a boy of no more than twenty and an old man, a girl with a bent back, an woman with long blonde hair, a man with only one hand.

She did not see her father fall, but perhaps she had only been looking the other way—perhaps his was one of those dark shapes upon the ground. Or perhaps he was on the Lower City's other side; perhaps he was even now terrorizing refugees far beyond the reach of even her brilliant light.

Perhaps, perhaps, perhaps.

Yet for all the blood, wine-dark in shadow, brilliant ruby in the light she cast, there were more walkers still standing. More walkers, truly, than bullets or spells might reach.

So Shai walked, a blazing torch shaped like a person, out into the ruins and away, a tide of walkers trailing behind her.

Chapter Nineteen

Xhea slowly pushed herself off the floor.

"I am going to get a new knee," she muttered. "I'm going to cut this one out and throw it in a hole and leave it there until it dies." Because it was that or scream, and she would be blighted if she let Lissel know how much her little spell had hurt.

"Should have hit her harder." Didn't matter how young she looked; didn't matter that, without magic, Xhea could probably break her like a twig. If she let the girl keep playing to her strengths, Xhea would be the one broken.

Leaning heavily on her cane, she limped into the hall.

It was quiet, no hint of the laundry machines' swish and tumble, the only sound the distant patter of departing feet and the chime of Xhea's hair. Xhea turned, spotting Lissel and Abelane farther along the hall. Abelane was walking first, stumbling as if pushed by invisible hands.

Xhea's heart pounded, and she bit her lip as she hurried after them, her knee protesting every step. She had not found Abelane just to lose her. Not again. Not like this.

She could not catch them, only staggered in their wake until they vanished beyond the hall's slow curve. Yet she saw where they'd gone: one of those doors, which she would have thought only another bedroom, was open a crack. Bright light spilled into the hall beyond.

Xhea pushed the door open and stepped inside, her arrival announced in a clatter of charms.

The room was large by Lower City standards; here, it probably counted as small. There was a sitting area in one corner, plush chairs gathered around a wooden table, with a long, low bed nearby, a folded blanket at its foot. There were two doors in the far wall: one seemed normal, though it bore three locks, while the other came only to Xhea's waist and was as wide as it was high.

Yet it was the object in the center of the room that drew her eye. It was long and black and rectangular with curved edges and corners. It had a lid that opened on invisible hinges and now gaped wide like a long, toothless mouth.

A coffin.

Abelane stood before it, bound, Lissel at her side. Only Lissel's ghost showed any true fear; at the far end of his tether, he cowered behind one of the plush chairs as if it might shield him.

Lissel stroked the coffin's open edge, her touch gentle, almost reverent. Without turning, she said, "They bring the prisoners in here, through that door." She lifted a hand, gestured. "One prisoner, two guards. Sometimes the prisoner is drugged or restrained; those times they're taken to the bed and tied down. Sometimes they come willingly."

Not fighting, Xhea thought, *is not the same as being willing.*

"They sit. Sometimes they talk and we have cookies and tea. They can be pretty funny, prisoners, and it's nice to get to know them a little first."

Still Lissel did not turn, only stood touching the coffin, her dark waterfall of hair streaming down her back. Next to Abelane, she looked so small, almost inconsequential.

Abelane stared at Xhea, her expression intense, as if she could send silent words flying between them with that look.

And perhaps she could; for Xhea wanted to recoil, age-old habit commanding: *Run. Find shelter. Defend yourself.*

But this was not the Lower City market; this dark magic child was like nothing that she and Abelane had faced together all those years ago. What good would running do? What good was hiding? Xhea would not be like the ghost in the far corner, a spirit so damaged that he could do nothing but crouch and cringe and hope that this time the pain passed him by.

"What are you doing?" Xhea asked instead.

Lissel glanced over her shoulder, the movement slightly stiff. She'd have bruises soon.

"Isn't this what you wanted?" she replied. "You had so many questions about the prisoner transfers. Secret questions. The easiest way is just to show you."

"I know what you do. I don't need to see it again."

At last Lissel turned. "Then why did you want to come here? Why all the questions?" Her tone was light, innocent; her expression was anything but. *How old is this girl?* Xhea suddenly wondered. She looked six; Xhea had thought she was probably eight or nine. But there was something hard and vicious under her sweet, young face—something that transcended age. Defied it.

"Shouldn't I want to know about the Spire?" Xhea asked, deflecting. "About why I'm here?"

Lissel refused to be distracted. "How are the bodies transported, you wanted to know. How to open the door." She stared at Xhea, her dark eyes intense. "You want out."

"I—"

"And I want you gone."

Xhea blinked, surprised. Abelane, too, started within her bonds, then looked from Lissel to Xhea and back again in no little confusion.

"You're rude," Lissel continued imperiously. "You're a disruption. You're old and untrained and I don't like you."

"Well, then," Xhea said. "I guess we have something in common."

"There are spells on that door." She meant the smaller door, Xhea saw; the door that was designed for a coffin. "Tell her, Laney."

Abelane swallowed, struggling to school her face to calm, but her voice was almost steady. "There are detection spells that scan the bodies as they go. If they find active magic, the exterior doors won't open."

"Active—?"

"Bright or dark."

Because, Xhea realized, pulling the spirit from a living person stripped that person of their magic; she'd seen enough walkers to know the truth of that. But if she couldn't escape through that door, then what was the point?

"But you—" Abelane started, only to break off with a cry as Lissel tightened the spells that bound her.

"That's enough," the girl said dismissively. She looked back to Xhea. "I could disable the spells."

Xhea snorted. "If it was that easy, why wouldn't you leave?"

Lissel looked at Xhea as if she had lost her mind. "Why would I want to?"

She rested her hand on the coffin's edge. Except, Xhea suddenly realized, it wasn't just a coffin, no matter the resemblance of its shape. For, looking, she could see the glimmer of bright spells within it; faint, dormant spells, that nonetheless made her think of an elevator.

Xhea shook her head. "Why would you help me?"

"I don't have to. I could call for help instead. I could have the bosses down here in minutes, and tell them you tried to escape." Again that smile, slow and knowing. "But you have something I want."

Lissel's eyes were intense. She stepped toward Xhea, her hands curling at her sides, tangling in her white nightgown.

"I heard you talking," the girl continued. "In your rooms before. I heard you talking to Laney."

Xhea felt a sick weight in her stomach that had nothing to do with magic. She knew what Lissel was going to say; watched her lips shape the words, helpless to stop their flow.

"You have a Radiant."

Oh, the longing in that voice. The need.

Xhea looked to the ghost of the man bound to Lissel, that ghost worn thin and gray, cringing at the end of his tether. Not her first bondling, to be sure; not her parent or any other willing sacrifice. Nor, she was willing to bet, would he be her last.

"No," Xhea said, but Lissel was not listening.

"I could live," she said, almost whispering. "I could live for *years*. Just think of what I could do, how powerful I could become."

That Xhea could imagine all too easily; it was a horror. Yet it was not the thought of what Lissel might do or become that made Xhea recoil, but the knowledge of what she'd do to Shai.

The binding forces, Abelane had told her; the binding takes. It could steal and twist a ghost's will until there was nothing left—until the ghost was only an extension of the child's will.

Perhaps that was what Xhea had done to Shai already, little though she wished to believe it; perhaps Shai only wanted, only cared—

No, Xhea thought. She would not believe that, no matter the fear that beat at her chest like a dying bird's wings. She and Shai had been together long before Xhea had known to make a dark magic binding, before the hunger had risen. They had been separated, Shai wholly free, and *still* the ghost had come for her, and fought for her, and cared.

But Lissel would destroy Shai utterly—the person she was, the person she'd become, if not her ghostly being.

"You can't just take someone's bondling," Xhea protested, grasping desperately for any reason the girl might understand. Remembering Ieren's rage when she'd so much as come close to his bondling.

Lissel said, "Don't worry, I've already got a replacement for you." She pointed at Abelane. "You won't even have to do it—I'll give her spirit to you. I'll even show you how to do it, quick and clean. You'll never have to be hungry again."

Xhea laughed, sharp and bitter. Abelane flinched from the sound.

"Look," Lissel said, reaching out, her magic flowing. "I'll bring down the detection spells. There. You can just get in now," she said, gesturing to the coffin, "and go. All the way to the ground. That's what you want, isn't it?"

It was.

Xhea was the only one who could speak to the Lower City—the only one who could possibly tell it what it had not yet realized: that it was as powerful as the Central Spire. As powerful, perhaps, as dozens and dozens of Towers combined. The City above wanted to hurt it, yes—but *it could fight back.*

It could even win.

Perhaps there was a way to protect their homes, all that they had built; and perhaps those buildings would fall, destroyed by magic, bright or dark. But they didn't have to die. All the people of the Lower City: Edren and Orren, Rown and Senn and broken Farrow. It loved them, in its inhuman way; the Lower City would not want them harmed. It would save them if it could.

All she had to do was give up Shai.

One girl, already dead; one spirit, fuel to years of dark magic. And everyone else might live.

Surely Xhea's own pain, her agony at that betrayal, was nothing against the weight of so many lives. *Children*, Xhea thought. Kids who were like she had been: poor and desperate, never given a chance. *I could save them.*

Perhaps it was the only decision that made sense. Perhaps she was a monster in truth, selfish and twisted and every horrible thing that anyone had ever said about her; perhaps she was, in her way, no better than Lissel.

But Xhea said, "No." The words came out but a whisper, cracked and broken. She drew a deep breath and looked Lissel in the eye; she saw the threat of the coffin and the threat of Abelane bound, and she said, "No." Stronger this time, louder. "You cannot have her."

"Her?"

"My bondling. The Radiant. My friend. You cannot have her; not now, not ever."

She would, Xhea suddenly knew, die first. She would cut the spelled tether and let the dark magic come boiling up; she would condemn herself to a slow and awful end. But she would not yield.

Lissel sighed. "I did offer." She looked to Abelane. "You heard me, right Laney? I gave her a chance. I was even nice."

The innocence seemed to fall from her expression like a mask discarded. Something blanker waited behind, cold and uncaring, and Xhea felt the girl's magic build.

"No one stands in my way." Lissel smiled and Xhea could not believe that she had ever thought the girl's expression sweet. "Not for long."

Lissel reached for Xhea and her magic flowed between them in a thin, tight beam of darkness. It struck Xhea in the center of her chest, where Shai's tether bound, then dug in, deeper and deeper. A hand of dark magic, grasping.

Xhea cried out and swung her cane; yet the magic was inside her, undoing her from the inside out. The cane fell from her grasp, and Xhea crumpled at Lissel's feet, writhing, gasping.

Xhea felt the moment Lissel's magic connected with the bindings on her magic; there was a short, sharp jerk in the pit of her stomach. The bindings writhed, like her belly was filled with cold, small snakes. The binding moved, changing, rewriting itself.

No, Xhea thought. She threw all of her power against those bindings and Lissel at their other end.

Perhaps Lissel was more powerful than Xhea; perhaps all of Xhea's strength was as nothing in the face of the girl's ability and training. But it did not matter, for Lissel was just a spoiled, powerful child who'd had everything given to her. She did not know what it was to struggle or to have desperate needs go unanswered. She did not know what it was to fight.

As Lissel made to tighten those bindings, cutting off Xhea's magic entirely, Xhea let her power rage. All her hope and fear and desperation went into that magic, fueling it. She threw her magic against the bindings and felt them crack.

And again. And again.

A thousand hairline fractures appeared in Lissel's spell, breaking and disrupting the spelllines as fast as Lissel could weave them.

Xhea felt as her magic washed over her, giving her a strength of focus she'd not before known. It was no great rush of power— most of the whole remained bound—but it was *something*.

She drew, too, on Shai's strength, and felt as some portion of the ghost's Radiant magic flowed into her, purified by the binding into a form Xhea's body could accept. Other things came with it: fear and determination, shock and horror—the image of a blinding light, and a flash of Shai's father's face, gaunt and ruined.

Then: surprise. Hope. Longing.

A word, her name softly spoken: *Xhea.*

More power, purer power, flowed into her without asking—a gift, freely given. Some of Xhea's power, too, flowed from her in return, and it swept away Lissel's magic and the small, unraveling pieces of the binding spell.

Suddenly, the pressure was gone. Xhea opened her eyes, blinking, and stared at the blank ceiling above her. Her ears echoed with a sound half-heard: Lissel's cry of frustration.

Then there was another sound, another cry: Abelane. No frustration in that sound, only fear.

"Abelane!" Xhea rolled, trying to see what was happening. She struggled awkwardly to push herself up on her good leg; she could not see her cane.

Lissel now had eyes only for Abelane, who twisted and struggled within the bindings that held her. Those bonds had burned dark lines across Abelane's uniform, like scorch marks; where they touched Abelane's skin, she'd gone a bloodless pale shade that reminded Xhea of a corpse's waxen flesh.

Lissel was small, and Abelane was not; even on the tips of her toes, Lissel's outstretched hand barely made it to Abelane's chin. Not as high as her eyes. It did not matter.

Lissel's magic closed the gap that her arm could not. Power, dark and sinuous, flowed from Lissel's outstretched palm and into Abelane's eyes. Abelane's mouth was open, caught in an unvoiced scream; her expression spoke only of pain.

This was not an offering; not a ghost to trade for Shai. Only vengeance.

If Lissel had heard Xhea speak of Shai, then how much else had she heard? Enough to use Abelane against her.

"No!" Xhea cried, pushing herself to her feet—but neither of them moved, neither of them noticed Xhea's existence anymore.

Already Lissel's magic was deep inside Abelane's body, flowing through her and digging hooks into her spirit.

Xhea could not find her cane, had no weapon—but she thought of Daye crashing that aircar into Ieren, breaking the boy's hold, and with a scream she threw herself on Lissel and bore the girl to the ground. Lissel's head bounced off the carpeted floor and she gave a small, high sound of pain, then blinked, dazed.

Xhea's magic was still bound, no matter how many cracks she'd put in the binding; even so, she drew power into her hand and slapped Lissel full across the face with all her strength, flesh and magic both.

And again. And again.

At last Lissel's eyes closed and stayed closed. Not dead, not anywhere close, though she'd have some good bruises come morning. No reaction to that thought—neither guilt nor triumph.

Xhea rolled off the girl's limp body. *Ah, there's my cane,* Xhea thought as her leg hit the twisted length of wood. She grabbed it and pushed herself to her feet.

Abelane leaned against the coffin's open edge, shaking and shuddering and bent almost in half, her hand clutching desperately at her face.

"Abelane," Xhea said, and she flinched, afraid. Again Xhea said her name, "Abelane," softer this time.

"Is she dead?" Her voice was thin and terrified, shaking as much as her hands.

"No," Xhea said. "Only unconscious." She glanced back at Lissel, sprawled on the floor. Her nightgown was twisted around her, and her long dark hair spread like a tree's broken branches. She was so small.

Abelane looked up. She tried to pull her hand from her face— then covered her eyes again, cringing. But it had been enough; Xhea had seen the faint glimmer of light about her eyes. The glimmer of her spirit dislodged.

She was not as bad off as Torrence had been; she was conscious and speaking. Even so, it was not an injury that would heal on its own.

Xhea lifted her hand, thinking to help her—but there had been screams, she realized. Lissel's, Abelane's, even her own. Perhaps this room was totally soundproofed, but the door was open a crack—and if anyone had heard? They had but moments before others arrived.

Abelane clutched her face. "I'll be fine," she managed, panting. "Just . . . *go!*"

Xhea couldn't leave her. Even if she were healthy and whole, Abelane would not be allowed to live until morning—not when one of her charges lay hurt on the floor and another was escaping. One of the children would finish what Lissel had started—perhaps even Lissel herself.

Looking at her, Xhea knew that Abelane understood. Still she said, "You have to go." She gestured, half-blind, at the coffin. "Get in."

A sacrifice, Xhea thought. *A willing sacrifice—her life for mine.* The same as six years ago.

Except Xhea was not a child anymore, not that little girl asleep in her blankets who could be left behind unknowing.

"You're coming with me." Xhea pushed Abelane toward the open coffin. It was testament to Abelane's pain that she didn't flinch from that touch, didn't seem to feel Xhea's hands on her at all. Even so, she struggled as Xhea tried to force her inside.

"No," she said. "You can't—I can't go, no—"

Xhea ignored her, toppling her into the coffin's bare interior. No pillow there to rest one's head, no soft lining, only a surface as hard and smooth as the black exterior.

Only then did she remember what Abelane had said about the spells on the door: they responded to magic. Lissel said she'd removed the protections against dark magic—but though Abelane's bright magic sputtered and flickered inside her, damaged by Lissel's attack, it would surely be enough to trigger a detection spell.

The sound of running footsteps came from the hall.

She was out of time.

Xhea looked back to Abelane, who struggled even now to push herself out of the coffin. She had no choice.

"I'm sorry," Xhea whispered, and reached for Abelane's eyes.

Xhea pulled hard on her power, fighting the binding. A thin stream of magic flowed down her arm, through her hand, and into Abelane. She could feel Abelane's spirit there—she could see it, her ghost just slightly out of synch with her body. It would be so easy, Xhea realized, to push it back, align her ghost with her body and make her whole again.

Instead, Xhea dug hooks into Abelane's spirit and pulled.

Abelane gasped, trying to cry out—and then collapsed into the coffin.

Xhea peered down. She had not yanked Abelane's ghost free of her body, only disconnected it. There was no light flowing anymore, no flickers; only her limp body and her spirit dislodged, struggling desperately inside her flesh.

Quickly, Xhea pushed the coffin toward the small door, grateful for the spell that made it float just above the carpet. There was no handle on the door, no touchpad, nothing she could try. She prayed to absent gods that there was a sensor in the coffin.

Behind her, the door to the hall swung open.

"What are you—?" A man's voice. Xhea ignored it—ignored his cry of protest a second later—only jumped into the coffin and pulled the lid shut behind her.

Felt as it shuddered and kept rolling; heard the grinding sound that could only be the door opening.

Please, Xhea thought, staring at nothing. *Please, please, please.*

Spells flared to life around her, dormant lines suddenly activating. Bright lines, dozens of them, hundreds, wrapped around them like ribbons. Xhea had been trying to keep from lying too heavily on Abelane, but now she threw herself flat against the other girl's body and wrapped her arms around her. She drew her magic to her, coiling it inside the binding spell, tighter and tighter, and fought to breathe.

Because the coffin was not the transporter; it was only the casing for the spells. A show, perhaps, to demonstrate the concern that the Spire had for the prisoners' bodies. As Xhea stared, aghast, the coffin broke apart into large pieces—lid and sides and bottom—that fell away entirely, leaving them wrapped only in the bright ribbons of an elevator spell.

"Sweetness, no—" Xhea whispered. They were cast into the open air beyond.

Xhea blinked at the spell around her. Unlike the other elevators she'd seen, this one created an opaque bubble, shielding her from the view outside—though it was surely meant to shield City traffic from the sight of a lifeless body being transported to the ground.

They were moving. Xhea felt their momentum build as the elevator swooped to enter the traffic lanes, and she tried not to think of the empty space below her. Tried not to think, either, of the last time she'd attempted to use an elevator: all those bright ribbons burning as they touched her, then sizzling away to nothing. Instead she clung to Abelane's body and told herself that it was only to protect her friend that she held her magic so tightly within the ache of the breaking binding.

Her breath sounded loud in that closed space, Abelane's shallow breathing like a reverberating echo. Xhea felt the warmth of that breath as it puffed over her cheek, and could not help but think of the many nights she had curled close to Lane's warmth as a child. Lane's presence had meant safety and security. Protection.

In the darkness, Xhea looked at Abelane's soft, slack features, and thought, *Let me protect you now.*

Around them, the spell shuddered as it swooped; already it seemed to be dropping toward the ground. Refocusing her eyes, Xhea peered beyond the spell's opaque barrier, trying to gauge their direction. She saw Towers first, the massive shapes nearly close enough to touch, shining like moons above her. Towerlight undulated around them, huge sheets and waves of power that moved like fabric on the wind.

It was the Towers that first drew her eye, but the Spire that held it.

Earlier, she had seen the Spire cast in light—all that bright magic channeled through the Spire's length, and the countless spells, countless people, in its untold hundreds of levels. Now, while Xhea saw glimmers of bright magic along the Spire's length, the brilliant light of that pure, raw power had been replaced.

Night had fallen, and now the Spire channeled not bright magic, but dark.

First from Farrow's peak, then Edren's rooftop, Xhea had watched the Spire gather wisps of dark magic from the City—from all the Towers, spread across the sky—to pour them on the ground below. She'd thought she understood—but she'd been wrong.

The Towers spun, slow and graceful, around the Central Spire. Xhea had never questioned that motion, no more than she had questioned the rise and fall of the Towers' political dance as they fought for position and altitude. Only now did she see the reason for it.

It created a vortex.

The Central Spire was like a magnet that drew dark power from the whole of the City above—and as that power gathered, the Towers' motion sent it swirling. Faster it flowed, until it formed a tight, rushing spiral of power around the Spire, and poured toward the ground.

A tornado of dark magic; black water circling a drain.

All the bright magic that she'd seen—so much wealth that Xhea could not begin to comprehend it—had been to reinforce the Spire: its walls and floors, its homes and gardens and people. To strengthen and protect it against the rush of dark magic that the Spire called once night fell.

She could see those bright spells along the Spire's length, straining beneath the onslaught.

Once she had wondered why the Spire had no defensive spell generators like the Towers bore. It did not need them; the whole thing was a defensive spire—a structure designed only to channel magic.

And its heart?

That evening Xhea had stared, struggling to see the Spire's living heart in the midst of so much bright magic. She'd thought that its glow must have been lost in the light from its channeled power. Now, with only dark magic flowing, she could see the truth: it had none.

Ahrent Altaigh had once explained that enough magic changed a thing—made even inanimate objects come alive. Made them wake.

She'd seen how much power the Spire channeled, in daytime and at night; there was nothing in the City, proper or Lower alike, that had touched so much magic as the Central Spire. Yet it did not live, not truly. Because for all the force of that bright magic, dark magic equal in power replaced it each night, undoing all that the light had wrought.

Born at dawn, Xhea thought. *Alive in the sunlight . . . and dying each night as darkness falls.*

Or did it live again before dawn, a dark magic creature like the Lower City? She did not know.

Yet she could see and hear the truth of it—it had no heart, neither light nor dark. It had no song. Despite the strength of that power as it flowed, there was not enough time for awareness to grow.

In all the City above, the Central Spire was the only thing as inert as she had once believed the Lower City. It was a vessel for power, a channel for magic, nothing more.

Xhea's breath caught. *A channel for magic . . .*

Something in that thought, or the sudden images that the words made bloom within her mind, made her magic push against the boundaries of the binding spell and struggle against her control. Beside her, Abelane flinched, unconscious though she was. Xhea opened her eyes, seeing only the elevator spell once more, and made herself breathe careful and slow.

Still she held to the thought—repeated it—as she and Abelane fell in darkness the long, long way to the ground.

It was only as they were nearing the earth that Xhea realized where the elevator was taking them: not to the Lower City or the ruins beyond, but the badlands.

It was possible to make it from the Lower City to the badlands and back again in one day—if barely—but one had to run near-constantly over uneven ground to do it. She'd been told that in the badlands, there was little sign left of the city that had come before; far enough out, there were only trees. She wanted to see it one day—but not now. She'd never make it back to the Lower City before the Spire's attack.

She reached up, and tried to pull a thin thread of dark power past the bindings. It fought and writhed. *Too upset*, Xhea thought. She was angry and overwhelmed, relieved and exhilarated and hurting; even the magic's calming effect did little against the adrenaline surging through her.

She meant to target just one of the elevator's lines of intent at the nexus of all those bright ribbons. Instead, her targeted strike unraveled near half the propulsion spells entirely. The elevator shuddered and dropped; suddenly they were no longer swooping toward a distant landing but spinning in an uneven circle.

"Down," she told the elevator, as if it might hear and understand. Xhea glanced toward the ground, looking past the shielding magic, and swallowed her sudden fear at the sight of that drop. Forty feet? Thirty? Too far to fall.

The elevator's ribbons flickered. Without changing her vision, Xhea could see beyond the spell's bubble to the shapes of the ruins around them. Broken buildings jutted like black teeth, and waist-high grasses and stunted trees clogged the spaces between, leaves shivering in the wind.

The elevator spell dropped and dropped again, its propulsion spells chirping and flickering as they failed.

It's dying, Xhea realized. She only had time to grab hold of Abelane's limp body before the elevator broke. They fell, tumbling.

Xhea screamed—she was falling, falling—and then suddenly they hit the ground. She rolled—not on hard stone but soft earth and moss. She tried to cling to Abelane, her arms wrapped around the unconscious girl's head, but Abelane was torn from her grasp. Xhea reached out, trying to slow her tumbling descent, praying to absent gods that the brace would keep her knee from twisting.

At last, she came to a stop and lay panting. Somewhere nearby, there was a faint sound as the dead elevator port fell to the ground and bounced once, twice, before rolling away into the darkness.

"Ow," Xhea whispered.

Everything ached. She would be black and blue, she judged; yet when she moved, shifting her arms, her legs, the pain did not worsen. Nothing seemed broken.

Slowly, Xhea pushed herself up and looked for Abelane. The young woman was sprawled on the ground nearby; Xhea pulled herself across the ground to her side. Careful to keep layers of cloth between them, Xhea rolled Abelane over. She was still unconscious, her spirit out of synch with her flesh. Her ghost glimmered about her eyes, her lips, her hands. Abelane's face and clothing were scuffed with dirt, and a shallow cut marked the span of one cheek—but she, like Xhea, was mostly unscathed.

"Sometimes you have to leave someone behind, right Abelane?" Awkwardly, Xhea tried to push the hair from Abelane's eyes. "Sometimes you're the one that gets left. But not today. Not ever again."

Xhea spread her hand across Abelane's face, not touching, but letting a thin stream of magic flow through the space that separated them. She took hold of Abelane's spirit and *pushed*, feeling as her spirit connected to her body with the ease of rain soaking into soft ground.

Xhea sat back, checking her work carefully; there was not so much as a flicker of spirit beyond Abelane's body.

But Abelane did not move.

"Lane?" Xhea said softly. "Come on, wake up."

Nothing.

Again she checked those connections, spirit to body, wondering what she'd done wrong. It had felt the same as when she'd put Torrence back into his body—and then, Ieren had almost ripped his soul entirely free. It had felt the same as when she'd brought Marna back to consciousness, despite the drugs running through the woman's veins—that same sense of a connection made. That same sense of rightness.

There was nothing right here. Abelane lay unmoving beneath her hands, and her skin, when Xhea touched her cheek with tentative fingers, felt almost cool. No reaction to that touch, either; no flinch or sound of pain.

Even with the evidence plain before her, it took a long moment to understand: Abelane was dying.

"Don't you dare," Xhea told her. "Sweetness save us, don't you *dare*. Sometimes everyone lives, Abelane. You, me—everyone. Sometimes we fight back and we win. Do you hear me? *We win.*"

Abelane's chest rose and fell, but the rhythm of her breath was slowing, faltering, and Xhea's sense of Lane's ghost, still bound to her body, weakened.

What have I done? She'd been so certain, so sure—and yet, despite her confidence, it seemed that Abelane had been right all along. Right to fear Xhea's talent and her instinctive reach for Abelane's eyes; right to fear the consequences that Xhea had only just begun to grasp. What was the point of freeing her from the Spire if she was just going to die now?

"Abelane." Xhea's voice was low, despairing. "Abelane, please. You have to come back, you can't—"

You can't leave me. She couldn't say the words. *Not like this. Not again.*

Worse, she didn't understand. Had Lissel done something more—something that Xhea had not seen? Abelane's heartbeat was slowing, her breaths growing shallower; and deep within her body, the candlelight glow of her magic dimmed.

What did I take from her? That's all she could think of as she watched Abelane's magic die—that she or Lissel had stolen some part of Abelane's spirit. She would give it back, if she could, whatever she had taken. She'd give some part of herself or her magic if only she knew how. As it was, she could only watch and try not to weep as she struggled to find something, anything that she had missed.

It was growing colder, the chill night wind making her shiver as it stole the sweat from her face and neck. Or perhaps it was only shock that made the summer air feel so cold. The air—and Abelane below her. It seemed almost as if being near to her body, touching her, drew the heat and life from Xhea's hands.

No, Xhea realized suddenly. *Not her body—her collar.*

That ring had been bright to Xhea's eyes, lit by the spells woven through the metal. It was dead now, inert but for a single line of dark power. It was not a powerful spell, not a complex one; Xhea might have woven its dark strands, little though she'd want to. For all that she'd been called callous and uncaring—for all her myriad faults—she never would have made something like this.

The dark spell in the collar was dug deep into Abelane's spirit and drew now on her power, draining it. The bright spells had protected her, Xhea realized; and in leaving the Spire they had been destroyed, whether through design or contact with Lissel's magic, she did not know. Now there was only that dark working tied to her spirit, and it pulled and pulled and gave nothing back.

Desperate, Xhea reached with her weak, strangled magic and snapped the binding thread.

Abelane shuddered, her breath heaving in with a huge, spasming gasp. Her magic, too, surged, flaring brighter as it flowed through her body once more. Abelane's cheeks darkened; flushing, Xhea thought, as her heart and circulation suddenly remembered their jobs and got busy with the work of not dying.

Xhea ran her shaking hands through her hair and sat back heavily. *Too close.* She only wished she had the strength to remove the collar entirely.

Abelane opened her eyes. She blinked in confusion, struggling to see in the dark. She saw Xhea and made to pull away, mouth opening—

And stopped, staring. Her hand flew to her neck and clutched the collar. No magic there, now; only inert metal. Slowly she looked up at the Towers spread across the darkened sky and the magic that moved between them. She turned until she could see the Central Spire, that great pillar of light so far distant.

"Am I dead?" Her hand moved from her neck to her head, then her chest above her heart—places where a tether might be bound. "Is this what it's like? Did you—?"

Xhea shook her head. She couldn't suppress the grin that curled the edges of her lips.

"I'm afraid not." She nodded toward Abelane's hand, resting above her heart. "Your heart's still beating. Lungs still breathing. Just flesh and blood like the rest of us."

Praise absent gods for that.

Xhea wasn't ready for Abelane's reaction: she reached out, grabbed Xhea by the shoulders, and pulled her to her chest in a tight, desperate hug.

"I don't want to hurt you," Xhea protested, trying to pull away. *No more than I already have.* "I don't want—"

"Shut up, Xhea," Abelane muttered, and though Xhea knew her touch had to hurt, Abelane only held her tighter.

Xhea bowed her head to Abelane's shoulder, and Abelane rested her forehead against Xhea's collarbone, and for all the discomfort in that touch, all the strangeness, all the pain, Xhea never wanted to let go. At last she drew back, and rubbed her hands and face to help return the feeling to her numbed skin. Laughing softly, unsteadily, Abelane did the same.

"Don't you ever do that to me again," Xhea said. "No more dying." She'd mourned Abelane too many times already.

"No more trying to kill me."

"Fair enough," Xhea conceded.

"Six years." Abelane shook her head. "I can't believe you actually did it. That you got us out."

"I can't either." The very idea was so preposterous that she couldn't help but laugh—and then she couldn't stop laughing.

She laughed at the idea that they'd escaped from the Spire; she laughed at her own giddiness, and the preposterous realization that she was safe on the ground with Abelane beside her. Abelane who she'd given up for dead a thousand times over; Abelane who she'd believed abandoned her. Xhea laughed and laughed until she sagged helpless on the ground, arms thrown out to either side, staring through tears at the sky.

And, laughing, it all made sense, the pieces clicking together as if they'd always been whole.

The Lower City and its magic, its size and its threat.

The Central Spire's ultimatum—and the Spire itself, not a living creature but a channel for magic.

All the dark magic of the City above, spinning around and around as it was channeled into the ground.

And the gray light from Farrow's struggling heart—bright magic tarnished from its proximity to the ground and the living Lower City, though the newborn Tower still lived.

Xhea laughed and laughed until tears streamed down her cheeks and the ruins around them echoed with the sound. Finally she managed to get control, wiping away her tears, and grabbed her cane so she could make her awkward way to her feet.

"I know how to stop them," she said when at last she could speak. "I know how to save us all."

In the ruins around them, it began to rain.

Part Three

Chapter Twenty

The Lower City had seemed far away. Walking, that distance felt a thousand times farther. As the rain continued, the ground underfoot became treacherous, slick with mud. Their footsteps did not crunch anymore so much as squish, the rain's steady patter punctuated by the miserable clank of the charms in Xhea's hair.

"You're veering again," Abelane told her. Xhea looked up.

It was true. She thought she'd been walking directly toward the Lower City, and yet as she blinked the rain out of her eyes, Xhea realized that the distant shapes of the skyscrapers were no longer in front of her but somewhere to her right. Xhea glared at those small buildings, as if she could make them be closer through sheer force of irritation.

She sighed and corrected her steps.

They'd been walking for a little over an hour, yet it felt like a day, a year, an age. She felt weary and sore and entirely out of sorts, the drenching rain making her clothes hang off her like weights. Even her cane felt too heavy, its slick metal top somehow rubbing a blister onto the inside of her palm.

Abelane had found the broken elevator port and carried it with her, turning it over in her hands every time she paused to let Xhea catch up. Abelane swore the elevator could be fixed. At this point, Xhea didn't care; she wanted to throw the blighted thing into the ruins just so she wouldn't have to look at it anymore.

Xhea bowed her head in an attempt to keep the wind from blowing the rain into her eyes and trudged onward. The world narrowed to the patch of ground before her, rocks and chunks of concrete, weeds bowed by the downpour. Water ran nearby like a small river, rushing alongside what had once been a curb; and if she listened, she could just hear the sound of that river falling and splashing into a deeper pool. A basement, most likely.

Even staring downward, she could feel the Lower City before her, urging her forward, drawing her on. Again she glanced up, correcting her steps, and tried to see her home through the rain.

Something was happening, that much was clear. The skyscrapers were lit, yet so were many of the other buildings in the core, their windows shining in defiance of the night. As she watched, aircars flew over and around the skyscrapers, spell exhaust shimmering behind them like silvery threads.

It reminded her of nothing so much as a dead animal, flies swirling about the bloated body.

Stop that. Whatever had happened, it was not too late. If they could stop the Central Spire's attack, then surely they could find a way to stop the poorer Towers. And if they could not find a way to undo what they had done? *We'll find a way to make them pay.*

The thought kept her marching resolutely forward, heedless of her braced knee's unhappy ache, the chafing of her wet clothes, the squish of her sodden boots.

Marching resolutely forward, Xhea realized, in the wrong direction. Again.

"Sweetness," she muttered. "What's the matter with me?" Because she could feel that pull, could feel where she was supposed to be going, and yet . . .

Xhea hesitated. Stopped. Touched the spelled tether bound to the center of her chest.

Shai?

It was hard to call on her magic; her power felt bruised by its long confinement, and even the new cracks in the binding weren't enough to ease that hurt. Even so, she conjured a whisper of dark, wrapped it around the thought, and sent it down that link.

She felt a surge of something in reply: images, thoughts, feelings, Xhea knew not which. They were all tangled in a way that made no sense to her tired brain. Yet one thing was clear: Shai was closer than she'd thought. Much closer.

Xhea wiped the rain from her eyes and held her wet hand before her, as if Shai's presence were heat that she might feel on her upraised palm. She moved her arm until she felt the stretched-thin length of the tether at the farthest extent of her reach; it pointed not toward the Lower City itself but somewhere to her left. The direction that her steps kept veering.

She sent a sudden wave of welcome and happiness down their link—or tried. Like Shai's sending, it was probably more like a muddled mix of happiness and weariness, mud and fatigue and that faint, desperate hope. *I'm over here*, she tried to say in that wordless way; or maybe, *We might not all die tomorrow!*

It probably just felt like rain.

Even so, Xhea grinned and turned in the direction the tether led. "This way," she said and went tromping forward, leaving Abelane scrambling to catch up. For once.

"What is it?" Abelane asked. "What are you doing?"

"I can feel her," Xhea explained. "My friend. She's this way." At Abelane's blank look, she said, "My bondling."

She didn't like the word, but supposed it was true—or at least a description that Abelane would understand. Abelane just shook her head, her expression darkening. She walked reluctantly in Xhea's wake, the broken elevator port clutched in her white-knuckled hand.

Eyes now on the ruins instead of the brightly lit Lower City, Xhea noticed more. The ruins, too, were lit—but in flashes and flickers, patches dimly glowing as if illuminated by a dying fire's embers. From a distance, she'd thought those lights were only reflections of Towerlight—magic glinting off rain-slicked walls, shimmering in swampy pools. Closer, she could see that they weren't reflections but *people*—encampments, big and small, lit with a thousand small spells.

Closer, there was a light. It seemed at first glance like a single point, but grew as Xhea came nearer. She could feel the tug of that light, as if part of her very self were out there in the ruins; and as the glow brightened and became the shape of a young woman walking some ten feet off the ground, Xhea could not help but smile.

Behind Xhea, Abelane said, "Someone's coming."

"I know." Surely Shai was glowing into the visible spectrum—surely that light was true light, brighter than anything but the lightning that now flickered along the far horizon.

And yet as she said the words, Xhea realized that there was something else. She could hear footsteps—many footsteps—splashing through puddles, squishing through mud. Footsteps grinding against the rocks and rubble, footsteps swishing through the high grasses and weeds.

Slow footsteps, steady footsteps. The step of numerous people walking to the same unwavering beat.

No. Not people.

Xhea stopped. Still Shai came toward her, arms outstretched, walking across the air and shining like magic incarnate. Xhea saw the moment that Shai recognized her, sodden with rain and mud, weeds reaching her waist. She saw Shai's eyes flicker to Abelane, who stood beside Xhea with the elevator port held like a weapon.

Shai saw them both and did not smile, did not wave, only walked. All those footsteps followed.

"I don't . . ." Abelane rubbed her eyes with her free hand. Looked again. "I don't understand what I'm seeing." Xhea could hear her fear.

"Xhea. Are those . . . are they . . . ?"

Even after six years, Abelane knew enough to fear the night walkers—or perhaps her fear had only grown. Again Abelane rubbed her eyes and squinted; confusion creased her brow.

Her eyes, Xhea thought, remembering Torrence's near-blindness after Ieren's attack. Remembering that his eyes had become sensitized to magic.

"What do you see?" she asked quietly.

"I see a woman made of pure light," Abelane said, "and on the ground, people made of shadow."

Xhea blinked, turning. She had always been able to see in the dark, even in places where no light fell; seeing by magic, she now knew. She could see the walkers behind Shai—their gaunt bodies, their ragged and dirty clothes, their hollow-cheeked faces staring upward. Four of them—no, five.

"Shadow?" Xhea asked.

But even as she spoke she shifted her eyes' focus—and understood. Viewed only in magic, she didn't see people following Shai, only shapes of purest black. Absence, pure and absolute, walking toward her in the shape of a woman, the shape of a man. A cluster of human-shaped nothing.

"They've been hollowed out," Abelane said. "I'd seen it, I always knew, but this . . ." She shook her head as if words had left her entirely.

Shai led them closer, until at last Xhea called out: "Is it safe? Will they come after us?"

Unspoken beneath that: *Will they hurt us?* For there was nothing that the walkers could do to Shai; but Xhea and Abelane were flesh and blood. There was no way that Xhea could run—and Abelane? Exhausted as the girl was—sore and disoriented from Lissel's attack, bruised and battered from their unceremonious fall to the ground—Xhea doubted she would get far before a walker caught her.

Only then did Shai pause, then stop altogether. She stood for a moment as if roused from a trance, then lowered her hands to her sides. She was, Xhea saw, weeping.

As one, the five walkers trailing her stopped. They stared at the shining ghost above them, their blank faces rapt.

Even so, Xhea held still, not wanting to move—never mind walk, never mind run—lest she draw their unblinking attention.

Beside her, Abelane had frozen—all but her hands, which trembled. Her breathing was fast and shallow.

"Shai?" Xhea said. Though she pitched her voice to carry, the walkers did not turn at the sound, did not sniff the air to catch her scent; they only stared unerringly at Shai.

"I couldn't save them," Shai said softly. Too softly; the words were almost lost under the sound of the rain.

"Who?" Xhea's heart was suddenly in her throat. She did not see blood on the walkers' hands or clothing—or, at least, no new blood. But it was raining; even fresh blood might be washed away by this steady downpour.

She glanced again at the Lower City—and those glints and glimmers that lit the ruins. She was asking the wrong question, she realized. Not, "Who did the walkers catch and kill?" but, "How many?"

"There were more." Tears ran unchecked down Shai's cheeks. "Twenty at one point, maybe more. I drew them out, drew them away, but the defenders *followed*. They shot them, one by one, and what was I supposed to do?"

She means the walkers, Xhea realized, eyes rounding. She looked again to the five gathered behind Shai, light and rain falling across their upturned faces.

"The people cheered for me, Xhea. I screamed and I wept and I watched them fall, and the defenders cheered for me. Because I saved them from the walkers. Just like I'd wanted to."

Xhea understood.

Shai knew what had been done to create the walkers—knew, too, what had happened to her father, though she rarely wished to speak of it. *I know he's dead*, Shai had told her once. *Truly dead.*

But to let them fall? It was an end, not only to their lives, but to that small, secret hope that Shai had held buried in the ghostly chambers of her heart.

That she might save them.

That she might help them, all of them. That she might let them rest.

"Your father?" Xhea asked quietly.

Shai shook her head. "I didn't see him," she whispered, as if that made it worse.

Beside Xhea, Abelane had begun to shiver. Her arms were pulled tight to her stomach, white-knuckled hands clasped to the elevator port. *Not just fear*, Xhea realized. *Shock.*

"Is it safe?" Xhea asked again.

Shai glanced behind her; she looked at the walkers for a long, slow moment, seeming to see them for the first time. "They're drawn to magic," she said at last. Her words came slowly, as if Shai was returning to herself from a very long way away. "As long as I'm brighter and closer, you should be okay."

Xhea let out the breath she didn't remember holding. "See? It's okay." Only when Abelane looked at her blankly did Xhea remember that seeing Shai's magic did not mean that she could see Shai, or hear her.

Of course. Oh, she was tired. Xhea felt like she could curl up somewhere in the dirt and ruin and sleep, rain and mud and all. She tried to ignore the feeling.

"She says that if we stay back, they won't hurt us."

Shai seemed to truly notice Abelane for the first time. "Xhea, who is . . . ?"

"Shai, this is Abelane." Xhea watched Shai's face—watched as the ghost processed the name and then memory sparked. Her mouth fell open and her magic flickered, her unthinking radiance briefly dimming in her shock.

"Abelane," Xhea continued. "This is Shai."

Shai blinked and recovered enough to write in the air between them, *Hello. I've heard so much about you.*

As if this were a normal introduction, rather than a meeting between Xhea's dead best friend and Xhea's one-time sister who she'd long thought to be dead, a crowd of staring night walkers as audience.

"Hello," Abelane managed. Nothing more. Her gaze flicked from Shai to the walkers and back again in disbelief, as if sure this was a terrible dream from which she might wake. Then she froze, gasping.

Her hands, clenched tight, fell to her sides; the elevator port slipped from her limp fingers and rolled across the uneven ground.

"No," Abelane whispered—and in spite of everything, she moved toward the walkers. It was just a step, but one she seemed to have made without thinking.

"Sandro?" Abelane raised a hesitant, shaking hand toward one of the walkers.

It was a man, little older than Abelane herself. His clothing had once been white—not the gray Spire's uniform that Abelane wore, but a simple shirt and pants that were nonetheless familiar. *Ieren's bondling wore clothing like that,* Xhea realized, remembering the screaming man with his vanishing hands. Little of the cloth's original shade remained; the pants were darkened almost black to the knee, the rest stained and ripped and hanging from a frame hollowed by starvation.

His hair had fallen out in clumps, and his dark skin was ashen. His eyes were like two gray holes in his face. He wore no metal collar; yet when she looked, Xhea could see scarring around his throat that such a collar would have left.

As Abelane moved again, Xhea grabbed for her. "Abelane, no," she hissed.

The walker she had named Sandro stood on the outside edge of the small group. Perhaps the movement drew his attention, or it was only that Abelane's magic was a lure he could not resist— for he looked around, eyes questing. He sniffed as if magic had a scent he might pick from the rain-wet air.

He turned to Abelane.

His blank stare did not change; no life came into his empty expression. Abelane whimpered nonetheless. Her hand, reaching for his face, froze; she pulled it to her chest as if her fingers had been burned.

She said, "Sandro. Sandro, please." There was no hope in that voice, no true plea. She knew what he was.

Only now did Xhea think to wonder how many walkers Abelane might recognize—how many she had once known. Of all the walkers that roamed the ruins, many would have been strangers; many she would have never seen, even as they passed through that small room and were thrown out in a darkened elevator, cast like a rotten seed to the ground.

But she would have friends here. People she had worked with and known; perhaps for years. People she had eaten with, laughed with; people with whom she had struggled through unknown daily horrors, side by side. She would have recognized Ieren's ghost, too, Xhea realized; would have known his name.

Now that she thought to look, Xhea realized that she too recognized one of the walkers. There, on Shai's far side, was a pale-skinned man with his hair cut short, crisscrossed scars marking the expanse of his scalp—one of the older kids' bondlings. No sign, there, of the bruises that had marked the ghost's face; no sign, either, of the young girl that he'd tried so hard to protect.

The walker—the empty creature that had once been Sandro—stepped toward Abelane. Abelane stumbled back. Xhea did not know who Sandro had been to her in life; all she needed to know was written in the horrified lines of Abelane's face.

As the rain fell, glittering in Shai's light, Xhea suddenly understood that in those six years there had been more to Abelane's life than just the dark magic children. More than just those halls, and her responsibilities, and her fears. She, like Xhea, had lived a life the only way she could; she had fought and struggled and loved.

Xhea had thought that this time, finally, no one had been left behind—and she had been wrong. Yes, she and Abelane were both free—but how many other beloved people had Abelane left in the Spire?

The walker took another step, leaving Shai behind.

"Shai? A little help?"

Shai glowed brighter, beams of magic shining from her like sunlight as she attempted to recapture the walker's attention—to no effect. For all that she held four captivated, one walker now had eyes only for Abelane.

Xhea pushed forward, trying to put the older, larger girl behind her—trying, in her growing apprehension, to bid her power to rise. Bound, it had no attraction; even as she forced a thin stream of power up and out through her hand, the walker did not so much as blink.

"They shouldn't—I mean, I didn't think—" Shai's hands twitched, fingers moving as if weaving a spell; none formed. "I was just trying to lead them away from the refugees' encampments."

Xhea spread her arms, shielding Abelane; yet the other girl grabbed her by the shoulders and dragged her back, their footing uncertain on the wet, rocky ground. The walker followed.

"And then what were you planning to do with them?"

"I don't know."

"Well, now might be a really good time to figure it out."

Another step, and this time Abelane stumbled to a stop, Xhea all but colliding with her. Xhea glanced back: a ruined wall spread stretched behind them, its broken edge higher than her head.

The walker came closer.

Step, step, step.

Xhea lifted her cane, held it in both hands. It was her only weapon—and would be useless against a walker.

She looked at the walker and something in his face, something in his eyes . . .

"Shai," Xhea said suddenly. "Give him some magic."

The ghost hesitated, surprised. Xhea had no easy answers; it was only a thought, half-formed, that had wormed its way into her head.

She tried nonetheless. "They're drawn to magic—their spirits have been stolen, and their own magic with them. Maybe they're just hungry."

It was the wrong word, *hungry*, but close enough. Because beneath the walker's slack, blank expression, that's what she imagined she could see: some need that transcended thought or emotion; a wordless wanting that drove him. Him, and all of them.

And they *moved*. They walked. They ate and drank, if poorly. They could, Xhea knew, reach out and grasp things—they could rend and tear—when they should have been helpless. Seeing the emptiness of their bodies, that echoing hollow where a spirit had once resided, Xhea knew: by all rights, these people should be comatose, struggling to even breathe.

There was nothing left of them; spirit and magic had all been torn away. *But perhaps*, she thought, *there's a wound.* How could one's spirit be ripped free and leave no hurt behind?

As the walker raised his hands, Xhea remembered the walker that had reached for her down in the tunnels, months ago. He'd gripped her shoulders as if he meant to tear her apart—and she'd sent her new, uncontrolled magic flowing into him. It had killed him—and yet it had also seemed to ease his pain. The release of death, she'd thought. But what if it had been more?

Shai frowned—and the walker that had once been Sandro grabbed Abelane by the shoulders. Abelane cried out, a sound that had more fear in it than pain—and then again, louder, as the walker's fingers tightened.

Shai's magic struck the walker like a beam of errant sunlight. He froze, Abelane caught in his grip.

Shai sent more power to him, brightening the beam until it seemed he stood lit by a spotlight. That magic shone on him like light—and yet, as Xhea watched, it transformed. Magic flowed over him, not like light but water, banishing the shadows from his cheeks and beneath his eyes, running over his bare arms and across the rain-slicked expanse of his chest.

Magic flowed over him, and sank into him.

The walker—the man—took a long, shuddering breath. His cracked lips parted as if he wished to speak, but all that emerged was a low groan. He blinked, and for a moment Xhea thought she saw something in his face: a flicker of confusion; sadness tightening his eyes, pulling at his mouth's corners.

"Sandro?" Abelane whispered again. She leaned forward, peering at the ruin of his face.

Again he tried to speak, mouth opening as if through movement of lips and tongue he might find a word in the air; as if he might taste it, swallow it down. As if he might ever do anything but walk and stumble and stare, always yearning for that which had been taken from him.

His bound and broken other half.

His fingers loosened from Abelane's shoulders and fell, limp, to his sides. His head sagged, as if his neck had lost all strength.

As his knees buckled, Abelane grabbed him and tried to lower his body to the ground. She fell, and yet she held to him, as if he were the one who might hurt upon landing.

He lay sprawled, staring not at Abelane's face as she bent over him but at the sky above. His lips moved as if he was trying to whisper, but no sound emerged. Shai's magic poured into him until it seemed that he glowed from the inside.

Slowly, slowly, his eyes closed. As they watched, tension left his body, flowing from him as he gave a long, wheezing breath.

For a moment, there was only silence.

"Is he . . . ?" Xhea asked.

But no: he inhaled slowly; and, looking at the hollowed length of his throat, Xhea could see the flutter of his heartbeat.

"No," Shai said. "He's asleep." A sleep, Xhea realized, from which he would not wake.

Bent over that gaunt body, Abelane shuddered and pressed a hand to her mouth. She closed her eyes; she struggled to breathe. But never, not once, did she allow a tear to fall.

The rain slowed.

Xhea watched as Shai moved to the next walker in her dwindling group and poured her magic into him. The walkers did not fight or jostle, only stared, their unrelenting silence broken by the quieting sound of the rain.

In the distance, lights flickered in the ruins—spells, maybe, or spotlights. But the Lower City shone brighter, aircars hovering above it, traveling back and forth to the City with their treasures. Even from so far, it hurt to watch them.

Abelane knelt by Sandro's side, her head bowed. Xhea had found and brought the elevator port back to her. Xhea wondered, if it flared to life once more, brilliant and shining, would Lane let it take her back? Up to the Spire and the life she'd led, the people she'd known; a life more familiar, if no more safe.

Abelane did not look up. She only reached, soft and slow, and pushed the rain-wet tangles of Sandro's remaining hair from his face. He was only sleeping—a sleep that would turn, over the next day or two, to death. No one could last long without water.

Except his breathing was already slower, the pauses between breaths longer. Xhea was so tired; she wanted to lie down against the mud and stone; wanted to close her eyes and rest. Instead she watched as Sandro's breathing faltered.

Kept watching, long after his body had become still.

A long, quiet moment passed.

Abelane did not look up, only said, "Near the end of their lives, the children kill a very many people. Sandro was taken four weeks ago." There was an untold weight in her voice.

At Shai's feet, another walker sagged to the ground.

"Why keep them?" Xhea asked quietly. "When they're dying. When they're killing. Why not let them go?" At what point did the cost of the children's lives outweigh the benefits? How many nobodies did it take to tip those scales?

Xhea looked at Sandro and the walkers gathered around Shai, and thought, *More than this.*

Abelane shrugged, a hopeless gesture. "Some because of their skill, their training. Others, the strength of their magic." At last she turned to Xhea. "Does it matter?"

"No," Xhea said, wishing she had words that might be a comfort. "We're free of them now."

As if anyone could ever be free of the things they'd lived and witnessed. They could only move forward, hoping for a time when memory's sharp edges would be blunted. A time when all the wounds of the heart and the spirit would turn slowly, slowly, into scars.

Chapter
Twenty-One

Shai stood before each of the walkers as if she were in a dream. She looked into their faces; she met their bloodshot, staring eyes. Three men and one woman, one of the men so starved and battered that she could hardly believe he could stand.

She poured her magic into them. Felt as that power flowed through them, filled them; saw their eyes widen, and their mouths try to work. Listened to the sounds they made that were not, could never be, words.

She watched them fall. One by one, they lay on the ground at her glowing, ghostly feet.

Asleep.

Asleep and then . . . gone.

At last, she was finished. It should have been a relief.

Bright magic could kill, she knew the truth of that; and she had given each more than a mere spark. More, truly, than any Lower City dweller might bring to bear, even if they scrimped and saved. More than a City citizen would want to spend.

As if death, or the rest it might represent, needed to be purchased.

Shai bowed her head. She was not crying; her tears had stopped some time ago. Somehow, that made it worse.

She should cry for these people, whoever they had been. She did not know them, would never know them; could only guess at the years that had been their lives. But she knew without question that they deserved better than this, left to rest in the cold mud, abandoned.

Rest, she thought again. It was a death gentler than that which might be earned with blades or bullets or in tearing, ripping spells.

They deserved better, and yet she'd given them all that she had. But it had not, in the end, felt like a gift. Neither had it felt like killing.

It had only felt like an ending.

Shai turned back to where Xhea waited, and she tried not to think of her father.

Xhea had fallen asleep, leaning against a broken wall. Her head was thrown back at an uncomfortable angle, and the dark tangle of her hair hung over one shoulder. The strange young woman sat perched on the wall above her, looking only at Xhea.

Abelane, Shai thought. Even thinking the name felt a surprise.

It wasn't that she hadn't believed Abelane had existed; yet now, seeing her here, Shai did not know what she had expected. Not this woman, young and bent and tired all at once. Not that long, wet hair, or the sodden blue Spire uniform; not even the way she looked at Xhea as she slept, as if she did not know whether the girl was a gift or curse.

Or perhaps it was only that Abelane had been a figure from Xhea's stories, someone idealized in thought and memory, when in reality she was just a person.

Abelane glanced up as Shai approached, squinting as if Shai's light hurt her eyes, and then looked back to Xhea. Yet Shai did not expect the words that followed.

"I'm sorry for what she's done to you," Abelane whispered. Her eyes did not stray again from Xhea's face, but Shai knew that the words were meant for her. She frowned, knowing that Abelane wouldn't be able to see the expression, and moved closer.

As if that movement was a reply, Abelane continued. "She doesn't understand what she's done by binding you. Doesn't understand what it will mean for you." A pause, then the woman laughed, a thin and tired sound. "And maybe I don't really either, but I've seen enough. Far more than either of you."

Shai wrote in the air, *She has not hurt me. Would not hurt me.*

"Perhaps not intentionally."

Abelane reached out to brush away the strand of rain-wet hair that stuck to Xhea's forehead—and then hesitated, drew back. Even so, Shai felt a twist of jealousy. For all that Abelane could not touch Xhea without discomfort, she could touch her, flesh to flesh, whole and real.

She's my friend, Shai wrote. *She's my family.* Both words felt true and right—and yet they were too small to encompass the entirety of her feeling. Friend. Family. As if either were large enough to say the whole of what Xhea was to her, little though she understood it herself.

She could see that Abelane did not understand—or, understanding, still thought Shai a fool.

"The binding," Abelane said. "It forces Xhea's will upon you—makes her will into yours." As if Shai's affection were coerced; as if trust or loyalty could be taken by force, or love twisted from her heart like water wrung from a rag.

Shai shook her head. *No. I have been unbound, the link between us cut. Three times I was alone, and three times I chose Xhea.*

Abelane glanced at Shai, but her expression was different, almost a recognition of futility. She seemed to swallow back her reply.

A pause, then: "It will kill her, you know. Even weak, even bound, this magic will kill her. But it will destroy you first. Everything you are, she'll take from you, whether she wants to or not."

Abelane tried to meet Shai's eyes. "My job was caring for dark magic children. Kids far younger that Xhea, and far more powerful. I can't see ghosts, but I know what's done to them before the end. People the children loved, sometimes. She will take and take and give you nothing in return."

Then, infinitely softer: "Love is not a defense with one such as her. It is only a knife, and it will twist deep before the end."

Shai looked at her, this woman who was once Xhea's everything, and did not know what she felt. Abelane was not trying to cause hurt, Shai realized; she was not trying to pry Xhea from Shai, no matter that it felt that way. She was only afraid. Afraid of what Xhea had become, what she'd done, and what she might do. Afraid, in some way, for Shai.

Maybe Abelane was right. Shai and Xhea had spoken at length about the link they'd formed, though neither knew the truth of it; it was so new, a joining but weeks old. There was so much they did not know.

But Shai looked at Xhea and could not bring herself to pull away, nor to nurture that thin thread of fear into something that would build a barrier between them.

Shai said only, *I hope that you are wrong.*

Maybe this woman knew Xhea when she was younger; maybe she knew children who had Xhea's power—but she did not know Xhea now and she did not know Shai. Did not understand any part of what they'd created together.

And it was true that Xhea took from her; Shai felt the faint, steady pull of the spelled tether even now, drawing some essential part of her away. But even bound, some part of Xhea flowed back to Shai down that link. Magic, yes, but something else, something deeper. Shai believed that, for all that her very self was bound to Xhea, so was Xhea's spirit bound to her.

Shai moved to wake Xhea, but Abelane held up her hand.

"Wait." Abelane raised something on the flat of her outstretched palm. It was a moment before Shai recognized it as a wet and slightly battered elevator port. "Can you fix this?"

Shai hesitated, then peered closer.

One look at the remaining spelllines and Shai knew what had been done; she could see the unique degradation of both the magic and metal casing that spoke of dark magic. Despite that damage, only a few key guiding spells had been snapped; the whole had not unraveled.

Xhea's control is getting better, Shai thought; or maybe it was that she had only a thin thread of power instead of an unbound torrent. Either way, the port could be fixed—even reprogrammed.

She had not been able to create a working such as this, but as Shai studied the lines of intent that remained and their stabilizing anchors, she understood where she had gone wrong. Carefully she added her repairs, watching how each added to the whole, and memorizing its shape so that she might recreate it. A moment more, and she refueled the empty storage coil that fueled it.

She drew back.

"Thank you," Abelane said, and rose.

Shai watched, eyes widening, as Abelane made to activate the elevator port. And yet she looked back to Xhea, hesitated, and then gave a small, shuddering sigh.

As one, Abelane and Shai said, "Xhea, wake up."

Abelane stood back as Xhea opened her eyes and pushed herself to her feet. She muttered about the ground's poor comfort and the foolishness of falling asleep—words that neither Abelane nor Shai truly listened to.

Shai saw Abelane holding the repaired elevator port behind her back, fingers tense. Abelane tried to smile and nod as Xhea spoke of her plan to return to the Lower City—her plan, she said, to save them all.

"Look," Abelane said at last, holding out the elevator port to show its blinking lights. "It works again."

"I fixed it," Shai said quietly.

Xhea looked from one to the other, and did not speak.

Abelane broke the silence. "I can't do this. I can't go with you." She held her hand flat before her, as if it was an explanation; it was shaking. She was sweating, Shai realized, and her skin looked far too pale.

Xhea seemed to notice none of these things. She stiffened at the words, as if Abelane had slapped her—and Shai watched as that sharp, sudden shock bled into anger.

"Xhea," Shai said, understanding—and wanting to interrupt the argument before it started. "She's afraid."

Xhea just glanced at Shai, yet Shai understood the question nonetheless.

"Of you, yes, but mostly of all the rest. Think of what she's walked into." A pause, then, "I know where Edren's encampment is. They have spelled walls, they have food, and I'm sure they have work that she could do. She could even help protect Edren's children.

"It's not about you, Xhea," Shai added softly, and hoped that her words were true. "We're going to the besieged Lower City on the dawn of the Spire's attack with no plan, no allies, nothing. Who in their right mind would want to come with?"

Xhea laughed at that; the sound was tight. But she nodded and looked back to Abelane.

The woman stood with her brow creased in worry; she knew that Shai had been speaking and had no sense of her words. She all but sagged in relief when Xhea told her, "You should go somewhere safe."

The rest was only details: Shai's map to Edren's encampment, Abelane testing the elevator's new controlling spells, discussions of who to find and what to say. At last the spell ribbons arced up and over Abelane, enclosing her in an opaque, white bubble. It rose.

A moment, and then Xhea turned away, looking to the light of the Lower City. Only Shai watched the elevator as it skimmed over the ruins until it vanished. Some part of her was glad to see Abelane gone.

Then Shai turned, returning to Xhea's side, and they planned their return to the Lower City.

If Shai had missed the underground—and she had, strange as it seemed—she had not missed the tunnels.

"Ugh," she said, staring down the long, dark length of what Xhea insisted was the perfectly stable Yellow Line subway tunnel.

"It's an express line," Xhea said. "Runs deep and straight. At this end there's hardly any flooding."

"Hardly any is not the same as none."

Xhea shrugged. "It was just raining. What do you expect?"

Sure enough, the tunnel roof was patterned with rivulets of water, some running along the tunnel's curved ceiling, others dripping to widening puddles on the ground. Nearest the tunnel entrance—marked by a wide bridge, mostly standing, where the trains had surfaced—the tracks had long since been dragged away; yet within sight of her light, Shai could see rails where the tunnel deepened, descending underground. The ground itself was flat, made of gravel, and covered with decaying leaves.

The Yellow Line, Xhea had explained, ran directly into the Lower City through Rown's territory. It was the deepest of the tunnels, and while within the core it was often flooded to impassibility, it would bring them close to the underground tunnels that they needed. Close to the Lower City's heart—or, barring that, Farrow.

It was a good approach—faster and easier than walking through the ruins. Even so, just stepping inside the mouth of the tunnel made Shai wrinkle her nose at the smell.

Xhea, seemingly oblivious, tromped forward.

As Xhea walked, Shai spread her hands and wove the beginnings of an elevator spell. It was delicate work—far more delicate than the brute-power spells she'd managed to date. To make matters more difficult, she was attempting to create the spells without the physical structure of the elevator port to support the anchors, while simultaneously trying to modify the spell to their needs.

Frowning over her work, Shai said, "Tell me the rest of your plan."

Xhea told Shai what she had seen: the dark magic of the City above swirling toward the Spire in a vortex of power. The Spire, Xhea explained, was not alive, only a channel for magic.

"Everything seems to make dark magic, if only in small quantities—part of the spell exhaust, I think. Part of the power itself, like a balance to so much light. Because bright magic might be the power of life, but there is no life without death, right? There's nothing that lives that does not die."

Shai looked down at her ghostly hands and the half-woven spell within her cupped palms; she glowed as if she were made only of light. There was no darkness, there; no shadow.

She had no more than opened her mouth to dispute Xhea's claim than she thought of the way that magic now flowed between them. Filtered by that link, Shai's magic and ghostly essence stabilized Xhea, fed her in a way that mere food could not—and Shai? Unbound, she had all but lost her magic entirely, before the link to Xhea—and the power that came to her through it—brought it rushing back.

Each a balance, one to the other.

Yet if that were true, where was the balance in the City? Like her, it was made only of bright magic; bright magic its foundations and its walls, its power and its life.

Xhea was still talking. "So they take all that waste power, and they dump it down here. I don't think they realized that it, too, could create a living being. And why would they? The Lower City was almost dormant—until Farrow fell, anyway.

"But all that dark magic that they pour on us, night after night. What if we gave it back? Repel the dark power and let them deal with it."

From everything that Xhea had seen, there was no reason that channel couldn't work both ways. They could funnel all the dark magic of the Lower City up through the Spire and out into the City beyond.

"Poison the Towers?" Shai asked, incredulous. "All of them?"

Right now, she wouldn't mind if the people of the poorer Towers faced retaliation—and knew that those she saw here, stealing and scavenging on the ground, would only be the most visible set of culprits.

She thought, too, of her conversation with Allenai: its massive complexity, its strange understanding of the world, the purity of its joy. Though they profited, the Towers themselves were ignorant of many of the their inhabitants' choices; and she shied away from the thought of making them needlessly suffer.

Xhea said, "Think of Farrow. It's alive, isn't it?"

"It's dying," Shai countered.

"But not because of the Lower City. Not because of the dark magic."

"Its heart is tainted." She had felt that, holding it in her hands: the otherworldly shiver of its magic across her palms, its softly golden radiance turned gray. It had not hurt—yet it had not felt quite right, either.

Was it wrong? Shai asked herself. *Tainted, poisoned? Or just different?*

"And if the Towers became tainted, what then?" Xhea asked. "What do you think will happen?"

"Well, obviously something that they're concerned about, otherwise they wouldn't be dumping the magic in the first place." Even so, Shai considered.

Dark magic in a Tower—a tainted heart—would mean, what? Her mind went right to the people: any dark magic in their surroundings would affect the Towers' citizens—tainting not just their magic, but the health and long life and prosperity that they took for granted. The people of the Lower City had lived in close proximity to a high concentration of that power—but for all that they were poor and sickened and died, she would not have said that it was only the dark magic that made them suffer.

If not the people, then what? It might hurt the workings, perhaps—the internal structures of the Towers that supported people's lives and luxuries; it might affect their defenses, or perhaps the Tower's ability to shape and reform itself.

Or was it simpler than that? Dark magic unmade light, as surely as bright could burn away dark. Combined, even in such small quantities, the magic would be less powerful. To keep any amount of dark magic was tantamount to throwing away renai—unraveling the very fortunes upon which lives in the City were based.

Lives, Shai thought, and economics. And politics. Always, always politics.

"I think it would be a disruption," Xhea said when Shai explained her thoughts. "But I don't think anyone would die.

And the Lower City is bigger and stronger than any of the Towers. Maybe we can't stop the Spire or the Towers themselves—but *it* can. If it wants to. If it knew that it could."

"You need to speak to it, then. Convince it."

"Not convince it," Xhea said. "But . . . show it. I don't know what I could say, but there's so much it doesn't understand."

Shai understood; she'd spoken now with a Tower. She remembered that feeling of opening herself up and all her truths pouring out—little good that it had done in the end. If Xhea could just reach the Lower City and connect with its heart, it could learn what stood against it—and what it might do to defend itself.

They walked in quiet for some time, though the tunnel around them was anything but silent. Water dripped, and Xhea's hair chimed, and the gravel beneath Xhea's feet crunched with every step.

Give the magic back. Xhea's idea was simple, and yet . . .

"If the Lower City sent all the dark magic back to the City above," Shai said slowly, "how would it live?"

Because that magic was the Lower City's body and soul, its blood and breath and life. To stop the flow of dark power to the ground—to send it back—would leave the Lower City no better off than Farrow: sickly and starved, slowly dying.

"Sweetness," Xhea muttered. "I don't know."

Shai frowned. "Or would it just reverse the flow for a day, an hour?"

"A night," Xhea replied absently—and stopped dead in her tracks. She turned to Shai. "The dark magic only flows at night. And the Spire attacks tomorrow."

"How long is it before dawn?"

Xhea didn't bother to reply.

If Xhea could have run, she would have. As it was, she pushed to the edge of what her body could handle: her breath came short, her limp more pronounced, and sweat beaded across her already damp forehead.

"Here," Shai said at last. "Stop a minute."

She held out her hand and the elevator spell bloomed from her palm. Xhea's eyes widened as bright ribbons of magic arced up and around her. Shai felt the sudden tug on her magic that meant that Xhea was trying to compress her own power as tight as she could.

As spells went, it wasn't beautiful. It was, if anything, slightly crooked; and as it lifted Xhea unsteadily into the air, jerking and sputtering, it leaned precariously to one side. Xhea, clinging to her cane, looked alarmed.

But they didn't need it to lift her very far from the ground—a few inches above the tracks and flooded sections would be high enough. Shai controlled the spell's speed and direction. Even so, Xhea yelped as the spell leapt forward.

In her mind, Shai tried to measure distance. She did not know this tunnel, its markings or its curves. *How long until we reach the Lower City?* The tunnel descended, deeper and deeper, and soon the tracks beneath them were lost under a foot of stagnant, swampy water. Shai wrinkled her nose, pushing the spell faster.

Then, ahead, there was a glimmer of light—true light. Shai's brow creased in confusion as they drew closer, and she tried to make sense of what she saw.

"Xhea," Shai said, and only then did the girl look up.

In front of them, the flooding did not end; it had been filled in. There was a hole in the tunnel roof—a hole, and just beyond it, no tunnel at all. Rubble filled the tunnel from side to side, a great mound of dirt and concrete that created a long sloping incline before them. The smell of dust and smoke was suddenly strong in her nose.

"I thought you said this tunnel was safe."

"I did." Xhea's voice was quiet, so quiet. "It was."

Carefully, Shai set Xhea down on that pile of rubble, banishing her spell. Xhea steadied herself and took a step forward. Another. Her eyes had gone wide.

"What is this?" Shai asked. "What happened?"

Xhea walked forward as if in a dream, her steps unsteady even with the cane's aid. Partway up that slope she paused, bending so that she could touch the rubble before her. Concrete blown to dust and ashes, Shai thought—all of it wet with rain, clumping together and clinging to Xhea's fingers as she dug.

Beneath that surface, Xhea found a bit of metal, a small fragment of wood. She fished out a shard of what seemed to be flooring tile and held it before her, turning it over slowly before letting it fall back to the pile.

Xhea straightened and looked to where the pre-dawn light now filtered down from the hole in the tunnel roof, the rubble leading toward it like a huge, uneven ramp. She took a step, and another, until she stood beneath that hole. A band of dim light fell upon her face, illuminating her features, slack with horror.

She did not speak, could not speak.

"What is it?" Shai asked. "Xhea? What's happened?"

"It's . . ." Xhea hesitated, swallowed. Tried again. "It *was* . . . Rown."

Chapter Twenty-Two

Xhea staggered up the ragged incline, smelling smoke and dust and rain-wet earth, hoping she was wrong. Knowing she was not.

She had to crawl the last few steep steps, clinging to her cane. She rolled onto the ground beyond, then pulled herself away from that gaping hole. Sat and stared at Rown.

Or, rather, where Rown had once stood.

Where that dark, hulking mass of a skyscraper had been, blockish and battered, there was only rubble. It made a small mountain, its long sloping sides crushing other, smaller buildings that had yet to fall. No wires in that mess, though; no rebar. If she were to sift through that broken pile stone by stone, she knew she would find no sign of a storage coil, no jewelry, no plants or organic materials of any kind.

Such things a Tower might use. Of the rest, there was only dust.

Xhea pushed herself to her feet, staring. She felt like she could not breathe.

Magic still glittered on some of the pieces before her—anchors for the spells that had brought the skyscraper down, collapsing it floor by floor, or those that had sorted through the pieces, claiming the good from the bad and letting the rest fall.

She stepped closer. Something dark pooled on the wet pavement before her. Oil, perhaps, or fuel.

No blood, she thought, the words a prayer. If the poorer Towers had planned on bringing down the skyscraper, surely they had emptied it first; surely Rown's citizens were all out in the ruins somewhere, huddled together against the rain.

But, knowing Rown, they had not been.

In the Lower City, a skyscraper meant life—but to Rown's citizens, their skyscraper had been more. Rown took those broken by life or circumstance and gave them a home—a community—when no one else would.

Or they had.

Being part of Rown was like a religion, or so she'd been told. Loyalty was like blood and breath there, the good of the skyscraper their unthinking mantra. To abandon those walls, that hard-won territory? Many would choose death first.

Xhea walked on, climbing, and it was not the broken ground that made her unsteady.

She felt as Shai followed, rising into the empty air; felt the ghost's shock and horror, twin to her own. They did not speak. What was there to say?

Xhea looked up. Atop nearby buildings, she could see landed aircars, people moving. One structure, a low warehouse that had once stood behind Rown, already glittered with a pale network of spells, ready to come down. Above, the cloud-covered sky had gone from black to darkest gray, while the Towers danced against that empty backdrop.

"There won't be anything left," Shai whispered at last.

Nothing for the Spire to destroy; nothing for them to save.

From the Lower City's far side came the low thump of an explosion, then the roar of a building falling. It echoed through the city streets like thunder, deafening; the buildings around her trembled with the impact. A moment, then a great cloud of dust bloomed above Senn's territory.

They can't do this. Xhea realized that she was gritting her teeth so hard that her jaw ached, and her hand was wrapped into a white-knuckled fist around the top of her cane. *They can't do this*, she thought, but demonstrably she was wrong. There came another low thump that felt like a punch to her gut, another cloud of dust rising, and somewhere in the Lower City another building fell.

Too late, she thought; *Too slow—*

But already she was running, or trying to, forcing her tired leg to hold her as she rushed down the rock-strewn street toward the burned-out market, and the dark magic heart that lived beneath it.

The streets were deserted. Doors stood wide, and windows were thrown open, unbarred, unshuttered. Laundry hung from snapped lines, the precious clothing dangling into the alleys below.

Behind her, Shai wove another elevator spell—but slowly, so slowly, and Xhea couldn't stand to wait. She walked and with every jarring step she grew angrier. No words to shape that anger, nor the need to speak it; it only swelled within her, and her magic tried to rise on that tide.

The binding felt like wire bands dug deep into her flesh, cutting into her, making her bleed; it constricted her every breath, the beat of her heart, the movement of her limbs. And despite its cracks and the thin wisps of magic that escaped, it held.

Xhea stumbled from the pain, gasping, and caught herself with her cane. She grabbed the wall of a nearby building, pushing herself up, scraping her palm bloody against the rough brick. Her magic pushed against its bonds, writhing and fighting, and the spell did not yield. She wept with the pain, with the rage, and staggered onward.

Some part of Rown's territory still stood; these streets with their low buildings and reclaimed shops had never been the most prosperous. There was more damage as she moved toward Senn's territory—broken Senn, burned Senn, its one-time riches in ashes across the ground.

Senn itself remained standing, its smoke-stained sides whole—but the rest? Xhea turned a corner and found a whole stretch of Senn's territory just . . . gone. It might have been a bomb site. Only piles of rubble remained.

And Edren? She could not see the ancient hotel from where she stood, or Edren's arena; she could not see any part of their territory. *And Orren?* From that direction, she heard shouts and laughter and the sound of something grinding, stone on stone.

The market, she thought. *Just get to the market.* If she could reach Farrow—if she could touch its living sides, all that twining black—she could speak to the Lower City. She could make it understand. There was still time, she could—

Another explosion rocked the streets, echoes reverberating, and a cloud of dust rushed skyward from Orren's territory. The sound rang in Xhea's ears. The buildings around her trembled, shaking free small pieces of stone and brick and concrete that smashed on the ground. Xhea made a sound, low and pained— she brushed the tears from her cheeks, angrily, messily—and kept walking.

"Almost got it," Shai said, holding aloft her new elevator spell—but she, too, wept. Her ghostly fingers slipped and fumbled with the spell lines.

Just get to the market.

"People in the street!" came a call from nearby. Xhea stopped and stood swaying, shivering, looking around as she attempted to pinpoint the speaker.

A sentry.

Another voice called in reply.

She followed the sound, and there they were: sentries on the rooftops and balconies of the nearby buildings.

The bridges that had once spanned from roof to roof had been cut away. The laundry lines and prayer flags were likewise gone, cut or left to hang, limp and dirty, from broken railings.

She thought she saw a body, too, in one of those alleys, limp and unresponsive. She did not look closer.

Xhea looked from one sentry to another, watching their weapons rise. They held this territory safe not from the Lower City dwellers anymore, she realized, nor from any fear of the walkers, but from each other.

Shai abruptly cut her light, dulling her natural radiance to a faint glow. But they had already been spotted.

"This is claimed territory!" called one. "By right of Tower Helta, I order you to turn around."

By right of Tower Helta? Xhea's magic strained against its bonds. *This is my home.*

Other sentries took up the call, repeating the threat even if they could not see her, a small girl in the middle of the empty street. They named other Towers in other voices: Lozan, Elemere, Jhen, Tolair. The names meant nothing to her; she blocked them out.

Xhea said only, "Shai?" Her voice strained and quiet.

"Ready." The elevator spell bloomed.

Xhea did not see who fired upon her, or only fell, screaming, to the street. The elevator strands wrapped around her, bright, glittering—and repelled the spells that attempted to surround her. The air burned, smelling sharp and metallic like the wake of a lightning strike.

Shai's elevator enclosed her and lifted her up. But it wasn't just an elevator anymore, and at last Xhea understood Shai's delay: it was elevator and shield both.

"Are you hurt?" Shai was saying from outside that bubble. "Xhea, talk to me!"

Xhea licked her lip, tasting blood. "I'm okay," she managed, and tried to send reassurance down their link. But all she felt was anger—anger and fear, one twisting into the other until she did not know which made her hands shake or her breathing shudder in her chest; did not know which bid her magic to rise. Thin streamers of black lifted now from her skin, and for all that they were faint and weak, they sizzled against the bright ribbons of the spell around her.

Another shot hit the exterior of that spell with a sharp crack, and Xhea shuddered from the impact.

"I should have done them separately," Shai was saying in distress, not seeming to realize that she was speaking aloud. "I should have—"

"Shai, hurry," Xhea said, and Shai pushed the spell forward.

They skimmed across the broken streets, through the rain-wet rubble and damaged buildings.

The market, Xhea thought again, the words a mantra. *Just get to the market.* As if once she reached the ring of burned structures—as if once she stood in Farrow's shadow—everything else would stop. No buildings falling around her, no loss of everything she had ever known—no attack coming on the heels of dawn's light.

No one shooting at her in the blighted streets of her own home.

Get to Farrow, she thought, as if those words could drown out the others that echoed through her mind, their chorus deafening: *Too late, too late, too late.*

In the distance, she saw glimpses of Edren and Orren: the peak of dark Orren, its broken crown of girders stabbing upward; and, briefly, the top few floors of Edren, the former hotel.

Each had been, if not her home, then her one-time shelter. Memories crowded within those walls, good and bad and in-between. Her stomach twisted as she saw spells covering both structures—spells that glittered across their façades like stars pulled from the darkened sky, faint lines between those bright points like the markings of constellations.

They stood, but not for long.

Then the market was before her, a stretching wasteland of burned-out black. The elevator slowed.

Nothing new there; even the ghosts had fled this place. No sign of sentries—no sign, even, of the poorer Towers' presence. There was only Farrow. Xhea imagined that whatever resources of value might pulled from Farrow's walls would be mitigated by the cost of drilling through the Lower City's twining embrace—and the effects of the dark magic that infused those vines.

Even so, she felt exposed as they crossed that open stretch. At last Shai set her down at Farrow's base and allowed the modified spell to disperse. A moment, then another flared above Xhea—brighter, stronger, and infinitely simpler. A shielding spell, like the one Shai had used to protect the market.

"I'll watch over you," Shai said. She shone, her eyes fierce and angry for all their tears, and Xhea had the sudden feeling that everything could fall—Farrow and the market, the whole of the Lower City—before Shai let anything cross that barrier.

Xhea reached for Farrow.

Beneath her fingers, the smooth, black surface of Farrow's side vibrated. She could hear the living Lower City's song if she listened—it shivered in the air around her—and yet it was so hard to let herself fall into its rhythms. Her heart was too loud, her breathing too ragged; she leaned forward, resting her head against those black vines, and conjured calm.

Steady, she told herself. *Focus*.

It hurt to call her magic. She'd thought of her power as a cold, dark lake, as a smooth, hard stone—yet those images were wrong. A lake could not be bound by chains of power; a stone could not bleed. And she felt as if she were bleeding; the ribbons of power that slipped through the cracks felt not so much like magic escaping, but some part of her draining away.

Still she called upon that power, drawing it up past the pain and sending it into the dark structure that held Farrow aloft. Into the living Lower City.

I'm here, she whispered. *Hear me*.

Her thin stream of magic flowed into the entity below and all around her. The Lower City's song was louder now, clearer, seeming to echo not from the air but from the corners of her mind, surging through her like a second heartbeat.

Hear me, she said, but it did not. There was only that song, echoing on and on.

Xhea pulled harder on her magic, fighting the bindings. She needed more magic, stronger magic. If she couldn't even get the living Lower City to hear her, she had no chance of telling it what she'd learned—no chance of making it understand.

The effort made her gasp, the pain of the bindings twisting inside her as if the spell was a blade, seeking her heart. But her power rose—darker, blacker, as if it had been stained by her blood—and she poured it into the living Lower City.

Once she had been oblivious to the Lower City's song, no matter that it had surrounded her, waking and asleep; now she tried to clear all else from her mind, as if the whole world had been reduced to that sound. No pavement below her, no cool, damp air; no sound of buildings falling, one after the other, to the broken ground.

Please, Xhea said. *You have to listen. Can you hear me?*

But that song, she realized, had changed. Where once it had seemed slow and constant, its rise and fall speaking of sleep and stability and the slow turn of seasons, it was now quick and hard and faltering. Again there came the sound of an explosion, a hard clap like thunder directly overhead, and again the Lower City's song rose, the sound low and aching. Almost a groan.

It's hurting, she realized. She remembered its pain when Farrow had been torn from the ground; remembered, too, the pain of the market fire and the line that Rown's weapon had scored across its living heart. No weapon had been turned upon it yet—not directly—but it hurt nonetheless.

The living Lower City was part of these buildings. Its magic and awareness filled each structure in the Lower City core, each skyscraper and warehouse, each apartment and shopping complex and stretch of broken ground.

Now they were falling. One by one they were falling, and the entity felt each loss the way she might feel the loss of a finger or a toe, her hair ripped out by its roots. If those wounds, those losses, were not enough to kill it, they were nonetheless enough to fill almost the whole of its awareness.

Yet at last, Xhea felt a shiver of recognition. Some small part of the living Lower City's attention turned toward her, and it heard in her magic what she felt—the shock and horror of seeing the rubble that had been Rown, the helpless pain of watching the buildings fall. It song swelled in acknowledgment.

Listen, Xhea said, *you have to listen—*

But somewhere, a bright magic spell was tearing a structure apart, brick from brick, walls from foundation, and the living Lower City turned away.

There was a sound; Xhea opened her eyes to see that the black vines beside her hand had once again parted and a small space waited just beyond. She took a deep breath. The Lower City could protect her, she knew—it could draw her down into the underground as surely as it had opened that passage for her to rise to Farrow, no matter how weak her magic.

And, weak, she needed to go closer. She needed to be *there*, right by its living heart, if she was to have any chance of convincing it to fight back. It, too, wanted her there—for the comfort of her presence, it seemed, as everything fell apart.

She turned to Shai, and she did not have to speak. The ghost only looked at her, and said, "No." No discussion, no opportunity for rebuttal: only that flat, hard denial.

"No?" Xhea shook her head. "What do you mean, no?"

Shai shook her head, the magic of her shield a shimmering veil between them. "I mean we're too late, Xhea. Too slow. There's no way we can stop them anymore."

Xhea glanced up past the shielding spell, only just realizing that her attempt at communication may have taken more than the bare minute it had felt. Above, the sky was not black anymore, not darkest gray, but a pale shade that spoke of dawn's approach. Towerlight still shimmered, countless shades of gray that mixed and clashed and faded one into the other. Towers rose and Towers fell, and the City spun on, oblivious.

It was the power between those Towers that Xhea sought—power so faint that even she struggled to see its presence. All those wisps of dark magic swirling toward the Central Spire, that spinning vortex. She turned, and there was the column of black falling from the Spire's lowermost point, a great waterfall of magic that cascaded down and blanketed them all.

There's still time, Xhea thought. *Time to send it back, time to make them pay.* She raised a defiant hand, meaning to show Shai—

But even as she watched, those faint streamers of power thinned; the vortex slowed. And that column of power—the one that, over and over, she had imagined surging back into the City in a huge, powerful blast—trickled slowly, slowly, to nothing.

Around her, the scavenging Towers did their work, taking the Lower City apart piece by piece and claiming the poor treasures found within. The buildings were crushed, they crumbled and fell, and the living Lower City cried out, its song one of pain and loss.

If that song had words, it would only be the one that Shai had spoken; the one that echoed even now through Xhea's heart: *No. No, no, no.*

Even so, she said, "We have to save it."

"Xhea, no." Shai pushed the shield wide and reached for her, struggling to hold Xhea's shoulders, to draw Xhea toward her. "We have to go. There's nothing left to save!"

"You're wrong," Xhea said, because it was *here*, it was right here. The Lower City was the ground beneath her feet, it was the buildings as they were falling. It was singing and singing and she was not going to let it die. Not now. Not after everything.

But dawn was coming.

Xhea looked over Shai's shoulder at the Spire and she could see no change—no new surge of magic, no sign of a spell building—and yet she did not know what to look for. Three days, they had said; they had to have meant three full days. Surely the Spire would not attack until sunset.

She did not know. Oh, she did not know.

"I have to get closer," she said instead, glancing back to that small space opened within Farrow's supporting vines. "It'll hear me then. I have to go toward its heart."

Even the thought of it drew her: all that dark power, magic incarnate. She remembered its pull urging her forward without thought or reason; remembered its welcome, that comforting darkness.

"It will kill you," Shai said. She was not wrong. "And for what?"

"Because," Xhea said—and her words vanished.

"Because," she tried again, and struggled, fighting to give shape to what she felt. If she screamed and screamed, perhaps that would express some small part of what burned inside her, the rage and the hurt and the injustice of it all. She took those feelings and made to wrap them in magic and push them down the tether to Shai, raw and fierce and true.

But no. Even Shai did not need that from her, no matter its truth.

"Because no one else will," she said instead. "Not now, not ever. This." Xhea pointed to the destruction around them. "This is what they do. They kill and they wound and they maim. They tear away people's souls and think it just. They bind people to their walls for their power, their luxury, and think that the pain of a few is sufficient coin to buy the happiness of the many."

They. Did she mean the Central Spire, the Towers—the whole of the City above? All of them, none of them.

"How long, Shai?" Xhea whispered, her voice breaking. Her heart breaking. "How long have they been doing this?" The city that had come before was in ruins; its ancient bones were even now falling. A hundred years. A thousand. An age of life and death, and beneath it all, this misery.

"How long will we let them continue?"

"We cannot stop them," Shai said. "Not the whole of the City." She said it as if the City were the whole of the world, the whole of everything—and maybe she was right.

"No," Xhea said. "But we could try."

She met Shai's eyes, and just . . . looked at her. She had such perfect eyes, pale silver to her vision, and brimming now with tears. She was, Xhea thought, the most beautiful person she'd ever known.

See me, Xhea thought. If anyone could see her and understand her tangled truths, it was Shai. Her truest and unlikeliest of friends. The light to her dark. The missing piece of her hurt and broken heart.

Because Xhea could not turn away. She could not stop, could not flee. She would rather die attempting to save what little was left than know she had stopped trying.

Was that weakness? She could not pretend it was strength or bravery. But it was the only way she knew how to be.

Shai wept then, those tears spilling over and cascading down her cheeks, bright, glittering—because she knew. Oh, she knew. She clung to Xhea's shoulders, or tried to; she bowed her head, sobbing, as if she might rest her forehead against Xhea's own.

At last she straightened and met Xhea's eyes.

"Okay," she whispered. "I'm with you."

Shai's acceptance should have been a relief—and it was. Yet it was a weight, too, that settled on Xhea's shoulders and bowed her neck, and when her hands shook it was not from fear or anger, but something she could name only dread.

Xhea did not long for death; did not court it, for all that her behavior drew her time and again to death's door. If she could, she would grab for a life like she'd always dreamed: a life of leisure and luxury, of long sleep and plentiful food. A life like the ones people lived in the Towers.

Xhea looked at the people tearing apart the buildings around her—she thought of the walkers, blank-faced, falling—and she thought, *No. Not like the Towers.*

It wasn't just that she did not know what she would do with herself if she had nothing to do but nap and eat and lounge, for all that she ached for such rest now. It was that she had seen more of those lives than she had thought possible—had understood, truly, the payment tendered for their comfort—and deemed the cost too high. Little though City citizens seemed to agree. Or perhaps it was just easier to reject something she'd never had than to give up everything she'd ever known.

But if not a life of luxury like the Towers then . . . something. Xhea found herself thinking of the far horizon and what might lie beyond. She'd never strayed far from the Lower City, never thought to wonder about the world as it existed beyond this small place; not until now.

Perhaps once that was the choice she would have made, to take what she might carry and walk away, Shai at her side. Some part of her yearned for that unknown—the mystery of it, the challenge—even though that path, too, would likely lead to her death. But oh, the things they might have seen, the things they might have done. Even the idea was enough to make her smile.

Doesn't matter. Not now, not anymore. Xhea put such thoughts carefully aside, each like a delicate artifact that she did not wish to break. There was so little left, but at least she might have this: the thought that once, if things were different, she might have been happy.

Xhea clung now to Shai, trying to hold the ghost's incorporeal shoulders as Shai clung to hers, and if their fingers slipped and slid and fell through—if holding tight was impossible—then at least they had something that felt almost like touch. Xhea took a long breath, and another, trying to steady herself.

I don't want to die. It was the simple truth. She did not want to die and yet there was no other choice; not unless she was willing to stand back and let the Spire win, let the City and its Towers crush them all.

She was not.

And so she drew in a deep breath and straightened. *I can do this*, she thought, but what she said was, "We can do this."

Shai nodded.

Together they stepped into that small, dark space, and let the living Lower City pull them down.

Chapter Twenty-Three

Xhea stepped from the Lower City's embrace, emerging from the wall in the food court beneath the market. That wall was black, now—black like Farrow's wrapped vines; in moving her, the Lower City had claimed that space as its own. She was not far from its heart.

The tunnels were cool and dark, as they always were, but they were not silent. The ground rumbled and shook and shuddered, and the halls took those sounds and amplified them. It sounded worse than thunder, worse than any storm; the impacts felt like they were going to shake the walls to pieces. Decades of accumulated dust rained from the ceiling, dislodged from exposed pipes and ceiling tiles, to cover the tile below.

Xhea knew that parts of the underground had already collapsed. She did not know what or where—did not know which of her familiar halls and passageways were gone forever. Only knew the truth of it. These structures were old, ancient, failing; they could not withstand such force.

The Towers were taking her home piece by piece, and she could not stop them.

But the Lower City could. It had to.

Xhea walked, letting her cane take most of her weight, the chime and clatter of her hair lost beneath the sounds of buildings falling, crumbling, smashing. Louder even than those sounds was the Lower City's song: its living heart wailed, echoing down into her flesh until her bones shivered.

No, there was no silence here. Not anymore.

Xhea tried to stop at the end of the long corridor that led to the Lower City's heart, staring at the darkness at its end. But the draw of the Lower City's heart was no longer a subtle call that could slip past her defenses and urge her onward. It felt like a physical force, as if the entity wrapped an invisible hand around her and *pulled*, dragging her nearer step by staggering step.

She clung to the wall, fingers grasping, trying to find purchase to fight that pull. Trying to fight the part of herself that wanted let the darkness sweep her away.

"Here," Xhea managed. "This is far enough."

The Lower City's dark magic was thick in the air; it was in the walls and the sagging ceiling and the tiled floor beneath their feet. Even now its power sank into her as if her flesh was parched ground; surely it would hear her from so near.

"It's in pain," Shai said, looking toward the heart. Xhea could see only dark magic incarnate—yet Shai saw something more. The ghost stared, brow furrowed, seemingly torn between her own discomfort and the Lower City's distress.

"Yes."

It was in pain, and so was Xhea; part of her cried out in perfect time to the song's rhythms, slipping into its quickening cadence of hurt and despair.

Instead of pushing the sensation away, Xhea embraced it. She drew her magic up through the cracked binding in countless thin rivulets of power, and sagged against the wall as she yielded to the Lower City's call. She did not allow herself to move forward, and yet her breathing shifted, becoming slower and deeper. Her heart, too, slowed, its beat falling into time with the song.

She pressed her hand harder against the wall and let her power flow. But this was no simple ribbon of magic like she had attempted before. Instead, she sang in time, her voice and magic rising in wordless harmony to the Lower City's song.

She did not say, *I'm here.* Instead she said, *I know.* It was no simple confirmation, not sympathy, but empathy, true and strong and bonedeep.

Xhea's magic sank into the Lower City's, all those wisps of black vanishing into the wall before her, the floor beneath her; into the very air.

I know, she said, for she heard in its song the agony of Rown falling, only dust and ruin where once had stood a skyscraper. It spoke, too, of structures for which she had no names: buildings too small to be so defined.

I know, Xhea said, for the Lower City cried out for its lost people. It had felt as they were killed in the streets and in their homes; felt their deaths as they tried to fight back. It felt their absence as they moved beyond its limits and into the inanimate ruins beyond.

Its people, leaving, dying. Its body crumbling, torn up, fallen, destroyed.

Oh, such betrayal. Such hurt and loss and pain.

I know, Xhea said. *I know, I understand; I hurt, too.*

And it heard her; she felt that glimmer of recognition as it turned and saw her—truly saw her, if only for a moment. She felt as the Lower City drew her magic into itself and sent some thin streamer of power back in reply. But there were no words there, no thoughts or images or knowledge—and when she tried to send more than that brief connection of empathy, it did not reply.

It was not enough. Even here, even so close, it was not enough.

Xhea opened her eyes, suddenly seeing the shopping corridor before her once more: its dirty, flooded floor, its glass-fronted stores, its sagging ceiling. And the darkness, living, roiling, at its end.

"I need to go closer," Xhea whispered.

Because she didn't have enough magic to speak as she needed to—didn't have enough *power* to tell it what it needed to know. Against its rising chorus of song, she could only whisper; and if it acknowledged her presence, it could not hear her. Not truly.

She needed to touch the Lower City's heart.

"Xhea—" Shai started, but Xhea did not need those words. Did not need to hear the truths they would contain.

She knew what that touch would mean; they both did. For all that Xhea was a creature of dark magic, her body was only flesh, only blood and bone. Dark magic—so much of it, so strong— would kill her, and if it was not the slow death of years that the dark magic children experienced, neither would it be quick.

A death of minutes, perhaps. A death of hours.

She and Shai had stood here before, in this place, teetering on this edge—only now there was every reason to step forward and so few reasons to step back.

Xhea shook her head. *I know how to save us all*, she had said. That sharp and glorious hope.

It was not true; not anymore. She had been too slow, too late, too weak—did it really matter which? Her failures compounded, piling one atop the other as if she wished to rival the Spire's height.

She could not save anyone but herself.

Walk away, she told herself in silence. *Step back and get out.* Perhaps there was time enough for her to get clear of the Spire's marked zone of impact, that circle drawn on the Messenger's map. Perhaps she could escape the poorer Towers' notice—her and Shai both; perhaps she could find a way out through the broken streets to the ruins.

But she did not think so.

"I know," Xhea said to Shai—the same words she'd said to the Lower City, with the same weight.

"If you have to do this," Shai said softly, "I will not stop you."

Xhea looked at the ghost, her pale eyes and paler hair, her glorious light.

"No," Shai said then, and drew a deep breath. "If this is what you have to do, you have my support. My everything."

We cannot be anything other than what we are.

Except that once she had not been this person. Once she had thought only of herself—only of that day, that moment, that meal, that moment of warmth. Xhea would not have run from the idea of sacrificing herself for others; she would not have had the idea to run from. Or was it that she'd only ever believed herself to be as others had seen her: small and helpless, powerless, useless.

Yet here she was, still standing as everything fell to pieces around her. So maybe this was the truth of her, her whole self laid bare. Not her selfishness and sharp words, not her hurt or loneliness or the countless mistakes of her life. Only this.

"You saved me," Shai said, as if in answer to a question that Xhea had not asked. Or perhaps she'd asked not in words, but magic; for power flowed between them now, strong and steady.

"No," Xhea said. "You saved me." For whoever she was, whoever she had become, none of it would have been possible without Shai.

"Try, then. For all those who had no one to save them."

Xhea thought of them: Edren and Orren and Senn, fallen Rown and black-bound Farrow. She thought of the Lower City market in the height of summer, the vendors and their stalls, the roar of their upraised voices. She thought of the children playing in the street while their parents washed clothes in a nearby fountain. She thought of the hunters and the thieves, the would-be business people and the leaders, the guards and the grandmothers and the gangs. She thought of the kids like her, the kids who had no one and nothing, and fought to live nonetheless.

She heard buildings falling, shaking the ground beneath her.

Somewhere overhead, dawn was breaking.

Xhea looked again at the Lower City's heart and the corridor's far end, all that roiling black. She shrugged then, and smiled. There was no point in stopping.

Shai took her hand and they walked together, step by careful step, toward that darkness.

Xhea could feel Shai's strain as she tried to stay by her side. Shai's steps had grown smaller, came slower, as she forced her way forward; and every step she made was claimed with the force of her Radiant magic.

The dark power of the Lower City's heart pushed Shai back as if it were a storm wind: her hair flew wild about her face, and her clothes fluttered and pressed against her body. She clung to Xhea, or tried to, as if the pressure of the magic forcing her back was nothing. Shai's expression was intense, fearful, determined. There were no tears there, not anymore.

At last, Shai could go no further.

"Shai," Xhea started, and did not know what to say.

Shai only smiled. "If you can, wait for me. We'll go together."

She reached out and touched Xhea's cheek with the backs of her curled fingers, gently, so gently. Xhea closed her eyes, because it was suddenly that or weep. She swallowed and took a deep breath, and when she'd found the strength to open her eyes once more, Shai had already stepped back.

Shai moved away as if it was the only thing she could do; as if, without Xhea to cling to, the darkness swept her back, caught in its tide. Xhea was drawn the other way, away from Shai and toward the darkness that waited at the hall's end.

There should have been something to say, some words that would express—

But no. Magic flowed between them, and her heart could say all the things her lips could not.

Xhea turned.

Perhaps it should have been easy; all her choices had been made, each decision weighted with finality. She knew what she was doing.

Perhaps it should have been easy, but it was not.

She looked down at her hands, one empty and shaking, one clenched tight, white-knuckled on the metal top of the cane that Daye had given her. Slowly she loosened her grip on her cane, then bent and laid the twisted length of wood on the ground. Straightening was hard; she hurt, and her body fought her, failing in a thousand small ways.

She stepped forward, not bothering to hide her limp. Not trying to hide what time had done to her, or magic; not fighting the power that tried to rise within her, or the pain that it engendered.

She only walked.

One step. Another.

That dark shape grew before her. So rarely had Xhea seen color, and so often had she mourned its absence; yet now she was grateful for the lack. There was no color here, no light or shadow. Only power, black and absolute.

Yet in that black, she could see details. The magic swirled and twisted into countless fractal shapes, and they were so beautiful some part of her wanted to shy away. They were the entity's thoughts writ large, the truth of her home written before her in black so dark it hurt.

"Hello," she said, in voice and magic both, but even here it was not enough. Not compared to so much power; not compared to so much pain.

So Xhea took a long, deep breath, and walked into the Lower City's living heart.

Dark magic.

It was, Xhea thought—strangely, foolishly—the wrong word, dark. For darkness spoke of the lack of light, as if it might only be shaped by that absence.

This black had a presence, stronger and brighter than any light she had ever known. It was not light's absence but its equal, its opposing force; and it *burned*.

She felt as if she had stepped not into darkness, but fire. Her flesh singed and burned away, and that fire poured into her, deeper and deeper with every breath. No air anymore, only magic, devouring her. She could not scream, could not think—

Her magic unfurled, its bonds burned away, and suddenly the pain eased. Magic flowed and Xhea let her consciousness go with it, leaving the agony of mortal flesh behind. Face and hands, blood and breath; she struggled to remember what they were, how they felt. Struggled to remember why they mattered.

Because there was so very much magic. There was no peace there, no calm—and yet she gloried in the feeling nonetheless, letting herself expand to her very limits. She felt the earth beneath her as if it, now, was her flesh; she felt the foundations and the tunnels that wove through that earth, and the cold weight of their age. She felt the streets and the buildings, so many buildings, all reaching for the sky.

Magic ripped through her, sharp and bright, and she shuddered with the shock of it. Magic tore into her, glittering like daylight, and she could not shy away, could not escape. She screamed as parts of herself were lifted and ripped apart—

No, Xhea realized, pulling herself back. That was not her pain—those were not her wounds—but the Lower City's.

As if that thought were a call, the entity's awareness turned toward her like a great, black eye. She'd felt her power to be vast, expanding; this creature dwarfed her unthinkingly. She was no more than a speck, a mote of dust tumbling through the darkened air.

But, it seemed, a beloved speck. For all the Lower City's hurt and grief, it embraced her, held her.

I know, she told it again. She shared what she had seen, what it had felt and already knew: Rown, fallen. The streets taken. The people scattered, hurting, dying.

Pain and sorrow echoed between them, amplified, shared. Oh, all the things they had lost.

It was only then that Xhea realized she could feel something else: power rushing into her, a strength not her own. That power seemed almost foreign; it spoke of light and spirit.

A name rose then, blooming in her mind like a bright flower. *Shai.*

She remembered. She was not the Lower City, not these buildings and homes, not this magic. She was not even a speck.

She was just a girl, small and broken, and she had come with a message.

Xhea thought of the Spire and the dark magic that flowed to the Lower City, night after night; she conjured the memory of that magic twisted, changed, in an attempt to poison the living Lower City.

She thought of everything she had learned since their last conversation—the Spire's ultimatum and its intent, the reason why the poorer Towers had claimed this ground and why, even now, the buildings were being torn apart.

The truth about the dark magic that poured down on the ground every night.

And the belief that underlay it all: that if the Lower City just tried, it could rise up and fight back. It could take on the power of the whole of the City above, and it could win.

Oh, it was a relief just letting that knowledge flow from her. She did not control it, did not try to shape it into words or thoughts or images, only opened herself entirely to the Lower City's magic.

It was worth it, she thought. All she had gone through, all she had seen. If it helped the living Lower City fight back—if it saved some fraction of her home, saved its people—then it was worth it. Such joy in that thought. Such hope.

The Lower City pulled away.

What? she thought. *What is it?*

Silence.

No, that wasn't quite true: the Lower City's song rang on unbroken, rising and falling with the rhythms of its life and thought, the flow of its magic through the territory it claimed. But in response to her sudden surge of magic and the knowledge it contained, there was nothing. No chords played in echo or answer, no sound of its sudden understanding.

She felt its attention upon her nonetheless.

The Spire will kill you, Xhea said, trying to wrap the words in her magic and send them flowing toward that awareness. *Do you understand?*

It did not reply, only reached for her, as if her mind and power—as if whatever might remain of her small and failing body—might be swallowed down like a pill.

Images rushed at her, too fast to understand—too many to tell one from the other. A tunnel, wings, something growing—

Sensations assaulted her, pain and light, color and sound and heat—

The taste of wild raspberries and the smell of rotted wood burning—

It was becoming harder to focus; harder to keep her thoughts from dissolving entirely. She wanted to rest, let go of her hurt and struggle, and just lose herself in the Lower City, dark magic to dark magic, no division between them.

Only her link to Shai held her steady, an anchor against the raging storm. Shai's magic flowed into her, more and more, giving Xhea shape and substance where she might otherwise have none.

Xhea drew upon that power, using it to build walls to separate her from the entity that surrounded her. By will and magic she created a barrier that said, *This far, no further.*

It was difficult. It hurt. But then, everything did these days; pain was her renai, the coin by which she paid for any progress.

Slowly, the Lower City drew back. It seemed to look at her, considering the messages that she had sent the way one would puzzle over a letter written in a particularly difficult hand.

It will kill you, Xhea said again, more urgently. *It will destroy you utterly. But you can stop it. You can fight back.*

A torrent of magic in reply, black on black, all but overwhelming her. The living Lower City battered at the walls she had built between them. She felt a surge of question, of confusion; it was grasping for answers. For understanding.

No, she thought. *Too much, stop—*

It drew back, but not, it seemed, because of her words. The Lower City shuddered then, pain rippling through it; another building had fallen. She could feel it, too: the sudden shape of that absence; chaos and disorder where once there had been wholeness, form, structure.

Orren, Xhea realized, interpreting the rush of sound that rang around her, through her, and the entity's grief. *Orren has fallen.*

It should have made her glad, that destruction; once she would have laughed to see the broken skyscraper fall, and danced on the rock and rubble of its walls. Not now. Now she felt its loss as the living Lower City did, as a piece of her torn free.

If she could have, she would have wept. She would have screamed.

Instead she cried: *Stop! You can stop this, you're stronger than them.*

Slower, anguished: *Why are you letting them do this? Why won't you make it stop?*

In wake of her words, there was only confusion.

At last, Xhea understood. Despair welled—her despair, the Lower City's, it mattered little which.

Xhea had thought the living Lower City was like a Tower, and it was—and yet it was so very different. Its magic infused the streets and buildings of the Lower City like a Tower did its walls; yet, unlike a Tower, the dark magic entity did not claim those structures for its own. It lived within them, but did not change them; did not make them anything other than they were. The only exceptions were the black tendrils that held Farrow aloft and the path of her recent decent into the underground. In all the Lower City, that was a slim triumph indeed.

Like having a great house, Xhea thought, and living only in the bathtub.

This entity was ancient—as old, perhaps, as the City itself. Yet for all its age, its size, and the dark complexity of its thoughts, there was so much it did not know. So much it did not understand.

Towers, in the City above, were connected to a very many people. They had their Radiants, bound to them in life and death; they had those Radiants' knowledge and memories, their hopes and dreams, flowing into them throughout their lives. They had their *citizens*, which numbered in the thousands; and each sent some portion of their magic into the Tower.

More than that, Towers interfaced with their people countless times per day: they ran the systems, the heat and water and power; they managed the myriad spells that City citizens relied on unthinkingly. They spoke with other Towers; they battled against each other, spell to spell, as they danced across the sky.

But the Lower City had always been alone.

The magic that had birthed it had come only from the Central Spire. No guiding hand, there; no intelligence with which it might communicate, or from whom it might learn. And yes, that dark magic fell on the people of the Lower City, and perhaps it had picked up some small flavor of their lives. Flavor, only; not knowledge. Not truth.

What it knew it had learned on its own. Scraps and pieces of countless lives, assembled into a picture that it thought was reality. Its understanding of the world bore little resemblance to the City Xhea knew.

Life it understood, and change. Pain, too, was clear—though it seemed that only now did it begin to understand the depth of the concept, the layers of meaning that pain might have, physical and otherwise.

But it had no knowledge of death, or even of endings. It had always been, growing, changing; it, like the world around it, knew no end.

Confusion rose, swirling around her. *No*, it would have said if it knew the word; it made do with shape and shade and emotion. *You are wrong.*

A kinder person might have found a way to speak to it calmly, patiently—might have shared an understanding of death in a way it could understand. Xhea had never been terribly kind, and of her slim collection of virtues, patience had never been among them.

Frustration welled, twin to the Lower City's confusion, if dwarfed entirely in magnitude.

What could she do but let down those walls that she had so laboriously built? She reduced the division between them, let their magics mingle freely once more, so that it might see into the heart of her—see into her mind and her memories, and understand.

Xhea opened herself to the Lower City. Its magic washed over her, a rushing torrent of power. It had no concept of its own strength; it grabbed the whole of her and pulled.

Xhea huddled in an alley, shivering, her breath a fog before her face. He was coming, the man was coming, and she had nowhere else to run. She stared up at the sky so she did not have to see his shadow as it darkened the ground before her—

Xhea sat in the morning sunlight that poured through the apartment window, and looked down at the torn clothing spread across the floor in front of her. "Here," *Lane said, passing her a scrap of cloth and a needle—*

Xhea coughed, choking; she could not breathe for the dust in the air, she could not see. She clawed at the broken ground before her, fingernails splitting as she pushed handfuls of dirt aside. "Abelane," *she sobbed.* "Lane, where are—"

Xhea froze as the spells dragged the ghost down into the broken body that awaited him. There was so much magic in the air that her hands and face had gone numb with it. "No," *she said, but Orren's casters did not listen, only pushed her back against the far wall. The ghost screamed—*

Xhea tried to push herself away from Ieren's body, away from Shai, but the ghost stepped toward her, her hand outstretched. "Xhea," *Shai said.* "You won't hurt me." *And the shining ghost came closer and closer—*

All the facets of her life, bright and dark and glittering; and there was no life without death. The Lower City ripped memories from her on that black tide, turning them over and around as it tried to understand, yanking Xhea's consciousness in countless directions.

Ghosts, so many ghosts; ghosts of the young and old, the sick and the wounded—

Shai lying in her bed, her body thin and wasted, her Radiant glow dimming as she exhaled and did not breathe again—

Dark magic washing over a nameless young man in Tower Eridian, his face going slack and empty as he fell—

Screams in the darkened streets as the night walkers caught a man and tore him slowly to pieces, and no one could help him, no one could even try—

Xhea screamed. She had no mouth, no throat, no voice; and yet something echoed from her—some soundless, wordless cry—and at last the entity drew back.

Darkness, then; a moment of perfect black. Xhea was not fool enough to name that calm peace.

Then: a swirl of shadow, a wash of sound. A question.

Yes, Xhea said in answer. *It will kill you.*

This time, it understood. Or, at least, it understood death as she did: as one who had fought and scrabbled against its inevitability; one who had turned it away time and again with stolen food, a fire built from scraps, a thin blanket wrapped around her shivering body like a shroud.

Only now, death was not such a distant concept, nothing that life still held at bay. For while Shai's magic flowed into her, that power was as thin and weak as she now felt. Too much dark magic killed a person, even her; and all her flirting with wisps and ribbons of black had not prepared her to face this.

But then, nothing could have. Mortal flesh could only bear so much power, bright or dark; Shai had taught her that. What better way to teach the concept of death than by dying? She would have laughed if she could; it seemed, in that moment, a wonderful joke.

Again that swirl, a rising sound of inquiry.

Xhea had no need to reply; the entity knew the whole of her life, the whole of her self, all the things she had ever learned. There was no need to repeat what it already knew.

She felt her death approaching, and if it was not welcome neither did she need to fear it. She had known so many ghosts, seen and spoken to so many of the dead. No wonder death felt like a friend, coming to sit at her bedside and read to her for a short while.

Wait for me, Shai had said. *We'll go together.*

Only now did Xhea understand those words. Again she wished to laugh, or perhaps to cry, and neither mattered now; because somewhere she'd once had a small, frail body, and it was surely gone. Burned to ash and embers; burned to the smoke of dark magic rising.

No, the living Lower City said suddenly—its song growing louder, faster, its darkness condensing in a single black surge of denial. It reached for her, wrapped around her and lifted her up—

But it did not matter. It was already far, far too late.

Chapter Twenty-Four

Shai watched as Xhea walked into the Lower City's living heart.

In the underground, so much was dim and dark and gray, as if time had leeched the color from all things. Yet the heart itself was black—black the way that Allenai's heart had been light—and in its swirls she could see some hint of the mind of the creature that the City's waste magic had birthed. No order there, as she had seen in Allenai; no true pattern.

Instead, it was like looking into the heart of a storm. Only there was no lightning or glimpse of light; just a clot of ebony cloud, swirling and raging like an unbound force of nature.

It swallowed Xhea whole.

Shai stared, wishing she could grab the girl back from that swirl of power; wishing she could clutch Xhea to her chest, as if her arms or magic might keep her safe. As if safety existed anymore.

Of Xhea she could see nothing, not a glimpse of her hand, the shape of her silhouette, a swirl of her charm-bound hair. She was simply gone.

Only the spell-bound tether remained, stretching into that dark. A rope to lead her back to the living world.

But against so much power? It looked so very thin.

A moment passed. Another.

"Xhea?" Shai called. Her voice echoed unanswered.

She felt Xhea's binding burn away.

A sudden flood of power surged down the tether, so sharp and strong that Shai gasped as that magic poured into her. Shai would have said that she did not feel the effects of Xhea's binding, and she would have been wrong; it was only now, with the binding gone, that Shai felt the difference.

Her power flared, bright, effortless. It rushed through her, and it felt not like magic but blood, its surge a heartbeat. The heart's dark magic pushed at her like a howling wind—but now her own magic pushed back, a beacon shining into that storm.

Just as suddenly, Xhea drew on Shai's power.

Shai had expected it, had braced against it, but even so that pull almost made her lose her footing. She reached out—as if physical walls would be any help, as if anything might hold her unmoving but will alone. She concentrated, steadying herself, feeling that glorious power rush out of her.

"Stand strong," she whispered—to herself, to Xhea, it mattered little which. She was the anchor, Xhea the ship lost to the storm; only together would they get through this.

Shai was not so naive as to believe that meant Xhea's survival. She hoped only that Xhea might tell the Lower City what it needed to know before its power unmade her entirely.

For she herself, standing near Allenai's heart, had felt the lure that pure magic offered: the peace, she might have said; the ability to surrender all shape and form, and the worries that came with them. Though she no longer had a physical body, neither had she stepped into that heart entirely; she'd had a way, however small, to retreat.

Xhea did not.

Shai could not see the girl, could not hear her, yet somehow she felt the way the heart drew around her, and some aspect of Xhea's loss of place, of body, of self. Shai felt as that magic unmade her, cell by cell; felt the echo of her pain as she burned.

No, she did not hope for Xhea's life now; it was too great to wish for, and the hope of it would be sharp enough to cut. She could not afford such wounds, not here, when all else was already breaking.

She hoped only that Xhea's spirit would survive. That Xhea would stay in the living world, as Shai had stayed, if only for a time.

We'll go together.

Around her, the underground trembled, and Shai blinked. A fraction of a second passed and then came a great, distant booming, like thunder. She tried not to think what that sound meant, what was happening somewhere above her; she only stood steady against the storm.

Harder Xhea pulled on Shai's bright magic, and harder still. Shai sent all her light and power into the tether, willingly yielding to that pull. The halls around her grew dim.

Shai thought again of her realization in the warehouse at the night's beginning: that she stayed in the living world for Xhea. She stayed, she knew, for other things, too. For the chance to learn more, see more; for the chance to help people.

For a chance, truth be told, for the life she had not had—or whatever semblance of it she might find.

It was only a chance. Knowing Xhea's magic and what it did to all living things, Shai understood what she had never put into words: Xhea would not live long, no matter what they did. A span of years perhaps, with Shai at her side to keep her strong; or maybe only months. A season's slow turn.

She did not know. No one ever did with a terminal illness, though some predictions were better than others. Death kept its own schedule.

Because that's what Xhea's magic was, she thought—an illness. Whatever its use, good or bad, it meant only death for its bearer. What else should she call something that caused the slow wasting of flesh, the withering of life in what should have been its prime?

It was, in the end, the same as her own.

They were so very different, she and Xhea. They always had been. And yet, in this—as in so many other small ways—they were alike.

Death hurt—or dying did. Of her own end, Shai remembered only peace. She only hoped that Xhea's death, lost in that dark entity, shared that moment of grace.

Again the underground shuddered, harder this time, as if in an earthquake. Shai struggled to look up—the movement was an effort. Cracks appeared in the walls around her, and dust rained down; bits of ceiling tile fell to the ground and scattered.

Stand strong, Shai told herself again, but already she felt the strain. No, more than that: for the Lower City's heart pushed her away, relentless; yet the tether, and Xhea at its end, dragged her back. She was caught between those two forces, pushed and pulled in equal measure, and had no way to fight either.

Shai grit her teeth, clenched her hands into fists, squeezed her eyes tight—as if anything, anything, might make her strong enough to meet Xhea's need.

Stand strong.

But she could not stand anymore. She could barely breathe.

She hung now in midair, her feet some empty span above the floor. Her hands were lifted from her sides, her head thrown back, and she knew not when she had moved.

Shai knew that her power was not endless—it had never been, for all that it had always seemed such. Unbound, she had come once and again to the end of her strength. Now her magic did not flicker, did not fail; it was only pulled from her, so fast, so brutally, that its leaving hurt. Its *absence* hurt.

It hurt—and Shai knew pain. She remembered it, though she tried not to: the agony of her slow death. The pain that no spell, no drug, could wholly mask. This pain was the same, a pain that slipped beneath her consciousness like a knife; it cut out sound, sight, thought.

She did not have enough power to fill Xhea's need, but the tether pulled and pulled and pulled nonetheless.

"Xhea," Shai whispered. The name left her lips like a whimper. "Xhea, please . . ."

She did not know whether she spoke the words or sent them down the tether with her magic, and perhaps it did not matter: there was no reply. No hint, even, that Xhea remembered her existence. There was only that relentless pull.

A pull on her magic—and on something else. For Shai reached out, her hand stretching toward the dark heart, and realized that her fingertips had grown transparent.

She knew, then, what was happening; she understood the cause for her pain. She didn't have enough magic to keep Xhea alive, and so Xhea drew on Shai's spirit instead.

Shai had seen the ghost Ieren devoured; now she understood that spirit's pain and his rage. His helplessness. For there was nothing that she could do to stop that inexorable pull that was tearing her apart and consuming her in pieces.

But it wasn't true, was it? For she, unlike that ghost—unlike the other ghosts that Xhea had seen bound to dark magic children—she had the power to make a choice.

Cut the tether, Shai thought.

She could not. No—she would not. It was the only way she might save herself, but would doom Xhea in an instant. Xhea would burn. So much dark magic and nothing to protect her from its power? She would be smoke and ash without time to cry out.

Shai cried out in her stead. She wept. She whimpered. She had died once; now she was dying again, and for all the slow pain and horror of that first death, this one was infinitely worse.

And still she stood.

Xhea had, in asking for Shai's help, accepted her own death; Shai, too, had allowed her to make that choice. She had understood some small fraction of what her friend was asking of her. Now she understood the rest, even if Xhea did not.

Her own unmaking.

Was it too great a price to pay? In that moment, it felt that way.

Yet Shai thought of the refugees in the ruins, the children sheltering in the warehouse. Lorn and Emara and Mercks,

Torrence and Daye, Edren's useless councilors—all the people she had met here on the ground. All the people she had never met, all the names she'd never learn. Surely, they deserved a chance to live—a chance to survive.

One life—one person's pain and suffering—traded for the lives of so many. Was it worth it?

Once she had said no—she had rejected that life and path and pain. A Radiant bound to a Tower, perpetually dying; it had seemed the worst thing she could imagine.

Now she was being unmade entirely. She tried to see her hands, and could not; glanced down through her tears and saw no feet anymore, no calves, no knees. She would have screamed for the pain had she any voice left—and still she stood. For them. For Xhea. Because she was the only one who could.

Her choice. Xhea's choice.

Perhaps it was the same in the end.

Shai stood, weeping, unraveling into nothingness, as the Lower City crumbled around her.

A tunnel collapsed. There came a rush of soil and stone, a cloud of choking dust that washed through her—or through what was left of her. All went suddenly dark and Shai did not know if it was because the hall in which she stood had collapsed, or her magic had been extinguished, or she had been struck blind.

Xhea . . .

No words left. No hope.

She could not see, could not scream. She could not feel anything anymore, not even pain.

All that was left was darkness.

Chapter
Twenty-Five

Dust.

Dust in her mouth, dust gritty in her eyes; the smell of dust in her nose.

Slowly Xhea raised her head and blinked, tears washing away the grit. She coughed. Tried to spit and choked instead.

Everything hurt.

It took a moment to get her arms under her; her muscles ached and trembled and slipped across the dust-coated tile. A moment more, then she pushed, slowly rolling herself over. She just lay there, staring at the ceiling.

Or, rather, where the ceiling had been. Above her was only a span of dirty plumbing pipe and structural girders, the ceiling having fallen entirely.

Well, Xhea thought, dazed, *that explains the dust.*

Again she coughed and tried to force herself toward sitting. Her hands shook, and her breathing was thin and ragged; her heart pounded too hard in her chest, trying to beat its way into oblivion. But it was her skin that hurt the most, as if the flesh of her whole body were raw and burned, sensitized to every touch, every movement.

The magic. She did not know where the thought came from; did not understand what it meant. Yet she looked down and saw dark magic clinging to her hand. Dark magic rose from her in wisps and tatters like early morning fog.

And behind her—

No, she would not look. Something in her quailed at the thought, making her shudder and whimper.

She could not stand, and so Xhea dragged herself forward with her arms, scraping her tender body across the gritty, dust-coated ground. Suddenly she could breathe again. She pulled herself forward once more, leaving a trail in the dirt. Again. Again. At last she let herself collapse, sagging back to the tile and resting her trembling arms.

It was an effort to keep her eyes open.

But there was something, something . . .

"Shai?" Her voice was a raw croak. Xhea coughed, choked, spat dust and tried again. Louder this time: "Shai?"

No reply. The tether was still there, bound to her sternum— weaker, somehow, and thinner, but undeniably present. She reached for the tether—and touched flesh. Tender, aching flesh— her own.

Xhea looked down in confusion.

She had been wearing her too-large jacket with its many pockets, and a thin shirt beneath. The pants she'd gotten in Orren: dark and strong with pockets down both legs. Now she wore only rags and tatters. What fabric remained was thin and ashy and shredded at her touch.

She raised her hand, and only then realized that, as she moved, her hair was silent. No braids there amongst the tangled dark; no coins and charms bound into its length. It was all gone—lank and unbound, the strands' natural volume was weighted down by sweat and dust.

The heart, she thought, and looked behind her.

The Lower City's living heart flared, a swirling mass of black. Just looking at it hurt her eyes; hurt, she realized, her skin. Every wisp of dark power that washed over her felt like sandpaper across her tender, scalded flesh.

She remembered walking into it—remembered being lost to it, mind and magic and body alike. She remembered dying.

Yet she was here.

Again the magic pushed her: *Go*, it seemed to say, urging her onward. *Go*.

She flinched from that touch, but tried to comply. It had, she realized, saved her—drawn back and deposited her on the floor, outside its flaring boundaries.

It understood death now, and it did not want her to die.

I've never been terribly big on the idea myself.

But there was no safety in its dark nimbus. She turned and dragged herself farther down the hall, until her outstretched hands encountered something hard. Not debris—something long and twisted, buried in the dust of the ceiling's collapse. Xhea reached for it, drew it forth. Her cane.

She wanted to laugh, but could not remember how. Wanted to stand, and did not have the strength. So she only pulled herself, body length by body length, all the way to the hall's end.

It was so quiet. She could hear the Lower City's heart; and yet its song was like an echo of her heartbeat, its rise and fall like the rhythms of her breath. Constant, comforting—and a sound her conscious mind need not heed.

Xhea did not let herself think about what that implied.

There were sounds, too, of debris falling, of walls cracked and crumbling, of rocks hitting the ground like hail. But no voices. Not so much as a whisper of the one voice she needed to hear.

"Shai? Where are you?"

Her aching eyes followed the tether to its end.

Xhea stared for a long moment, uncomprehending. Shai hung in midair, seemingly unconscious. Or, at least, what was left of her.

Her arms had vanished to above the elbow, her legs to above the knee. Those limbs did not end bluntly, only faded to nothing.

The rest of her seemed whole, but not untouched; for when Xhea looked at her, she realized that she could see *through* her to the broken hall beyond. There was no sign of her Radiant glow—not so much as a glint or a flicker of that light.

Shai's eyes were closed, her lips slack and unmoving, her pale hair hanging limp about her face and shoulders. There was no pain written in Shai's expression. It should have been a relief, and was not; for neither was there hope or joy or sorrow. No sign, in those familiar, beloved features, of awareness at all.

Xhea made a sound that was too low, too pained to be a cry, and dragged herself to her friend's side. She pulled on the tether; she could draw Shai down to her, could even almost touch her, but she did not think that it was just a lack of magic—hers or Shai's— that made her fingers slip through that ghostly flesh unfeeling.

"Shai," she whispered, trying to touch the ghost's face; and, "No, no, no." Words stopped having meaning, though she spoke nonetheless, quickly, unthinkingly, as if she might come across the word or phrase that would spark life in the fading ghost. As if something, anything, might undo what she had done.

Abelane was right. The thought fell into Xhea's mind like a stone, cold and heavy. Abelane's fear, her anger, her insistence that Xhea did not understand what her power might do had not been so groundless after all.

Xhea cried, hard and fast and ugly; her sobs stopped her breath, if not her hands' desperate attempts to bring Shai back toward consciousness. There was so little of Shai to touch, to hold; she seemed to be made more of mist and memory than ghostly flesh. So little of her left.

Xhea remembered what Abelane had said of the binding: it takes and it takes and it gives nothing back.

It wasn't true—or it hadn't been true. Not until now.

Xhea realized that, standing in that living heart—despite the magic flowing around her, through her—she'd had no magic to spare. She'd needed all of her power to speak with the entity; she'd needed it, too, to build those barriers, trying to keep herself separate and sane while the Lower City pulled her apart, one curious bit at a time.

She remembered drawing on Shai's power and that power filling her, holding her to life. She would have died if it wasn't for Shai's support. She would have died a thousand times over.

Xhea looked at Shai and knew she would have taken those deaths and the pain that would accompany them—would have unspoken her message, swallowed back her magic and bound it hard and tight—if only it might have undone this.

No, she thought—not bind her magic, but give it back; return power in kind for what she'd taken.

Her heart hammered in sudden hope as she fumbled for the tether. Her power was no longer bound, and yet it felt weak and quiescent within her—exhausted, she thought, by her time in the Lower City's living heart. Yet it rose, dark black and coiling like sinuous smoke: her full power, her real power, responding to her demand and the fear that drove it.

She funnelled her magic into the tether. Slowly at first, the way one might spoon broth into a sick person's opened mouth, then faster. She felt as Shai absorbed that power, drank it hungrily down—and so she sent more magic, and more.

As she watched, Shai solidified. Her ghostly flesh gained more substance, bit by bit blocking out Xhea's view of the debris-covered floor beyond. Shai drew in a slow, shallow breath, and another—the first breaths Xhea had seen her draw in some long minutes.

But her limbs did not return, not her hands or feet, and there was not so much as a flicker of her magic returning. Shai did not wake.

Xhea released her magic and sagged back to the ground, exhausted. She reached for Shai, pushed that pale hair from her sallow face. Wept, and watched the tears fall through her.

"I'm sorry," Xhea whispered, over and over. "I'm so, so sorry."

Is this how the children feel the first time they destroy a bondling? She would have said no—that they couldn't have felt like this, wouldn't. If this was how they felt, how could it have not destroyed them utterly? How could they continue, day after day? How could they destroy another ghost, and another, and another?

They only love the first one. After that, it would be too hard to care for another ghost, knowing what they were going to do, slow or fast or all at once. Knowing that this unmaking was any bondling's eventual end.

This wasn't supposed to have happened to Shai. She was Radiant, and Xhea had always assumed that the bond they had was different. Stronger. Better. Yet Xhea had pulled everything from her nonetheless, all her magic, her very existence—

Xhea hesitated, then drew back. She could not stop her tears, but she could look through them at Shai's lifeless face. There was no glimmer of magic there—but then, she thought, normal ghosts, normal bondlings, had none. It was not just power that she had stolen, but Shai's ghostly flesh.

It was not just magic Xhea had to return, but something else. Something deeper.

Her spirit. Her very self.

Magic she could call forth with will or effort, no matter how painful the experience—but spirit? Xhea did not know how to grasp that, nor how to draw it from her. At least not her own. For, she realized, she had always manipulated spirit, the bodies of ghosts, even when her magic had been but a cold, dark lake in the pit of her stomach.

Xhea looked down at her trembling, dust-covered hands. She reached for her arms, her chest, the dusty confines of her face— touched her skin as if she might reach beneath and grasp her own ghost within that living flesh. Magic was at her fingertips and drifted about her lips as she whispered quick, desperate words of encouragement. But she felt only skin and dust and sweat, and the ashy threads of her once-beloved jacket decaying to nothing. No hint of the ghost that lay beneath.

The tether, then.

Xhea reached inside herself with mental hands, trying to draw forth not magic, but—what?

Not her anguish. Not hurt or sorrow or regret, but something deeper. Something truer.

Love, then? All her complicated joy and yearning, her secret hopes and happiness.

All of them, she thought, and none of them. For she was not her thoughts or her emotions, as much as she was shaped by them; she was not her history, or her memories, or her fears.

But she was afraid. In that moment, fear coiled through her, stronger even than her magic. There had always been parts of herself that she'd been afraid to share with Shai—to share with anyone. She'd feared what the tether might send to Shai without her knowledge, what stray truth might make its way down that length; for Xhea had known at a level beyond words that if anyone saw those darkest, most secret thoughts and feelings, they would be horrified.

If Shai knew who Xhea truly was in the depths of her own spirit, then she could not care for her, could not love her. She would draw away as if burned by Xhea's touch.

Draw away as everyone else had, leaving Xhea alone.

Oh, she was afraid—and yet that terror was nothing beside the fear of losing Shai entirely. Xhea looked at Shai's face—her pale eyelashes resting on her cheeks, the smooth lines of her jaw and chin and throat, the lips that she wished would smile—and she could not imagine Shai abandoning her. Not anymore.

Xhea knew: she was just . . . a person. Good and bad, light and dark. And if anyone already knew the truth of her, unspoken, it was Shai.

Before, she would have said that she had built no barriers in her heart or soul to protect her from her link to Shai. She would have been wrong. For now Xhea opened herself fully to the binding and the ghost on its other end, and felt those mental walls fall away, one by one.

Xhea wrapped Shai in her arms and drew the ghost to her, holding her as best she could. Her head bowed, Xhea's tears fell upon the ghost; her breath whispered across Shai's face and hair. She closed her eyes.

The living Lower City had opened her up and hollowed her out, searching through the whole of Xhea's life and identity for understanding. It had taken from her, even as she allowed it; but this? She did not allow Shai to take from her so much as she gave herself, all of herself, like a gift.

She felt something flow away from her like heat or breath or blood, and despite the weakness of its passing, she did not mourn the loss. Magic flowed too, and emotion, and the light that she could only name hope; each greater and smaller than mere words.

She felt, too, as something began to return to her through the tether. Slowly at first, a mere whisper, then more.

And she felt—

And she knew—

Xhea choked back a sob, and her tears flowed harder; she tasted their salt on her lips. They were not sad tears anymore, not anguished tears. What flowed into her was more than magic, more than spirit; it was the whole truth of Shai's self, known and shared.

She knew that Shai—oh, she knew—

Not alone, Xhea thought at last, struggling to find words for her joy. *Not ever again.*

She heard that thought echo back from Shai; the same truth singing from two different hearts.

Xhea opened her eyes.

Shai no longer sagged limp in the awkward circle of Xhea's arms but rested there calmly, her breathing steady and slow. Carefully, Xhea pushed Shai back, holding her by the shoulders—and she *could* hold her. Her fingers no longer sank through Shai's ghostly flesh but held, the pressure of their conflicting magics making that contact feel real.

Shai's face no longer looked empty, but merely as if she was sleeping. Her face—the whole of her body—was lit once more with the steady light of her magic. Shadows fled.

All had not been undone, Xhea saw. The ends of Shai's fingertips seemed hazy, as were the ends of her bare toes. But she was *there*, and if she was not whole and untouched—well, neither was Xhea.

Xhea laughed then, a faint chuckle that was nonetheless filled with wonder. At the sound Shai opened her eyes and looked at her. Slowly, slowly, she smiled.

I'm so sorry, Xhea thought, for she could not move, could not speak. Sorry for the pain she must have felt, the betrayal—

No, Shai said in silence. *It's okay.* The thought was gentle, understanding; it did not stop the pained, guilt-ridden tangle of Xhea's thoughts—but it eased them. Shai reached for Xhea's cheek as if she might brush away the tracks of her fallen tears.

Don't go yet, Xhea thought, and the words flowed between them, one to the other. *Wait for me. We'll go together.*

But what she said was, "That looked like it hurt."

The first words that Shai had ever spoken to her.

Shai laughed, the sound echoing around them in the dim, dusty underground, and said the only thing that she possibly could: "A good observation."

Dawn was long past. Already, the sun was rising high; a span of hours had passed while Xhea and Shai were underground. But it was not the light that made Xhea stagger to a stop and stare—not the light that made Shai gasp and cover her mouth with her hands—but everything else.

Before, though the streets had been undeniably changed—if, captured, they had become a nightmare version of her home—they had at least been recognizable. The world that she saw upon rising from the underground was not.

It was not like the ruins, for all that what surrounded her was ruined. The ruins had been worn by time, by age, by rain and wind and snow; their edges had been blunted, the memory of what they had once been grown over by vines and weeds. Here, there was no such softening. There was no forgetting.

There was only destruction.

Logic told her where she stood, upon which street her feet rested. Memory told her what she should see—only memory. Because, staring, there was nothing of the buildings she knew in the rubble that remained.

Brick and stone lay in great piles, uneven, crumbled; concrete and plaster dust covered everything like a layer of fine, gray snow. She recognized little: the rounded arch of a doorway, the twisted metal of a balcony's rail. The glitter of glass, glinting like lost diamonds in the midst of so much dirt and dust.

Xhea turned, looking around her. She could see farther than seemed proper for any vantage on the Lower City streets. There was little left to obscure her view.

Orren had fallen. She remembered the *feel* of it falling, and suddenly had to close her eyes, disoriented by the Lower City's memory and the contrast to her own flesh, so small and warm and fragile. She pushed the memory away.

Orren had fallen, yet Edren remained, the ancient hotel standing defiant against the wreck and ruin around it. Defiant against the whole of the City above. But its facade glittered with Tower Lozan's spell, a net of bright magic waiting to tear it down.

It's all that's left, she thought—but it was not true. Farther, there were other, smaller buildings still standing. There was less worth in the materials that might be claimed from those walls than the magic needed to tear them down. Xhea had felt them when she had, however briefly, been the whole of the Lower City; she heard their presence, even now, in the living Lower City's echoing song.

But as she turned and turned again, that was all she could see: Edren and black-wrapped Farrow standing like sentinels, guarding their broken domain.

Gone, so much of it's gone. The thought echoed as if it had been spoken, reverberating across the landscape. But for all her despair, Xhea felt hope, too—she felt, strangely, like laughing. Because across the Lower City, smoke had begun to rise.

No, not smoke—magic. Dark magic curled and spiraled as it lifted into the air, like summer rain turned to mist above sun-hot pavement.

"It's working," Shai said, looking around. "The Lower City is fighting back."

Xhea nodded—though the growing fog of dark power had little to do with the plan she had attempted to communicate with the entity. No matter; whatever its intent, it was having an effect.

Despite the destruction, it was clear that the poorer Towers had not finished ransacking the rubble. But as that magic rose from the streets and the buildings and the earth beneath them all, they abandoned that work—they had to. If even weak Lower

City dwellers shied away from the touch of the magic in the underground, Xhea could only imagine how that power felt to City citizens.

Voices cried out. From nearby, Xhea heard the sound of running footsteps, cursing, a door slamming—then an aircar shot skyward, spell exhaust shimmering in its wake.

Farther away, another aircar rose, and another. Xhea laughed then, watching as they lifted into the sky, one by one, fleeing the ground. Fleeing the power that flowed into the air, faster and darker with every passing moment.

"That's right," she called after them. "Run!"

Higher, in the safety of the remaining buildings that were two stories, or three, others lingered. Xhea saw shields pop into being, like bright glints in the morning sunshine. People protecting themselves so that they could continue their work.

Anger surged at the sight.

Xhea did not need to speak; she reached for Shai's hand and found her fingers already there, waiting. Magic leapt between them as if their joined hands were a second tether; magic flowed through them, bright and dark, in an endless loop that built and built as it moved from one to the other and back again.

Shai's light flared beside her, while Xhea's power, dark and heavy and slow, rose from her body in a great roiling pillar. A figure of light; a figure of shadow. Hand in hand they walked down the broken street, and people cried out as they drew near.

No words passed between them; words were not needed anymore. As one they reached out, and their coiling magics twined together into something that was almost a spell. It gleamed like tarnished silver.

That magic grabbed hold of the spell wrapped around Edren, distant though the skyscraper was. As one, they lifted their hands and ripped the spell away, leaving its spell lines to unravel in midair. It had been no small working, and yet they unmade it in an instant.

A sentry on a nearby rooftop leveled a weapon at them. Xhea felt no fear, no hesitation; only reached toward him and clenched her hand into a fist. Shai mirrored the action, and the man's weapon fell from limp fingers to smash on the ground below. Another gesture, and his protective shield popped like a bubble.

"Run," Xhea said to him, and he did.

They did not kill. They did not want more blood and death, only for the scavengers of the poorer Towers to run and hide— to run like they'd made the Lower City dwellers run.

Around them, the Lower City's magic grew and grew. It rose in huge black columns toward the sky, like Xhea's power writ large. The living Lower City reached toward the Towers, reached toward the Spire with great, black arms made only of dark magic, as if it wanted to pull them, one by one, to the ground.

And it sang. Xhea heard herself reflected in that song—some hint of her anger, perhaps, or her determination. In its rise and fall it seemed that she could hear her voice, her laughter, the edge of her sharpened tongue.

Of all the teachers that the Lower City might have had, she wished now that there might have been someone other than her. Someone not quite so bruised and battered by life; someone without so much unspent anger hiding beneath their skin.

Or maybe hers was the truth it had needed.

She did not know, only laughed as its power rose, twining, and reached the Central Spire's lowermost point. The Spire was a channel for magic; as Xhea watched, the Lower City's power entered that channel and surged upward.

Higher on the Spire, there was a flash of magic.

Later Xhea would think, *There was no warning.*

But it was not true. The Spire's warning had come three days before, announced by a light-clad Messenger. It had reverberated through the whole of the Lower City and the ruins beyond; its echoes were felt, even now, in the buildings' collapse.

What Xhea saw? It was only a flash, like sunlight glinting from a gladiator's descending blade.

As they stared upward, bright and dark, feeling as if the City itself should fall at their feet and beg forgiveness, magic rushed across the sky, from Tower to Tower and into the Spire itself.

The Central Spire attacked.

Chapter
Twenty-Six

The Lower City was its buildings, and its buildings had fallen. The Lower City was its people, and its people had fled. The Lower City was its streets and its tunnels and the earth beneath them—the Lower City was its singing, flaring heart of dark power—and the Central Spire attacked them all.

How would you kill a Tower? Lorn had asked, trying to understand what the Spire might do. He might well have asked, *How would you kill a person?*

A spell, a shot, a blade: these were, in the end, only tools; only methods of achieving that deadly end. To kill, one had to strike at an exposed weakness. To kill quickly, instantly, one aimed for the head or neck or heart.

The heart, Xhea thought—it was all she had time for.

A blade of bright magic stabbed down.

She was not the target, but instinct made Xhea cringe, raising her hands. Magic flared around her, bright and dark; magic clashed, warring, until it suddenly merged, layer after layer of protections springing into being.

"Shai," Xhea said, but she could not hear her own voice or pull her scattered thoughts together. There was only the sound of that impact—a great, terrible clash like blades meeting, and the shock of an explosion as debris flew skyward.

The concussive wave sent Xhea tumbling into the rubble, dragging Shai in her wake. Xhea's instinctive attempts at a shield failed as she rolled across the broken ground, but Shai's held, protecting her as rocks and shards of asphalt fell like hail. Yet even those shields shuddered beneath the force of the wave of magic that followed, bright and burning like a wash of noonday sun.

Xhea blinked, blinded, staring at after-images. The Spire had attacked with a spell, one larger than anything she'd imagined possible. Its lines of intent had been huge, each woven by one of the channels along the Spire's sides; airborne, each line was larger around than a person with their arms stretched wide. Together they created the blade that she'd seen, a massive beam of power that had formed beneath the Spire's lowermost point and stabbed toward the ground fast as thought.

Yet something had deflected the blade, or dispersed its power; for even as she struggled to regain her feet, dazed, within the embrace of Shai's shielding magic, Xhea could hear the Lower City's song.

"Are you okay?"

Xhea didn't hear Shai's words so much as feel them, like a thought spoken with the ghost's voice. Xhea's ears were ringing, and she staggered, disoriented—but she nodded. She was not harmed; no more than before.

But the Lower City?

Smoke rose—real smoke, thick and choking, twin to the dark magic that even now covered the Lower City in a haze. That power was no longer shaped into columns, nor into hands that reached skyward, but aimless coils of magic that scattered in the wind.

Like blood, seeping from wounds.

"We have to get to safety," Shai said. Xhea nodded, because the ghost was right, for all that her words seemed impossible to implement. They were blocks from the Lower City's living heart—blocks from the point where the Central Spire's lowermost tip hovered poised above that heart, bright magic gathering for another strike.

Blocks, at such a time, felt like no distance at all.

Xhea's hand tightened on her cane and she stumbled forward, trying to put as much space between her and the Lower City's living heart—as much space between her and the Spire—as possible.

"Edren," Xhea managed. The word was almost a cough, tasting of concrete and ash—but Shai understood.

Before them the skyscraper stabbed skyward. Its surface was pitted and scarred, the flourishes and details of its ancient façade scrubbed away by spell and impact. Most of its precious glass windows had been blown out, leaving only dark holes that gaped like mouths filled with glittering, ragged-edged teeth.

But Edren had been her home when all else had been taken from her; and if she could not name it hers, hope rose in her nonetheless at the sight.

Safety, Xhea thought, in spite of everything. *Shelter.*

The road to Edren was not clear. Debris covered it: huge chunks of fallen walls, bricks and breeze-blocks, scattered pieces of what had once been chairs, beds, clothing, dishes. Navigating those pieces turned the street into a maze, while scrambling over them was an impossibility. Even if she'd been whole and undamaged, Xhea knew the danger of such piles. They were as likely to fall and crush her, trap her, bury her, as they were to allow her safe passage.

Behind her, Xhea felt the Lower City's defenses rising. Like her, it had no complex spells, no allies that might grant it power; like her, it had no great knowledge of the workings of dark magic. The Lower City had only its own power, ancient and raw; countless decades of magic poured from the City above, pooling deep into the ground.

It should have died. Oh, she knew it; she had seen that blade of power. Blinking, she could still see it: a harsh white line bisected her vision.

The living Lower City should have died, and yet she had warned it. Xhea had given all of herself to tell it of the Spire's intent; she had given, unknowingly, all of Shai. And as she'd held what was left of the ghost of her friend, she had thought it a mistake—the effort useless, the sacrifice wasted.

Now she glanced back and watched as the Spire's spelled blade stabbed once more into the ground—and was repelled.

Shai could not stand against that spell, nor could Xhea; they did not have to. It was not the two small, fleeing girls that the Spire targeted, though they were so close to its line of fire. Xhea stumbled and fell, crying out, and Shai followed her down, her protections flaring bright as Xhea curled and cringed and covered her face with her hands.

Again there came that terrible sound, and a concussive gust of wind and dust and magic passed over them. Beneath it was the Lower City's song. But it seemed not like a song anymore so much as a scream, a cry that echoed out as if from a thousand inhuman voices. A scream of pain, yes; but also a scream of defiance.

It understood death as Xhea understood it—death as she had seen and known it.

And it did not want to die.

There was so much magic. Even with her eyes closed, Xhea was blinded; even with Shai's shields, it scoured her tender skin as if it wished to scrape flesh away to bone. But this time, Shai stood strong, not bowed beneath that onslaught as Xhea was— and as magic and thoughts passed between them without barrier, Xhea saw through Shai's eyes.

Color. The overcast sky was white and palest gray, the sun's glow but a brightening of that haze—but beyond? The Towers shone like jewels, blue and red, purple and green, each lit from the inside. Each sent magic to the Spire, and that power shone in pale echo of those tones, turning the sky into a rainbow wash of color.

The Spire absorbed the Towers' power, channeled it; and through Shai's eyes the blade of power that the Spire stabbed downward was not the harsh, blinding white that Xhea saw, but purest gold, edged and glittering.

A thought rose that felt like Shai's, appalled: *They're loaning power from so many Towers. The expenditure—the debt—*

Xhea cared little for the long-term political and financial ramifications of the power she saw—that Shai saw—cast across the heavens. She cared only that so much of the City was arrayed against them. Arrayed, in truth, against the heart of the Lower City.

The ground shook and Xhea's view abruptly shifted; she saw only from her own magic-dazzled eyes the gray patterns of the rock-strewn street.

From the point of impact came the smell of burning—but not smoke and ash, like the market fire, but something darker, hotter, its scent sharply metallic. *Not burning*, she realized. *Melting.*

Again the ground shuddered, and Xhea looked up to see chunks of glowing rock and molten metal arc overhead to smash and splatter across the rubble some span distant. Magic, too, sailed over her in a great rope-like stream: one of the spelllines that formed the Spire's blade had been deflected, and unraveled as it flew.

Xhea watched as the spell smashed into Edren's side.

The ancient hotel's peak exploded, the top ten stories turned to fragments that spewed out like a firework of stone. The rest of the skyscraper shuddered, swaying beneath the force of that impact. Cracks appeared, deep and fast, and a whole section of Edren's façade suddenly fell away, unmoored from its walls.

For a moment, the broken skyscraper stood, its top stories missing, its front stripped bare and its inner workings exposed. Then, like a weary person sagging to their knees, it fell.

Compared to the battle between the Lower City and the Spire, the crash of Edren's collapse was a small sound, for all that its impact shook the ground. Even so, for a moment it was all that Xhea could hear, all that she could see. She watched as a great cloud of dust billowed up and out, and could only stare in blank-faced shock.

Everything had fallen, everything—yet somehow she had thought, somehow she had believed—

But no. There was no safety here, no shelter. For she stood within the ring drawn on the Spire's map—and the territories that the Lower City claimed by right of magic—and she should have known better than to believe there was any other ending. She should have known better than to hope.

Xhea turned away from the rubble that had been Edren and looked back toward the Lower City core. Darkness rose, thick and dark, pushing back the shining remnants of the Spire's latest attack. Yet the Lower City was weakening. Xhea heard fatigue in its song, while in the City above, more magic flowed into the Spire from the Towers, and more magic, and more.

Already the Spire glowed as it readied its next strike, light building along its length like mirrors reflecting the sun.

The Lower City could not form a shield strong enough to stop the Spire's blows. It could not make a weapon to strike back. It did not know how—nor did Xhea.

Yet it had her knowledge of the workings of the Spire itself. It understood what she did—and, struggling to understand why the Spire would consider the Lower City a threat, Xhea had looked down and seen the vast expanse of ground that was the Lower City core. She'd seen the shadow of the magic beneath it—and had known that that power was just a dim reflection of what waited, sunk deep into the earth.

Xhea had not understood how much of that magic was unshaped, unclaimed, untested. Had not known how much the living Lower City would have to learn to make good the threat she'd seen in its vast depth of power.

She'd only had that sudden insight, and instinct had said that the Lower City was, or could be, dangerous. That it was, or could be, a threat.

The living Lower City had rejected some part of her knowledge, she understood now; it had not believed that the Spire would truly strike it—or, in striking, that the Spire's aim would be to kill. The Spire had been its everything: its life and breath, its food and warmth and comfort. Now, it knew itself betrayed.

At last, the Lower City believed her.

And, in believing, the threat that Xhea had imagined became real.

"Sweetness," she breathed, aghast. "Sweetness and blight."

The rising magic seeped into her, and in that power Xhea saw its intent, as if the Lower City whispered into her ear. Oh, yes, the Lower City understood death—hers and its own; it understood the Spire's desire. But what she heard echoing now in its song would only be suicide.

"Shai," she started, "it's going to—"

Shai had already drawn away, her eyes wide. "I know." That knowledge reverberated between them, one to the other; so, too, did a sudden thought of the refugees out in the ruins. Xhea had never been to those encampments, yet she saw them now in quick, confusing flashes. Barricades with spelled walls, makeshift barriers with people huddled behind.

Little to protect anyone from falling debris, or magic, or fire. And there would, they knew, be all three—and that was a best-case scenario.

"The defensive spell generators—I asked Torrence and Daye—"

Xhea nodded. "Yes," she said. "Go."

Because if those spell generators had been brought to the refugees in the ruins, then Shai could power them. And if she could not protect everyone, then at least she could protect some. There would be a future for people here, one way or another.

But Xhea needed to stay, because only here did she have any chance of speaking to the Lower City, guiding its actions or shifting its course. She couldn't move away from the destruction, couldn't head to the ruins or the badlands beyond; she had to move *toward*.

There was no shelter here, not in a building or its remains, not in the tunnels. No, she could only think of one place that she might go; she thought of dark walls turned liquid as they wrapped around her, protecting her, drawing her inward and letting her rise.

Farrow. Not the skyscraper itself, but the tendrils that surrounded it; the only part of all this vast ground that the Lower City had truly claimed.

Shai nodded, accepting her decision. There was no way around it. To speak to the Lower City Xhea had to remain within reach of its magic—within reach of its heart—and there was nowhere left within the Lower City's boundaries that might be called safe. Not anymore.

And death? That was inevitable. Already Xhea knew that her body would not long withstand the damage that had been done inside the Lower City's living heart—or the power that poured from her even now. For all that she, too, was a creature of dark magic, she was also but a girl with a small, failing body.

No words, then; no need to speak them.

Shai reached for her, and Xhea accepted her embrace. Arms wrapped around one another, they rose. No elevator spell, now; no attempts at a shield. Only Shai's power, raw and shaped by her will.

Xhea did not watch the ground fall away, though it was not her familiar fear that made her turn away. Instead, she rested her head against Shai's shoulder and felt the other girl's pale hair whisper across her face, soft as breath.

She closed her eyes and tried not to think.

At last her feet touched Farrow's rooftop, feather-light. It took Xhea a moment to find her balance; her legs shook, and her knee was weak, and for all that she felt calm her heart pounded frantically inside her chest. But magic flowed through her, hers and Shai's, and she would not be afraid.

Much had changed since she'd last stood here. From Shai's expression, that change had occurred overnight; it had not looked this way when she'd attempted to claim the spell generators.

The roof had been flat and covered with small gravel pieces; in places, that gravel had been pushed back or worn away, revealing a hard surface covered with years of flaking, sticky black—tar, perhaps, or paint. Now, though it was black, no hint of that surface remained.

There were only vines—that dark, grown substance. The garages, the chained enclosures where the skyscraper had kept its battered collection of aircars; the welded blocks upon which the spell generators had been mounted; even the rooftop door to the skyscraper itself—all gone, or covered so entirely with black vines that it made no difference.

Briefly, Shai knelt and pressed her hand to that black surface. "Courage," she whispered, the word almost lost in the Lower City's song. But it was not the Lower City to whom she spoke, but Farrow itself—small, pale Farrow, living and struggling within that dark embrace.

Shai's hand brightened as she poured magic into the skyscraper. A moment, two, and then she rose.

Xhea looked at the now-barren wasteland around them; at the Towers above, spinning and spinning, their magic flowing inward. She looked at the Spire, that great pillar of light, as it brightened and prepared another shot.

She laughed. In spite of everything—or maybe because of it—Xhea laughed.

"We've caused such trouble, you and I." Her voice was almost lost in the sound of the ground breaking, cracking, falling in upon the tunnels far below. "You ever think that maybe things would be easier if we just gave up and died?"

"Tried it," Shai said. "Didn't solve anything." Her smile was a flicker of light across her otherwise grave expression.

For a moment they looked at each other, and then Shai lifted into the air, heading out into the ruins. Xhea did not watch her go, only took a deep breath and walked toward the edge of Farrow's rooftop.

Xhea could not see the ground; she did not try to. Instead, she looked across the whole of the Lower City, or what was left of it. Dark magic covered most of the destruction, hiding it beneath a layer of swirling gray fog. Light flashed and flickered within that fog, like lightning dancing within clouds—the remnants of the Spire's most recent spell, spending itself to nothing as it burned.

Here and there, bits poked above the fog's roiling surface—a jutting wall, a broken rooftop—but most was lost to shadow.

As if that magic was oxygen, Xhea breathed it in. She felt it deep within her lungs, felt it shiver across her skin; felt it, too, in the ground beneath her feet, all those black and twisted vines.

She exhaled, and her magic flowed with her breath. Magic swirled from her fingertips. Magic dripped from her cheeks—tears she did not remember crying.

She poured some of herself into that power; it felt, now, almost second nature. Words and emotions and thoughts flowed into that darkness, and sank into the black structure beneath her.

Listen, Xhea said. *I'm here.*

She felt the Lower City's acknowledgment, but it was faint and distant, a sound nearly lost in the deafening chorus of its song. No swell of recognition or greeting, no joyous echo sung in harmony: the entity's attention, now, was almost entirely elsewhere.

Magic, too, had begun to rise—but not in streamers, as before, nor in columns of black, but in a single dark swirl centered above the Lower City's heart. Centered, too, directly beneath the Central Spire's point. It swirled faster as she watched, rising higher.

Xhea had seen the vortex of power that the Spire poured upon the Lower City night after night. This was its opposite: a tornado of black that pointed not down but *up*, reaching for the Spire as if it might consume it entirely.

You can't, she told it.

Yet demonstrably it could. For its power rose and rose, darker now, faster, all the waste magic of the whole of the City suddenly surging into the air and reaching for the Spire. It drew the fog-like haze of power from the ruins and pulled it upward; it drew strength from the very ground, and from Farrow's living walls.

The Lower City sang, loud and triumphant, as if with force of sound and power it could drive out all pain and sadness.

You shouldn't, Xhea corrected.

It heard her, she knew it did; their magics mingled. They were joined now in thought and power and memory, as surely as she was joined to Shai.

It heard her—and it did not agree. It pushed her words and the magic aside as if they meant nothing, as if it could not even stand to listen.

Xhea could listen, and did; and suddenly within the rise and fall of its wailing song she heard a sound that had not been there before. It was not voice or melody, rhythm or harmony. It was the beat that underlay it, the truth that had become the bedrock for the whole of the Lower City's being.

If Xhea had a word for that sound, it would be only this: *Gone, gone, gone.*

Its walls were gone, its people were gone. Its streets and buildings, its skyscrapers and tunnels—they were gone, all of them gone. The Lower City was breaking, it was broken, it was gone and still it lived. It lived and it fought back because it could do no less.

In the echoes of that pain, Xhea heard something else.

Alone, the Lower City sang. *Alone, alone, alone.*

The City that had birthed it wished only for its death; the Towers had turned against it. The Central Spire, which the living Lower City had always thought of as the giver of life and sustenance, formed the blade that sought its end.

Of everything else, what was left? Only rubble, each stone torn apart. Only dust and ash and ruin.

Xhea knew that pain. She had given it the words that now echoed through the fallen structures of her home.

Gone. Alone.

But it was not true. No matter how it felt, no matter how that truth seemed to echo down through the very core of its heart, it was not true.

No, Xhea said. She sank to Farrow's rooftop and pressed her hands to that black surface as if she might press her meaning into its very being. *I'm here. Your people are here, in the ruins just beyond. We have not abandoned you.*

That inverse funnel of power twisted higher. It was beyond the height of Farrow now, reaching into the empty space that separated the Lower City from the City above. It did not hesitate at her words; it did not even slow.

You are not the buildings, she told it. *You can shape yourself, as the Towers do. You can make something new—something stronger, something better. But please, don't do this.*

Again, that light flashed midway down the Spire—a precursor, only, to its final attack. And it would be the final attack, Xhea thought; for all the Lower City's magic, all its sudden rage, it could not withstand the City's concentrated power.

But the Lower City was not going to give it a chance to fire again. The vortex of dark magic reached the Spire's lowermost point.

"You *can't!*" Xhea cried. Her voice echoed, thin and breaking, across the broken landscape.

It did not listen. Instead, the Lower City reached up with all its strength, all its dark power, and began to pull the Central Spire from the sky.

Chapter Twenty-Seven

Shai fled toward the ruins, and it took all of her strength not to look behind her. She felt the pressure of the Lower City's rising dark magic, sure as Xhea felt the pain of the bright magic of the Spire's attacks.

Xhea had given the Lower City her life. Her understanding, yes, and her knowledge—but her years, too, of anger and loneliness. It did not live those experiences as she had, one at a time and growing slowly from each. Instead, it gained them in a single gulp, and the things she had learned these past months must have seemed small against the pressure of the rest.

Or maybe it was only that those were the experiences that spoke to it, twin to its own.

It is not wrong, Shai thought—for she could almost hear the edges of its song; a hint of its meaning echoed to her from Xhea. So much loss, there; so much anger and betrayal. The Lower City lay in ruins. The Spire had turned on it, and many of the richer Towers.

They meant to destroy the Lower City and now the Lower City was bent on destroying them in kind. There was symmetry in that. Not justice, not peace. But symmetry.

Shai had seen the refugees' camps in darkness; daylight was no kinder. Though the ancient, broken walls were stronger now than anything left in the Lower City, they offered poor shelter.

But people were moving, she saw as she rushed past. They no longer huddled behind the walls but ventured beyond them. Hesitantly, in places; in obvious fear of the uncertain ground around them, and wary of conflict with their new neighbors, but moving even so.

There was work to be done.

While some of the refugees stared at the clashing magic at the heart of what had once been their home, others turned resolutely away. Shai saw tears on a woman's face as she bent over her work, building a wall with stones and rough mortar. A father held his child close, rocking her, shielding her eyes from the light of the Spire's strikes, while next to him an older boy stirred the watery soup that was to be their breakfast.

Shai's heart lifted as she approached Edren's encampment. The walls still stood, and Edren's people worked to make them higher, stronger—and towering above those walls like a bare flagpole stood a defensive spell generator.

Shai looked at that pitted length of metal—its cross-spars twisted and broken, its directional controls all but gone—and smiled in relief. It did not mean salvation—but it meant they had a chance.

"Ghost incoming," said a voice as Shai approached. She looked down at Torrence.

A bruise marred the left side of his face, its mottled red already darkening toward blue; his left eye was nearly swollen shut. He had been lying in a nest of blankets near the generator's mounted base, his head pillowed on his arms, as nearby others stood and argued.

Or, rather, Lorn, Emara and Councilor Tranten argued. Daye stood beside them, her arms crossed, looking like nothing so much as a disapproving statue.

At Shai's arrival, Torrence's lips lifted in a lazy grin and he pushed himself up, as if rest could be denied in light of whatever entertainment Shai now offered.

Others, too, turned toward Shai's light; she shone into the visual spectrum without meaning to, so much power flowing through her now that she could not bear the thought of holding it back. No matter—she would need all this power and more if she had any hope of pushing the generator's defensive spells wide enough to cover even a fraction of the refugees.

"Shai," Lorn started, and as he turned toward her glow she was surprised to see that Torrence wasn't the only one with a damaged face. An angry cut sliced across Lorn's forehead, swollen and pulling against the hasty stitches that held it closed. "We were just—"

Torrence, of all people, cut him off. "Perhaps you can help us," he said, the sharpness of his gaze belying his lazy tone. "We were discussing what to do with these."

He kicked aside the dirty fabric that had covered the second spell generator.

No, Shai thought, her eyes widening in surprise. There were two more spell generators. Torrence and Daye had retrieved the two generators from Farrow's rooftop, as well as the one from Rown. They'd reached Rown before it had fallen—or had stolen it from Rown's refugees, and right now it mattered little which.

Lorn brought forth a rough-sketched map of their encampment, a variety of symbols sketched in ash indicating proposed placements of the second two generators. "We thought," he began—but this time it was Shai who cut him off.

She wrote in midair, *You need to take them to the refugees on the Lower City's other side. There.* She gestured at a location roughly a third around that encircling ring from their current position. *And there.* Another third.

Voices rose to debate and again Shai gestured, cutting them off. She wasn't interested in discussion.

Already she could see a swell of dark magic in the Lower City's center, a rising vortex of power. She saw its intent written in those swirling patterns, black on shadowed gray; the Lower

City spoke only of vengeance now. It spoke of death—its own, and that of the City above.

Shai pressed her hand to her chest where the spelled tether was bound. She felt Xhea's distress as if it were her own; felt the girl's urgency building beneath her breastbone. Whatever Xhea was doing to calm the Lower City's anger, it wasn't working.

Closer, on the edge of the Lower City's limits, there was a detonation—a flicker of the Spire's last attack, the spell striking out as it died. Magic discharging, nothing more. Yet rock scattered from that point to fall upon the refugees like hail. Most chunks were small, little larger than a tooth or eye—but she saw, too, bits of brick and concrete that were the size of a man's fist, a person's head.

Shai moved without thinking. She reached, fingers spread wide, and knocked the pieces from the sky with a surge of bright magic. She wove spells fast as thought: spells to break apart the larger pieces, turning them to nothing but dust and fragments; spells, too, to slow their dangerous velocity. Bits rained down on Edren's encampment.

Farther, where there were no such protections, Shai heard screams.

Faster, she thought, looking to the spell generator. She had to work faster.

Below her, conversation had stopped. She lowered herself to the ground at Torrence's side, feet touching down as if she might stand on that rocky ground. They were looking at her, staring.

As if a flaring protection spell were anything at which to gape. But here, now, amidst so many exhausted protectors? Perhaps it was.

Shai pointed toward the Lower City core and the dark magic rising above the ragged ruins of the buildings.

It wants to destroy the City above, she wrote. *The whole City.*

Lorn stilled; beside him, Emara reached for her knives. Daye, as usual, did nothing. It was Torrence who spoke.

"Well," he said. "That sounds messy."

That was one way of putting it.

For she looked up, and saw Towers arrayed above them; Towers moving, spinning. She did not know what any of them might do when the Lower City's dark magic reached them—did not know whether that magic *could* reach them, or what else the Lower City had planned. Even so, she feared it. It wouldn't take much to destroy what was left of these people, or the little they still had.

In the City's center, magic spread across the sky, gold and green and blue, flowing toward the Spire. Light built along the Spire's length, and Shai knew they were readying another strike.

Shai wondered what the Spire told them, the officials who now ruled those Towers—that the Lower City was a danger, a threat? It hadn't been—not until the City had tried to destroy it, the buildings and entity both. More likely, she realized, they had simply offered terms for those loans that only a fool would turn down. For Shai knew fortunes when she saw them, the riches of untold thousands pooling across the sky.

"No rest for the wicked." Torrence was laughing. "Give it here," he said to Daye, who had already lifted one end of the heavy spell generator. She passed him the end, moved, then heaved the other end into the air. Shai knew the weight of those spires; she had tried and failed to lift them herself. Torrence grunted as he took its weight—but Daye? She didn't even flinch.

Wait, Shai wrote, and reached for the generator. *Don't think*, she reminded herself; she didn't need a careful weavings as with the elevator, only a shape woven on instinct. She sent a spell into the metal—not quite a tracking spell, but something similar. She thought of a length of chain broken into three pieces, and attached one of those pieces to each battered generator.

She nodded and let the second two spell generators be taken away. As Torrence and Daye carried theirs toward a battered aircar, Lorn called for an aide and for another car to be brought from the encampment's interior. Shai left them to their planning.

She went to the base of the spell generator already mounted within the encampment. She placed her hand on that cold metal, then let her fingers sink slowly within it.

There were spells there—not spells like the ones that she wove, all unthinking, in bright magic; not spells, either, like trained spellcasters used, those careful patterns of magic and intent. These spells were part of the metal itself; the spire *was* the spell.

It was inert now; no magic flowed through it, latent or otherwise; and the storage coil installed at its base was dead. But spell generators weren't meant to be fueled by such things; they were grown parts of the Towers themselves, used to power flowing through them the way living flesh was used to blood.

The analogy was more apt than she first knew, Shai realized as she let her awareness sink deeper into the metal. For the spell generator was not just a structure grown by a Tower, but was— or had once been—*part* of a Tower, as much a piece of that living being as her arm or leg was part of her.

It was not alive anymore; yet it remembered the flow of power the way Shai remembered living.

As Shai funneled magic into it, it shivered in response. Magic twisted around the generator, through it, weaving complicated patterns before arcing up in a great fountain of light. It created a dome. At first it was small, protecting only a span of some twenty feet or more, but as she poured magic into it the spell spread, becoming wider, arcing higher with every passing moment.

Shai had seen this spell generator and its twin working on Farrow's rooftop as the doomed skyscraper had attempted to rise. Then, the domes of protective magic that the two had created had been bright, glittering, and tinged with gold.

Despite the similarity in the shape that now opened over Edren's refugees like an umbrella, this spell was different. For she was no mere storage coil, feeding the generator raw power; she wove her magic as it left her, shaping and changing those spells in turn.

She thought of protection—a wall against the dangers of the world, a barrier past which no blade might fall. But she thought too of gentler things: of the peace she'd found in the safest moments of her life, lying curled in the grass beneath the glorious light of Allenai's living heart. She thought of beginnings. Of the children sheltering in these ruins; of the trees out here reaching for the sky.

Of new leaves unfurling.

The spell that arced now above her was not gold but green, and it shimmered the way leaves did in a breeze.

A surge of emotion from Xhea—fear and awe in equal measure—made Shai look away from her working.

There, beyond the boundaries formed by the glowing green spell, she saw a pillar of light and darkness. The Spire. Light formed its peak, and light gleamed down its sides all the way to the central living platforms that held the gardens Shai had so loved as a child. Beneath that, light gave way to shadow.

Dark magic crawled up the Spire's golden sides from the Lower City's great funnel of power. That magic seeped into the Spire, running up the channels that Xhea had seen, and unraveled all in its wake. Dark magic, too, wrapped around the Spire's exterior in a long, lazy spiral, twisting around and around as it reached ever higher.

As Shai watched, that power dug deeper into the Spire, clenched tight, and *pulled.*

The Spire was impossibly huge, impossibly powerful; but within the Lower City's grasp, it shuddered. Even from such a distance Shai could see the motion that reverberated along its length: it trembled, as if in fear. At that motion, the Spire's uppermost peak snapped in two.

Shai was not the only one watching in shock; someone screamed, a sound that was echoed by countless voices in the ruins. Echoed, she felt sure, by countless voices in the City itself.

It was just a small piece that fell, spinning, toward the ground—a small piece, that is, for the Spire. Yet that length was at least a third of the size of many Towers, perhaps half of the height of some of the poorer Towers out on the City's edges; and what it lacked in mass, it made up for in momentum.

It hit one of the Spire's uppermost living platforms, carving out a deep chunk and sending glittering shards raining down. The fragment of the Spire's peak tumbled, end over end, into the Towers below it.

Defensive spells flared from the nearest Towers, red and violet and a roiling, twisting blue. Towers pushed that piece aside—pushed it, truly, toward their neighbors, though whether by accident or design Shai could not tell.

The fragment struck the side of one Tower, and another; and despite the defensive spells that shone like burning wings, she could see it had done damage. Down the fragment fell, bashed from one Tower to another before at last tumbling into the empty air between the City and the ground.

"Protect them," she whispered to those Towers, as if her words might fly from her lips and to the Towers' hearts; as if she could not already see their grown flesh turned liquid, healing the damage that piece had wrought. Protect the people, she meant. For in that moment, her goal and that of the Towers' seemed one: to save the lives of those who counted on them.

One defensive spell generator was already working, its green-tinged fountain of power arcing across the refugees' shelters. She could feel, too, the spells she'd placed on the other two generators; they were like little sparks of herself, held at a distance. Both had stopped moving.

"I hope you've got them anchored," Shai whispered to Torrence and Daye, and whomever Lorn had sent in the other direction. She hoped that the other refugees had allowed the generators to be placed in their own encampments—or that they had been mounted somewhere safe nearby. For as she watched broken fragments of the Spire and Towers alike rain down, she knew she had no more time to spare.

Shai had stretched the protective dome from the single spell generator to its limits; she could feel the spells in the metal protest as she tried to twist their lines to go a little farther, a little wider. This, then, was what she had to work with.

Now for the hard part.

Shai reached for the spells she'd placed on the generators. She envisioned those three pieces of a chain linked once more together, one to the other in a single whole, unbroken and strong no matter the distance between the links. Felt them, as if they were things she might grasp in her outstretched hands, and joined her power to them.

In the far distance, roughly where she had pointed, she saw first one then the other spell generator flare to life. They, too, were green, though the haze of dust and dark magic between them shadowed that color.

Like this, she told the generators, pushing at the spells woven into their metal. The spell that she held was the template, and she struggled to get the second two generators to follow suit.

Shai felt stretched, as if her ghostly body and not just her magic were being pulled in three directions. She staggered and held to the metal and magic of the generator beside her, as if it might steady her.

Focus, she commanded, and let her breathing fall into a familiar pattern that spoke of calm and steadiness. Despite her fear, her exhilaration, her magic steadied in response, no longer flowing out in a rush but in controlled beams of pure power.

Once those domes had been spread to their full extent, Shai linked them. Suddenly they were not three arcing domes of power but a protective ring that circled the whole of the Lower City and the refugees that sheltered in the ruins around it.

Shai gasped as the working took hold, feeling magic pour out of her almost as fast as she created it. *Steady*, she thought, changing her breathing pattern to one that spoke of strength and stability. *Steady.*

But it was not enough. For all her strength, all her power, it was not enough.

That great ring of green light flickered—and though the part to which she was connected flowed unbroken, her hands held deep within the metal of the spell generator, the defenses in the distant parts thinned and stuttered. Too much distance between the spell generators; too little magic spread too thin.

She was no Tower. Her heart was made not of pure magic but only the memory of human flesh, weak and fallible; and for all that her unthinking magic turned her into a pillar of blinding light, she was just a person. One person.

Shai could not save them all, and she wept to know it.

She barely noticed when another spark of power joined hers. So very little magic; it was hardly a glimmer, especially compared to her flaring light.

But then came a second spark, and a third, centered around the spell generator that was anchored out near the far edges of what had been Rown and Farrow's territories. A fourth spark, a fifth, each tiny bit of magic holding a different signature.

Torrence, she recognized suddenly. Something in one of those pale sparks spoke of the bounty hunter. *Daye.*

Then again, a spark, this time on the other spell generator on the Lower City's far side.

And another, and another.

Lorn. Emara. Mercks. Councilor Tranten.

She would not have said that she would recognize their magical signatures, but she did—she knew them as the weak, flickering sparks of their power entered the spell.

They were joining her, she realized; the people of the Lower City were adding their magic to hers. She could not see them, they were too far distant; but she could *feel* them, feel their magic as surely as if those people had stood beside her and placed their hands over hers.

None were powerful. None, not even the strongest, would have been considered anything of true value in the City above. Certainly not on their own.

But together? More power flowed into Shai's working, and more, and the failing spell surged once more to life. It grew stronger and wider, rising to encircle all of the fallen Lower City, a ring of arcing, flaring light that stretched far out into the ruins.

She could almost hear it singing, the way Xhea might.

The spell was not green, now, or not only green. Other colors filled the working: the leaf-like glow of her magic was joined by threads of red, twists of orange, a soft haze of blue. Colors twisted over it, through it, dancing like oily rainbows across a puddle's surface. No boundaries, there; no way to tell Edren's people from Orren's or Senn's, Rown's or Farrow's. No way to tell one person's magic from another.

Tens turned to a hundred, then more, and more.

And so they stood, Shai and the people of the Lower City, holding high the shelter that protected them from the dangers of the City above as the Spire fell from the sky.

Chapter Twenty-Eight

The living Lower City grasped the Central Spire and dragged it toward the ground.

It was not easy. Magic poured from the ground, more magic, dark magic, as the Lower City struggled against the countless spells that held the Spire aloft. Spells, too, flared along the Spire's length, fighting to maintain its altitude.

The ground shook with the force of the power rushing through it. The broken bits of the few buildings that still stood began to crumble, and dust rose in clouds across the Lower City's surface. Farrow, too, shuddered beneath her, swaying like a narrow tree.

Xhea screamed and stumbled back from Farrow's edge.

"No!" she cried, in voice and magic alike. "No, please—you *can't*. You'll break it, you'll destroy everything!"

But that, she knew, was its intent.

No matter that dragging the Central Spire from the sky would kill the Lower City too. The Spire hovered directly above the Lower City's living heart; there was nowhere it could go but down. To pull the Spire from the sky was like Xhea placing a long knife against her chest, positioning its blade between the curving arches of her ribs, and stabbing the blade directly into her heart.

Her living heart, her beating heart. Was a heart of magic any different?

It did not matter what she tried to tell the Lower City, or what words she used; did not matter what images she tried to shape or how desperately she pleaded.

It would not listen. It did not even try—only held the Central Spire with countless hands of grasping dark magic, wrapped each one tight, and pulled.

Xhea screamed as part of the Spire broke free and fell, tumbling, toward her. It bounced from one Tower to the next, pushed by defensive spells, until at last it fell with a great booming crash to the earth some span of blocks distant. *Senn's territory*, she thought—not that such things had meaning anymore.

The Spire towered above her, so close that much of its length was lost to her sight, nearly vanishing into the overcast sky high above. But she saw bright magic at its peak, flaring, flashing; all else had already turned dark.

She could not see the whole of it, but what she could see was coming closer. Harder the Lower City dragged at it, and faster, until suddenly the Spire was not slipping some span of feet but falling.

As much as she despised the Spire—or, rather, the people who ran it—she did not want them to die. She did not want this. And so Xhea reached out with her magic, not lifting it toward the sky, but sending it down.

Down into Farrow beneath her, running through the skyscraper's embrace of vines; down into the underground beneath, all those broken halls. Down into the Lower City's heart.

But not to merge with it this time, not to speak, but to bind.

She no longer had Lissel's binding as a guide—had not examined the intricate weavings of that spell, only felt its terrible constriction. Yet she knew what she had to do.

Quickly, before the Lower City noticed or understood her intent, Xhea wrapped bands of dark power around its heart. Those bindings hung loose at first, while she added more and made them stronger. She imagined that they were not just magic but metal, braided and strong; not just bindings but a strong hand holding the Lower City back. Magic rushed out of her, dark and cold, and she felt her panicked breathing slow in response.

It's not enough, she thought, as her power as it wrapped around and around. But it was all she had.

With a sudden jerk, she pulled the bindings tight.

Xhea had struggled to break Lissel's binding—had struggled, even, to crack it. The Lower City had no such difficulty. Though she'd poured all of her magic into those bindings, everything she could spare, the Lower City just seemed to shrug, and her bands of power fell away.

Xhea gasped as that magic was torn from her grasp. Her head spun, dizzy, disoriented.

She'd known that the Lower City was stronger, infinitely more powerful, but she had thought—

It didn't matter now.

Xhea stared up as the Spire plummeted, stabbing deep into the earth—and into the Lower City's flaring, beating heart.

Xhea was cast to the ground and tossed as everything shook and shuddered. Everything was screaming, tearing, grinding, crashing.

She screamed and could not hear her own voice. Debris fell around her, striking her exposed head and hands, and only her magic—rising thick and dark around her—protected her from worse. It burned away the pieces as they rained upon her.

At last, Xhea could open her eyes. Farrow should have fallen. It would have fallen a thousand times over if the Lower City didn't hold it, those dark vines twisting and turning and reshaping themselves around the ancient skyscraper's structure, holding it aloft after all else had turned to dust.

Still the Spire fell, on and on, that once-brilliant pillar of light turned dark as it stabbed ever deeper. Dark magic boiled into the air, thick and black: the Lower City's heart's blood. The Lower City should have screamed, Xhea thought. But though its song rose and rose, unstoppable, it sang not of pain but triumph.

And the Lower City lived.

The Spire shook and shuddered and cracked. Xhea thought of what she'd seen of the Spire, that bare, magic-free space and the dark magic children that lived within it. Lissel and Amel, the kids playing and reading, and all the ghosts bound to them. The Spire's servants, the other attendants—Abelane's friends. She could only imagine what was happening to them.

And the Spire from Shai's stories? All those gardens, so much growing and green—all those places, level upon level of homes and offices and public spaces, stretching from near-ground to sky. She could not see them; only watched as the Spire cracked and crumbled.

From the Spire's peak, more pieces broke away and tumbled through the City. The Spire should have broken, Xhea thought. It should have cracked in half and fallen like a felled tree, crashing through the Towers all the way to the ground.

It should have fallen, but it did not. For, Xhea realized, the power that she saw rise into the air was only some small portion of the Lower City's magic; the rest surged up through the Spire itself, and wrapped around it, through it.

It held. The Central Spire stood like a sword plunged into the ground, and though it swayed and shuddered and threatened to break, it held.

If the Spire was a sword, it was one held now in the Lower City's hand.

The Spire was a channel for magic, and now it channeled only dark. Xhea leaned back, farther and farther, and watched in horror as dark magic flowed from the Spire's center and stretched across the sky.

It reached for the Towers and twined around them, one by one. And, one by one, they grew dark.

It was her plan, she realized; her plan achieved. But now she reached out, small fingers grasping at nothing, as if she might take it back. As if she could gather that magic and draw it down.

As if she could stop the Towers from dying.

"Please stop," Xhea whispered to the Lower City. She was so quiet; she could not even hear her own voice.

There was no point in arguing anymore. No point in begging or pleading or crying. She could hear in its song: the Lower City would not be turned from its path. It would pull the Towers from the sky one by one, as long as it was able.

Vengeance. Justice. The City cast to the ground as she had been, as so many Lower City dwellers had been, as if they were nothing. Shouldn't she have cheered?

Not anymore.

Xhea sank to Farrow's dark-covered rooftop, feeling the smooth vines against her palms; she rested her aching body and her throbbing knee. She settled to the ground as if it were her bed, some soft nest of blankets where she might rest in peace, for all that she did not let herself surrender to sleep.

There, she began to sing.

Xhea had never had a good voice; she had learned long ago that even her tuneless humming when she washed her clothes in the communal basins would earn her only dark looks or mockery, depending on the audience. She had never *wanted* to sing, for that poor voice was just a vulnerability, and the last thing she'd needed was another weakness.

Now, that song came without thought or hesitation, the words falling from her tongue. The melody was slow and simple, the words rhyming; it was a song that Abelane had sung to her during the longest, darkest nights, when the walkers had been outside their building and neither of them could sleep.

A lullaby.

Her voice did not carry, nor did she try to make it. Yet it was not only her voice that she raised, or that echoed now across the broken landscape. Her voice was but the vessel; it was her magic that held the true power, the sound only giving shape to the black.

She lifted her voice, and yet she sang, too, the way the Lower City did: letting her power flow from her without words. Magic rose from her lips and tongue; it rose from her hands and outstretched fingers; it lifted from the whole of her bruised and battered skin and swirled in midair, its patterns complex and slow.

She knew the Lower City's song, that furious chorus that shouted: *Betrayed, gone, alone.* She knew those pains; she knew that anger, burning so hot and fast that it seemed it would consume all and leave nothing in its wake.

She knew how it felt to want to tear everything down, *everything*, as if in destruction one could be avenged; as if fury might purify, might wash one's heart clean.

It was not of such things that she sang now.

The Lower City's song was inhuman, too beautiful and terrible to have ever been birthed from a human mind or throat. Xhea's song was the opposite: thin and weak, her voice warbling, breaking. Her magic, too, for all its glorious power, was nothing compared to the dark magic that rose even now from the ground, thick and black, as if it meant to turn morning into night.

But it was the heart and soul of her. It was inherently human; and though it was not beautiful, it was true.

Xhea sang not of pain or death, not of vengeance or destruction—not even of the sorrow that was left when such things were past. The words were simple: they spoke of the laying down of burdens and closing one's eyes to rest until the next day dawned. But it was not, now, the words that mattered; and into their simple, repetitive phrases she put other meaning.

Xhea sang a song of farewell.

Farewell to the place she had known: the market and the skyscrapers, the tunnels and the streets and the ruins beyond. Farewell to the world she'd known and the people that had filled it; farewell to the joys and horrors of her time in the Lower City, its petty frustrations and small triumphs.

Farewell to her life, and the lives of countless others. The people in the Towers, guilty and innocent alike. The Towers themselves, great and unknowable creatures of magic, airborne structures dancing across the sky.

Xhea felt as the Lower City hesitated, confused—for she wasn't trying to reach it now, wasn't trying to speak or reason with it, wasn't trying to change its path. She only sang.

There was guilt there, too, woven in amongst her goodbyes, but she did not let it settle on her shoulders; that weight was not hers to bear. She had tried, in countless small ways, to fight the things that occurred as much as she had set them in motion, she and Shai alike.

Xhea had tried to fight, and she had failed. A thousand times over she had failed.

Yet for all her mistakes and missteps, there were some things that she would never do differently. If she could live her life over, her mistakes unmade, her sorrows washed clean, she would still accept the hesitant, fearful ghost that had been brought to her one rainy spring day. She would still try to save her.

Shai. Her hand rested on the tether, though she did not need the physical touch to connect her to that ghost anymore. They were far apart, but Xhea felt her friend as if she stood by her side, her hand resting on Xhea's shoulder. Xhea felt Shai's struggle to achieve some great working—felt the pull on her own magic. But beneath that, beneath thought or image or emotion, there was only Shai.

Goodbye, Xhea sang, repeating her lullaby's simple melody once more. For here it ended, and though tears coursed down her cheeks to wet the blackened rooftop beneath her, it was not only sorrow that she felt.

Her life had not been gentle; it had not been easy. It had not, at times, even been good. But it had been *hers*, and for that she would be forever grateful.

Her song finished, the last whispered note vanishing into silence. Xhea took a deep breath and closed her eyes.

The world around her stopped.

Xhea sat unmoving, caught in a moment of perfect quiet. Silence was a bubble that rose to surround her. She could not hear the earth shuddering, the Spire cracking, breaking; there was no hint, even, of the Lower City's song.

She opened her eyes.

The Lower City's magic surrounded her like a wall. It was poised, waiting. Confused.

Then sound rushed back in a wave of magic, and she winced from the force of it. Again that power spiraled around her as if to draw her attention, then swooped skyward, toward the Towers.

Bright power surrounded those structures, flashing like blades of light as they attempted to beat back the dark magic that assaulted them from the ground and Spire alike.

Look, the Lower City seemed to be saying. *Here.*

As if she had not already seen what it was doing, or understood its intent. As if, understanding, she would cheer for that destruction, and join her magic to the flood of power that now rushed skyward.

Xhea shook her head. She moved her hand, and the dark magic that flowed from her fingers did not join that upward rush but cut through it, pushing it away in a gesture of sharp, swift denial.

Again the Lower City hesitated. She could feel its attention on her like a pressure, for all that it reached skyward and battled the Towers. Its song stuttered in confusion and inquiry.

Why did she not join it? Why did she just sit there, looking out and not up?

Why did she not watch its fight with the Towers above, that coming triumph, and instead only stare at a lone Tower on the City's fringes?

It had been so difficult, once, to understand this entity. To understand not just that it sang, but that the song was its voice; to understand the meaning that was—and was not—in that melody. To understand the rush of magic and image, emotion and sensation that came with every note.

It wasn't sound, not in truth. Sound was only the way that her brain interpreted what it sensed. She knew it, and it did not change the way that song thrummed through her body and ears alike.

Once it had been difficult to understand the living Lower City—but then she had lost herself in the whole of its mind, and it had, in turn, lost itself in her life. Her memories. Her emotion. However briefly, they had been a single entity.

Now she struggled to imagine hearing what she heard, feeling what she felt, and not understanding it.

It was puzzled, almost hurt by her reaction. A cloud of dark swirled around her, and in its song she heard the words that might shape that questioning sound—the words that she would have spoken.

What are you doing?

"I'm bearing witness," Xhea whispered.

Confusion.

"I'm watching. I'm seeing the effects of what you've done— what you're still doing."

Confusion compounded. Sound and power swirled, probing, questioning.

"If they're going to fall, they'll fall—but I will not let their deaths go unmarked."

No more hidden lives, like the one she'd lived; no more ignored deaths.

Xhea did not know the name of the Tower that she watched slip from the ranks of the City. Perhaps she would have known the name if she had heard it spoken; perhaps it was one of those whose names had so recently echoed through these streets, reviled. Lozan or Helta, Elemere or Jhen or Tolair. It did not matter.

The Tower was from the City's edges; no debris should have reached so far. Yet it had, and the Tower's defenses were too weak—the Tower itself was too poor—to push it back. A piece of the Spire hit it hard and the Tower shuddered, sliding on air.

As Xhea watched, its grown-metal flesh turned liquid, shimmering as it attempted to heal that wound. Attempted, too, to stay aloft.

But it was falling.

Just one casualty in this fight, but not, she thought, the last.

As it fell beneath the level of the other Towers, that unnamed structure gave up its attempts to struggle back into the sky. Instead, its whole surface changed to that shimmering liquid, and Xhea imagined that inside, its citizens were being absorbed into the walls or floors or whatever other surface they could find as the Tower prepared for impact with the ground.

Xhea winced as that huge structure hit the earth of the distant badlands, far beyond the brilliant protective ring that now encircled the raging Lower City. A moment, then she heard the sound of it, echoing across the landscape. Its long, tapering point crumpled as it hit; its defensive spires cracked and exploded in a shower of sparks. But maybe, just maybe, it had managed to slow its descent enough to protect its citizens. Maybe, just maybe, it would live.

"You did not deserve what they did to you," Xhea said to the Lower City. She did not have to try to speak in magic anymore; that power was like air to her, its calm filling her, its taste perpetually on her tongue. "And that Tower? It did not deserve what happened to it."

A rush of sound, of anger, of denial.

The Lower City was a vast creature, ancient, unknowable. She knew it. Yet, hearing that voice, she suddenly understood that it was also a child. A child lost and ignored—just like Xhea's younger self.

Despite its strength and power and rage, that's how she suddenly imagined it. The Lower City was a hurting child, just a small girl curled in upon herself, weeping angry tears. Angry, lost, betrayed.

And because Xhea had been that girl, she understood. Once she, too, would have burned the whole of the City to the ground. She would have watched the Towers fall, and she would have laughed.

"This doesn't fix it," she whispered now. "This death? This destruction? It doesn't make it better."

Again she hummed the lullaby's refrain, as if to remind it of all that had come before; not just of loss, but of life and home and stability.

A pause, then: *Too late*, it said. The sorrow ringing through that chord did nothing to ease the sense of inevitability. *Too late, too far.* As if now that it had begun this destruction, everything had to fall. Every Tower just a domino, tumbling one after another from the sky.

"No," Xhea told it. "You get to choose. Every moment you get to choose."

The words themselves were simple, even trite. There had been a time when hearing them would have made Xhea roll her eyes at best. At worst? She wouldn't have listened at all.

But if the Lower City was now like her younger, angrier self, it had within it, too, the memories of everything that came after; the seeds of growth, and the person she had become. It was choosing the anger, as she once had. It was choosing to cling to that hurt and betrayal, and no matter how truly it had been earned, it was not of use here.

Dark magic poured from the ground, up through the Central Spire, and into the City above. It wrapped around the closest Towers, the richest Towers, and for all their wealth and status and affluence, they struggled. They sputtered. They began to slip from the sky.

Farther the Lower City's magic reached, and farther. No triumph there anymore, only a slow weight of grief. It would see through what it had started. It did not see any other option.

A surge of thought and emotion came from Shai, flooding into Xhea like the sudden memory of a dream. Home and conflict and youth; a flash of leaves; a living, flaring heart.

Allenai.

Xhea looked up.

Amidst the chaos of the Towers and the black, smoke-like tendrils that reached for them, it took her a moment to find Allenai. The Tower had changed much since she'd first seen it, when she'd thought that it was to blame for every ill that befell her since Shai's death. It had changed, too, since its forced takeover of Eridian. But it was not Allenai's new appearance that made her blink in surprise, but the magic that surrounded it.

Xhea knew Towerlight—could see Towerlight, even against the overcast sky, the Towers' defenses shining like a brilliant gray aurora. The magic that spread from Allenai was different.

For all their beauty, the defensive spells of the other Towers seemed sharp, forming great blades that swept through the air. The magic around Allenai was gentler in its movement; and it did not press against the spells of the Towers surrounding it, but seemed instead to flow around them.

Allenai reached for the Spire and the dark magic that surrounded it not as if it wished to attack or defend. *No*, Xhea thought. It was like a hand reaching out.

An offering. An invitation.

A plea.

Xhea saw only magic; she was too far to hear any sound if Allenai was, indeed, singing. But Shai saw something different.

Meaning filled that magic, thought and color and intent, and if Shai did not read such things with the ease that Xhea now shared meaning with the Lower City, she nonetheless understood.

"It's calling," Xhea said. Her words felt like an echo of Shai's, as if they spoke in unison no matter the distance between them. She felt pride in those words, joy; she felt Shai's sudden smile.

To the Lower City, Xhea said, "It's not an attack. It's a greeting."

As Towers fought and struggled and fell, Allenai called out to the Lower City. Called out, too, to the Towers that surrounded it—and one by one, they stopped fighting. The Lower City reached for them and they did not engage. They pulled away, not battling that touch, but evading it. Around them, the other Towers shifted and moved to make room.

Xhea thought suddenly of standing within Eridian as Allenai crashed down upon it, the walls tearing away and becoming liquid, swirling and merging. In the City they spoke of hostile takeovers in human terms; yet there, listening to the Towers as they merged, Xhea had heard only joy. It was joining of thought and mind and power, as much as it was of physical, grown-metal flesh.

They want *to join*, she'd thought then in sudden understanding. But now she realized something more: despite their human inhabitants, the Towers were lonely.

They battled, one against the other across the sky, fighting for altitude, power, position—but not because they wanted to. Not because such things had meaning for the living Towers themselves, but only because it was the will of the people who created and fueled them.

The people who ruled them.

All her life, Xhea had seen the Towers move in the City above, rising and falling, turning and shifting and clashing. Only now did she see the Towers move of their own volition.

If their magic was a song, then this was a dance. Spells flared around them, but not like blades; Xhea could not help but think of the twist and flutter of silken veils.

Again and again, one reached for another and they changed. Xhea did not know what passed between them in that magic; she saw, too, that whatever was said, some obviously disagreed. Some Towers fought back, or struggled against the damage already caused by dark magic. Some slipped slowly, slowly, toward the broken ground below, pieces falling from their sides like rain.

The Lower City hesitated, all that dark power suddenly frozen across the sky.

"Listen," Xhea said. "Hear them."

But what she meant was, *Trust them.* And oh, it would be hard; she knew that more than anyone. How many times had she rejected help because she would not, could not trust the hand that offered it? There were too many strings attached—too many times when everything had gone horribly, dangerously wrong for her to place faith blindly.

The Lower City was stronger than she had been, but also lonelier. It *wanted* what was offered in that outstretched field of magic, no matter that it feared it in equal measure.

Though its power surged through the Spire like breath and blood, no longer did it strike out. Instead it reached—slowly, hesitantly—and touched the swirling magic that Allenai sent.

Allenai, and so many other Towers.

Power flared, bright and dark, and Xhea thought of her hand touching Shai's. Sound rose in a great inhuman chorus.

What the Towers said, Xhea could not understand, nor could Shai—neither in sight nor sound. But the Lower City, could— and did—and Xhea heard the echoes of their meaning in the sudden rush of the Lower City's song.

Our sibling, the Towers said. *Our friend.*
Beloved stranger.

We welcome you.

As if the Lower City were not an attacking force, not a threat or danger, but the family member they had never known they'd had. Such joy in that sound—and such joy in hearing it.

Beneath Xhea's feet, Farrow shuddered. Not an earthquake; compared to all that had come before, it was little more than a shiver. Xhea looked down and placed her hands once more against that black-wrapped surface, thinking of the magic Shai had sent down to the small, starving Tower. If she concentrated, she could just feel a faint whisper of bright magic against her palms, faintly warm, like the touch of sunlight on a cool day.

Farrow, living. Its bright heart tarnished with shadow.

She did not mean to speak—and yet she did nonetheless, though her lips were silent. Magic lifted from her skin like steam, and it seemed that power now held her every thought, every whisper of memory that skittered across her consciousness.

Xhea felt some fragment of the Lower City's attention turn back to her—and to small, black-bound Farrow beneath her. Felt as it plucked that image—Farrow's heart, shining gray—from her mind as if it were but a fresh, ripe apple, left unattended in the market.

For a moment, she felt only its surprise. Then there came a rush of sound, a surge of dark.

"What are you—?" She had no chance to finish.

Because the ground in every direction was suddenly moving—not shaking, but *melting*, sinking into the earth. There were no ruins, no heaped piles of rubble that had once been homes, buildings, skyscrapers; there was, very suddenly, only a great sea of roiling black.

Then the Lower City reached again, its magic pouring up through the Spire to blanket the City above. It was speaking, she thought, as if the power that spread like a dark stain across the sky could truly be understood as words.

This time, only a few Towers struggled to evade that grasp, defensive spells flashing. The rest surrendered to it, or welcomed it, she knew not which.

She had thought—

She had believed—

It didn't matter, because they were falling—the Towers were falling, dark magic guiding them toward the ground.

Something vast blotted out the sky. Xhea looked up—and gasped. Allenai was directly above her, descending, its lowermost defensive point stabbing down as if it wished to pierce Xhea's heart.

She lifted her hands on instinct, as if hands alone might do anything to stop the weight of that massive living building from crushing her as it fell. She wanted to scream but could not shape the sound; it caught within her throat like a hard, round stone.

Xhea wanted to scream but instead she laughed, for she had been here before. In dream she had relived this moment over and over, standing beneath Allenai when all had seemed lost. Sometimes, in dream as in memory, Shai was there, her power flaring around her like wings. Sometimes Xhea fell to safety. Sometimes she only fell.

Shai was not here now. Out in the ruins that defensive ring blazed bright, protecting the refugees from the destruction of the City, and Shai was the key to that spell. There would be no last-minute salvation at her friend's hands.

Yet Xhea looked up and touched the tether, sending that image of Allenai above her wrapped in shadow and light, falling, falling to crush her.

Together, was all she said—and the reply? Beneath the sorrow, beneath the fear, Shai sent only a rush of emotion in reply: love and acceptance and pride that wrapped around her like arms, holding her tight and never, ever letting go.

It was, in the end, all that Xhea had ever wanted.

She closed her eyes and lowered her hands, and in the final moment before Allenai's impact, Xhea smiled.

Chapter Twenty-Nine

Xhea lay quiet, magic shining full upon her like sunlight.

Thoughts were slow in forming. Perhaps she slept; perhaps she dreamed. If so, she did not want to wake.

She heard a sound like gentle music, a sound like water flowing and wind through leaves. The air smelled like it had been washed clean by rain. Her hands rested at her sides, her legs stretched out, her head pillowed by something soft. And for all that magic shone down upon her, brilliant and flaring, it did not hurt.

She did not hurt.

Not her skin or her heart or her knee; not the countless cuts and bruises on her hands and arms. Not any of it. The lack of pain was a relief beyond words, and for a moment longer Xhea just drifted, lost and glad for that oblivion.

At last, she opened her eyes.

Shai stood above her, smiling down. She shone, her light Radiant—but above her was something brighter. A horizon of light, stretching as far as she could see.

"Am I dead?" Xhea asked. She was surprised how hopeful she sounded. But then, death could be a gift, too, at the end. A laying down of burdens. A last breath, soft and slow.

Maybe she didn't have to fight anymore. Maybe she didn't have to hurt.

Shai said, "Not quite. Not yet."

The ghost held out her hand and Xhea took it without thought or hesitation. Shai helped her to sit.

No, not dead, Xhea thought, looking down at herself. For though she was clean, she still wore the ragged remains of her clothing, the fabric of her beloved jacket, her practical pants and top, worn down to thin scraps by dark magic. Her knee brace was but bands of decaying fabric that wrapped around her leg like ribbons, crumbling pieces all that was left of the plastic spars that had once joined them. Her boots were gone entirely; she wiggled her bare toes.

Her hair fell about her shoulders and down her back, unbraided and unbound. As she turned her head, looking around, she was surprised at how light it felt, shorn of its coins and charms. In this quiet, she missed the old chime and clatter of her movement.

She sat now upon a smooth, dark gray platform; her legs, dangling, did not reach the floor. There were walls, also gray, yet they seemed impossibly far away.

She blinked, frowning at those walls. They were not smooth, not flat and featureless, but made of countless strands like vines, twining around each other as they rose. No, she thought, looking higher. Not vines but trees. Their dark branches arched high overhead, leaves rustling.

Beneath that ceiling of branches and leaves flared a living heart of bright magic.

"Where am I?"

"Allenai," Shai said. "Or Farrow. Or maybe the Lower City." She smiled, as if this made any sort of sense. "It's a bit confused about what to call itself right now."

"It's not the only one who's confused."

"Look down."

Xhea did, peering at the ground beneath her dangling feet. The walls were dark tree trunks, the ceiling those trees' leaves and branches; she expected the ground to be roots. It was not. Instead it was smooth and dark, polished almost to a mirror shine; looking down, she could see a hint of her own reflection, and the tangled halo of her unbound hair.

She opened her mouth to speak—and hesitated.

For beneath the reflection of her face and the bright light of the heart far above her, there was something else. Xhea gripped the edges of the platform on which she sat, because suddenly she felt as if she were falling. The floor seemed to fall away and she could see down, down, as if that ground wasn't there at all. There was only a deep, empty hole.

No, not a hole—but darkness. Living, flaring darkness.

But it was not a heart—or, rather, not just a heart. Not a single point of darkness, as the heart above was a point of light, but something larger and more diffuse.

That power, too, had fundamentally changed; she did not need to conjure magic of her own to see the difference. It was still dark, but less so than the magic that might rise from her outstretched hand. It was no longer midnight black, no longer the darkness that waited in the deepest tunnels where no hint of sun or moon might shine. It was the dark hour before dawn; it was the night sky, glittering with stars.

Slowly, Xhea looked up.

The Tower heart that flared above her was bright; she had to raise her hand to shield her eyes from the glare. But she could look directly at it, and, staring, saw patterns in that light. Perhaps, to anyone else, those shapes had color. For her? It seemed only that, within that swirling heart of bright magic, there flowed ribbons of darkness.

Tarnished, she had thought, seeing Farrow's heart; *tainted*, she had said. This was neither. It was beautiful.

And, she realized again, it did not hurt.

Perhaps it would be different, were she closer. With that magic like a fog in the air around her, drawn deep with every breath—with that magic sent straight into her, like a shock of lightning—she was certain it would be different. But here, now? That power was only warm, gentle light.

As she watched, power flowed from the ground up through those reaching branches to the bright heart; and power shone down, down, soaking into the darkness. Power flowed between them, one to the other, as it did between her and Shai.

Xhea had thought that they could not exist in the same place; that they repelled one another, unmade one another. She unraveled bright spells, destroyed things with a touch—while Shai could burn away even a hint of that darkness.

And it was true—at least for raw power, pure magic shaped only into spells. But living power? The magic not of things, but *people*, freely shared? That, it seemed, was something else entirely.

Magic, she thought, *and spirit.* Each a part of the other.

Understanding, Xhea had no words. She looked to Shai, her face alight with wonder.

"I think we were an inspiration," Shai said softly.

Xhea laughed, and felt tears prick her eyes. "Me," she said in disbelief. "An inspiration. Imagine that." Perhaps stranger things had happened, but she could not think of any.

"What did they do?" she asked instead. "How did they—I mean, when . . ."

Instead, Shai offered Xhea her hand once more, helping her stand. "Come," she said. "I'll show you."

Xhea's cane had not been found; or if it had, it had not been returned to her. Of all the things lost, for a moment that seemed the worst. Or, rather, that loss was easiest to understand.

Lacking its support, she clung to Shai's hand as she walked, and she felt the subtle spells that Shai wove to bear the weight that neither Xhea nor Shai's ghostly arm could hold. Spells, too, wrapped around her knee, and their presence just tingled; they did not hurt.

Oh, the wonder of that.

At the far side of the vast room there was an arch that led out to a hall and, eventually, a balcony, daylight just beyond. Xhea stepped cautiously outside.

The sun was setting. For a moment, that was all Xhea could see—the only thing that made any sense.

"How long?" Xhea asked at last. The words came as if from terribly far away.

"Three days."

"Three . . . ?"

It seemed impossible.

Three days for the Lower City to fall into ruin. Three days, in truth, for the whole of the City to fall, for all that the Towers had not been warned of their impending end.

Three days for the City to fall, and three days for the City to rise. For it was the City that stretched now before her in all its glory—but a City fundamentally changed.

Closest was the Central Spire, its lowermost point embedded deep into the ground. Xhea did not need to see color to know that it was not gold anymore; instead, it was purest, deepest black. It had no living platforms, only stabbed skyward, forming a single, tapering point high above.

Above that, and all around, there was nothing. The sky was empty but for clouds.

Except, Xhea saw, that wasn't quite true. Squinting, she could see a few Towers floating in midair, most so high that they were little more than glints of light, like stars.

Despite those presences, the sky *felt* empty, almost desolate. Never before had Xhea looked up and seen anything but Towers. Now? Bare sky. Fluffy clouds. The dark and whirling shapes of birds.

Some of the Towers had smashed; Xhea saw them out in the badlands. Some were stabbed into the ground, as the Spire was; some tilted or rolled or leaned. Some had shattered entirely, and she cringed at the thought of those impacts and all they entailed.

Yet those Towers were few. The rest stood as the Spire now stood, joined to the earth.

Joined to the Lower City.

Some Towers had clearly merged; they were huge structures now, impossibly vast. Others seemed to have simply landed as they were. Towers great and small rose skyward, their varied shapes making them look like sculptures, glowing against the setting sun.

She stood, Xhea realized, almost where she had stood before, watching everything crumble and fall around her. This was where Farrow had been; below her was the patch of ground that had once been the Lower City market. Steeling herself, she stepped forward and peered over the edge—gasped and stumbled back, grabbing at Shai and closing her eyes to stop the sudden feeling that the whole world was spinning.

But even that brief glimpse was enough. This *was* Farrow; she recognized the black-wrapped shape upon which she stood, reinforced though it was by countless other strands of the Lower City's grown vines.

And above? Slowly, Xhea looked up.

More of those dark vines, that substance made from concrete and asphalt, soil and rock and rubble: the grown-earth flesh of the Lower City itself. They coiled upward, ever higher, and in their grasp was Allenai.

Except as she looked, Xhea saw that the division was not quite so clear. The Lower City didn't hold Allenai so much as merge with it, the darkness of those vines giving way to Allenai's smooth, undulating sides.

"Allenai claimed Farrow's heart," Shai said, answering the questions that Xhea didn't know how to ask. "They're one structure now—and growing and changing as we speak."

Xhea nodded. Already she could see the truth of that: the Tower shifted shapes as she watched, its movement like cold honey pouring.

"And the Lower City?"

"Joined to the Towers. All of them." Shai touched the spelled tether that even now joined them, one to the other, as if that gesture was explanation enough. Perhaps it was.

"Three days," Xhea said again, and shook her head. Even with the City stretched before her, it felt unreal, as if she were only caught in the grips of some weird and wondrous dream. "And me?"

She did not know how she could have survived, not as she was. Not alone and unprotected; not with the damage her flesh had taken.

"The Lower City held you," Shai said. "When it raised the tendrils to take hold of Allenai, it wrapped around you first, like a cocoon. Together, they healed you—or tried to. Even in the midst of everything, it did not want to let you go. But I can be very persuasive." The ghost smiled at that, the expression only hinting at what those days had been like for her, all the worry and fear and confusion.

Xhea reached again for her hand. Squeezed. *I'm sorry*, she thought.

It's okay, came the reply. *Everything's okay.*

Xhea touched the rippling gray wall at her side, a whisper of power flowing through her palm and into the structure beyond. A moment, and then she heard it: a slow and rising song. It was so different, its sound and rhythms wholly changed, and yet she'd know it anywhere; it was a new song, sung by a familiar voice.

"Hello," she whispered, in voice and magic both, and smiled as that sound swelled in greeting.

It wasn't just the Lower City that she heard; other voices, too, sang in recognition and echo. Dozens more, hundreds. All the Towers, new and old alike; all the flaring power of their living hearts, and the structures that were their bodies.

For a moment, Xhea let her awareness flow into them.

She felt the Towers and the countless lives they held as if they were her body, all their homes and businesses, the gardens and walkways, briefly as much a part of her as her lips or throat or hands. And oh, the chaos that must have reigned in those halls; the structures disrupted, the people displaced, the financial and political systems alike wholly in uproar.

But those problems were for the people. The Towers themselves just whispered and sang to each other, some speaking and debating, others simply singing. They were, Xhea thought, happy.

Yet, for all the wonder she felt—seeing the Towers, hearing them, touching some part of their essence—it was in the lower levels where she felt most comfortable, now as in years past. Down she let her consciousness sink, deep into the Lower City.

Never before had that name been so appropriate.

The living Lower City had taken possession of all the materials its magic had touched; it owned that space now, the way the Towers owned their walls and floors, and it shaped them into something beautiful. No longer was the Lower City a broken place, every structure on the crumbling edge of ruin; it was something wholly new, a city grown from the ground up.

Xhea felt as the Lower City shaped homes there—streets and passages, some like buildings and some open to the sky, some reaching up into the Towers themselves—and it sang all the while.

Home, it sang. *Home, home, home.*

Xhea took a deep breath and returned to herself. She was, she found, weeping. No shame in that; no embarrassment, no sorrow. Only joy.

In silence, she reached once more for Shai's hand. Side by side they stood, fingers interlaced, and watched the sun set over the City.

Epilogue

The next morning, the people of the Lower City gathered to bury their dead.

In the three days she'd missed, there had been other gatherings, other funerals, other holes dug and other unmarked graves. But this, Xhea thought, was theirs.

Out in the ruins, there was a ring of land untouched by either the newly risen City or the debris that had fallen in the destruction of the old. A ring where all was as it had once been: the broken buildings of the city that had come before, and the people who chose to shelter within them.

A place where the dead might rest.

For a time, the people of Edren had dug in silence. There were spells to help with digging, with turning the rocky earth and lifting it away; but most chose to take turns with the shovels. No magic could replace the cleansing power of sweat; and, watching, Xhea knew that more than one set of callused hands ached for work to drown out the sound of their thoughts.

Then the preservation spells on the wrapped bodies were whisked away, and the bodies lowered into the waiting earth. The bodies of Edren's dead, yes, and the bodies of other Lower City dwellers—but also the walkers. Those that had been killed attempting to reach the refugees, and those that Shai had lulled into death.

During those three days, Shai had combed the ruins for any remaining walkers. They were here now, lined up side by side— among them Shai's father.

Of Abelane, Xhea had seen little.

"She's here," Emara had said when Xhea asked after the young woman. "She's working." But not, as Xhea had expected, with the children. Instead Abelane worked in the makeshift kitchen, preparing food. Xhea had not gone to greet her, only met her eyes across the distance that separated them, and nodded.

Abelane seemed grateful for that distance. There was no hurt this time—knowing that, in her way, Abelane had moved on and left her. Xhea thought that she understood. Sometimes a person needed to forge their own path. Sometimes, they needed to leave the past behind.

Besides, she had her own paths to walk.

At last, the work was finished, the graves filled in, the prayers said, charms and spells laid upon the earth that spoke of peace and rest and remembrance. In groups and pairs, Edren's citizens walked away.

Only Shai lingered, standing above her father's grave, and for her Xhea was willing to wait forever.

Xhea settled herself in the shade of a fallen wall and braided a strand of her long, dark hair. As that braid reached its end, she drew from a pocket of her new jacket an ancient, battered coin. She turned the coin over in her hands, and rubbed its surface clean with her fingers. Its markings had all but worn away— only hints of numbers and script remained around its edges, a softened shape in its center that might once have been a face.

From another pocket she pulled a piece of narrow ribbon, then leaned back against the wall, her legs stretched before her, and bound the coin to the braided length of her hair.

"Where did you get that?" Lorn asked, gesturing to the coin. There was a council meeting later today, Xhea knew, for Edren to decide what to do, where to stay, what to ask of the living Lower City. What to negotiate with their new neighbors, and how to decide the new rules of their lives.

But for now, his dark skin glistened with sweat, and in his arms he held the shovels.

Xhea shrugged, a grin lifting the corners of her mouth. "I have my ways."

An echo of that grin flickered across Lorn's expression, then he nodded and turned away.

Xhea looked again to Shai. The ghost stood with her head bowed, motionless over that freshly turned earth. Her lips moved in speech or in prayer, and for that moment Xhea gave her only silence, privacy in mind and voice.

Even so, her eyes lingered on the graves' fresh earth, dark in the morning sun.

It was not yet her time to lie there, silent and still. *But soon,* Xhea thought. *Soon.*

Already she could feel the tired burden of her body, a weariness that had nothing to do with rest or sleep or their absence. She did not have long before her body gave out. Weeks, she guessed; perhaps days.

It should have been a weight, that knowledge. It wasn't. For she looked to the sun above the far horizon, watched its light shine across the City—a City reborn—and she could not help but smile.

Shai turned away from her father's grave and returned to Xhea's side.

"Are you okay?" Xhea asked softly.

Shai nodded, face wet with tears. "I will be." And that, in the end, was all that any of them could hope for.

A moment passed between them, soft and slow. There was nowhere they needed to be but here.

"Are you ready?" Shai asked at last. Xhea nodded, and slowly, slowly, pushed herself to her feet, the coins bound into her hair chiming.

No, it was not yet her time, but soon.

Wait for me, she thought to the ghost, her friend, her everything. *We'll go together.*

Together into the unknown, and everything that might come after.

The End

Acknowledgments

A little over ten years ago, I wrote the beginning of Xhea and Shai's first story—the story that grew to become *Radiant*. And now, at last, I've reached the story's end, envisioned all those years ago.

Finishing is a joy and a sorrow. Even now I want to reach for the words as if I might change them, fix them, add to them; as if to deny that I am, in fact, done.

To all those who have walked this path with me, or had a hand in its shaping: thank you, thank you, thank you.

In particular:
To Greg, now and always. For reading, yes, and for listening to my incessant book-related rambling, but mostly for all the rest. Because for months, *everything* was terrible . . . except you.

To Jana Paniccia, Jessica Leake, and Julie Czerneda for your friendship and help far above and beyond the call of duty. I don't know how I could have reached this point without your assistance.

To the excellent writers of the "War Room"—Catie Murphy, Michelle Sagara, Laura Anne Gilman, Robin Owens, Lana Wood Johnson, Chrysoula Tzavelas, Di Francis, Mikaela Lind, Earl Miles, Patricia Burroughs, and everyone I'm forgetting. You helped this book exist, half an hour at a time.

To my publishing team: Sara Megibow, Kelsie Besaw, Jason Katzman, and the others at Skyhorse for your hard work and support.

And to you, dear reader, for sticking with me for three books. I am grateful beyond words to everyone who gave these stories a chance, shared them with friends and family, wrote reviews, and shared ratings online. I hope you feel it was time well spent.